ALL
THIS
TWISTED
GLORY

Novellas
Destroy Me
Fracture Me
Shadow Me
Reveal Me

Novella Collections
Unite Me
Find Me

Furthermore
Whichwood

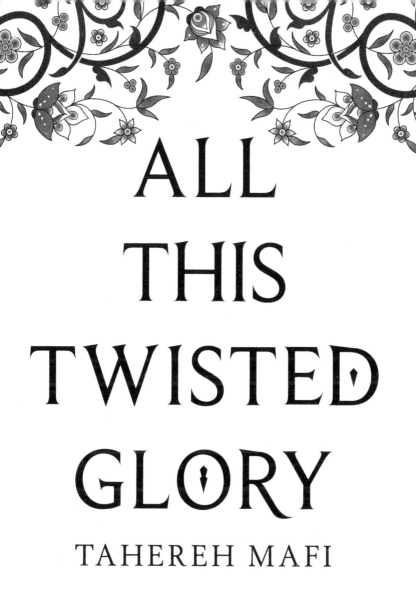

ALL
THIS
TWISTED
GLORY

TAHEREH MAFI

HARPER
An Imprint of HarperCollinsPublishers

Library of Congress Control Number: 2023942522
ISBN 978-0-06-297250-7 — ISBN 978-0-06-337831-5 (special ed)
ISBN 978-0-06-337553-6 (intl ed)

Typography by Jenna Stempel-Lobell
23 24 25 26 27 LBC 5 4 3 2 1

First Edition

For Ransom

"But, my lady, I have sworn an oath to the moon to paint the earth crimson with his blood."

—Abolghasem Ferdowsi, *Shahnameh*

"Speak your name and tell me, who shall cry over your headless body?"

"You will not last long enough to benefit from knowing my name. But if you must know, my mother named me 'Your Death.'"

—Abolghasem Ferdowsi, *Shahnameh*

ALL
THIS
TWISTED
GLORY

PART ONE

IN THE BEGINNING

در آغاز

THE HEM OF HIS INKY cloak scissored through tall grass as he moved, his frantic pace inciting small riots of sound that seemed to scream between his ears with every footfall. Hands of heat grasped at him, his heavy attire stifling. Cyrus of Nara could feel his heart clamoring in his chest, panic breeding panic as he fought the impulse to run. He felt much like rain in search of a river, trying in vain to orient home. Occasionally he stiffened—head turning in sharp, birdlike movements, breath catching as if he'd been startled by a ghost.

No. Not a ghost.

Far worse.

It was unproductive to panic, he reminded himself. There was no benefit to losing one's mind. If there were, Cyrus would've happily mislaid his mind at the palace, where it might've lived forever with his father, the king, and the surfeit of oppressions the older man had earlier laid at his feet. Instead, the young prince had done the more reasonable thing in a crisis and promptly retched into a nearby planter.

Now Cyrus took a shaky breath.

He forced himself to slow down, to assemble his thoughts. The overgrown lane was perforated by gopher holes camouflaged by weeds and wildflowers; he'd twisted an ankle too many times along this path, and no matter his desperation now, he could not afford to be injured.

The route he traveled was marked by the bones of a deserted train track, these origins all but invisible save two parallel beams of steel corroding in the expanse, the drama of so much floral anarchy ablaze around him. Among other creatures, thick neon snakes were known to doze in the warm grass, their appetites easily awoken. How many times in his youth Cyrus had limped onward in agony from here, poison brimming in his blood, he'd lost count. As a child, he'd found such heart-pounding adventures exciting; he'd learned over time how to catch a serpent by the throat with a flick of his wrist, how to uncurl smoke from his fingers and send it slithering into the distance. He'd once loved stomping through these wilds: challenging trees to duel, digging for treasures he'd buried himself. Each caper had exposed a new challenge, a new beast, a new agony to conquer. The trek was now nothing more than an essential commute—and nothing short of devastating.

Life, he feared, would never be the same.

His heart thundered harder as he approached the mouth of an obsolete train tunnel, its crumbling interior choked by a tapestry of climbing vines, the scent of life so fragrant it chafed the mind. Blue-winged birds and shafts of brilliant sun stole through fissures in the rotted structure, drowsy blooms unfurling in this gloss of light, dust motes suspended and glittering. The tunnel was a portal to another world— one in which, once upon a time, he'd intended to live forever.

A green locust latched onto the young man's shoulder as

he entered the underpass, the contrast of bright on black like a shriek in the void. Cyrus pulled his cape more tightly about his body as he moved, something akin to grief webbing between his ribs.

In the narrowing distance, the sight of so much green spiraled into a blitz of white. A thicket of waist-high clouds rose up from the ground, and he traversed this odd stretch with care, for the experience was not unlike wading through frost. It was just as his legs began to freeze that the cloud path thinned beneath his feet, and Cyrus suppressed a shiver.

A palpable veil of magic hung always above the many acres encircling the Diviners Quarters in Tulan, shrouding the central temple and its many outbuildings. There were few indeed who knew the old train tunnel ran perpendicular to this ancient site, and fewer still who were granted permission to enter from this path.

The Tulanian prince had been three years old the first time he'd visited these hallowed grounds. From birth he'd been a frustrated child: he'd cried easily, screamed freely, and though he knew himself capable of speech, he'd been uninterested in the performance. The day his nursemaid had lovingly stroked his head and said he was *quite beautiful for an idiot*, the child had thrown a wooden block at her face. Only when the woman responded in fury did Cyrus remember that violence was frowned upon, and as she rounded on him, he'd bolted for an open window, registering the nanny's horrified shriek only as he tumbled out the other side like a potato. He'd bounced three times off the hip of the fatally steep roof before plummeting to the ground, where he'd landed with a final, unexpected bounce.

The boy had badly scraped his hands and knees; a bruise blossomed along the back of one arm and part of his cheek. Still, he'd not cried. Like a fern uncurling, Cyrus had risen slowly and with surprise, pushing copper locks out of his face with small, dirty hands, only to discover himself at the center of a halo.

Never before had he seen Diviners up close.

They'd stared down at him, faces obscured, black cloaks so dark they seemed to leave holes in the world.

There you are, little one, he'd heard someone say.

The child had rubbed his head in wonder, marveling that they'd managed to put the voice inside his mind. It was only then that Cyrus laughed, that he spoke aloud his first words with delight.

"That was magic," he'd said.

The nanny was still screaming as she ran out into the gardens, half the palace staff at her heels, all wild with hysteria. Her services, she'd later discover, would no longer be required.

It was that fateful day Cyrus had decided who he wanted to be, and every year the conviction had rooted more deeply inside him. The king and queen had felt this a fortuitous discovery, for the boy had not been born to ascend the throne and would require some lesser, dignified preoccupation in life.

Cyrus of Nara was the spare, of course; never the heir.

It was his older brother who'd shadowed their father from

infancy. It was his older brother who'd prepared for a life of decadence and power.

Cyrus, on the other hand, had spent every free hour in his youth tearing down the secret train tunnel with abandon, flowers blooming in his hair as he hurtled himself through the clouds and into the arms of the Diviners. Over the years, he'd devoted himself to the study of divination, forsaking the high shine of the material world for the hazy wonders of the ethereal—and was endlessly mocked for it by his royal family. Learning the basics of magic they could understand, but no one believed a prince would willingly strip himself of a title and refuse an inheritance of riches only to join the ranks of nameless Diviners.

Cyrus hadn't cared.

He'd locked away his gold and jewels, cut off his hair, and whittled down his wardrobe to simple black garb. He took preliminary vows on his eighteenth birthday and spent the next year and a half living exclusively at the temple, seldom leaving the grounds as he prepared for the final ceremony. He was among the youngest students allowed to advance to this first rung of priesthood, and now, as he approached his twentieth year, he was only weeks away from being given official robes, from having his lips sealed with a magic that would bind him forever to—

Stop.

Cyrus froze, his breath catching. The icy cloud path had connected, ultimately, to the roof of a stone cottage, one of several in the crescent of outbuildings on the Diviners' land.

The young prince stood atop one such building now, a spongy rug of moss yielding under his boots. His fears hardened as he lifted his head; never had Cyrus been denied entrance to these grounds.

Slowly, he looked his old teacher in the eye.

The man glided forward, his dark robes mesmerizing in motion. Tulan's Diviners were distinguished by their black cloaks, the curious material shimmering like liquid metal, heavy with secrets. The elder pulled back his hood an inch, baring a hint of his face to the cold light. What was visible of his brown skin was smooth despite his advanced age, though his eyes were milky with cataracts. Still, there was no censure in his energy; in fact, there was a compassion that emanated from deep within the man, even now. At once, Cyrus understood.

You already know, he said soundlessly.

The Diviner canted his head. *We have always known. But we were not meant to interfere.*

The young prince felt his heart wrench at this revelation, the words landing as a betrayal even as his mind knew better. To be a Diviner was to be burdened by knowledge and bound by brutal limitations; powerful as they were, the priests and priestesses were not allowed to obstruct the free will of others, and they were not allowed to offer unsolicited guidance. Cyrus understood this better than most.

Still, his eyes flashed with heat as he stood there, for he knew now, with a categorical certainty, that his dreams had died; his role had changed forever. Never would he become a

Diviner. All he'd ever wanted, all he'd ever worked for. His life, his future—

The teacher tilted his head once more, this time the small motion delivering Cyrus to the ground, where the violet walls of the temple rose behind them to breathtaking heights. With fresh heartache the prince registered the press of a barrier between their bodies, magic keeping him at bay.

These hallowed quarters would never be his home.

Please, he said desperately. *I've come to seek your counsel.*

Slowly, the Diviner shook his head. *There are only two choices, little one.*

Cyrus moved to speak, a fragile hope gathering in his chest, but his old teacher lifted a hand to stop him. It was with unmistakable sorrow that the man looked him in the eye and said—

Few can die. Or many.

ONE

یک

"WHAT ARE YOU— ARE YOU *eating an orange?*"

Kamran turned as he spoke, his face taut with dismay, to study the young woman seated in the night sky beside him. For hours now they'd been soaring through the heavens, and whereas he'd only grown frigid with disquiet, Miss Huda half reclined atop her magical bird, staring up at the stars and eating a piece of fruit for all the world as if she were the heroine in some impassioned novel.

"Yes, why?" She'd paused in the act of lifting a section of orange to her mouth and suddenly startled. "Oh! Forgive me, Your Highness—would you care for a piece?" She held out her sticky palm, upon which sat a sticky wedge, and Kamran recoiled.

She'd offered him the fruit she'd been about to put in her own mouth. It was as if the girl had no manners at all.

"No," he said curtly.

How Miss Huda had procured the citrus, or why she'd thought to tuck away an orange in the midst of so much mayhem, he'd never know, for he'd no intention of—

"I filched a few from a passing tray before we left the palace," she supplied, pausing briefly to chew and swallow. A wash of starlight illuminated her artless movements, her eyes glassy as she stared at him with ill-concealed admiration. "I hope that's all right. I grow a little light-headed when I take too long between meals."

Kamran made a noncommittal sound, turning away.

Of all things, he'd not meant to encourage conversation. All this time their unlikely troop had been little able to converse—the constant noise and turbulence of their journey making long chats impossible—but the headwind had finally settled, and the relief among their quintet was nearly palpable. The stunning winged beasts that carried them drew together in a tight formation as they began their slow descent into Tulan. Not long before they touched land.

Meanwhile, Kamran's mind was waterlogged with fear and weariness. Grateful as he was for the extraordinary circumstances of his escape, the shine of their journey had begun to dull under the steady scour of his thoughts. He'd no interest in holding forth with anyone.

"Oh—can I have some?" came Omid's eager Feshtoon. "I'm so hungry."

The boy had recently decided to communicate exclusively in Feshtoon while the others responded in Ardanz. This new system of communication had lately given their conversations an interesting texture, developed only after the child had discovered, to his supreme delight, that all in attendance were fluent in Feshtoon.

Even, apparently, Miss Huda.

Kamran had been surprised to discover the illegitimate miss was properly educated. He knew the assumption made him seem cruel, but neither could he condemn himself for the thought; it was, quite frankly, bizarre for someone of her uncertain station to be brought up with a governess. Then again, her father was known to be an eccentric.

"I'd love a piece as well, if you've enough to spare," added Deen, the apothecarist. "It smells heavenly."

This much was true.

The air around them had been scented by the spritz of orange oil, and as Miss Huda broke apart her rations to share with the others, their excited voices and ensuing conversations served only to provoke the prince. He'd barely tolerated most members of this unlikely group even in the best of spirits, and now, rumpled and unsettled, his patience had worn thin.

"Leave her be," came the whisper of Hazan's familiar, scolding voice. "She doesn't mean to vex you."

"Who?"

"Miss Huda."

Kamran registered these words with surprise, turning to face his old friend as if dealt an insulting blow. "*Miss Huda?* You think I preoccupy myself now with thoughts of Miss Huda?"

Hazan did not smile, though his eyes indicated some private amusement. "Do you not?"

"If I think of her at all, it is only to marvel at the many inelegant turns of her mind."

Now Hazan frowned. "That seems unfair."

"Earlier," he said, lowering his voice to a hiss, "she tried to *eat* her way through a cloud. Her jaw, can you imagine?" He mimed a biting motion with his hand. "Snapping her head around, making some ridiculous voice, just to entertain the child. She appears to have no sense of propriety whatsoever."

Hazan's face remained impassive as he said, "I believe she called it *the hungry cloud monster* voice."

"Oh, and you approve of this, do you?"

"Not everyone takes themselves as seriously as you do, sire. They have neither the energy nor the interest."

"Are you implying that I'm vain?"

"I'm not implying it, Kamran. I'm delivering the statement to you directly."

"You're an ass."

"It's a mercy I don't stare too long in the mirror, then, contemplating the contours of my face."

Reluctantly, Kamran cracked a smile.

"You've never been allowed to drop the crushing weight of imperial expectations," Hazan said quietly, staring now into the distance. "Others are not so encumbered as you. That does not make them inferior."

Kamran gave a small shake of his head, appraising Miss Huda once more from afar. When he forced himself to imagine her beyond the outrageous crime of her gown, he was able to glean the finer details of her features. It was not that she was an unattractive girl; it was simply that he found her lacking in refinement. She was loud and indelicate and childish, and being in her orbit made him feel restless, as if his clothes were two sizes too small.

She laughed, then, laughed until her body shook, and he turned sharply away, the cheerful sound grating his nerves. "If only I might experience the luxury of being so unencumbered," he muttered. "A cold day in hell that would be."

Hazan offered him a grim look of understanding, and Kamran, deciding he deserved some relief from his mental punishments, allowed himself to slouch a little in his seat.

He sat astride Simorgh—a legendary bird who'd offered him escape in his most desperate hour—while the others had settled upon the steady backs of her four children. The Ardunian prince hadn't known what to expect when he'd first climbed aboard the magnificent, towering creature, her wingspan as wide as a room. He'd been so overwhelmed with awe and gratitude for the privilege of her company that it hadn't occurred to him to wonder whether the long journey from Ardunia to Tulan would be easy. It was bad enough that he'd been tossed together with these motley souls—all of whom had been lodged into his life by virtue of knowing the same enigmatic young woman—but the addition of exhaustion, hunger, fear, and unprocessed grief had made the very occupation of his body nearly intolerable.

Kamran had wanted Alizeh—Alizeh and nothing more—and instead he'd been forced to collect the orphan, the by-blow, and the misanthrope; as if his life were some children's quest game and he'd been dealt a set of cards he had no choice but to play. Considering how rarely Alizeh seemed to allow others a glimpse into her life, these characters were precious indeed—but had he not been so blinded in his pursuit of a young woman, he might've known the bliss of an existence apart from these people.

To compound his churlish mood, the prince had heated unevenly. Despite the warm engine of the bird's body, his extremities were all but numb with cold, the bow and its quiver of arrows slung across his back slowly digging into his flesh, and—though he'd never admit this aloud—he'd been carefully ignoring a need to use the facilities for nearly an hour.

Still, Simorgh had proven a mount both unshakable and shockingly plush; her silky, iridescent feathers were a gratifying cushion for his tired body. He'd hardly slept in days, so upended had been his life. If only he could be certain he wouldn't topple out of the sky, Kamran might've dozed against her neck. Now, as the steady, gentle motions of flight threatened more than ever to lure him to sleep, he struggled to keep his eyes open. Silently he was grateful for the occasional, bracing slap of cold against his face.

"Are you still hungry?"

Kamran looked up, a soft wind tousling his hair, only to realize the question had not been addressed to him. Miss Huda had procured a banana from some secret pocket in the billowing folds of her horrifying dress and was now straining across the dark expanse of the universe to hand the fruit to Omid, whose eyes had lit up even as his mouth was still full. He scrambled eagerly to accept the offering and, in a moment that caused Kamran to stiffen in alarm, the two of them knocked heads and nearly fell out of the sky.

Omid and Miss Huda promptly dissolved into gales of laughter, delighted to have nearly killed themselves with stupidity. Even Deen, the grouchiest of the four companions, had managed a smile.

It made Kamran irrationally furious.

He didn't understand that what he felt as he watched them was not anger, exactly, but a mix of longing and resentment.

Omid, Huda, and Deen had come on this journey only for a bit of adventure, for a touch of the magical. They were not here as he was: in a desperate fight for his life, his throne, and his legacy. That they might laugh so easily, recline so freely, snack as they chatted—it made him seethe with indignation. Secretly he longed to know such cheeriness; but being unable to express these feelings even to himself, he simmered in his frustration instead, allowing the familiar arms of anger to bolster him as he sat in the sky, slowly eaten away by unknowns.

His thoughts of Alizeh, of course, loomed largest.

TWO

,,

ALIZEH TOUCHED A FINGER TO the ground, drawing shapes upon the coarse terrain, the texture softly abrading her skin. She sat alone and exposed in the icy dark, planted in the eye of an expansive salt flat that seemed to whirl toward infinity in all directions. The white crystals were packed upon the earth in a hard crust, minerals glinting in the moonlight with the glitz of crushed diamonds.

Absently she licked a bit of salt from her thumb, grimacing at the taste as a dull heat flared along her tongue. Her thoughts churned as she gazed up into the pitch, where the thick of night was freckled all over by stars. Alizeh knew that fireflies, too, lived in Tulan's atmosphere, and the shimmer was so dense this evening it blurred in places. It was as if a child had pressed a hand to the heavens and smeared its glitter across the sky.

Still, these marvels would not distract her mind.

Scenes of the last several hours continued to haunt her, sounds drumming incessantly against her bones, memories of remembered sensation quickening across her skin. Even now, surrounded by quiet, she could not find silence.

Just hours ago, she'd done the unthinkable.

After eighteen years in hiding, Alizeh had finally stepped out of the shadows. Exposing herself as the lost queen of

Arya had been a dangerous move for several reasons, chief among them that she was ill-equipped for the role. She possessed no throne, no army, no plan, and not an ounce of the powerful magic she'd been promised for the part. At this juncture she was more likely to be murdered than venerated for popping her head above the parapet, yet she felt she'd no choice but to emerge, unfinished, into the spotlight. After rumors of her arrival in Tulan had choked the royal city, thousands of Jinn had stormed the castle in search of her, demanding proof of life. The mob had been wild and frenzied, clamoring for a glimpse of the fabled queen, threatening violence if she'd come to harm. It was a good thing, then, that the cut at her throat was too faint to be registered by a distant crowd.

Unfortunately, it had drawn Sarra's attention at once.

The Queen Mother had phased through shock and horror upon sighting Alizeh, who, prior to facing the masses, had emerged from Cyrus's bedroom in a short, bloodied dress and a bleeding throat with as much dignity as she could summon.

Sarra had taken in Alizeh's flushed and battered state, then her son's wild eyes and naked torso, and her expression had darkened to something like murderous disgust. Alizeh had nervously unknotted her soiled gown, shaking out the hem to its full length before hastening to explain the situation—but Cyrus had flashed her a look so severe it lit the nosta tucked inside her corset, the soft burn startling her into silence. Sarra gave a derisive laugh at this small exchange, though ultimately the matter went undiscussed, for the woman seemed too agitated by the urgency of the waiting crowd—thousands of Jinn still rioting outside the palace walls—to delay the moment with talk. Her only indulgence had been to aim a pointed look at the far end of the hall, where four gaping young snodas had toppled into one another in an almost comical state of shock, before turning her grim smile on Alizeh.

"Sharpen your mind, girl," she'd said with menacing softness. "If the mob doesn't kill you tonight, the gossip might."

Alizeh squeezed her eyes shut at the memory, her skin heating with the residue of mortification. The greater part of the truth was far from scandalous, of course; in fact it would've delighted Sarra to know that she and Cyrus had only been trying to kill each other.

Theirs had been a dizzying evening.

After hours of tending to Cyrus in the aftermath of a brutal assault from the devil, the half-delirious king had magicked them back to his bedchamber where, shortly thereafter, they'd had an explosive fight. She and Cyrus had crossed swords, exchanging blows and heated words until, in the end, he'd vanquished her not with a weapon but with a sequence of passionate confessions that had left her all but decimated.

Absently she touched her neck, wincing as the dusting of salt on her fingers seared the open wound. Alizeh pulled her knees to her chest and held herself tight, biting the inside of her cheek to keep her teeth from rattling in the cold.

How would she ever keep her thoughts in order with so much sensation to file and sort? So many desires to manage and extinguish?

She'd not known what to expect when she finally asserted her right to the ancient Jinn throne, though she'd once thought it reasonable to imagine any claim would be met with suspicion and anger. She'd prepared to defend herself against accusations of fraud; she thought she'd be forced to prove, somehow, that she was the rightful heir.

Instead, the moment she'd stepped onto the balustrade the crowd had appeared to flinch, as if struck in tandem by an unseen force. Their deafening roars dimmed to a silence so complete Alizeh had been able to hear her own shallow breaths. The first moments had been more than terrifying; seconds ticked past as if in slow motion, her heart hammering against her ribs as panic swelled within her.

She'd not thought it through—she hadn't enough time to prepare—and she worried then that she must say something grand, or else inspiring. Her first public words would doubtless be remembered in their history, repeated in the streets. She'd thought, at first, to rally them.

Then she'd looked more closely.

What she'd seen was a sea of Jinn worn out from long hours of standing and shouting. Only the muted cries of infants were still detectable, exhausted parents with their children in arm, older kids asleep at their feet. The elderly leaned on canes or otherwise sat painfully on the ground, while the young and hale stared up at her with strained, feverish eyes. Every face she looked upon was taut with fatigue, trembling hope—and a hunger born of simple dehydration.

Gently, she'd said, "My dear people, let me bring you water."

The result was a breathtaking chaos.

How they'd been so certain of her identity, she couldn't know; it wasn't a question she might ask without injuring her credibility. But at her words, they'd seemed to glean the necessary proof and grew hysterical once more, some sobbing uncontrollably, others fainting into the arms of strangers and loved ones.

Alizeh had made to go to them, resolved that she would find a way to provide nourishment to these thousands of people, when Cyrus stepped at once out of the shadows, staying her movement with a familiar, thunderous look.

"You will not endanger yourself," he'd said.

She'd hardly registered her irritation, had hardly opened her mouth to protest before he'd turned to a nearby servant and issued orders she couldn't hear. No longer shirtless, the king of Tulan wore a plain sweater and overcoat, his only indulgence a thick fur cap pulled low over his brow, the article all but hiding his copper hair.

Everything, everything, black.

She'd been unable to look away as he performed this small task, fascinated by his unshakable bearing. Just hours ago he'd been battered nearly to death by the devil only to be dealt further blows by Alizeh herself, his mother, and the threat of violence against his home. These strikes had rained down on him one after another without pause and still, he remained composed. He wore a slight smile as he spoke quietly to a footman, his mannerisms easy but firm.

He had not collapsed.

His business conducted, Cyrus had looked up, arrested by

the force of her gaze upon him. She, too, had changed before addressing the crowd, wearing now one of Cyrus's cloaks, which he'd insisted would be both a protection from the cold and a cover for her stained dress. Soon she felt the heat of his inspection elsewhere, lingering first at her neck, then drawing down the hidden lines of her body. He took in the billows of her borrowed garment, the too-long sleeves, the several inches of hem pooling around her feet.

His eyes held all the inconstancy of an eclipse: his anger nearly overwhelming his need.

Alizeh had grown light-headed under this careful gaze, her skin prickling with awareness where his eyes had touched her. She didn't know how to describe this feeling, this breathless languor. No one had ever looked at her the way he did, as if the sight of her might be fatal. Her lips had parted under the weight of his silent want, her mouth growing heavy with the sound of his name and a desperate, foolish impulse to whisper the word against his skin.

Mercifully, sharp gasps and cries of astonishment punctuated the melee, and the trance was broken; Alizeh turned, startled, to witness palace servants winding through the mass of Jinn with gilded trays, each piled high with cups and pitchers of water.

Presently, Alizeh sniffed against the chill numbing her nose, squeezing her eyes shut against the dizzying night sky. The scene that ensconced her was beautiful, no doubt—but neither her head nor her heart were equipped to appreciate the present.

Besides, she knew not where she was.

She'd found this site only after haunting Cyrus through midnight turns of the royal city. After the mob had been settled—after the people accepted that she was well, that she'd only just arrived in Tulan, that she'd made no firm decisions about marriage, and that she'd address them officially just as soon as she rested a while—the crowds had very slowly dispersed. It was when their small party withdrew into the castle—Sarra's face contorting as if she might scream and Alizeh thinking of nothing but sleep—that the young king had spoken an efficient five words to the wall:

"I'm afraid I must go."

Without further explanation, Cyrus had left her in the custody of his horrified mother.

Sarra had made a choking sound before staring at Alizeh with wide, blinking eyes, and for a moment, Alizeh felt sorry for the woman. In a shocking reversal of character, Sarra, once a shrewd and complex adversary, had lost her nerve. After witnessing Alizeh's quiet power before the unruly crowd, the woman now appeared terrified even to share oxygen with the girl. It seemed the Queen Mother was worried she'd made a dangerous mistake asking Alizeh to murder her son.

If only she were able, Alizeh might've laughed at the absurdity.

Instead, she'd bid good night to the trembling Sarra and, once she'd found herself alone in the hall, quickly donned invisibility and trailed Cyrus at superhuman speed, taking care to evade all eyes, for fear of being spotted by Jinn servants. It wasn't long before she'd followed him off the palace grounds, foreign scenes melting into blackness as they traversed the chilling night.

Now Alizeh sighed.

There were peculiar woodlands here, bone-white trees with bone-white branches that shone from within, a small stand of which glowed softly at the edge of the salt flat. *This* was as far as her search had taken her, for Cyrus had soon evaporated into a literal puff of smoke upon approaching the illuminated forest, and here—alone and off course—was where she'd landed, cursing herself for her stupidity.

She pulled the borrowed cloak more tightly about her shoulders, struggling against the urge to inhale the familiar scent of its owner. She'd come to know this cologne of him, the floral notes of rose infused with the masculine spice of his skin—though she wasn't entirely sure how. It was perhaps the hours she'd spent holding Cyrus's body, breathing him in even as she cried. She could still feel the silk of his hair sliding between her fingers, the down of his cheek under her hand. For her efforts she'd been rewarded this unrelenting burn beneath her breastbone, a ripple of feeling so powerful it spasmed without reprieve, refusing to settle even when her thoughts turned to anything and anyone else. Her body had never felt so alive, so electrified.

When had she allowed Cyrus to take up so many rooms inside her?

Nothing had even *happened* between them.

The paroxysm of feeling she endured now, the emotional wreckage she was forced to sift through in the aftermath of what was, by most metrics, a nonevent—

It made no sense.

Worse: Cyrus was under the command of the devil. This statement alone should've been conclusive enough to condemn him, but heaven help her, she had other reasons, too. Among other horrifying crimes, he'd stolen her precious Book of Arya and refused to return the item, holding it hostage under lock and magic. He'd slaughtered Ardunia's Diviners, murdered King Zaal, killed his own father, and crowned himself her enemy whether she liked it or not. So when he'd fled the palace on a mysterious—and likely nefarious—quest, she'd felt compelled to follow.

Too bad, then, that she'd been a fool.

THREE

OF COURSE CYRUS KNEW HE was being followed.

She possessed all the subtlety of a dragon in slumber. As if she could draw near him without his knowledge—as if he couldn't hear the dragging hem of his borrowed cloak on her body. It was torture enough to imagine her wearing his clothes, but it was an altogether different torment to envision her determined stride, her furrowed brow, the slight pout to her lips that appeared only when she was thinking too much. The resolve with which she pursued him now—as if she had any idea what she was doing—was so endearing it angered him. For as long as he lived he feared he'd know the scent of her, the sound of her walking toward him. She was a fool to think otherwise.

He was a fool to think of her at all.

Cyrus sighed and strode onward, the icy eve raising puffs of frost from his lips. Towering evergreens glinted along the path, ghostly fingers of moonlight pushing through branches as if to seize him. Night birds jeered; oblivion threatened; the clean fragrance of pine filled his head. The hour was late and unusually frigid.

If only she would leave him.

A ghastly journey lay ahead, and after all he'd endured this night, Cyrus had hoped for a single mercy: solitude.

He wanted a moment to collect himself—to steady himself before entering the next phase of torture. Her clinging shadow made this small dream impossible.

Several times already he'd heard her soft *oof* as she tripped over the hem of her cloak, and he'd gritted his teeth to keep from turning to help.

The young king had no need of this long, glacial odyssey; Cyrus intended to reach his final destination by way of magic. He'd been leading Alizeh in an aimless wander on purpose, hoping she'd eventually tire of the cold, or at least give in to her own exhaustion and turn back toward the castle.

She could not know his dilemma: that her inexpert shadow infuriated him even as it soothed him, that he wanted to vanish even as he couldn't bear the thought of abandoning her here, in the frigid dark. He wanted her closer than he could express in words, wanted her bare and trembling in his arms, wanted to excoriate these sensations from his skin. He wanted to lop off his own head and hurl it into the river.

He wanted to shout at her.

There was a sudden sweep of wind then, the sharp rustle of leaves. Cyrus ducked his head against the chill and heard the barely perceptible sound of a sniff, which only provoked his fury.

He knew his anger was irrational, but he was compelled nonetheless to turn around and accuse her of being senselessly stubborn; she was all but freezing to death for no reason at all, torturing him beyond the bounds of humanity. At first he'd been astonished that she'd followed him, unarmed, into an unknown darkness—and his first thought, naturally, had been to stop her. He'd nearly done as much, nearly whipped around and demanded she return to her rooms.

As if she'd listen.

He felt certain that if he indulged such a fantasy she'd only return his displeasure in full. She'd shout and stamp her foot like a child, angry to have been discovered. She'd refuse to leave and accuse him of using magic against her—for how else might he have gleaned the presence of such a masterful spy?—and when, inevitably, he left her behind anyway, she'd hurl insults at his back, first demanding he return her book, then accusing him of being a dissolute bastard and a jackass to boot.

No, slight correction: she'd not use such vulgar language.

She'd more likely call him a scoundrel, a charlatan, a common miscreant. The thought almost made him smile before it broke him.

The dam shattered.

Pain came for him in a brutal siege, radiating from his core until his mind was forced to submit to an invasion of memory. He was bombarded by scenes of the last few hours, scenes he wished he might banish forever from his history, to no avail: Cyrus could think of nothing now but her small hand at his brow, the home of her arms as she'd held him, the delicious agony of her skin against his face. His throat worked at the remembered feel of her, how he'd touched her in his delirium, drawn the intoxicating scent of her into his head, where it would live, forever, with the whisper of her voice as she'd cried. Her tears had fallen down *his* cheeks as she'd repeated his name, over and over, begging him to wake. He clenched his fists.

He couldn't believe he'd told her the truth.

This was still inconceivable to him, that he'd confessed to dreaming of her night after night; that for eight agonizing months he'd known the taste, the heat, the silk of her in his sleep. Nothing more than an attack of madness could've driven him to such a state. He'd been painfully fatigued, still under the fading influence of dark magic, his mind and body not fully recovered from the devil's most recent assaults. It was the only excuse he had, that he'd been broken—his locks unbolted by shock, his weak body pushed over the edge by her tenderness. At any other hour in his life he'd have been stronger. He'd have walked away, sealed his mouth—he'd have died before disgracing himself with a pitiful exhibition of his own desire.

Hells, he'd known better.

Eight months ago, Iblees had planted Alizeh in his head on purpose, had built in Cyrus's mind a narrative that left him nearly powerless before her. No doubt the devil had hoped to use her to break him—and Cyrus had fallen into this obvious, avoidable trap.

He struggled then to breathe.

Something had irrevocably changed inside him tonight, and he feared for who he'd become in the aftermath. Gone was his mask, his veneer of indifference, his wilting ability to withstand her proximity with an acerbic wit and a wealth of contempt. From the moment of their first encounter Cyrus had patched the myriad holes in his chest with the imagined evidence of her evil; she was, after all, the chosen bride of the devil—certainly this was reason to believe she was corrupt and dishonorable. He assumed she'd claimed the devil as a friend, that she was complicit in the scheme to force herself upon his empire. He'd held this conviction to his heart even as his doubts about her had been swiftly disproven, each reveal of her innocence casting devastating cracks in his armor. That her character was faultless—that she'd made no bargain with the devil—that she was just as haunted by Iblees as he was—

This was worse, infinitely worse.

Her ultimate show of compassion toward him had been his undoing, for this, layered upon all else, had proven she was every inch the angelic figure he'd cherished in his dreams. Not only had he been horribly wrong about her, he'd treated her cruelly. He knew now that she was so far above him he wasn't even worthy of standing in her shadow. Certainly he had no right to desire anything from her.

He came to a sudden halt then, his heart pounding against his ribs.

All this time he'd been able to endure the agony of her presence only because he'd braced himself with hatred; knowing now the depth of his error, how could he bear to be close to her again? How would he even bear to look upon her face when he no longer possessed the defenses necessary to shield his pathetic heart?

He dragged frozen hands down his face, reminding himself to remain composed—that she could still see him. He felt he might combust if he did not decompress, and yet:

How was he meant to deal with his roiling mind while she watched him?

He'd hardly paid attention to his surroundings these last many minutes and realized only now, upon looking up, that he stood before an illuminated copse of trees at the edge of Tulan's largest salt flat. It was haunting in this vast expanse, and he was more aware than ever that he and Alizeh stood alone under this dome of darkness, their movements followed by the stars. A feverish part of him dared to imagine her there in the dark, watching him.

God, he'd wanted her.

He'd wanted her with an all-consuming thirst, with the desperation of a man waiting to die. No doubt the devil had been delighted to see him so debased. *This* sobering thought drove the heat from his head at once, and in its absence Cyrus felt cold and stupid.

Numb.

If only he could go back to hating her, mistrusting her— everything would be safer. If, instead, he allowed himself to carry on in this desperate manner, the Book of Arya would be the least of his troubles. He might be driven to kill a man just to improve her view out a window. He might renege on the entire deal, just as the devil desired.

Oh, he would be sorry then.

Cyrus was in danger of losing control. Alizeh had done him a mercy by walking away, by putting an end to the dawn of what might've destroyed him. He could never again allow himself to get so close to her. It was ludicrous even to entertain the idea that she felt something for him. Even now she followed him only because she didn't trust him; she had no idea she was attempting to accompany him tonight on a trek into hell, where a dark master impatiently awaited his arrival.

No. His was a blighted soul.

Watching her address a desperate, devoted crowd of thousands—all ready and willing to die for her—had driven home this final blow.

He would always be the villain in her story.

Many months ago he'd made peace with the sacrifice his life was meant to be, for it was the only way he'd been able to fulfill the tasks set before him. For Cyrus, hoping for anything more than death was a treacherous game, one that would end only in tragedy. He had no choice but to relegate his impossible dreams to the dusty bins of childhood.

Besides, the devil was waiting.

With that final, bitter thought—he vanished.

FOUR

چھار

MELT THE ICE IN SALT

BRAID THE THRONES AT SEA

IN THIS WOVEN KINGDOM

CLAY AND FIRE SHALL BE

Over and over these words rang through Kamran's mind. He was thinking of the mysterious book he'd discovered in Alizeh's carpetbag, its cryptic inscription having since seared into his memory. It was the last two lines that plagued him.

Woven kingdoms, clay and fire—

Despite everything, Hazan had managed to plant the seed of a dangerous idea in his head: that Alizeh might yet be destined to marry him. Kamran was wracked by indecision as regarded Alizeh, for there was so much he still didn't understand, his heart and mind hopelessly knotted by the betrayals she'd left for him to untangle. And yet—his memories of her remained so ardent he struggled to think rationally where she was concerned. In defiance of his doubts, the thought of having her as his queen was so tempting he couldn't help but indulge the fantasy. He'd never met another young woman to

equal her, not in beauty or composure, in elegance or intelligence. It hadn't been entirely surprising to Kamran that
the enchanting, unassuming snoda had turned out to be the
long-lost heir to an ancient kingdom. There had always been
something regal about her—a dignity in her bearing—

A snort of laughter interrupted his thoughts, and Kamran
turned irritably toward the sound, his mood darkening as he
watched Miss Huda fail to get ahold of herself. The young
miss clapped a hand to her chest as she chortled, her mouth
still half-full as she said, gasping, "Oh my goodness, I'm so
tired I could die."

It was impossible then not to compare the two women in
his mind. Miss Huda was the antithesis of Alizeh, unpolished
and unrestrained. One had been brought up to be queen,
the other to be tolerated; and yet Alizeh had been raised
in relative poverty, Miss Huda in an aristocratic home. The
differences between them were vast, and though both young
women had suffered negligence, only one had emerged with
self-possession and grace. Kamran flinched as the sound of
another snort pierced the quiet, his expression growing only
more dour.

"Oh, I daresay Tulan is a horrid place," she was saying.
"I doubt anywhere in the world could measure up to the
beauty of Ardunia—"

Something about the sound of her voice bothered him,
burrowed under his skin. He gave his head a sharp shake, as
if to dislodge her from his mind. He didn't want to think on
the many irritations of Miss Huda.

Instead, he sunk his hands into the soft, dense silk of Simorgh's plumage, taking comfort in her nearness. The legendary bird had come to Kamran's aid in deference to Zaal, who'd bequeathed his grandson a single, enchanted feather in his will. The plume was meant to summon the magical creature only in a moment of great and devouring need, and Kamran—having been nearly stripped of his crown by Zahhak, the defense minister, then locked in the tower dungeon by the Diviners—had been in dire straits indeed. Still, he didn't know the parameters of the arrangement. Would Simorgh remain with him for some undetermined length of time? Or would she assist him with this single journey only, flying off again as soon as they touched ground?

Once again, his thoughts lurched back to uncertainty.

Kamran was supposed to use this journey to prove himself a worthy inheritor of his own throne—the Diviners had said as much—yet they'd given him no clear guidelines on how to accomplish the task. He wondered whether Zahhak had worked out where he'd gone; he wondered what the Diviners were doing and saying in his absence. Unless the priests and priestesses intended to stop the defense minister from crowning himself king, there was little time left before Zahhak took control of Ardunia.

"Actually, I've heard Tulan is quite beautiful," came Deen's quiet objection. "Several of my vendors are based in the southern empire, and they've never had anything but praise for—"

"Well, naturally," said Miss Huda, cutting him off.

"They're probably terrified to speak a word against their own land, and who could blame them when they're governed by such a beastly king—"

Kamran stiffened at that, his disparate shards of anger coming together in a single, focused blade of hatred.

In all the disorder of his mind, one thing was absolutely clear:

He would kill Cyrus.

Whereas Kamran filled with uncertain dread at the prospect of seeing Alizeh again, he experienced a refreshing flood of adrenaline at the thought of seeing the bastard southern king. High among the many horrors repeating on a loop in Kamran's mind were the gruesome images of King Zaal's death, for the scenes had branded forever upon his memories. Over and over he returned to the stomach-churning sound of the sword slicing through his grandfather's heart. Kamran would never forget the shock, the horror, the ensuing chaos.

The murderer himself.

The Ardunian prince was on a mission now, above all else, to right the scales. He would exact retribution for his grandfather's death or perish in the effort. The brutal king of Tulan would finally be delivered justice. Preferably hacked to pieces, his organs fed to vultures.

"Kamran."

At the sound of his name, the prince nearly startled. He fought to calm his bloodthirsty heart as he turned to face his old minister.

"I've not meant to interrupt," said Hazan quietly, "as I see you're preoccupied. But the sun appears to be struggling against the horizon, and I can hear the distant rush of water growing louder, which can only mean—"

"Yes."

By air or sea, the approach to Tulan was distinguished by the din of cascades. Kamran, who'd led many water journeys to this part of the world, was more than familiar with the sound, the roar of which was a hateful reminder that Ardunia had perhaps two more years before they'd need to start rationing water and three years before the crisis overwhelmed the empire entirely. They'd recently had good snowfall and a brief deluge of rain—but Ardunia would require a great deal more than a few days of precipitation if they were to stave off a drought. *Tens of millions of people* would soon look to him for protection—and one day, under his leadership, they might die of thirst.

It was yet another crushing problem for which Kamran needed to conjure a solution; yet another blade of fear pressed constantly against his throat. His grandfather, King Zaal, had managed to keep this secret from the people, insisting there was no need to inspire panic when there was time yet to resolve the issue. Only now, as the burden fell upon his shoulders, did Kamran recognize this silence for what it truly was: *cowardice.*

Devils above, his grandfather's failings continued to bludgeon him.

"By my estimate, we'll touch ground in roughly thirty minutes," Hazan was saying. "I'd been hoping to discuss the results of my earlier expedition with you before we arrived.

However, if you'd rather wait—"

"No." Kamran stiffened, his back straightening. For so many hours they'd been unable to find calm or quiet in the tumult of the flight, and this most essential conversation had been so delayed it was nearly forgotten. Yesterday, as a hedge against possible expulsion from the castle, Kamran had dispatched Hazan to the north of Ardunia, charging him with the task of securing a safe house, where they might one day take shelter, if necessary. "No, let us discuss your discoveries straightaway. You mentioned you saw my *mother*? In the countryside?"

"Yes."

"Did you speak with her?"

Hazan shook his head even as he said, "Yes."

"Where was she? Was she well?"

"Yes."

"And will you force me to pluck each word of explanation from your mouth like so many blasted splinters? What is the matter with you?"

"Your mother is a strange woman," Hazan responded, fighting a smile. "I traveled north per your request and headed directly to the largest township. I figured the local tavern would be the best place to find an unsuspecting farmer willing to exchange his acres for a small mountain of gold—"

"Yes, very good, Hazan, you went to a tavern and found a farmer. Do you intend to tell me you then went to a butcher and discovered a side of beef?"

Hazan narrowed his eyes. "If you're in too dark a temper even to have a simple conversation, declare it now and spare me the desire to knock you off your mount so I might watch, at my leisure, as gravity does the noble work of snapping your neck."

For reasons inexplicable to him, these words cheered Kamran slightly. "Is my mood always so obvious to you?"

"Your mood is obvious to a corpse."

The prince looked away as he fought a smile, saying, "Go on, then. You went to a tavern and found a farmer."

"No. I found your mother."

Kamran lifted his head sharply.

"She was, by all accounts, awaiting my arrival. The moment I pushed open the door I saw her—though to be fair, she made no effort to conceal her presence. She was so weighted down by jewels it was a wonder to me she hadn't been robbed in plain sight."

"Mother has always been a master of discretion."

Hazan gave a dry laugh. "In any case, she was looking at me as I entered, and indicated at once that I should join her at her table, where she proceeded to tell me she'd secured us a safe house."

"*What?*"

Hazan nodded.

"My mother—*my* mother, the languishing princess of Ardunia—took it upon herself to do a bit of business with a common farmer? In the interest of my protection? Don't say she took a room at the village inn?"

Again, Hazan nodded.

"No," Kamran breathed.

"I confirmed this fact with the owner."

"But how did she know I'd require a safe house?"

Hazan looked suddenly troubled. "I don't know. As I said, your mother is a strange woman. She didn't seem at all surprised to discover me alive; did not ask whether you'd survived the dagger she'd generously planted in your shoulder; did not seem disturbed by the death of your grandfather; and asked me only whether we'd made plans to go to Tulan. When I said yes, she demanded I spare her the details."

Kamran turned away, dragging a hand down his face as an icy breeze sent a shiver through his body. Dawn had not yet broken, but the dark was lifting like a stubborn stain. Blue and gray smeared at the horizon, the promise of golden light just beyond, and the prince drew a deep breath, relishing the mist as he tried to make sense of these revelations.

Hazan hesitated before adding: "She also asked me whether the devil had yet paid you a visit."

Kamran turned back, every muscle in his body tensing. "The devil?"

"I told her I had no idea, as we'd not discussed it."

The prince shook his head. He'd always had the good sense to be repulsed by the devil, but after witnessing the fallout of his grandfather's terrible bargain with Iblees, the very idea of meeting with such a creature revolted him to his core. "What reason would he have to pay me a visit? I've not yet been crowned king."

"I don't know," said Hazan, a furrow forming between his brows. "She did not expound on the matter. She only instructed me to tell you that she'll be waiting for us upon our return, that she has the situation in the countryside well in hand, and that I should direct any militia in her direction, to be managed under her care." Hazan hesitated. "She also sent you this."

Hazan reached into his coat pocket and retrieved a pale pink envelope, which he handed to the prince, who received this strange gift in a bit of a daze. He turned over the delicate paper in his hands, noticing that the flap of the envelope was open. Unsealed.

Kamran glanced up at his friend. "You've read it?"

Hazan exhaled, looking grim. "I suppose I should forewarn you," he said. "It's not a letter."

FIVE

پنج

ALIZEH TRAVELED CAUTIOUSLY, TAKING CARE not to tread on the overlong hem of her robe as she moved. Her extremities had deadened with cold; she'd finally admitted defeat and begun the trek back to the palace. The stars withdrew as a new day threatened, black skies now feathered with gray. Despite this promise of light, the journey seemed more menacing now that she traveled alone, and it was odd to think she'd felt safer with Cyrus about. Nevertheless, there had been no point in waiting for him to reappear; he was too wise, she'd realized, to retrace his steps upon returning home, and she'd refused to waste another minute waiting for him.

In fact, the whole business had left her feeling angry and foolish.

It had been hard to accept that her efforts to track Cyrus had come to naught; but it had been a grave error, too, thinking she could crack the enigma that was the king of Tulan, for he possessed advantages Alizeh was unable to match. She'd followed him and he'd *vanished*. His use of magic, she'd felt, was deeply unfair.

With a sigh she strode on, absently smoothing her hands down her cloak as she went, brushing away lingering salt from her garment. Her palms prickled, and she shook them, slightly, before pulling the heavy hood forward, hiding her face as much as was practical. She advanced in the direction of the castle, its magnificent spires beckoning in the moonlight, and wondered what more awaited her here, in this foreign land.

Both the king and his country perplexed her.

Tulan was a much smaller empire than Ardunia, yet its geography still managed to impress. Alizeh didn't know whether it was the abundance of magic in this region that made it so, but Tulan appeared home to various microclimates and geographical variations. From the middle of the salt flat she could count the teeth of a distant mountain range, savor the scents of night blooms, hear the muted hush of waterfalls, shrink from the eerie calls of jackals. With its dynamic landscape and elevation changes, Alizeh was beginning to see how rare such a piece of land might be, situated as it was along the Mashti River—and parallel to the sea.

It was no wonder to her that Ardunia desired to possess it.

Still, she struggled to understand how an empire as powerful as Ardunia had been unable to overtake the humble nation. No doubt many had tried and failed to conquer this fertile piece of land. Tulan seemed a place both accessible and unfathomable; diminutive yet vast. It was the kind of contradiction she often felt repeated in herself: that she was both useless and powerful; unimportant and essential.

If only she might learn how to reconcile all these feelings.

Then again, her life had changed so dramatically in so short a time that it was easy to imagine why she felt emotionally uncertain; indeed, if she agreed to Cyrus's offer for the

Tulanian throne, she might never return to Ardunia. Already she'd accepted that she'd never again see Kamran, whose own life had recently been eviscerated—and she stopped, suddenly, nearly tripping over her cloak at the thought of him. She wondered how he was managing in the wake of so much ruin. She wondered whether he would one day look back upon the days during which their lives had so serendipitously intersected, and she wondered how—or whether—he might remember her.

With her whole heart, she wished him well. Wished him peace, wherever he was. She'd always be grateful for his kindness. For truly *seeing* her when no one else had.

Alizeh shivered, curling inward as an icy wind blustered against her back. Her heart had grown heavy under the weight of her thoughts, making her body harder to carry. Never again would she see her trio of unlikely friends. Never again would she see Hazan, who was doubtless buried in an unmarked grave. Her breath caught at this last thought, her chest constricting as she felt acutely the pain of loss, of loneliness.

And yet—somehow—she was no longer alone.

Hours ago she'd addressed a crowd of thousands as their queen.

Even so, between her shocking scene with the southern king and her subsequent performance before a surging mass of Jinn, Alizeh had begun to worry that, upon her return to the palace, she might discover herself the center of extraordinary scandal. She didn't relish the idea of becoming fodder for gossip. Moreover, she had no interest in dealing with Sarra—whose recent insistence that she murder Cyrus remained an unresolved issue. Heavens, but the woman was peculiar.

With a final sigh, Alizeh summoned the last of her strength to propel herself, with preternatural speed, back to the castle. She all but flew as she ran, her murky surroundings bleeding together, and soon enough she was back on the palace grounds, gasping for air as the deafening roar of water inundated all with its clamor.

She took a moment, easing her shaking body against the trunk of a towering tree. It had been a hellish few weeks, and she wasn't sure she could go on like this, at this breakneck pace. She desperately desired sleep, but she needed a minute more before she embarked upon the final, impossible task of finding her rooms in the mountainous castle.

She clenched her teeth against the icy gusts of air lifting off the waterfalls, absently patting down the countless folds of her cloak in search of pockets. She'd thus far been curling her fists in the extra length of her sleeves, but the bitter chill was proving unconquerable, and it was with great relief that she shoved her frozen hands into the fleece-lined pockets, clenching and unclenching her fists to warm them. It was then that she felt something like a shock—an electric heat sparking painfully against her fingertips.

Alizeh froze.

Her heart thudding in her chest, she pulled one hand free, lifting the offending digits to the moonlight.

The tips of her fingers had turned blue.

Quickly she rubbed at them, grateful to discover a strange dust shifting from her skin. Still, there was no relief. The friction caused more sparks to course through her fingers, the feeling not unlike flint striking against stone until the pain crescendoed and she cried out, nearly doubling over as she heard the wisp of a familiar whisper, the chokehold of a familiar terror—

Pain exploded behind her eyes, seared her throat. She nearly fainted from the force of it, sweat breaking out across her forehead as her body shook with terrible tremors. A scream was building in her chest, fear snaking through her veins.

This was the devil.

She knew this feeling, knew this slithering terror, knew these horrors, and yet he'd never come to her like this, never broken her mind with such violence—

Alizeh didn't know when she'd fallen down, only that the earth was cold and damp beneath her face, tendrils of moss tickling the inside of her nose with every inhalation. Dirt and lichen nudged at the edges of her lips, but her head was leaden, immovable. She soon became aware that she'd injured herself in the fall—that there was a cool plane of rock wedged under her cheek where a separate pain had begun to bloom. Still, the discovery felt slippery; dreamlike. More present was a disembodied voice shrieking indistinguishable nonsense as her mind spun, sparks still flaring beneath her skin, pain expanding relentlessly inside her. She made only a pitiful sound as she lay there, pinned to the ground by an impossible gravity, when a single word finally separated from the noise. There was no doubt now that the voice belonged to the devil—but the sound was distorted, skipping as if caught in a broken loop, as if the rest of the sentence had been lost on the wind.

Eyes

Eyes

Eyes

Eyes

SIX

شش

CYRUS MATERIALIZED AT THE SAGGING mouth of a moldering cave, the smell of damp earth and cold air greeting him with the blunt force of a club. He drew in the heavy, musty scents as he stepped over a shallow pool of water, silt grinding beneath his boots. Ducking under a jut of rock, he was careful to touch nothing as he straightened into an antechamber, his eyes adjusting slowly to the darkness. The humble entrance had opened onto deep rooms of dizzying heights, the discrete spaces divided only by webbed columns of calcite formations. Coins of moonlight dropped through slots in the distant ceilings, casting spectral globes of illumination upon dripping stalactites and a set of crudely formed stairs that ascended, without end, into a smear of black.

Cyrus remained absolutely still.

He was no longer afraid of these visits—not the way he'd once been—but fear was a slippery thing. He'd been surprised in his green life to discover the manifold ways in which a person might experience terror, the creativity with which dread and horror might be provoked in a soul. He'd overcome one nightmare only to discover its child, outrun another only to encounter its twin. No matter his efforts he could not outsmart that which he could not anticipate, and his only comfort as he stared up at the familiar, sinister staircase was a cold one.

He either *did* or *did not*.

He would not live by half measure.

Cyrus had learned this sobering lesson on his first visit to this particular rung of hell. He'd been tender and unseasoned then, so colonized by fear he'd broken into a cold sweat before even entering the abyss. He'd vacillated at the bottom of the towering staircase for nigh on an hour, cowed not only by indecision but by the hostilities of the cave itself. His skin pallid, his limbs occasionally locking in protest, Cyrus had wanted nothing more than to flee this den of horrors; it had been his only clinging thought as he slowly mounted the steps, each advance more tentative than the last. Always he glanced over his shoulder at possible escape, never committing to his footfalls, and he'd nearly made it to the top when his wavering finally cost him.

Cyrus had fallen from the precipice without mercy, without grace.

It was a fifty-foot drop to his death, and he'd slammed bodily against every jagged lip of stone on the way down, landing with an impact so severe he broke his back.

The young royal had lain there bleeding on the cold, damp ground, enduring an agony of incalculable depths. He could see that he'd snapped two bones in one leg, that a jut of rib pierced through his shirt. His vision blurred; blood pooled slowly in his open mouth; his chest spasmed with some unknown damage and still he smiled, for what he felt in that moment was nothing short of joy.

It was over.

He would not have to face this terror, for Death had

come. He'd tried to do the right thing, but his efforts had come to naught, and now he could lie here until his blood ran cold and know no guilt. His world would unravel, countless innocents would die—but he'd be long departed by then, unaccountable for these tragedies.

He'd cried soundlessly, and they were tears of relief.

Cyrus couldn't have known that Iblees would animate his shattered body with the ease of a puppeteer, articulating his broken limbs in a display of breathtaking cruelty the young man had never even thought to imagine. The devil, Cyrus soon discovered, would not allow his debtors to default on a contract.

Inch by harrowing inch Cyrus was made to ascend the stairs by way of dark magic, his own blood choking in his throat. He was half-blind as his severed bones scraped together, piercing organs and tearing flesh. It was a state of suffering so excruciating he'd lost consciousness over and over, only to wake up each time on the slick ground in a shallow pool of his own gore, and made to climb the stairs again.

That day, Cyrus had learned cowardice was a luxury.

Only the privileged few could afford to run away, to lock their doors and close their eyes to ugliness. The rest lived in homes without doors to lock, looked through eyes without lids to shut. They confronted the dark even as their hearts trembled, as their souls shook—for even strangled by fear, there was no choice but to endure.

No one would be along to slay their demons.

Cyrus had been a sheltered royal the first time he'd

stepped foot in this cave, and he'd paid a tall price for the timidity of his heart.

He'd been careful never to make that mistake again.

Now he took a steadying breath and, very carefully, made his first move since arriving in the antechamber. He looked up.

It was like activating an alarm.

A swarm of sound enveloped him as he stared skyward, clocking the presence of several thousand bats hung like so many pendants from a neck of darkness. Their disembodied eyes watched him closely as they screeched, the eerie cacophony soon overtaken by the harsh, echoing skitter of small, hard legs rushing toward him. Cyrus, who'd experienced this spine-chilling phenomenon many times, knew he was being crowded on three sides by a clutter of arachnids and was careful to remain calm. A whisper along his spine alerted him to the growing presence of one in particular and, slowly, he turned to face his appraiser.

A spider roughly the size of his face peered at him from its perch in midair, the gleam of a silk thread barely legible in the light. Her long legs writhed not unlike the last, grasping reach of a man in need, several glassy eyes glinting in his direction as she assessed him. She spoke without precisely meaning to, relating her thoughts in a fractured communication that was never meant to be parsed by humans.

You are? You are?

No danger to you, said Cyrus soundlessly.

The spider only stared at him.

He held out his hand, palm down, and, after a brief hesitation, the massive arachnid lowered herself, then climbed
aboard his body with an eager scuttle of legs. She investi-
gated his fingers before climbing up his forearm, pausing at
his elbow to consider his face more closely.

You are? Before?

Yes. I've come before. You are in no danger from me, I swear it.

In response, the spider scaled the incline of his shoulder,
then his neck, the prickle of her hard, lightly-furred pins
raising goose bumps along his skin. Cyrus conquered the
impulse to recoil from the unnerving sensation, holding
still as she cautiously boarded his cheek, lifting her forelegs
slightly to better study his eyes.

It was a torturously long moment before she said—

You are? Sad. Sad. Sad.

Cyrus swallowed. "Yes," he whispered.

The spider regarded him a moment more before scurrying
from whence she came. She stepped off the plank of his arm
and into the unknown with a final judgment:

No danger.

The young king shook off a lingering unease as he waited
for the path before him to clear of arachnids. It was always
an unsettling business, being psychoanalyzed by spiders. He
did not want to ponder that the creature was able to dismiss
him with three words of shrewd observation; neither did he
did want to wonder how else he might've survived these trials had he not trained for so many years as a Diviner. If he'd
been unable to communicate with living creatures, if he'd
been unable to wield magic to fight for his life. It bothered

him to think of it as anything but coincidence; he didn't like to imagine he'd been born for this role, brought into the world only to endure this misery.

Fate, he thought bitterly, was only romantic when one was destined to be the hero.

Once his safe passage had been granted, Cyrus did not tarry; he thundered up the steep incline of the endless staircase, taking the steps two at a time. He was eager to be done with this hateful, infinite night. He reasoned that the sooner this fresh hell commenced, the sooner it might end—and before long, his destination came into view.

Towering above him was a colossal black archway suspended in midair, the structure as tall as a castle and half as wide. At the base of the ornate passageway spilled forth a herd of ominous gray clouds, within which Cyrus could make out only the spark of a familiar orange light. He headed toward this thick haze, pounding up the last few steps before launching himself, like a bird, into the rift.

SEVEN

هفت

WIND BATTERED HIS FACE, SOUNDS screamed in his ears. Cyrus spun until his flesh was wrung out, his face chapped by the currents, cheeks ablaze with color. He landed on his feet with a heavy thud that rattled his teeth before he straightened slowly, regaining his balance by careful degrees. The stench of rotting matter struck him swiftly, and he fought the impulse to gag, nearly doubling over as his eyes burned.

Before him loomed a curtain of charred flesh.

Iblees had never presented himself to the young king as anything but a whisper—a force transmittable from anywhere—and yet, too often Cyrus was summoned here. *Here*, the scene of every great missive and every great castigation, this decomposing suite of rooms separated only by patchwork veils of scorched human skin, was the devil's preferred place of communication.

It was, in Cyrus's approximation, a parallel to purgatory.

He closed his eyes now and braced himself, fighting not to inhale the putrid air as the familiar whisper blew through him, a voice like smoke pooling in the hollows of his body, curling around his joints, and tugging him downward—a suggestion that he fall to his knees. Cyrus fought this

compulsion, snapping the connection with a violent jolt
and straightening to his full height. He felt the haunting
impression of a laugh, and then—

Clay King was once a little boy,
and he would often cry
for milk and sleep and wooden rattles
and a soothing lullaby

Now he is a strong young man
and still we see him cry!
Poor heart is broken
Weak mind is weary
He simply wants to DIE

Cyrus's eyes flew open. His fists had clenched, unbidden,
but there was no one to fight; nothing to see.

"Did you bring me here to mock me?" he said quietly,
turning about the room. "What is it you want tonight?"

Oh, the jester is a lonely sort
who seldom gets to play
despite the jokes he loves to make
of witless, greedy Clay

Cyrus stiffened. He bade himself be calm despite a creeping instinct to panic.

With forced composure he said, "What does that mean?"

Clay girls and boys
my favorite toys!
Soon they'll come together
And she will choose
and you will lose
to a clod tied to a feather

A muscle jumped in Cyrus's jaw. "I don't understand your infuriating riddles. But I have reason to hope Alizeh is going to accept my proposal. She said as much to me earlier—"

Poor Clay brain is made of dirt!
It cannot solve a puzzle
Poor Clay heart
it falls apart
A frail, decaying muscle

"*Enough,*" the young king said angrily, fruitlessly searching the room for a face. "I let you spout your senseless rhymes at me for hours without complaint, but you've already forced me to endure your loathsome presence once this interminable night, and unless you intend to torture me again, I'll take my leave. Besides—I've lost nothing yet. I still have plenty of time to uphold my end of the bargain."

Time and ice are much the same
they slowly disappear

You may not see your failure, King,
but we can smell your fear

Cyrus felt a flash of rage. "Is that why you summoned me, then? To celebrate early?" He shook his head. "You're a vile bastard."

Afraid to close his eyes at night!
Afraid to see her face!
He hasn't slept a single wink
beyond a drugged embrace

At that, Cyrus gave a mocking, unhinged laugh. He felt like a caged animal. "You dare taunt me for my efforts, when it was *you* who planted her image in my dreams? You play dishonorably, resorting to manipulations beyond the terms of our agreement. What choice do I have but to protect myself?"

Poor Clay brain is made of dirt!
It cannot solve a puzzle!
Poor Clay heart
it falls apart
A frail, decaying muscle

"Why do you repeat yourself?" he demanded. "Cease hounding me with your nonsense if you won't explain your meaning!"

Never have we lost a match
We swear it by the stars
Never shall you have the girl
Her fate is twined with ours

You think to best the jester
in a game we have designed?
You mean to take away our toys—
and expect us to be kind?

Cyrus could hardly bring himself to speak through his fury, his fear, his wretchedness. Of all the ways the devil had thought to undermine him, this was by far the worst—and Cyrus could see now how easily he'd cleared the path for his own destruction. Iblees had endeavored over and over to break him with violence, yet these bleak efforts had only strengthened the young king.

But appealing to his parched heart?

Delivering him not merely the vision of an angel but the temptation of the real thing? He, who'd been discarded by all—shunned by the Diviners, hunted by his mother, betrayed by his father, abandoned by his brother, plunged into isolation and hated throughout the world? He, whose desiccated heart turned to dust before her tenderness?

Alizeh was the fulfillment of his most desperate, undisclosed desire. The constant, gnawing ache inside him—this pitiful need that grew only more fraught in the wake of every darkness that devoured him—

He longed for her warmth, for her radiance. She'd been, from the first moment she'd wandered into his dreams, an enduring flame in the endless night, his only haven in the madness that inhaled him.

This was his real weakness, and the devil had marked him easily.

The jester is quite delighted
to see you so distressed
For this pleasure you're invited
to make one small request

"I want nothing except what I'm owed!" Cyrus shouted, turning sharply as he spoke. He'd fully lost his temper now, glowering even as he addressed an empty room. "If you think I'd ask you for anything, you're a great deal stupider than you seem."

Oh, the jester is delighted!
To see you so distressed!
In exchange you are entitled
to this splendid bequest—

"No—" Cyrus tried to cut him off, fear branching up his spine. "I want nothing from you— I asked for nothing—"

The curtain of flesh evaporated without warning, and Cyrus went slack with disbelief. His anger changed, tenuous emotions braiding together in his chest. He saw the familiar orange light in the distance, its flickering glow acting as a beacon as he drew steadily forward, his heart pounding madly against his ribs.

He heard a muted rattle of chains, a ragged drag of breath. Cyrus pushed toward the sounds, following a long wall lit by an endless procession of blazing torches. A muggy heat clung to his skin and lingered, drawing beads of sweat down his throat as he turned a corner, and the scene came suddenly into view.

Chains as thick as fists were fastened to a cratered wall, shackles clasped around the hinges of an older man who hung unnaturally in the air, his emaciated body starved and tortured beyond recognition.

"Who's there?" came a hoarse, trembling voice. "Who's come?"

Seldom did Iblees allow Cyrus such a moment, and the sound of this haggard speech provoked a sting inside the young man's nose, his eyes heating foolishly. No matter how many times he'd come, this scene had never grown easier to endure.

Another desperate rattle of chains. Another terrified rasp of voice. "Who's there? I demand you declare yourself!"

Were he capable of humor, Cyrus might've smiled at the high-handed command, for it gave him reason to hope. The king had not yet lost his sense of superiority. He was not yet broken beyond recognition.

Cyrus approached his father then with a composure he could not explain. The young man did not feel as calm as he appeared, yet he knew no other way to face these horrors.

"Father," he said softly. "It's me."

"*NO!*" The true king of Tulan fought uselessly against his chains, his face contorting in terror, his eyes squeezing shut. "Leave here at once! I begged you—I asked you never to come back—"

"He took your other eye, didn't he?" Cyrus said thickly, pain lancing through his chest. "Tonight."

His father stiffened, then sagged, grief painted across his face. He did not open his eyes. He did not answer the question. "Never think of me again," the man said raggedly, the last dregs of energy leaving his body. "Imagine me dead and gone, child. This debt is not yours to bear."

"How can you say that," came Cyrus's quiet reply, "when it was you who asked me to bear it?"

A tense silence settled in the filthy chamber.

Cyrus cursed himself. He hadn't meant to say the accusing thought aloud—hadn't meant to waste this precious moment delivering emotional blows his tortured parent could not withstand. The young man had not paused to consider his words because his mind was splintering. The devil had not exaggerated: Cyrus had not slept since first laying eyes on Alizeh.

He hadn't dared.

He'd never forget the first time he saw her on that calamitous night, the way she'd stepped out from behind the dressing screen. She'd appeared in the golden lamplight of Miss Huda's bedroom like some impossible vision. Only when she'd lifted her eyes to his face and the sight of her had nearly killed him did Cyrus realize just how artfully he'd been outmaneuvered. He'd absorbed the blow with immaculate outward calm, letting the bomb explode inside him, liquefying his core. This inner destruction birthed a staggering, terrifying anger he'd been almost unable to conceal. He felt he'd gone mad, swinging wildly between desire and fury and disgust and fear, hardly able to manage himself or his reactions to her. He knew at once he'd been tricked; he knew at once she was an instrument of the devil, sent to ruin him. And yet, he weakened each time she looked in his direction. His need grew only more explosive as she solidified into someone real; always he desired another glance, another accidental graze of her skin—

He was terrified to ever dream of her again.

Cyrus had been using magic to keep himself awake for two days now. The drugged drowse of the devil had weakened his mind even as it revived his shattered body, and he'd awoken from that dangerous slumber only to betray himself shamefully. Exhaustion was even now pushing through the bonds of magic that held him upright, and the young king was not himself. Still, this was not the first time his father, Reza, had made such a ludicrous statement, and Cyrus should've bit his tongue. A wave of self-loathing washed over him as quiet sobs soon wracked his father's limp body. Tears fell from the man's closed eyes, streaking down his sunken cheeks.

Yes, Cyrus hated himself.

"Forgive me," came the older man's broken response. "I was a fool—I didn't know— Our weak, sheltered imaginations cannot fathom such corruptions of darkness— I never thought it would be like this— I never—"

Cyrus set his jaw. "I will see that this matter is resolved, and when it is done, you will return to Mother. The Diviners will fashion you a new set of eyes—"

"This matter will never be resolved!" Reza cried, hysterical now. "Don't you see? It's a trap—it's always a trap—"

"That's not true," Cyrus said, determined. "I've already completed most of the tasks. I have four more months—"

Reza would not stop shaking his head, his torment undisguised, his moods as sudden and changeable as the wind. "My son—you don't understand—"

"Tell me, then," said Cyrus, his chest heaving with barely restrained emotion. He'd all but destroyed himself in the pursuit of righting these wrongs, and always his father doubted him. "Why is it you won't put your faith in me? What is it I don't understand?"

Finally Reza opened his eyes, the rosy flesh of the empty sockets still wet with tears. "It's never been done," he whispered. "No man has ever wagered against the devil and won."

EIGHT

هشت

AT FIRST, ALIZEH THOUGHT SHE was dreaming.

Her head felt lush and heavy, mellowed by the honeyed sounds and scents of daybreak. It seemed as if people were speaking to her, but it was difficult to distinguish voices from the trills of chatty birds and the distant roar of moving water, and she was too distracted besides. Delicious sunlight warmed the wool of her cloak, a cool breeze coaxing her hood to rise and fall against her face. Her lips curved into a smile as her eyes slit open, a blur of amorphous forms crystallizing into an astonishment of color above her: vivid leaves of towering trees embroidered like lacework across a cloudless sky; a trio of bright red finches shooting through it all like fireworks. Alizeh made a gentle sound of contentment before closing her eyes again.

"No, miss—please stay awake—"

"She appears to be smiling," came a familiar, feminine voice. "Perhaps she chose to sleep outside?"

"If that's true, why does she seem incapable of waking?"

Alizeh giggled. It sounded almost as if her Ardunian friends were here—Omid and Miss Huda and even Deen. This was a possibility so absurd it seemed a stretch even for a dream. She rolled onto her side, blades of grass tickling her nose as her oversized hood fell forward and obscured her face entirely, plunging her back into a glimmering darkness. She drew in lungfuls of the damp soil and sweet air, delighting in the ineffable magic of dew. Oh it was heavenly here, wherever she was. The dream was generous, too, the confluence of so many things she loved—the serenity of nature, the soundscapes of early morning, the ebullient hues of life— with none of the ominous shadows that so often ruled over her in slumber. Alizeh thought she might sleep indefinitely, if only given the opportunity to stay right here.

"Your Majesty."

Alizeh startled at the strong voice. Her mind, which had not yet met the moment, was a step behind her heart, now pounding against her chest. Overwhelming intuition demanded she pay attention, but Alizeh could not place the speaker, even as she accepted he was important.

"Your Majesty." Again, but gently now. "Why are you lying on the ground?" The surprising weight of a hand landed atop her cloaked head. "Are you in danger? Have you been hurt?"

Then, like a key turning in a lock, she fit the voice to a name.

With a gasp Alizeh tore open her eyes, the action resulting in a magnified impression of grass, blades adorned by pearls of dew, and punished not only by the searing burn behind her lids but also by the bleak realization she wasn't dreaming. Her pulse racing, she perceived at once that this was not the landscape of fantasy, but the hard ground of reality, upon which she lay limp and disoriented. A shadow shifted, blotting the heat of the sun, and she shivered, the aches in her body awakening. The longer she held her eyes open the worse her head throbbed and her neck smarted; even some aspect of her face felt heavy with pain. Too soon the lift became too much, and her eyes fluttered shut once more.

It was when she felt the warm hand retreat from her head that she panicked, worrying she'd gotten it wrong, that this person was in fact a stranger, that her hopes were too wild to be realized. She summoned her strength, licked her parched lips, and compelled herself to whisper his name.

"*Hazan?*"

A beat.

Then, softly, "Yes, Your Majesty."

Alizeh thought she felt her heart stop. "Is it possible?" she breathed. "Are you really here?"

She did not imagine the tenderness, the faint surprise in his voice when he said, "I am really here."

The nosta flared to life against her sternum.

All this time, her fear and guilt over Hazan's fate had been trapped in a bauble of sentiment inside her, and the sudden compression of her chest shattered the delicately held emotion, wresting a terrible sob from her throat. She forced herself to turn over, lying flat on her back as she clapped a shaking hand over her mouth, hot tears curving toward her temples. Desperate for visual proof, she forced her eyes open again, her hands fumbling against the ground. When she turned an inch and saw him kneeling in the grass beside her, she was overcome.

She fell back against the earth and shook her head, over and over. She couldn't believe he was alive. Hazan, who was peerless in his loyalty to her, who'd gifted her the rare nosta that had saved her in a thousand ways from harm, who'd risked his life over and over for her safety.

She thought he'd been killed.

And now he was here? He'd come for her once again?

In all these years since her parents' death—years of screaming loneliness—she'd lost hope of ever finding another trustworthy soul. Yet Hazan had come to her without demands or expectations, parting veils of night to fall on one knee before her, setting into motion what might've been the great escape of her life. There was no one she felt safer with, and she'd done nothing to deserve his kindness.

He'd simply put his faith in her.

Blindly she grasped for his hand and pressed it between her palms, hardly able to see through her own tears to the mirrored emotion in his eyes. With great effort she swallowed, releasing him only to wipe at her face with trembling fingers. She fought to sit upright.

He moved at once to help, shifting her into a seated position. Her hood fell back as she lifted her head, and he stiffened at the reveal, his eyes widening as he looked her over. She felt an inexplicable tremor of alarm move through his body, but she struggled to connect to the feeling. Her mind was still so murky she could focus only on one thing at a time, and right now, she was having a hard time believing her eyes.

Hazan looked the same.

A bit fatigued around the edges but the same: hale, unin-jured. His hazel eyes were more brown than green in this light, an unruly lock of his ash-blond hair slipping over his forehead, grazing the slope of his broken nose. Alizeh had never seen him from such close proximity, and she was struck by the reminder that he was almost entirely freckled—a fea-ture that, were it not for the iron of his eyes, would've made him look rather young. Hazan was not traditionally hand-some, and yet his features were singular, his gaze alive always with feeling, his air of self-assurance so potent it moved with him like a second shadow.

She lifted her hands to his face, taking his lightly scruffed cheeks into her palms. He startled at the contact, the sudden movement of his chest betraying his reaction better than his eyes, which remained steady as she studied him. She couldn't explain her need to touch him, to know that he was real.

A single tear, the last of them, slid down her cheek.

"Hazan," she said softly. "How are you here? I thought he'd killed you."

In response, Hazan only shook his head, his eyes flaring with panic. "Your Majesty," he whispered. "You are gravely injured."

This statement surprised her.

Absently, Alizeh patted herself down as if to locate the source of this injury, first lifting a hand to her hair, which had hours ago come loose of its pins and adornments. The glossy bulk of her curls were trapped beneath the weight of her cloak, shorter sprigs springing free, dancing into her eyes. She frowned as she looked about herself, trying to ascertain where she was and how she'd arrived here, memories of the previous day and night coming back to her messily and out of order. Gently, she drew fingers along her face, wincing when she felt the welt of some fresh contusion along her cheekbone.

"Oh," she gasped, fighting a grimace. "Do you mean this? I don't know where—"

The words held in her throat, eyes widening in shock as she noticed, for the first time, the four looming figures planted just beyond Hazan's head.

Alizeh didn't know whether to recoil or rejoice.

Her mind had awakened enough, at least, to perceive that the scene was all wrong. Delighted as she was to see Miss Huda and Omid and Deen—all three of whom lifted hands in muted hellos—their presence here made no sense.

Finally she turned her gaze to the last of them, the most forbidding of the four standing just apart from the others. The crown prince of Ardunia was striking even in stillness, his gleaming sable hair and honeyed skin both novel and familiar to her.

Alizeh felt a quickening low in her stomach as she met his eyes, surprised to discover how much she'd forgotten about him in so short a time. He looked regal in the glow of a newborn sun, his expression inscrutable as he studied her, his mouth set in a grim line. She couldn't be sure whether it was the fatigue of her mind, but Kamran's face appeared different, one of his eyes glinting gold in the burgeoning light, the other as dark as it ever was.

Heavens, but he was devastatingly handsome.

He made no movement, no effort to reach her. He only studied her quietly from afar, one hand resting lightly on the hilt of his sword, the other curled around the strap at his chest, which connected to the quiver of arrows peeking out from behind his shoulder. It took Alizeh longer than usual to piece things together as she stared at him, but in labored seconds she gathered the threads of an explanation for his arrival—for the stoic, unflinching expression on his face—and when she did, she felt suddenly wide awake.

Mere days had passed since King Zaal had been murdered at Cyrus's hand—since the revered Diviners were slaughtered—and Kamran was no doubt dealing with chaos of extraordinary proportions back in Ardunia. He could have no business arriving, uninvited, at the Tulanian palace lest he was interested in one thing.

Revenge.

Alizeh drew a sharp breath, and Kamran's eyes narrowed. It was as if they'd communicated everything in those two movements. She could see now that he was not exactly pleased to see her, and in her head she tore through the tumult of the last thirty-six hours to recall the specifics of their parting, remembering, with an ache, the blaze of betrayal she'd seen printed upon his face before she left.

And yet—

Surely all that was sorted? Kamran must've forgiven

Hazan's secret efforts to help her escape Ardunia—for why else would the two young men have reunited? Why else would Hazan still be alive?

Her mind spinning once more, she returned her eyes to Hazan, who was looking at her with something like compassion.

"Fear not, Your Highness. I'll not allow you to come to harm."

Alizeh drew back. "*Come to harm?* You mean the prince has come to harm me?"

"In truth," Hazan said after a moment, "I don't believe him capable."

This was not reassurance.

Alizeh was unsettled anew, the revelation so confusing she struggled even to speak. "I don't— I don't understand— What reason could he—"

She was distracted by movement in the distance and lifted her head to discover Kamran coming toward them in swift strides, his face as impassive as ever. Alizeh shrank back reflexively at Kamran's approach, tensing even as she devoured the sight of him.

No, her eyes had not deceived her: his face was altered.

Something like a strike of lightning had bisected his left eye, splitting open a narrow, chaotic vein of gold along his skin, the peculiar striation glittering under the sun. His affected iris was now an inhuman color, the transformation somehow only heightening his beauty—rendering him otherworldly, and not a little terrifying.

"Your Majesty," came Hazan's low, urgent voice.

Alizeh turned back to him, her pulse refusing to calm.

"Forgive me, but I must ask you quickly: Have you consented to marry the king of Tulan?"

NINE

ALIZEH NEARLY ROCKED BACKWARD IN astonishment. She couldn't fathom how news of Cyrus's proposal had traveled so quickly to Ardunia, though she could imagine no other reason Hazan might've encountered such gossip.

"No," she said softly, eyes still round with wonder. "I've not consented to marry him."

"*Hells*," Hazan said on an exhale, the harsh word a contrast to his obvious relief. "I can't tell you how gratified I am to hear it."

"But—Hazan, I must tell you"—she placed a hand on his arm and he stiffened—"I've been giving his proposal serious consideration. . . . Cyrus has offered me his kingdom in exchange—"

"No," he said, brightening with alarm. He tossed a furtive glance at Kamran's approaching figure. "I beg you, do not consider it— It would be a mistake, Your Majesty—"

"What would be a mistake?"

Alizeh turned slowly toward the voice, steadying herself under the prince's imposing stare. She bristled with uncertain energy; she didn't know what to make of him, not now that she knew he harbored some wish to hurt her. He, on the other hand, remained implacable—just until he took inventory of her face and slackened in shock. His voice, when he spoke, was all the more lethal for its softness.

"Your throat," he said. "Your cheek— You are injured—"

"I'm quite well," she countered, not understanding her own impulse to lie. It was just that her head was so muddled and his mood so changeable that she felt at a great disadvantage. Alizeh disliked the way he towered over her, and she wanted space from his heated eyes, wanted a moment alone with her thoughts in the wake of these upsetting revelations. She attempted to lever herself into a standing position but lost steam in the effort, the unfinished action causing the unfastened flaps of her cloak to gape open.

Hazan swore loudly at the reveal of her bloodied dress, the epithet so off-color it shocked her—but it was Kamran who spoke, whose voice shook her with its fury.

"What happened?" he demanded. "What has that bastard done to you?"

Hazan, unfortunately, was no calmer. "Is this why you were on the ground? Were you in fact unconscious?"

"I don't—" she tried to say.

"Why is it you bear every indication of abuse?"

Alizeh shook her head, and a sharp pain pierced the back of her skull. She was dizzy and dehydrated, and her limbs were trembling, she realized, with much more than unease.

"Pray do not upset yourselves," she said breathlessly. She looked around, assessing the situation through new eyes. "Heavens, I wonder why we haven't yet been swarmed by palace staff. Or intercepted by the Queen Mother herself."

"Oh, the servants are all watching, miss," Omid piped in from afar. "Their faces are pressed against every window."

He waved at someone in the distance, and a faint chorus of giggles were issued in response.

"How nice," said Alizeh, forcing a smile. "More gossip."

Kamran's eyes were shrewd. "What do you mean?"

She was spared responding to this when Hazan cut in. "Your Majesty," he said, "where is the king?"

"I haven't the faintest idea," she said, and pressed the back of her hand to her forehead, which had broken out in a light, cold sweat. She felt nauseous. "But I promise you, the situation is not as it appears. He is no true danger to me—"

"I beg you do not make excuses for him in the interest of our protection. It is good of you to be concerned for our welfare, but you need not worry that we will prevail over such a brute."

"You must understand," said Alizeh wearily. "You, of all people, Hazan. *This*"—she gestured to her stained gown—"is not my blood."

"No—of course," came Hazan's stilted reply, his eyes sweeping over the endless spatter of red. "But the cut at your throat—"

"I know." She sighed, pressing the heels of her hands to her eyes. "It all appears rather badly, doesn't it?"

"It appears you've been physically harmed by the Tulanian king," said Hazan, who struggled now to moderate his voice. "Is this true?"

Alizeh winced. "Technically, yes."

Again Hazan swore loudly.

"But it's not as bad as it—" she started to say, before thinking better of it. "That is, to be fair, we both did harm to each other— In fact, I might've done worse to him if only afforded the opportunity."

"You mean you were involved in an altercation?" Kamran now. "With the southern king?"

"And did you aim to kill him, Your Majesty? Were you attempting to flee the castle?"

"No," Alizeh said, then hesitated. The throb at the base of her skull was making it difficult to think. "Well, yes. I mean, naturally, at first, I tried several times to kill him—"

"Wait."

At the tortured sound of Kamran's voice, Alizeh looked up. She found him staring at her with a pained expression, something between anger and anguish.

"Forgive me," he said, "it's only that I need to understand— If you tried to kill him— Are you saying it's possible you didn't leave with him voluntarily?"

The question was so strange, Alizeh fell silent.

"Leave with him voluntarily?" she finally echoed, a notch forming between her brows. "You mean did I leave Ardunia *voluntarily* with the king of Tulan?"

Kamran nodded.

"Of course not," she said, flinching as if physically stunned. The accusation was so insulting it lit like a firework in the tinder of her dry mind, supplying her a badly needed surge of adrenaline. "How could you ask such a question? I didn't even know who he was— He tricked me into coming here—"

"I told you!" came a chipper voice. Miss Huda was on tiptoe, holding a hand in the air like an overeager student. "I told you, sire, that she didn't know who he was!"

"*Quiet*," came Deen's loud whisper, shushing the young woman as he tugged down her hand. "Does this strike you as the time for gloating?"

"Yes, well, I did tell him, though, didn't I?" Miss Huda crossed her arms. "I tried to tell you all—"

"I believed you, miss," said Omid urgently. "I never doubted."

"No, you didn't," came Miss Huda's surprisingly tender reply. "You are the dearest boy."

Alizeh's thoughts were in chaos.

It had never occurred to her that anyone might question her reasons for tearing off into the night on the back of a Tulanian dragon. She'd been in the grasp of powerful magic, had screamed fearfully for her life for all to hear. That any person with a reasonable mind would attach a malicious explanation to her actions was baffling. She'd *defended* Kamran from Cyrus—had risked her life to protect him from the southern king's final, fatal blow—and still he'd doubted her intentions?

Knowing her own heart as she did, it seemed cruel to Alizeh that her good deeds had gone so quickly uncredited, that at the first chance to recast her in a poor light, Kamran had seized upon the opportunity. It made her realize how little she and Kamran knew each other—how tenuous was the bond between them. Only someone with a shallow understanding of her character could be so easily persuaded to malign her, and it was fortunate, then, that the guileless shock now printed upon her face was clear enough to all.

"I did not doubt you, Your Majesty," said Hazan softly.

She drew a breath, sparing Hazan a look of affection before turning to Kamran. "But you," she said to the prince. "You thought I ran off with him after—after all he did? You thought me capable of playing a role in the atrocities of that evening?" Despite her own injured feelings, her heart couldn't help but soften at the dawning horror in his eyes. After all he'd endured—what he must've thought of her. How he must've suffered.

"Oh, Kamran," she said. "How could you think that?" Then, more quietly: "How tortured you must've been to think that."

He absorbed her words with a stillness so complete it worried her, thawing only to close his eyes, to swallow. He appeared suddenly ashen with shame. Kamran was quiet a long moment, unmoving save the rapid rise and fall of his chest, and when he opened his eyes again there was a rage burning in the depths of his gaze, an inferno of fury that threatened to burn him down with it.

"I'll kill him," he said softly. "I'll gut him open and tear out his organs, and I'll make certain he lives long enough to endure the torture. When I'm done with him, he'll be begging for death. He will die, and he will die of his own agony." Kamran reached out an unsteady hand to touch her, his fingers skimming the tender bruise on her cheek. "You may depend upon it."

Alizeh shook her head in a sharp motion. "No," she said, stunned. "Kamran—you can't kill him—"

"It's what he deserves."

"No, it's—well, yes"—she frowned—"I suppose there

might be some argument for—"

She broke off with a gasp.

The fine hairs at the nape of her neck had risen in awareness, her skin seeming to tighten over bone. She knew he'd
arrived before she'd even laid eyes on him, and in the time
it took her to turn her head in his direction, Kamran had
already notched an arrow in his bow.

"*No,*" she breathed.

She finally caught sight of Cyrus in the distance, the lithe
lines of him appearing like an apparition through a veil of
mist. He struck her then as almost unreal; billows of morning
fog had gathered around him, his coppery hair gleaming like
a wicked halo in the gloom. He was following a narrow flag-
stone path along the edge of the cliff, having abandoned in
his wake an unopened steel chest—one that recalled another
from her arrival in Tulan, when Cyrus had taken time to feed
and water his dragon. Now, she wondered what he'd been
doing, where he'd been all night, whether he'd slept at all—
but her questions were silenced when their gazes locked in
place. He was too far to perceive clearly; she could not have
seen the hell and turmoil trapped in his eyes, his features
strained with exhaustion; but she saw the change in his body
as he registered, in real time, that something was wrong.

He fairly electrified.

Cyrus moved quickly, appearing altogether indifferent to
the presence of his uninvited aggressors, and if he had an
opinion on the matter of the arrow aimed in his direction, he
gave no indication. As he drew closer, it became obvious that
he focused on Alizeh to the exclusion of all else, his body

taut with restraint even as he moved resolutely toward her. He tried to hide a flare of panic as he studied the unnatural curl of her limbs on the ground—but she knew the moment he discerned the bruise on her face, for his eyes widened with undisguised alarm and he all but ran to her, now bolting down the narrow path at a dangerous speed.

"Stand down," came Hazan's sharp voice, cutting through the haze of her mind. "This isn't the moment."

Alizeh spun toward him, her heart in her throat, only to realize he was speaking to Kamran—who was carefully re-adjusting his aim, following Cyrus's movements.

"That is not for you to decide," said the prince.

"If you kill him now," Hazan responded angrily, "you are committing to war between our empires, which you know would be a mistake. There are any number of witnesses pressing their faces against the windows, and it is all but certain that one of the servants has alerted the royal guard— we are no doubt only moments from being intercepted, and we'll all be sentenced to death. You'll have little hope of sal-vation from the Ardunian side, especially as Zahhak seeks to destroy you. I implore you to think this through—"

"*Enough*," the prince bit back, sparing only a violent glance for his comrade. "If you think I will fumble an opportunity to exact revenge when it is within my grasp, you sorely mis-understand me—"

"I'm asking you only to *wait*, you fool! Your actions would incriminate us all—you put the child at risk—the young miss—"

"I warned them not to come," came his dark reply. "I

told them I wouldn't be responsible if they got themselves killed—"

Oh, this couldn't be happening.

Alizeh struggled to her feet; she felt as if the world were softly melting around her, as if she were trapped in a distorted dream. She saw the horror caught in triplicate on the faces of Deen, Miss Huda, and Omid; she saw the unflinching fury in Kamran's eyes, the resignation in the set of Hazan's jaw. It was wrong, all wrong. Cyrus couldn't die. Not now. Not yet.

Heavens, she thought.

Not ever.

She felt suddenly like she might scream at the prospect, her feelings on the matter so tangled they'd built a nest in her chest. Her own emotional chaos notwithstanding, Alizeh had every practical reason to keep Cyrus alive, too. She hadn't even realized how much she'd come to rely on him until just that moment. No matter her many protests and prevarications, Alizeh had begun planning her life around the prospect of marrying the southern king—and of taking over Tulan. Only hours ago she'd finally stepped into the light, holding forth with thousands of Jinn who were counting on her to address them again soon. If Kamran killed their king—if he sent Tulan into turmoil and cemented the prospect of war—

What would happen to her people?

With no empire, no crown, and no resources, Alizeh would have no choice but to flee, yet again, abandoning her flock just hours after she'd promised to lead them. All this flashed through her mind with breathtaking speed; she knew it futile even to attempt conveying these thoughts to Kamran, who had every right to want Cyrus dead. She could acknowledge this: she could acknowledge Cyrus's unforgivable crimes against Ardunia and its prince. She could acknowledge that he deserved retribution for these offenses. She could acknowledge that her reasons for keeping Cyrus alive were entirely selfish. It made no difference.

She didn't want him to die.

Oh, if only she had her own land, if she could find her own magic—she'd leave both these empires and their heirs behind, for Kamran and Cyrus had proven nothing but trouble. But without resources—without horses or supplies—the necessary journey into the Arya mountains could take months on foot. And even if she were to survive the trek, she couldn't do it alone. *Five people had to be willing to die for her* before the mountains parted with their magic.

Overwhelmed, Alizeh felt tears prick her eyes.

After all these years—and all this recent mayhem—the pieces of her life had finally, painstakingly, begun to fall into place. Now everything felt impossible once again.

She had to stop Kamran.

Much as she understood his pain, she couldn't stand aside and let him kill Cyrus and implicate the others in his murder. But something was the matter with her—with her head, her lungs, her bones. She couldn't understand why she was so tired or clumsy, and when she tried to move too fast, she swayed, as if the ground had surged beneath her. She felt the brace of Hazan's arms come around her even as she wheeled away blindly. She had no plan; she only knew she had to go to him, get between them somehow—

"Alizeh!"

Her head shot up at the sound of Cyrus's voice. He was still a dozen feet away, still following the path along the edge of the bluff, but he was close enough now that they could see each other properly. She met his wild eyes with panic of her own, absorbing his anguish just in time to witness the first arrow pierce clean through his leg.

She screamed.

TEN

CYRUS HISSED AS THE BOLT tore through muscle, the impact nearly knocking him over the cliff, parallel to which he stood precariously, even now. Mercifully, the shot had been so forceful the point made a clean exit through the back of his leg—a fact that would be helpful to him in a moment. For now he breathed, squeezing his eyes shut as he listened to the clamor of his heart, the swell of nearby water, the crash of the falls.

He was too tired for this.

In swift, practiced motions he snapped off the fletching of the arrow, wrapped his fingers just under the arrowhead and, without allowing himself to consider the repercussions, yanked the shaft out of his thigh. He gasped, blinking as the edges of his vision went briefly white. Still, he'd glimpsed the weapon: a broadhead tip with three barbed blades. Had the arrow not gone neatly through his leg, he wouldn't have been able to pull it free without tearing his flesh apart in the process. As it was, the pain was so extraordinary it was a miracle, even to him, that he didn't scream. To distract his mind, Cyrus bore witness to the maddening episode playing out before him; this mayhem, after all, was of his own making.

He deserved to be shot.

The evening prior he'd lifted the protective enchantments around the castle, all so Alizeh might return to her rooms without obstacle. She'd followed him off the grounds without knowing these expulsive shields went up after dark, and she had no reason to know: such defenses were technically illegal. The Nix accords drawn up long ago had made it criminal to place magical boundaries between lands, and Cyrus, who always sealed this magic right up to the escarpment, couldn't have cared less. Besides, he'd just killed a bordering sovereign; he had every expectation of a murderous visit from his neighbor and no reason to tread cautiously.

Yet his stomach had turned at the thought of Alizeh being forcefully repelled from his home. The devil, he'd reasoned, wouldn't have liked it if she were abandoned in the cold, vulnerable and exposed. Cyrus had done a bit of bad math as a result, convincing himself that an assault upon his empire—during the few remaining hours of night—was fairly low.

This optimism, of course, had been born of denial.

He'd lied to himself only so he wouldn't have to turn around, take her by the arm, and walk her back to the palace. It was too much temptation: the two of them alone in the dark, her body glazed in moonlight. He'd been afraid to go near her; he hadn't been ready to hear her voice, to look into her eyes. He was terrified she'd go and do something brutal, like smile at him.

Now, clenching against another contraction of pain, the heat of fresh blood pulsing from his wound, he knew this to be a fitting punishment. Indeed if the situation weren't so unpleasant it would be horribly amusing. Cyrus had been so sure he'd conquered cowardice; he'd been so sure facing the devil would be the greatest confrontation of his life. Never did he imagine he'd fear the subtle power of a young woman even more.

His land was now littered with fools, his hands slick with his own blood—all because he'd been too afraid to touch a girl.

He wanted to stab the arrow back through his leg.

All the same, Cyrus had anticipated such unpleasantries from the north; his only miscalculation was thinking he had more time. That the prince would barge onto his land without any apparent plan or imperial support, accompanied not by the might of his army but this bizarre assortment of allies, was baffling. More perplexing: there was no sign of their transport. And while he could imagine how these fools stood freely upon his land, he couldn't understand how they'd *landed*—for the enchantments around the palace were reinforced by numerous other protections. His team of dragons allowed no large-winged or otherwise aerial creatures to pass through the falls, and there was no chance the Ardunians had survived the battalion guarding the face of the castle.

How, then, had they come this far?

Cyrus was hounded by doubt, and yet, what preoccupied him most was a desire to go to Alizeh, to ask about her injuries, to discover what had happened in his absence.

His many questions would have to wait.

Currently, it was a wonder to Cyrus that he could think

at all. He took another breath, morning mist filling his head, and attempted to focus his thoughts.

Dregs of magic pulsed in Cyrus's veins—magic he'd allotted, for the most part, to keep himself awake, and which he would be forced now to expend keeping himself alive. His leg was so badly injured he'd begun to shake, and with great effort he cast a healing enchantment throughout his body, the sudden burn a comforting signal that flesh was painstakingly knitting back together. Even so, the torment was acute enough to render him unconscious; he felt a wave of nausea rise up inside him, and he forced it down just as he heard the distant, insistent shouts of a familiar voice.

He didn't need to turn to see her, for Alizeh lived always in luxury behind his eyes; he turned because the act of aligning his body toward hers was chased every time by a strange relief. Cyrus had spared little thought as to why the apothecarist, the street child, and the loathsome miss had invaded his territory; they were, to him, inconsequential players. The motives of the other two were of course obvious. As if the hole in his leg weren't indication enough, Cyrus watched through a haze of controlled suffering as the Ardunian prince notched another bolt in his direction. He and Hazan had arrived, naturally, for the simple pleasure of killing him. But Alizeh—

Alizeh, he couldn't understand. She was *defending* him.

Even then, trembling where she stood, speaking urgently with the prince, she fairly glimmered in the diffuse light of morning. As much as it tortured him to look at her, it tortured him more to look away. She was like no one he'd

ever encountered. The fact of her beauty was unimpeachable, yes—but one had only to behold her in motion to truly
understand her power. She was like an avenging angel come
to life, tender and magnanimous, serene even as she slit your
throat.

And he'd done nothing to deserve her mercy.

The Ardunian prince had yet to release another shot only
because she'd stayed his hand. Remnants of her words carried on the wind; she was visibly agitated, her movements
unsteady, and she'd clasped a fist around the bow, gently
turning the weapon downward.

Cyrus grimaced.

He estimated he had precious few seconds before Alizeh's
peacemaking efforts failed and the prince released another
shot. If only he could move his leg he might've gone to her,
might've advised her not to expend her energy arguing with
a wall. The thickheaded Ardunian had every right to try
to murder him; Cyrus would never be so unsporting as to
deny the young royal a chance at revenge. In fact, it was best
if she stepped aside and allowed Kamran to exorcise a bit
of this anger; the prince's mood would likely improve only
after drawing a few pints of Cyrus's blood. Perhaps then they
might actually have a conversation, after which he'd happily
stab the incumbent king straight through the eye.

In any case, Cyrus had suffered far worse than this and
survived. He needed only a moment to—

Another cry of warning, another arrow hurtling in his
direction.

With wicked quickness, Cyrus surprised even himself by

catching this one in his hand; he grit his teeth through a rush of breathtaking pain, an agonized gasp escaping him as the triple-bladed point tore open his palm like the pages of a book. The bloodshed was considerable, and as he watched the small crimson flood spill over the edges of his fist he almost laughed, though the sentiment was cold.

At least now he understood why the devil had been so delighted.

That bastard.

Clay girls and boys
my favorite toys!
Soon they'll come together
And she will choose
and you will lose
to a clod tied to a feather

This great oaf was meant to be the clod, then? Excellent. And Cyrus had clearly infuriated him by refusing to fall.

With an angry shout, Kamran released a volley of arrows in Cyrus's direction, one after another, the succession so smooth they seemed to come at him all at once. Even then Cyrus was able to appreciate his enemy's skill; the Ardunian was an accomplished archer. Cyrus bit through a fresh wave of torment, lifting his good arm to divert a bit of magic in his own defense, dissolving the incoming arrows while still healing his wounds. He was preoccupied with this—this and the effort to keep steady in the face of the many small deaths aimed in his direction—which was why he didn't notice, not right away, that she was running toward him.

When he did, he nearly lost his mind.

He watched the whirl of her draw closer and went light-headed with rage; he could hardly breathe around the feeling, so extraordinary was his anger. Alizeh had clearly spent the last of her strength, using what little energy she had left to rush at him with great speed—but whatever she'd thought she might achieve, she'd miscalculated, for she was not fully in control of her movements. He wanted nothing more than to shout at her for doing something so foolish. He couldn't fathom that she'd thought him worth such an effort, that she'd risk her own safety to spare his life. It made him want to do unforgivable things.

Indeed this anger might've been the only thing he and the stupid prince agreed upon, for Kamran's earsplitting cry of terror came just as Hazan and the others erupted in frenzied sound. Cyrus managed a choked cry before her soft body crashed into him, momentum rocking them both toward the very edge of the cliff, and if only there'd been time he would've pushed her out of harm's way, would've turned her in his arms—

With a sharp *thwack* the last arrow found its mark between her shoulder blades. Alizeh flinched under the force of impact, and her small, startled gasp rendered Cyrus absolutely, inhumanly still.

Panic inhaled him.

He felt blind with it, blind with madness. Alizeh whispered something incomprehensible against his neck, and he closed his eyes against a destructive swell of emotion, wishing desperately that he'd never been born. He didn't realize at any point that he'd stumbled, that he'd lost his footing, or that they were falling—not until he felt the wind, like a heavy hand, rise up beneath them.

And then let them drop.

ELEVEN

یازده

CYRUS ALLOWED HIMSELF ONLY A second to touch grief before his spine straightened as if wrenched taut, like the laces of a drawstring. The wind formed almost a cocoon around them, thick as it lashed their bodies, the calls of morning birds clashing with the thunderous crash of the falls. A heavy mist ensnared them as they plummeted, and though Alizeh shivered, Cyrus couldn't feel the chill; fear and fury seemed to be burning him alive. He'd just made a decision, and now he would see it through.

Alizeh would not die.

"*Look at me,*" he said wretchedly, pulling her close even as his torn hand shook in agony. It seemed some strange twist of fate that he should continue to bleed all over her, and if he'd more time to reflect on this fact he might've screamed for how much he hated it. "Alizeh. Please. Lift your head. *Look at me.*"

With great effort, she did.

Her eyes were glazed, flickering silver and brown in the rising light. She studied him like he might've been a dream. "Why? Because you're terribly handsome?"

"Don't be funny," he said, breathing hard. "This isn't funny."

She blinked, her head lolling softly to one side. "I can't feel my legs."

His heart heaved in his chest. That she'd lost sensation in her lower body meant the arrowhead had impaled her spine. Briefly, the southern king turned his gaze to the churning sea. They were falling at a dizzying clip, but the drop was so steep it was almost a mercy: they'd have nearly a minute before hitting water. If Cyrus had any hope of saving her he'd have to perform complicated magic before they made impact—but he was going slightly blind, his vision occasionally flaring with light. Worse, he was losing sensation in his left hand.

"*Kaveh!*" he called out.

The response was almost immediate. Cyrus heard the clamor of surging, crashing waves before they broke open to reveal the bulk of a shimmering dragon, its fiery hide emerging from the depths like a flame in flight. Every one of Cyrus's dragons was precious to him, but there were three in particular he loved as if they were his own family.

Kaveh was one of them.

By far the most sardonic of the fleet, Kaveh was also one of his oldest dragons, and Cyrus knew he would require the animal's careful expertise now, perhaps more than ever.

"Cyrus," said Alizeh suddenly, half gasping the word. "Where are you?"

His body was shaking as he held her, and he found he was grateful she'd turned away again, that she couldn't see his face. "I'm here," he said roughly. "I'm right here."

"I just—I just remembered," she said. "I can't swim."

There was no fear in her voice, only mild surprise—as if this were all a stroke of bad luck, a disappointing inconvenience. Cyrus didn't point out that she wouldn't have been able to swim anyway, given that she'd lost feeling in her legs. He only closed his eyes against her hair and fought the desperate crush of his chest, the violence of his affection for her. How she managed to disarm him even now, on the brink of death, he could not understand. She'd wept for his pain, wiped the blood from his eyes, taken an arrow in the back for him. She'd shown him more loyalty and tenderness in two days than he'd ever felt in his life, and he knew then, with a force that drove the air from his lungs, that he would never survive her.

"Don't worry, angel," he said quietly. "You won't have to."

Kaveh gave a small roar, exhaling sparks as he approached. Cyrus felt the dragon's confusion, then concern, and communicated without speaking, as he often did with animals—

I'll explain later.

Kaveh made another sound in response, a snort that nearly singed the king's hair. The flap of the beast's enormous wings was enough to whip Alizeh's curls across Cyrus's face, and as he struggled to push the tendrils out of his eyes, the animal swooped neatly beneath them, breaking their fall with a complete lack of finesse. Cyrus fumbled desperately for purchase with his injured hand, grasping at the dragon's hide to stabilize their bodies while he pulled Alizeh across his lap, hoping to absorb the brunt of the impact; given their tremendous downward speed, this proved nearly impossible.

Alizeh gave a sharp cry as they were seated, while Cyrus, who'd made no sound at all, nearly fainted from the pain. Of all things, he sensed Kaveh laughing at him. *You all right, sire?*

Cyrus did not dignify this with a response.

His every muscle taut with restraint, it was slow moments before the southern king could breathe again, before the haze cleared from his eyes. As they gently ascended through mist and cascades, Cyrus was able to discern screams from above, and when he craned his neck he could almost make out the shapes of the shouting idiots, their foggy forms tilting precariously over the crag, shrieks all but incomprehensible save a single: *"Dragon!"*

Kaveh was moving slowly for the sake of their injuries, and the higher they flew, the more Cyrus relented to an overpowering relief. The feeling hollowed out, however, when he realized Alizeh had grown lifeless, even as she trembled violently in his arms.

"Alizeh," he whispered. "Please. Wake up."

She didn't respond.

He knew he should inspect her wound in order to assess the damage, but Cyrus himself was in a horrible state of disrepair. His injured hand was now all but matted in blood, the affected arm convulsing as his fingers sparked and faded with sensation. His leg, at least, had received some magical care, but though the wound had stopped bleeding, it gaped open, a neat hole blown straight through muscle, radiating pain. Still, he couldn't do more for his own damage; he feared he might need to save what magic he had left for Alizeh.

His breathing was strained as he turned her slightly in his arms, the movement jostling her injury despite his best efforts to be careful. He expected her to gasp or at least flinch in response, but she remained motionless; her eyes were closed; her face drawn and pale. Even her trembling had begun to slow.

Cyrus struggled to hide his panic.

Urgently he whispered her name, willing her to speak, to open her eyes. He wanted her to yell at him, to threaten him, to pester him with her endless questions. There were no demands from her to know what was happening; no smart quips about the dragon; no threats to fling herself into the water just to be away from him. All this struck Cyrus like a blow to the sternum, and when he finally sighted her injury, he was dealt another: the arrowhead was lost in the folds of her borrowed cloak, at least three inches embedded in her flesh. Given the complexities of the barbed broadhead, it would not be a simple matter to remove the bolt—and he was in no state to offer her proper surgical and magical care.

There was only one other alternative—and Cyrus hoped she would forgive him for it, later.

"Kaveh," he said. "She needs to be delivered to the Diviners."

He felt at once the dragon's disapproval. *All due respect, sire, but you're not allowed there anymore. You know that.*

"Of course I know that," said Cyrus, his mood darkening. As if he needed such a reminder. "You will leave me at the cliff, then take her alone."

Cold quiet from the animal. They were hovering in mid-air now, stalled.

Please, Cyrus added silently.

But why, sire? Yaasi said you and the girl nearly killed each other on the flight back from Ardunia. Wouldn't it be better if she died? You said she was the devil's bride.

"A great deal has changed since we last spoke," said the king, wincing as his leg spasmed. "I was wrong about her. She's not allied with Iblees—and she was injured just now trying to save my life."

Kaveh gave no response to that, though his surprise was loud.

"I know," Cyrus said quietly. "I don't understand, either. I've given her nothing but cause to murder me."

More surprise. *And she doesn't know? About your father?*

Alizeh's eyelids fluttered briefly, and Cyrus hesitated. The bruise along her cheekbone appeared swollen and tender, the sight both devastating and confounding to him. He didn't know why she'd been lying on the ground this morning nor how she'd been injured; and given their collective response to the drama, it seemed unlikely her friends had been the ones to harm her, leaving no obvious suspect. It was yet another mystery he'd have to wait to unravel, and Cyrus, feeling both weak and helpless, finally allowed himself to stare at her. He studied the exquisite planes of her face, the fullness of her lips, lashes soft and inky against her pallid skin. It was dangerous to allow himself to linger, memorizing details—for the more he grew to care for her, the more unbearable it became to look at her.

Cyrus tore his eyes away, fresh bitterness fouling his mood further. "No," he said finally. "She doesn't know."

She would never know.

Iblees had forbidden Cyrus from speaking the truth to another person, but the southern king had not been precluded from confiding in nonhuman creatures. Such an exception was only possible, of course, because the young man possessed the rare ability to communicate using just the mind. Whereas nearly all others endowed with this skill were committed to the priesthood, Cyrus—whose deal with the devil had earned him an expulsion from the temple— had been unable to complete his journey as a Diviner, leaving him the unusual layman with this skill.

Still, few animals were interested in conversing with humans, and fewer still were capable of communicating more than basic information; which meant that his dragons, whose emotional intelligence encompassed an astonishing range of feeling, were his only confidants in the known world.

Sire, said Kaveh, his tone inscrutable. *I fear you're losing focus.*

"As if I don't know that," Cyrus muttered.

Days ago you would've considered this situation an opportunity. She put herself in harm's way through no fault of yours. Either let her die and be done with her, or make saving her life conditional upon accepting your hand. You need to marry the girl—this is your chance—

"You think this hasn't occurred to me?" he said. "I simply can't do it, Kaveh. I already had to drag her here, and that was when I thought she was conspiring with the devil to usurp my throne. Now that I know otherwise, how could I level such cruelty against her? Can you not see the difficulty—"

You murdered the northern Diviners without a second thought.

"You know that was different," said Cyrus sharply. "When Zaal was born the Diviners knew how the prophecy would end—they agreed it had to be done, and they set the terms—"

They may have been willing, but you were the one who cast the curse that killed them, just as you were the one who slayed Zaal. Was it for nothing? Everything you've endured? You would risk it all, sire, simply to please one girl's sensibilities?

Cyrus squeezed his eyes shut, suddenly hating himself. No matter what choice he made, he would lose. The devil had made certain of that.

No, came Kaveh's voice. *The answer is no. She's not worth such a price.*

Cyrus fell silent and was soon spared responding; Kaveh had started flying again, and they were now approaching the top of the precipice, where Hazan's angry cries rang out sharp and clear. They'd flown into the heart of an argument.

"—had a deal!" he was shouting. "I warned you—if any harm came to her—"

"Can you not imagine my agony?" came the prince's heated reply. "How can you bring yourself to accuse me when you know it was an accident—that I could never have meant—"

"You could *never?*" Hazan laughed darkly. "Are you quite certain? When you confessed to me just yesterday that you intended to kill her?"

Cyrus stiffened. As if he didn't have ammunition enough to murder the idiot.

"What?" The loud girl, Huda, spoke. "Is that true?"

"Oh, no," said the gangly boy too quickly. "No, miss, it can't be true."

"I had every right to be uncertain," Kamran shot back. "I had every right to doubt. It was never clear whether she could be trusted. The circumstances were disastrous—even you could acknowledge—"

"All right, I suppose it's true," Omid mumbled. "But I'm sure he didn't mean it."

"I'm sure he did mean it," added the older, wiry one.

"Be certain of one thing," Hazan said with quiet menace. "If she doesn't survive this, you will know the full breadth of my rage. I'll rip out every bone in your body before I *take off your fucking head.*" This last part he all but bellowed, the words echoing across the grounds.

Fascinated by this absurd exchange—between a crown prince and his lesser—Cyrus almost smiled.

"You are overreacting—" Kamran tried again.

"And you are not reacting enough!"

Prepare to descend, sire. Though how you hope to keep her seated on my back in your absence, I cannot imagine.

They were about level with the offending cliff now, Kaveh carefully hovering, and the entire unsavory scene came into focus. Hazan and Kamran were at each other's throats, so preoccupied with their anger they thawed a beat later than the others, the three of whom gaped in horror at Cyrus, then Alizeh, who remained unmoving in his arms.

The loud girl screamed.

"She's dead!" Miss Huda screamed again, shriller this time. "Heaven help us, she's dead—we killed her—she's *dead*—"

Cyrus turned away from this chaos.

He heard it all, of course—their collective shock, their shouted questions, their in-fighting—but he turned his back on it, feeling certain now that Hazan would keep the prince from any further attempts at murder. Cyrus needed to magic Alizeh upright so she'd survive the journey to the Diviners, and, as his mind was splintering with pain gathered from any number of grievances, he needed a moment to focus.

There were great risks involved.

Draining his store of magic would leave him deeply vulnerable to attack—and worse, would send him into a spiral of fatigue. He hadn't slept in over forty-eight hours; between sleep deprivation and blood loss, he wondered how he'd manage basic motor skills. He'd need to get to his rooms as quickly as possible after performing this last bit of divination for Alizeh, but how he'd accomplish that with this troupe of clowns to contend with, he didn't know.

Cyrus took a deep breath, a tremor rocking his body as he exhaled. He gathered Alizeh gently against his chest, pressed his good hand as close as he could to her wound, and, with great effort, transferred the remaining magic in his body directly into hers.

He felt the change in her, the pulse of energy returning to her limbs, and she cried out in response, this breathless sound sending his small audience into renewed chaos—*"She's not dead! She's not dead!"*—even as her cry soon dissolved into a whimper. He couldn't heal her, not with the arrow in her back; but he'd lent her some pain relief, at least, and he was certain she'd now remain seated until reaching her destination. It was enough for now—it had to be—because just as her eyes fluttered open, Cyrus nearly swayed. Without magic to keep him awake, he was suddenly so tired he felt he'd lost control of his limbs. Cyrus, who'd never touched spirits, imagined the feeling was akin to being drunk.

Miraculously, he lifted her off his lap and sat her on the dragon, satisfied when she didn't pitch sideways. Still, his thoughts seemed to slur. "Go," he breathed, digging deep for the last of his adrenaline. "Promise me—promise you'll take care of her."

"What?" Alizeh was squinting at him.

Cyrus startled. He hadn't expected her to speak, and he hadn't meant to say that out loud. Still, she appeared only half-awake, her head canting to one side even as her body remained upright.

Blearily, she said, "Who are you talking to?"

His heart was beating faster now. "My dragon," he said.

"Oh." A little line formed between her brows. "You have a dragon?"

"I— Yes."

"Just like you did before." She stifled a yawn, her eyes closing. "Do I get one, too?"

Cyrus frowned. "Would that . . . please you?"

"Yes, I think so."

"All right." He blinked slowly. "You can have a dragon."

Kaveh's head gave a sudden jerk, smoke curling from his nostrils. *Are you quite out of your mind, sire? You will not give the girl a dragon.*

Cyrus bristled. *You live under my protection, in service of the crown. I'll give her a dragon if I like.*

Well it won't be me.

"Cyrus?"

"Yes?"

"Why are people shouting?"

With effort, Cyrus glanced at the others. Kamran was threatening from afar to disembowel him; the three goons were in various states of hysteria; and Hazan looked as if he was contemplating a running leap off the cliff and onto the dragon. Terrible idea, that.

"I suppose people shout sometimes," he said as he turned to her.

"Cyrus?"

He felt delirious. He was staring at her with the awe of an idiot perceiving the sun for the first time. He nearly drew his hand down her cheek. Nearly kissed the side of her neck. Nearly slumped against her and fell asleep. "Yes, angel?"

"We died, didn't we?"

The question was such a surprise he briefly jolted awake, and was about to deny it when she spoke again.

"We died and we're together—and we're not in hell," she murmured. She nearly tipped over, but the magic yanked her upright. "And you got a dragon. Maybe I'll get a dragon."

He swallowed.

She patted his arm blindly. "That must mean you're not so bad."

Cyrus took this like a shot of poison; he couldn't bear to respond.

The idiot Jinn is going to jump, said Kaveh. *You must go, sire. You'll receive word as soon as she's safe.*

It was true; Hazan had a determined gleam in his eye. He was shaking off the child, whose futile efforts to pull the young man away from the ledge were almost endearing.

I'm entrusting her to your care, said Cyrus. *Please. Protect her at all costs.*

As you wish. I'd only like my disapproval noted.

He sighed.

With a last look at Alizeh, the king dismounted carefully; Kaveh had extended a wing toward the cliff, a veritable bridge to uncertainty. Cyrus cleared this distance as quickly as his dense head and injured leg allowed, and once across was rewarded for his agony with the dramatic excoriations of his unwanted guests.

"You sick fiend, what have you done with her?"

"—bad was the injury? How deep did it—"

"Carry her off the dragon, you demented ass!"

"Is she dead? Please tell me if she's dead? It wasn't clear—"

Cyrus glanced back just as Kaveh roared, he and his rider setting off into the morning light against a backdrop too beautiful to suit. He knew she'd be all right. He knew the Diviners would easily mend her. It wasn't fear for her life that gripped him now; it was fear for his own. He shouldn't care for her so. He *could* not. It would kill him before he was ready to die, and then— And then all this torture would have been for nothing.

With a heavy head, he faced his visitors.

Of the five who stood before him, it was Kamran whose gaze was impossible to ignore. Anger and hatred were so alive in the prince's eyes they nearly forged a separate soul.

It was the last thing he saw before he collapsed.

TWELVE

دوازده

"GOOD GOD," DEEN BREATHED.

"Is he dead?" asked Miss Huda, peering at the king out of the corner of her eye, as if she were afraid to look at him.

Omid ventured a bit closer, leaning down to inspect the cretin's face. "I don't know," he said softly.

"And what of Alizeh?" Miss Huda said with a cry. At the sound of her name, Kamran experienced a familiar shock of pain.

"What's happened to her?" the girl went on. "Where do you think she's gone? That madman probably shipped her off to a dungeon somewhere—"

"That seems unlikely." Hazan was stone-faced. "The dragon was heading west."

"A-And?" Miss Huda faltered. "Are there no dungeons in the west?"

"Don't worry, miss," said Omid reassuringly. "It'll be all right. I'm sure we'll find her. I'm not sure how, exactly"—he dimmed—"if the king is dead. He's probably the only one who knows where she went."

Deen dragged both hands down his face. "Do you really think he's dead? I feel terrible for the poor girl, but perhaps we should we run for our lives? Surely we'll be executed for this?"

"Executed?" Omid turned to the prince, his eyes wide with fear. "Sire?"

They all turned to face him, and finally, Kamran spoke.

"It won't come to that," he said irritably.

"Can you be sure, sire?" Deen again. "Because historically—"

"Oh!" the boy exclaimed. "Oh, I think he's breathing!"

Deen went slack. "Thank heavens."

"It does seem curious," Miss Huda mused, "that, despite the many faces pressed to the window, not a soul has stepped outside. I think if we were going to be tossed in the dungeons it might've happened already."

Hazan was studying the palace windows, the many wide eyes peering down at them. "Yes, very curious," he said quietly. "Where on earth is the royal guard to defend their king?"

He walked over to Cyrus's fallen body, crouching to get a better look. After a moment, he said gravely: "He's certainly not dead, though his health has deteriorated with astonishing speed—which is strange, as his wounds aren't terribly severe. His leg has stopped bleeding and the damage to his hand, while grotesque, is not enough to kill him. I can't imagine why he's lost consciousness."

"Maybe he fainted," offered Omid.

"I doubt that," Kamran said darkly. "He doesn't seem the type to lose his head over a little mutilation."

"Blood loss, perhaps?" suggested Deen.

Hazan, who was still inspecting Cyrus, said, "Not quite enough blood lost, I would say. Though it's certainly possible."

"Did you see the way he used magic?" asked Miss Huda, who was stepping cautiously closer to the king. "The way he made some of those arrows just . . . disappear?" A pause, while her brow furrowed. "Speaking of which: Has anyone else noticed that he seems to be rather frighteningly magical? How do you think he's able to cast spells so easily?"

"The devil," said Kamran. "No doubt he and Iblees are fast friends. I'm sure his power is a consequence of selling his soul to darkness."

"If that's true"—her frown deepened—"I wonder why he didn't use magic to spare himself of this moment now. He's in a horribly vulnerable position. Just think: anyone at all might come along and"—she made a dramatic slicing motion with one hand—"chop off his head."

Omid giggled at that, and she giggled back, as if it were entirely the etiquette to be making jokes at such a moment. Kamran turned away from the infantile pair, grimacing against the sharp blade of a fresh headache.

"It's possible he was dealt a blow to the head in the descent," Hazan said quietly. "If he's suffering from an internal injury he'll need assistance at once. His situation is growing more uncertain by the moment."

"Shall we let him die naturally, then?" More from the excruciating Miss Huda. "Or do you still intend to kill him?" This she asked as she whipped around to look at Kamran. Three other sets of eyes turned in his direction.

"Don't you dare," came Hazan's low warning.

Kamran shot his old friend a hateful look.

The insipid king had fallen to the ground at his feet almost as if he were offering himself up to be killed. How easy it would've been to drive a dagger through his throat; indeed Kamran should've been thrilled—and yet he was nothing less than furious. He wanted the blackguard to get up and fight; what satisfaction could there be in impaling a corpse? Then again, the entire morning had been a tragic disappointment. First, Simorgh had abandoned them almost immediately after alighting; then, Alizeh had been discovered unconscious. Kamran had only just digested the revelation that she hadn't betrayed him when Cyrus came into view, and it had been the perfect opportunity. He'd been inches from victory. Inches from exacting revenge upon the person responsible for the nightmare his life had recently become.

That Alizeh had tried to save the blighted king was hard enough to understand—but that Kamran had shot *her* instead—

For a terrible moment he thought he'd killed her. It would've been a tragedy—he knew that, knew it in his soul—but he was nursing a quiet anger toward her, too. Anger that she'd intruded upon a private matter, anger that she'd taken the side of his oppressor, anger that she'd foiled his plans. To make matters worse, she'd now complicated things horribly: she was injured and missing, and would require a second rescue. Lord knew what Cyrus had done to her, sending her off on the back of yet another blasted dragon to some godforsaken place.

"Why shouldn't I kill him?" said the prince ominously.

"The simple answer," said Hazan, "is that Alizeh begged you not to."

Kamran's expression grew only stormier. "Is that all? You think I should've let him live simply because she wanted me to?"

"Is that not enough? You did as you pleased and nearly killed her in the process—"

"A terrible accident!"

"And where is your remorse?" Hazan demanded. "Why do you express no concern for her well-being—why do you remain preoccupied only with your own disappointments, when we came here with the express purpose of saving her—"

"I came here with one purpose." Kamran cut him off, his eyes flashing. "And that was to avenge my grandfather."

Hazan fell silent a moment. "Even now?" he said. "Even after discovering your grandfather was wrong about her? Can you not relinquish your anger long enough to realize that Alizeh needs our help—"

Kamran flinched. "Stop saying her name!"

"My humble opinion?" Deen cleared his throat and lifted a finger. "You might consider killing the king now, Your Highness. It does seem a good opportunity. You could finish up, and we could fly straight home." He picked up a fallen arrow and offered it to Kamran as if he needed it—as if he didn't have any number of weapons concealed on his body. "If we move quickly, we might even be back in time for supper."

"But Simorgh and her children are gone," said Miss Huda. "And I suppose we haven't any way of knowing whether they'll return—"

"Alizeh did not betray you!" Hazan insisted, ignoring all

this. "She was wrongly accused by both your grandfather and yourself. You had proof of this today and still you persist in this attitude. Our focus now should be finding her—saving her—not wallowing in personal vendettas. How can you not see the damage you're doing?" He shook his head. "Your thirst for revenge has blinded you, Kamran."

The prince clenched his jaw, darkness settling inside him. "I *am* sorry she was injured. I'm sorrier to have been the one to cause her harm. But she had no business interfering, and I'm no longer certain she needs saving."

"She was just carried off on the back of a dragon!"

"She chose to protect him!" Kamran shot back. "She took an arrow in the back for the bastard who nearly killed me! Perhaps you can imagine why I'm struggling to feel sympathy."

"I trust that she had good reason for acting as she did."

"And your blind faith is going to get you killed."

"Watch yourself." Hazan's eyes had gone flinty. "You speak of her as if she's some capricious girl, and not the prophesied savior of my people. If she didn't want you to kill him, I'm certain she had justification. She felt so strongly that she pleaded with you—she physically turned down your bow and still you defied her wishes—"

"*Her* wishes?" Kamran all but exploded. "And what of mine? What of my dead grandfather, my dead Diviners, my broken empire, my disfigured face—"

"Oh, it's really not that bad, sire," Deen assured him. "Truly, I've seen quite a number of disfigurations, and yours—"

"—doesn't diminish your beauty at all," finished Miss Huda, nodding eagerly. "In fact, I think it suits you nicely—"

"Well *I* think he looks ugly," Omid countered. "And I don't think it's good to lie to him—"

"Are you raving idiots incapable of shutting your mouths for a single, bloody second?" Kamran cried, his chest heaving with fury.

Both he and Hazan turned to look upon their audience, all members chastened save Miss Huda, who was staring slack-jawed at Kamran with a disappointment so severe it bore a resemblance to heartbreak.

She didn't move except to blink her devastated eyes at him, and in the proceeding silence Kamran realized she was waiting for an apology—an expectation so absurd it cemented in his mind the unnerving fear that the young miss was, in fact, delusional. He witnessed the moment her light went out—naive hope extinguished—before she finally spoke.

"Come along, Omid," she said tightly, taking the boy by the hand. "I'm beginning to realize that princes aren't nearly as charming as I'd been led to believe." Then, more quietly: "This one, in particular, has fallen well beneath my expectations— which I fear were great, indeed."

Kamran reeled at that, his chest heating once more with indignation. He was clearly in the throes of a wretchedness that encompassed his very soul—and this ridiculous girl had the audacity to focus only on her own feelings, and the temerity to accuse him of incivility? If only she knew the number of times honor alone had kept him from acknowledging aloud the many indignities of her character. She'd no idea the self-restraint he'd already employed in her presence, and for his efforts he was granted no credit, only condemnation—

"It's clear we're not wanted here," she added with an arch of her brow. "Perhaps we should see about procuring some breakfast."

Omid frowned, even as he allowed the young woman to steer him away. "I don't understand your meaning, miss— I'm sure the prince doesn't want us to leave—but breakfast would be great, if I'm speaking honest. I'm starving."

"I'd love a cup of coffee," Deen piped up, joining the others eagerly.

"You were too harsh," Hazan said quietly to the prince. "They didn't deserve to receive the brunt of your misdirected anger—"

"They should learn to hold their tongues," Kamran snapped. "They talk too much. All of them."

Hazan, too reasonable to deny a proven fact, only sighed in response.

A cool breeze pushed through the grounds then, morning sun recasting the grim scene in a dazzling flare of light. Kamran turned his face up to the sky, exhaustion and uncertainty plaguing him in equal measure. He felt no remorse for his earlier speech. He would not allow Miss Huda's unwarranted feelings to affect his conscience. In fact, should the aforementioned idiots finally abandon him, he would be *delighted*.

He turned his head to witness the three walking off with great conviction in no particular direction, Deen's voice carrying when he said—

"Do you think it's all right to leave the king lying there?"

"I don't know, and I don't care!" sang Miss Huda. "I'm no longer interested in the lives, deaths, and bloated heads of royalty. I've put up with enough snobbery in my life, I think, and I've just decided I'm quite done with it. Besides, I didn't come all this way to manage the tantrums of an overgrown child, I came here to help Alizeh—who, despite her apparent crown, never once spoke to me in such an insulting manner." She turned to her companions. "Did Alizeh ever speak to either of *you* in such an insulting manner?"

Kamran flinched at the repeated sound of Alizeh's name, even as he listened to this exchange in mute astonishment.

"No, miss," said Omid with an eager shake of his head.

"No, miss," said Deen with an uncertain glance back at the prince.

He couldn't believe— *The nerve of her*— He never tolerated such insolence from anyone, much less an ill-tempered, illegitimate miss of no distinction. Even Omid, who'd once tested his patience to the hilt, had quickly learned deference. That she would dare insult him and speak of him with such condescension, as if he were beneath her—and he, the impending king to the greatest empire on earth— Hell, it was his prerogative to have her banished from Ardunia forevermore should he choose to do so, and yet, somehow, his bafflement was so complete he was unable to form the words necessary to express this outrage.

Very well.

His eyes narrowed. If this was how she wanted to proceed, he would more than match her ire. Kamran was nothing if not masterful in the pursuit of vanquishing his rivals.

"Ah, there's a fine lady coming toward us now," announced Huda. "Perhaps she'll know where we might find something to eat."

At once Hazan took advantage of his stupor to step forward, shielding Cyrus's crumpled body from view. "A final warning, Kamran," he said quietly. "I don't take orders from you anymore. My queen issued a command to keep this fool alive and I will honor that, even if I don't understand it. Try to kill him, and you'll have to go through me."

It was a moment before Kamran recovered himself, tearing his mind away from the horrors of Huda to this, the more present catastrophe, and when he did, disappointment dampened his fervor. "Of all the scenarios I might've imagined," he said finally. "I never thought you'd stand against me in this. That you would defend *him*."

"I never imagined I would, either," Hazan said with a long-suffering sigh. He dragged a hand through his hair before glancing again at the prone body of the southern king. "At the very least, I need him alive long enough to discover what happened to Alizeh—and what he did with her. Until such a time, he will remain under my protection."

"You would really fight me?" Kamran said, regaining a shade of his earlier temper. "If I challenged you now—you'd be willing to die for him?"

"For *her*," Hazan corrected. "Without hesitation. Though you flatter yourself if you think you could best me in a fight. You've never truly known me, Kamran, and I'd hate for you to make my acquaintance only as you draw your final breath."

The prince raised his eyebrows.

It was the way Hazan had said it—without arrogance or swagger—that gave him pause. In fact, Hazan seemed to mean the words sincerely, as if he'd indeed regret a bloody conclusion to their friendship. Except—

"If that's true," said the prince, "why didn't you fight back when the guards dragged you away at the ball? If you're as capable as you claim, you might've saved your queen then."

Hazan looked away. "I should have."

"And yet?"

"My greatest failing that night," he said gravely, "was that I didn't anticipate Cyrus. I'd no idea another plan for her had been hatched alongside my own; hell, I didn't even know Cyrus was in possession of her *name*, much less a scheme to spirit her away. My own plans for the evening had been compromised; all I wanted was her safety and anonymity, and I'd hoped the distraction of my betrayal would afford her an opportunity to run. Never did I imagine that in my absence she'd take her exit through the palace wall, on the back of a Tulanian dragon. Never did I imagine she'd end up *here*, in this godforsaken hell," he added angrily, meeting the prince's eyes. "I've gone through it in my mind dozens of times, hating myself more each time for failing her. Understand me now: I refuse to fail her again."

The prince was silent as he appraised Hazan a moment more: the set to his jaw, the grim resolve in his gaze. "I see that you're determined," he said finally. "And I'll grant you this one concession, Hazan, but never again. You may keep him alive until your queen is found, but when the time comes for him to die, be certain that I will set the terms."

"So that's it, then?"

Everyone turned at the sound of the new voice. Kamran was surprised to discover a regal, older woman drawing carefully toward them. Her fiery hair color and glittering diadem left little doubt as to her identity, and though Kamran knew he should bow, or at least incline his head, he refused.

He only stared, stonily.

She nodded at him, unbothered by his silent disrespect, then at the others who'd circled back from their breakfast search, now frozen in various states of debasement. Omid had attempted a curtsy.

"I am Queen Sarra," she said with a strange smile. "And you must be Prince Kamran, of Ardunia." Carefully she cataloged his fresh scar, the glittering vein of gold that split through his left eye. "I've heard a great deal about you, of course. My condolences."

Kamran maintained his silence, though he was resisting an urge then to destroy something. That she might stand there and offer him condolences as if she were remarking upon the weather—and her own *child* responsible—

"Are you quite certain," she said delicately, "that you're not going to kill my son?"

"There was a serious misunderstanding, Your Majesty," said Hazan, stepping forward. "The king appears to be unwell."

She glanced at Cyrus's collapsed, bleeding body. "I can see that."

At this cold reaction, even Kamran frowned. The woman's

son was half-dead on the ground, and she inspected him as if he were diseased. She was either demented or dangerously malicious; Kamran hadn't yet decided. When she continued to smile at him, he found himself leaning toward the former.

"Well," she said, and took a sharp breath. "I suppose you must all be tired from your journey. Do come inside. Breakfast is well underway."

"Breakfast?" Hazan echoed.

"*Breakfast*," Omid said eagerly, then hesitated. "Wait"—he stepped back—"you're not going to throw us in the dungeons, are you?"

Sarra tilted her head at the boy, then responded to him in his native tongue. "You speak Feshtoon, how lovely. And where are you from?"

Omid straightened to his full height. "I'm from Yent, of Fesht province, miss. I mean, Your Ladyship." Huda elbowed him and he squeaked. "I mean—Your Majesty."

The woman's eyes softened. "My mother was from Fesht," she said. "I haven't been back since I was a little girl."

"Forgive me," Hazan interjected. "But the king requires swift medical attention. Perhaps we should send for a surgeon, or a Diviner—"

"Are your parents still in Fesht?" Sarra went on. "Or did you move to the royal city with your family?"

Omid shot a nervous look at Hazan before answering the woman's question. "My parents are dead," he said, and in a gesture of respect for the deceased, he touched two fingers to his forehead, then to the air. "*Inta sana zorgana le pav wi saam.*" *May their souls be elevated to the highest peace.*

"As are mine," she said softly, mirroring the motion. "Inta ghama spekana le luc nipaam." *May their sorrows be sent to an unknown place.*

"I— Thank you, miss." Omid ducked his head in acknowledgment and, after another nudge from Huda he added: "I mean—Your Highness, ma'am."

Sarra appraised Omid a moment longer, her expression not unkind, then studied each of them with a shrewdness that sent Kamran's instincts into high alert. "Welcome, all of you," she said. "What an unexpected—but delightful— surprise. Please do join me—"

"I'm afraid we must decline," said Kamran, issuing his first words to the woman. He was now certain beyond a doubt that she was mad; there was no chance he'd be accompanying her anywhere.

"But, sire," said Omid, "she said there was breakfast—"

"I know the situation is unusual," said Sarra, her eyes sharp as she turned to Kamran, the smile on her face belying her next words. "But if you don't accompany me inside, there will be hell to pay. As you may recall, you came here this morning with the intention of murdering my son—"

"It was not as it seemed, Your Majesty," Deen said nervously. "Most of us meant no harm—"

"—and, having been unsuccessful, you think you might cut your losses and head home. You've failed to realize that you stand here now only because of me, because of the amnesty I am willing to provide. You need not understand my motivations, but you *should* understand this: your actions have been witnessed by all in the palace. Did you really think no one would note the appearance of five legendary, magical birds in our sky? That no one would observe them alighting upon our land?"

Deen made a strangled sound.

"Very clever of you, I should say," she added softly. "There's only one creature alive to whom dragons show such deference, else you never would've survived your descent onto the palace grounds. Though how you managed to secure the protection of Simorgh is a mystery I should dearly like to solve." She narrowed her eyes at Kamran. "I presume it has something to do with the fabled tale of your grandfather."

"Oh, yes, miss," said Omid, "it really is an amazing story—"

Five heads swiveled at once in his direction, and Huda quickly clapped a hand over the boy's mouth. Kamran nearly swore aloud.

"I see," said Sarra, whose anger appeared to spike in the silence that followed. "You intend to cling to your secrets until the grisly end. How unwise. But then I suspect you have no idea what kind of mayhem befell our home just last night, nor what devastation might befall us all if word spreads that the Ardunian prince stormed our palace in an attempt to kill the king."

"When she puts it like that," Huda whispered, her hand falling away from Omid's face, "it *does* sound awful."

"Hells," Deen breathed. "I just wanted to meet Simorgh."

"Hated as he might be in Ardunia," Sarra pressed on, "the Tulanian king is rather beloved at home. So unless you hope for our empires to go to war—or you wish to be murdered in the street—you will join me," she said through gritted teeth, "for breakfast."

Kamran was still contemplating this shocking speech, and still contemplating his response, when Hazan interrupted angrily—

"How can you stand there and monologue while your son lies bleeding on the ground? Your actions are so baffling as to confound the mind! Ma'am, the king is *dying.* I am asking you to call for help at once—before it is too late."

To this outburst Sarra showed no reaction, never even glancing at Hazan. Instead, she kept her eyes fixed on the prince, her strange smile now bordering on manic. As he met her gaze, Kamran felt a bolt of dread move through him.

It was true: he had no idea what they'd just walked into. He had no idea what Alizeh had experienced during her time here; he didn't know who this woman was, what her intentions were, or where the devil Simorgh had gone. Heavens, but he needed her badly now.

More than that, he needed his grandfather. He'd even settle for a kind word from his mother.

With a start, Kamran remembered the envelope in his pocket—the one Hazan had earlier pressed into his hand. It suddenly seemed more important than ever that he make sense of the communication from his mother, and he resolved to find an excuse to be alone at the first opportunity.

"Very well," he said, discreetly locking eyes with Hazan. It took this single look to confirm what they both understood: there was something deeply the matter with Sarra, and they should tread cautiously where she was concerned. "We'd be honored to join you for breakfast."

"*Wonderful!*" she cried, clapping her hands together. Then, turning to Huda: "Some things should be illegal for their offenses against the human eye, darling, and if you're to enter my home, I'm afraid you'll have to burn that frock." She appraised the girl a moment more, her brow wrinkling in distaste. "If you wear that abomination to dinner tonight, I might set it on fire myself, and with you still in it."

"Dinner?" said Kamran, alarmed. "When we've yet to endure breakfast?"

"I don't— But it's the only dress I have—" attempted Huda, who was blushing fiercely.

"Your Majesty, please—" Hazan tried again.

"*I* think you look real pretty, miss," insisted Omid, inching closer to the girl as if he might protect her. "Don't listen to her—"

"Dinner, of course," Sarra said, baring her teeth at Kamran in an unnatural smile. "Needless to say, you will all stay at the palace for the duration of your visit. What a fine show you've put on just now, what a lavish gift it was for the royal household to glimpse the glorious Simorgh and her children! It was the viewing of a lifetime, one even the youngest members of our staff will cherish forever. I should like to thank you for this spectacular performance—and for this unmistakable overture of friendship. How thoughtless of my son to try to catch a ceremonial arrow in his hand! And to think, most of our visitors merely offer us jewels."

"Oh, for the love of—" Hazan cut himself off with a foul

oath. He shot a final, disgusted look at the Queen Mother, stomped over to Cyrus, gathered up the king's body, and hoisted him over his shoulders.

Kamran watched this happen with no small amount of astonishment. Cyrus was taller and broader than even he was—the deadweight of such a man would be extraordinary. He knew Hazan possessed immense Jinn strength, but this was still a fairly new revelation, and Kamran marveled at the ease with which his old minister carried Cyrus now. Hazan pushed past their small crowd, circumventing Sarra to hurry toward the closest entrance. He tried the handle and, finding it was locked, bellowed a brief warning before kicking down the door.

It collapsed with an earsplitting crash.

Omid and Huda screamed. Deen muttered a faint *dear God* under his breath. Even Kamran was stunned. He glanced at Sarra for a reaction, and she revealed nothing more than irritation.

"*Your king is injured!*" Hazan cried as he stepped over the threshold, and he was swarmed at once by harried servants. "He needs medical attention immediately—"

"King Cyrus!" a snoda cried.

"I thought she said it was all a show—"

"Do you think—?"

"—been injured by accident—"

"But the king never gets injured—"

"Where is the surgeon?"

"Someone call for a Diviner!"

"—said to never call for the Diviners—"

"Hurry! Hurry!"

Kamran and the others hastened toward the scene, and the prince watched, transfixed, as Hazan was mobbed, many hands reaching up to relieve him of the king's weight. They carefully transferred Cyrus's body into their own arms before dashing off into the belly of the castle, a woman who was ostensibly the housekeeper trailing after them all, looking as if she might burst into tears.

Kamran couldn't help but compare this moment to one of his own: the night his grandfather had been murdered, when he'd been bested by Cyrus and left broken and dying. When his mother had finally freed him from the binds of magical paralysis, she'd disappeared—and he'd fallen to the floor. Not even a servant had been willing to step out of the shadows to come to his aid. In the end, only Omid had come to him; somehow, miraculously, despite receiving nothing but unkindness from the prince, the former street child had saved his life. It had been an enormous gift—one Kamran still struggled to appreciate—but it was nothing like the reception Cyrus received now. The hated king's servants appeared to truly care for him, which was so foreign a concept to Kamran it was difficult to accept as fact. It was also entirely at odds with the reaction the young man had received from Sarra, his own mother.

Kamran was studying the woman carefully now, sizing her up as he might an opponent on the battlefield. She was watching the scene unfold as if it were a great disappointment. Kamran's mother, for all her faults, had at least tried to help him in her strange way; Cyrus's parent, meanwhile, had done everything she could to *avoid* assisting her own child.

She shook her head, offered a fleeting smile to the prince, and said, "Well, there's always tomorrow," before stepping inside.

Kamran remained frozen in the doorway.

Indeed, he knew not what new horrors awaited him here.

THIRTEEN

سیزدہ

IN A COORDINATED EXHALATION OF fabric, the six of them were seated. Chair legs shuddered over a plush rug as footmen nudged the breakfast guests closer to the table— and then there was stillness. An awkward silence descended over the lushly appointed room, curious snodas peeping through the open doorway, heads bobbing in and out like so many chickens pecking. Sarra was seated at the head of the table, from where she watched them all with that unsettling smile. She seemed about to speak when there came a sudden jangle of silver; Omid had gathered up his flatware in one hand, inspecting the bunch as if it were a bouquet of flowers.

"Put those down," Deen hissed from across the table.

Huda, who was seated next to Omid, pressed nervously on the boy's arm, and he dropped the utensils to the table with a clatter.

Kamran closed his eyes in irritation.

"Why are there so many spoons?" he heard the child say. "And where is the food?"

Hazan shook his head at the boy, hard.

"But I haven't eaten since yesterday," he whispered loudly. "And she said there'd be breakfast."

"An interesting selection of companions you have," said

Sarra, subjecting Kamran to another uncomfortable inspection. "I imagine you'd only bring the finest entourage on such an . . . important journey. I expect they were the best Ardunia had to offer."

The prince clenched his jaw. He couldn't even bring himself to look at the members of this ridiculous ensemble. He'd been mad with grief—with fear—when he'd made the ill-formed decisions to allow them into his life, and he was paying dearly for the oversight.

"Quite," he replied coldly.

"Do you really mean that, sire?" said Omid, his head lifting. "Because I've always thought that you—"

Kamran shot him an ominous look and the boy sat back, his mouth snapping shut. Hells, it was like corralling cows.

Sarra turned her gaze to Omid. "What is your name, dear?"

The child startled, upsetting his silverware again. "I'm Omid Shekarzadeh, ma'am. I'm from Fesht province."

"Yes, so you said."

He nodded.

"How old are you, Omid?"

"I'm twelve years old, ma'am."

"And what is your business with the crown prince of Ardunia?"

Kamran visibly winced.

"Oh," said Omid, puffing out his chest. "I'm the home minister, ma'am. It's my job to keep the prince safe at all times."

Sarra lit up as if struck by lightning, eyes gleaming with

pleasure. She then projected the full force of this pleasure at Kamran, who, at that moment, wanted nothing more than to burst into flames.

"Indeed?" she said softly, eyes on the prince. "Twelve years old, far too many spoons, and your job is to keep His Highness safe. Of all the candidates the grand empire of Ardunia might've considered for such a position"—she turned again toward Omid—"the role was given to you. Goodness, you must be so proud."

"Oh, I am." He nodded eagerly. "Very proud, ma'am."

Kamran pinched the bridge of his nose and very nearly groaned.

"This is what happens when you don't listen to me," Hazan muttered under his breath. "Idiot."

The prince glared at him.

"And what is *your* duty here?" Sarra turned her cloying smile on Deen, who seemed to shrink under her attention.

"I'm—I'm an apothecarist, Your Majesty."

When she continued to stare, he grew nervous and began to ramble.

"I own and operate an apothecary in the royal square. In Setar. That is, in Ardunia. I learned the trade from my mother. Started when I was a boy. I come h-highly recommended. Excellent reviews. Customers are pleased."

Sarra drew back, *hmm*ing as she considering this, and seemed to decide he was a sensible choice for a royal retinue.

"*You*," she said to Huda. "What purpose do you serve?"

Huda blanched.

She looked around uncertainly, her brown eyes wide with

fear, and for the first time, Kamran studied her in earnest. Her hideous yellow gown was travel-worn and dusty, streaks of dirt visible along the frilly sleeves and high ruff, which was presently choking her throat. She appeared to have no neck. She wore no jewels save a small, glittering stud of an earring, and only in one ear. Her hair was scraped back from her face in an unadorned knot that did her no favors, and, in fact, gave her head the unfortunate appearance of an egg. Kamran had never spent long considering Huda, for he'd never felt there was much to consider. He was not surprised, however, to find himself observing her now, for it was his practice to form a thorough assessment of his adversaries— and it was safe to say that this infuriating chit had recently made an enemy of him.

She had some charms, however.

On a different occasion in her acquaintance he'd noted her elegant bone structure, but he noticed now that she had deep, inky eyes that looked perpetually languid, ready for bed. It was the kind of half-lidded gaze that reminded him, with a twinge of awareness, that her birth mother was a courtesan.

"*Well?*" Sarra snapped.

Huda flinched.

It was negligible—the way she jolted, briefly squeezing her eyes shut—and Kamran would've missed it had he not been staring at her directly. Yet he frowned at this, for it had seemed an involuntarily reaction of one bracing for violence. It made him wonder whether she'd been struck as a child, and he was shocked by the spark of anger he experienced at the thought. Huda clasped her trembling hands before tucking them out of sight; he watched as she drew breath before she smiled, as if she were summoning courage.

"I—well, that is—I'm not sure a person should be reduced to a single purpose," she said, "for the human heart is known to contain such diversity of feeling and expression—"

"She's here for the queen," Hazan flatly supplied.

Kamran glanced at him.

"Miss Huda is lady-in-waiting to Her Majesty."

Huda sank back in her seat with relief, staring gratefully at Hazan.

"Lady-in-waiting to the queen?" Sarra was saying, intrigued. She sat up straighter, then steepled her hands under her chin. "Is it she who requires you to wear such hideous clothes, darling? Has she demanded you diminish your beauty in her presence?"

Kamran almost choked. As if Alizeh's otherworldly beauty could ever be threatened by Huda, who continued to resemble an egg swaddled in the implausible scramble of its own yolk. He made a great effort to suppress a laugh, only for Huda to level him a glare so murderous it was practically treason. By the angels, Kamran was going to be a bloody *king*.

Men had been executed for lesser offenses.

He returned her glare with a furious glower of his own, briefly blinded by an outrageous desire to throw her over his shoulder, toss her in a boat, and send her out to sea.

"A terrible shame," Sarra went on. "You look about as absurd as a court jester. And that ghastly shade of yellow, with your complexion! It's very nearly criminal. Then again"—she smiled—"royalty can be odiously self-important. I would know."

"Forgive me, ma'am, but you're quite mistaken," said Huda, her face ablaze with heat. "This gown was selected by my mother."

"*Your mother?*" Sarra stared. "Good heavens. Does the woman hate you?"

Huda ignored this question with a thin smile. "Alizeh— that is, Queen Alizeh—"

Kamran winced.

"—is tremendously kind. I can't imagine she'd ever force me to wear an ugly garment. In fact," said Huda, warming to the idea, "in fact, she's an exceptional seamstress. Just days ago I'd commissioned her to make me a rather beautiful gown, but sadly there wasn't time to finish the job, and I'd no choice but to wear one of my older frocks on this journey."

Hazan swore under his breath again and Kamran was tempted to do the same. Sarra had gone still, staring at Huda as if she'd lost her mind.

"You *commissioned* her?" the woman echoed. "You com-missioned a queen, you mean, to make you a gown? Are you daft, girl? Tell me you aren't serious."

Huda looked around nervously before biting her lip. "No?" At the warning look from Hazan, she cleared her throat. "N-No. Certainly not," she said quietly. "I wasn't at all serious."

Sarra lost her patience then.

"*You,*" she barked, turning to Hazan. "You seem to be the piece most likely to finish this puzzle. Tell me what you know of the girl."

"What I know of her is none of your business."

Omid gasped; Deen paled. Kamran almost cracked a smile.

The Queen Mother straightened in her chair, appraising Hazan now as if she might eat him. She sent a fleeting look at the footmen lining the back wall, made a gesture with her fingers, and the footmen were at once dispersed. There was the *snick* of a door closing before she pasted on an angry smile.

"None of my business?" she said, her eyes glittering with fury. "I know nothing of her origins, nothing of her parents— The girl is to be my daughter-in-law, and I've only recently learned of her title—"

"Your daughter-in-law?" Kamran cut her off, alarmed. He nearly stood from the table. Hell, he nearly lost his head. "You mean— It's true? They are to be married—"

"No," Hazan said sharply. "It's not true."

"Of course it's true," Sarra countered. "That's why you're here, of course. To attend the impending nuptials as guests of my son's bride. To forge peace between our empires after all the recent ugliness. To prevent war." She shot a loaded look at Kamran. "Certainly not for any other reason."

The prince's heart was pounding too fast. "This is intolerable," he said, turning to Hazan. "She's going to marry him? Did you know about this?"

"She's consented to wed that foul man?" said Huda, looking ill. "That can't be right."

"*No.*" Omid was shaking his head. "Alizeh is a good lady, and he's an awful, horrible, murdering, OW—" The boy frowned at Deen. "Why'd you kick me?"

"You can't insult the king in his own castle, boy—"

"Kamran—listen to me—it's not true, she hasn't accepted him yet—"

"*Yet?*" he exploded. "What do you mean, she hasn't accepted him *yet?*"

For a moment, Kamran could've sworn he heard Sarra laughing; but when he looked at her, she appeared entirely composed.

"Here I was thinking I understood the motivations for your visit," she said to him, her smile growing wider. "Now I see why you've truly come."

"You spread unsubstantiated lies," Hazan protested.

"Lies?" Sarra's eyes widened. "Ask any servant in the palace what's preoccupied their time lately; they'll tell you they've been preparing for the arrival of the king's bride."

"That doesn't mean she's going to marry him—"

"Then why, pray tell, did I intercept her leaving my son's bedchamber just last night?"

Pain shot through Kamran's chest at that, radiating up his throat. He felt as if he couldn't breathe.

"You amuse yourself, ma'am," Hazan said angrily, "by planting seeds of discord. Her Majesty has no understanding with the king. Entering a bedchamber is proof of nothing."

"It's fairly damning," Huda said, biting her lip. "Much as I hate to admit it. What other reason could she—"

"You would stoop to assume the worst of her based on an unsupported claim from a woman clearly delighting in our destruction?" Hazan was furious. "Where is your good sense?"

"I didn't mean it like that," said Huda, shaking her head quickly. "Truly, I didn't—I just— Oh, please, I'm so very tired—"

"She lies, Kamran. I asked Alizeh this morning whether she was betrothed to the Tulanian king, and she told me emphatically that she was not. Despite having received an offer of marriage, she's still considering her options—"

"Considering her options? That she would even *consider* marriage to the man who killed my grandfather—who nearly killed me—who murdered our Diviners—"

"And who are you," Sarra said to Hazan, her eyes hardening, "to call me a liar? What purpose do you serve here in this royal court of misfits?" She held up a finger. "No, wait— let me guess. Things are becoming clearer, I see it now. At first I'd assumed that you, the boldest of these simpletons—"

"*Simpletons?*" Deen drew back, offended. "I was trained at the Royal Academy—my shop has been exalted in *The Daftar* numerous times—"

"—had traveled here in service to the prince. The only capable companion, the only one with a working brain—"

"I *beg* your pardon—"

"I took you for a knight. I realize only now that your allegiance is, in fact, with the girl—and I'd love to know why. Who are you?" She tilted her head at Hazan. "So fiercely impassioned. So loyal. Don't tell me you're in love with her, too?"

Huda drew a sharp breath.

"Good heavens," Deen said softly, then looked at Omid, who was shaking his head in horror.

Kamran, who'd never before considered this possibility, was entirely rattled. Slowly, he turned to face his friend.

It was a long, torturous moment before Hazan said, in a lethal whisper, "*How dare you.*"

At that, the room seemed to exhale, and Sarra appeared to blossom.

"Oh, I think I like you," she said. "I suppose I'll let your troupe live long enough to see the bride in all her glory."

"But I thought"—Huda gaped—"I thought you'd already decided to let us live. In fact, I thought we'd come here to have breakfast."

"I tend to change my mind," Sarra said dismissively, before eyeing the prince. "I think it might be interesting to see how all this drama ends. I love a tragic love story."

With controlled anger, Kamran said, "I'm *not* in love with her."

Hazan turned sharply in his seat. "What?"

It had been bothering the prince: the casual jabs, the crude suggestions that he'd traveled all this way in the pursuit of a woman who didn't want him. Kamran's pride could no longer bear such insinuations of weakness. It was still true that he cared for her; true that she'd moved him, deeply—

Indeed, how could he not have been moved by her?

She'd embodied eminence, traversed a harsh world with grace, and was possessed of a beauty that drove the breath from his lungs. She'd inspired in him a wealth of feeling he'd never imagined he might experience. Had she only returned his affections, Kamran might've known true happiness. But

he would never force his attentions upon a woman, and
Alizeh had refused him twice now, walking away from him
both times he'd pleaded with her to stay. Too, his cherished
memories of her had lost their shine under the tarnish of
recent disillusions, and, worse, Kamran wasn't even certain
he could trust her—she, who'd willingly risked her life trying to save his sworn enemy.

Given the tremendous uncertainties, Kamran would have
to be the worst kind of fool to declare himself in love with
her.

He would *not*.

He directed his next words to Sarra. "You seem to be
under the impression that I've come here on a mission of
unrequited love. That's simply not true."

"*Kamran*—"

"I just want to be clear"—he lifted a hand—"that while I
admire her a great deal, I'm not in love with her."

Somehow, this honesty seemed to anger Hazan. "You told
me you wanted to marry her!"

"What?" Huda froze in an almost comical state of shock.
"You wanted to marry her?"

"I did," Kamran said to Hazan, ignoring this outburst. "I
think I still might. But every minute brings me more confusion, and every revelation complicates her character. I'm
realizing I haven't the faintest idea who she is. It was a weak
thread that bound us if she's already considering an alliance
with the person responsible for destroying my life."

"But—the book— The inscription—"

"I need to see her again," said the prince, shaking his head. "Too much has happened in the time we've been apart. I'm no longer acquainted with my own mind. Or hers."

"I can't believe"—Huda was still blinking—"I had no idea you intended to make her your queen—"

Kamran briefly turned his gaze upward, for he was resisting the compulsion to do something as ill-bred as roll his eyes. He feared that if he allowed himself the indulgence of rolling his eyes at Huda, his eyes would eventually roll out of his head from overuse.

She turned to Omid. "Did you know he wanted to marry her?"

Omid shook his head with great force.

Then, to Deen: "What about you? Did you know?"

"Certainly not," came Deen's dry reply. "The prince does not make a habit of involving me in the emotional turns of his heart. Though I have to admit it's an interesting twist of fate, considering the way she once spoke of him in my shop."

"She spoke of me?" Kamran faced him at once. "When? What did she say?"

Sarra laughed. "Yet he claims he's not in love with her."

Kamran looked at the woman. "Do you presume to know my own feelings better than I do?"

"It wasn't altogether flattering, sire," said Deen, flustered. "I shouldn't have even mentioned—"

"What did she say about me?" Kamran demanded.

The apothecarist stiffened in his seat, his small dark eyes shifting. "She— Well, she seemed to question, sire, whether your lack of engagement with the general public spoke to an a-arrogance, or pretension, in your character—"

"*Arrogance?*"

Huda released a sharp, horrible chortle before clapping a hand over her mouth. "I'm sorry," she wheezed. "I just— Heavens, I already knew I adored her, but now—"

"Of course I vehemently disagree," Deen added hastily, "and to be fair to the young woman, I don't believe she'd made your acquaintance at the time of this speech, for she spoke of you as if you were unknown to her—"

"I warned you," said Hazan. "I warned you it was a mistake to ignore your public duties. Every function you skipped, every ceremony you avoided—I told you it would reflect badly on your character if you didn't make the occasional appearance to soothe the hearts and fears of the common folk—"

"That's enough," Kamran said ominously.

He'd never thought of himself as arrogant, and the fact that Alizeh had chosen, at some point, to define him as such was an unexpected blow. Certainly Kamran made no willful effort to be pretentious in his duties; he'd simply abhorred the ridiculous functions that defined the crown. He loathed the aristocracy and the pompous heads of the seven houses; he tired of the awestruck commoners desperate to catch a glimpse of him; he resented the performances that paraded him about like a show horse.

Then again, he'd never understood their point.

As a young prince with a direct line to the throne,

Kamran had been taught to consider himself vastly superior in the world and was seldom encouraged to look beyond the gilded tiers of his own domain. Only through Alizeh's interference was he inspired to examine the rotted structures that informed the suffering of so many. She was the reason he'd questioned, for the first time, the actions and motivations of his grandfather King Zaal. She was the reason he'd questioned, for the first time, the insufficient wages and protections of servants. She was the reason his eyes had been opened to the struggles of street children in their empire. Her perspective—her patient eye for the anguish of others— had turned his own gaze toward the less fortunate, inspiring him to see not only the social failings within his kingdom but also the ways in which he might be called upon to address them.

Nevertheless, the unfortunate truth was that Kamran had never thought to examine his own biases until his life had collapsed around him. It had never occurred to him that an unshakable belief in his own greatness might prove a weakness. Indeed, it had never occurred to him that life might one day deal him a lesser hand.

Perhaps, he thought with a pang, this was the very definition of arrogance.

Kamran stifled a sigh.

Even now, Alizeh had managed to deliver him a brutal lesson. Without fanfare she'd fallen from the heavens into the still waters of his life, and he wondered, uneasily, whether he'd feel the reverberations of her impact forever.

"The more I learn about this young woman," Sarra was saying, "the more I look forward to welcoming her into my family."

"Then you will be horribly disappointed," said Hazan. "Such a marriage will not take place."

"It will," Sarra countered.

"What do you care who she marries?" Kamran said, his eyes darkening as he turned to her. "What interest do you have in her union with your son?"

"I don't know that I do," she said evenly. "I only suppose that a girl desired so ardently by the rulers of two powerful kingdoms—a girl who can command a crowd as she does—must be worth something, and I'm suddenly curious to know what, exactly, that might be. I do like to look after my own interests, after all."

"Command a crowd? What are you—"

"She's not magical or anything," Omid said, confused. "We just like her a lot."

"A ringing endorsement," Sarra said drily.

"Actually," Deen said, leaning forward. "Her body has a natural healing ability—"

"I mean it," Omid insisted. "You've never met a kinder person. I tried to kill her in the street once, and instead of handing me to the magistrates, she offered me bread. I bet you've never tried to kill someone, ma'am, and had them offer you bread."

Sarra's lips parted in silent astonishment.

She blinked rapidly, first at Omid, then at Kamran, and,

sounding a bit breathless, she said, "I'm afraid you've just raised more questions than answers, child."

"She may not be magical now," Hazan interjected, "but she *will* have magic. And when she comes to possess it, the entire world will recognize her power."

"Is that so?" A flicker of unease moved in and out of Sarra's eyes. "And what kind of magic will she come to possess?"

"I don't . . . know yet."

"I see," she said wryly. "Sounds formidable."

Hazan sent her a black look, but Sarra turned away, studying the prince with renewed interest. "So you've come because you seek her rumored power, sire, and not her heart?"

"I came here to kill your son," Kamran said flatly. "Little else animates my interest at the moment."

Sarra clapped her hands together. "In that case, you *must* stay until the end of the season, at the very least. Though if you do manage to kill Cyrus, I beg you to make it appear an accident, for I detest war, and do not desire bloodshed between our lands."

The five of them, collectively, stared at her.

Gently, Huda said, "Are you joking, Your Majesty?"

"About which part, dear?"

Choosing to ignore this, the prince glanced at Hazan before saying, with great resignation, "We'll stay just long enough to find out where she is. Lord knows what he did with her." He felt dazed suddenly; exhausted. "Hells, she might not even be alive."

Sarra stiffened, color leaching from her face. "What?"

"Oh, don't say that," said Huda. "We must not lose hope—"

"She was injured," Omid explained. "Earlier, ma'am."

Sarra gripped the table for support. "What do you mean, *injured?*"

"Forgive me," said Deen. "But didn't you see the moment she and Cyrus fell off the cliff? When we were outside?"

"You fool," Sarra snapped, standing up so fast her chair fell over with a thud. "If I'd seen anything of the sort do you think I would've wasted my time with the lot of you? What on earth happened to her?"

Hazan, who appeared as disconcerted by this eruption as Kamran was, said carefully: "She was caught by a stray arrow."

Sarra made a guttural, mournful sound. "By whose hand?"

"Why is that important?"

"It's of the utmost importance!" she shouted. "If Cyrus had anything to do with it"—she shook her head—"oh, I'll kill him, I'll really do it this time. By the angels, they're going to riot again. They'll set fire to the castle—"

"Who?" Deen asked, eyes darting around. "Who's going to set fire to the castle?"

"When I'm upset," Omid said helpfully, "I like to take a walk, and search the streets for spare coin—"

Huda squeezed the boy's hand. "Not now, dear."

"It was me," Kamran said in an undertone. "I shot her by accident."

"*You.*" Sarra straightened in obvious relief, pressing a hand to her chest. "It was you. Yes, we'll tell them you did it. Your empire will take the blame. It was all your fault—"

"What are you talking about?" Hazan demanded. "Who are you referring to?"

"The Jinn!" she cried. "Thousands and thousands of them! I swear they were going to kill us all!"

"*The Jinn?*" Kamran echoed softly, stunned.

Hazan rose slowly from the table, his countenance visibly altered. His old friend looked shaken, his eyes burning with feeling. "What Jinn?" he said.

"Last night, they stormed the castle," Sarra said, her breathing shallow. "Our Jinn population is normally very gentle—unlike most empires, we allow them a measure of freedom to exercise their abilities without penalty—but yesterday—yesterday they were terrifying and violent. They threatened to burn down the palace. They threatened to destroy the city. They wanted proof that she was alive, that she was unharmed—"

"I need you to be clear," Hazan said to Sarra, a slight tremor in his voice. "Do you mean to say she was discovered? That she's been revealed publicly as the long-lost heir to the Jinn kingdom?"

Kamran felt a twist in his gut.

"So *that's* what she is?" Huda exclaimed. "I knew she was some kind of forgotten royal, but she never told me her true identity, only that she was running for her life—"

"It's not some courtesy title?" Deen asked. "She's a real queen, then? All that time I'd thought she was a servant . . . And that horrible housekeeper, the way she treated her—"

"*Servant?*" Sarra stood frozen. "Housekeeper? What in heavens can you mean?"

"My queen has been in hiding for nearly two decades," Hazan explained. "She's taken odd jobs since the untimely deaths of her parents"—he touched two fingers to his forehead, then to the air—"doing what she could to stay alive."

"How the drama unfolds," Sarra breathed, clasping a hand to her throat. "But why would she need to be in hiding?"

"The Ardunian throne has been threatened by her existence for some time," Hazan offered coldly. "Her parents—and most all others who knew her in childhood—died in a series of mysterious and calculated incidents. She's lived in hiding ever since."

At that, Kamran experienced a burn of shame.

It had been Zaal, his late grandfather, who'd hunted Alizeh as a child. The Diviners had foreseen Zaal's demise—had predicted his end would be orchestrated by a formidable enemy with ice in its veins—and Zaal, who'd been searching for any whisper of such a foe, had found her long ago, spending many subsequent years thinking he'd successfully murdered the girl. It wasn't hard for Kamran to imagine that Zaal had played a role in killing the others in her life as well. There were things about his grandfather he could neither reconcile nor condone.

"So she lived as a snoda?" asked Sarra. She'd picked up her fallen chair and was taking her seat when she glanced at Huda. "And a seamstress?"

"Yes," she and Hazan said together.

"And now she is queen," the woman said softly, her eyes

dreamy. "Now she has the sovereigns of two empires vying for her hand. Now she— Wait—"

Sarra turned sharply toward the prince.

"The Ardunian throne was threatened by her existence," she quoted. "Does that mean it was your grandfather who murdered her family?"

All heads swiveled to face him.

"Theoretically," he bit out. "Though there is no proof."

Sarra laughed. "You hope to *marry* the young woman whose entire family was slaughtered by your grandfather?"

"Again, it is not a certainty—"

"Your Majesty," Hazan interjected, his voice urgent. "I fear we're diverting from the subject at hand. Can you confirm that her identity has been revealed?"

Sarra met Hazan's eyes then, and in the feverish depths of his gaze, she seemed to find focus. "Yes," she said finally. "I don't know how she was discovered; I know only that they came for her yesterday. Thousands of them. Shouting for hours. They only settled down after I begged her to speak to them—"

"She stood before them?" Hazan asked, paling. "She acknowledged, out loud, that she was their queen?"

Sarra hesitated. "Was it the wrong thing to do?"

"No." Hazan blinked. "No, if she felt the time was right, then of course, it's just— By the angels, this cannot be undone. The consequences—" He lifted his head, looking suddenly unnerved. "You must prepare yourself, ma'am. By now, word of her appearance has likely spread halfway around the globe. They'll come for her from every corner of the earth—they've likely begun their pilgrimages already—"

"What?" Sarra said, visibly terrified. "How many will come?"

Hazan shook his head. "It won't happen all at once. They'll push through your borders in phases—"

"*How many?*" she cried.

"Millions," Hazan whispered.

FOURTEEN

چھاردہ

CYRUS HAD FALLEN INTO AN endless pit of darkness, the tug of sleep so severe that, at first, he wasn't even certain he was dreaming. He'd seemed to plummet from a great height for what felt like centuries, lengths of smog tightening around him like bands of steel. His chest constricted as he hurtled toward this horrible infinity, his terror so consuming he could hardly draw breath to scream before cleaving, suddenly, through a lacework of night. This grotesque tapestry unraveled only to promptly ensnare him, his body a veritable bobbin as inky, tar-like strands caught around his head, his legs, his torso. Then, just as suffocation seemed a certainty, he broke his arms free and tore the greasy webbing from his face, drawing a frantic breath before hitting the ground with a horrible *crack*.

His skull fractured as it struck stone, and pain exploded throughout his body. Cyrus made a sound of anguish as the crushed enamel of his teeth met his tongue, the grit growing slick as blood pooled in his mouth. It was difficult to ascertain the full extent of his damage, but he suspected his ribs were broken, and then, as he wheezed, that a lung had been punctured. One of his arms had effectively snapped, a jut of bone pushing through the dark wool of his sweater, and his legs—his legs felt wrong in ways he couldn't decipher.

But then, this wasn't new.

For eight months his nightmares had followed the same sequence, adhered to the same rules. Always, they began with darkness; always, they followed with agony. This imagined torture was as real to him as his mother's hatred, and echoes of these miseries lingered on in his waking hours with a verisimilitude that haunted him.

Like a wounded animal Cyrus dragged his body across the pitted floor of this unknown hell, searching fruitlessly for an exit. The smell of sulfur filled his head, and he spat, with difficulty, the strange cocktail of blood and silt from his mouth, dazed by the dull *plink* of a broken molar as it hit the ground. His jaw felt broken. A kneecap had shattered. He was breathing painfully, his head swimming as he struggled for oxygen. Somehow, he understood he was dreaming; somehow, his consciousness was able to break this fourth wall even as he heaved himself across the bleak planes of his imagination—and yet, the knowledge that he was dreaming offered him no comfort, for he could never be absolutely certain that a nightmare wouldn't kill him.

Finally, he met with resistance.

With his good hand he clawed at what proved to be an oily barrier, his fingers catching in a thick, gelatinous substance that refused to yield. Desperately he freed himself from the muck, his heart pounding in tandem with his head. Cyrus was drawing breath in small, frantic gasps, an immobilizing dizziness leaving him no choice but to surrender. He collapsed, hard, onto his back. Cyrus was fully drowning—his lungs filling with fluid as he stared into the lightless murk—when

Death reached a hand down his throat, grasping around for his soul. And then—

She appeared as the dawn did: a slow burn of light that soon suffused with color, focusing into a radiance that blinded him. Always, the sight of her was miraculous. Always, his body trembled in anticipation.

This time, he knew better.

Finally, he knew who she was; knew her name; knew, above all else, that these visions had been designed to break him—that in fact he'd already been broken. Cyrus could no longer afford to give in to her sweetness, not even here, in the privacy of his mind. Through the thick of incoherence, he fought to look away from her, curling inward as if he might blot her out of his imagination. This achieved nothing.

She came to him as she did every time, without fear.

"Cyrus," she whispered, drawing deeper into the dark. "Where are you?"

"No." He panted, kicking painfully at the ground to get away from her. He could hardly form words for the devastation of his teeth, tasting blood as he spoke. "No—please—stay away from me—"

She found him and touched him—a single stroke of her hand along his arm—and he cried out, his body seizing as a torrent of bliss drove through him, invigorating his body with a relief so intoxicating he nearly wept.

"Please," he said, begging now. "Please don't do this to me—not now, not ever again—"

"Don't be afraid," she said, crouching to look him in the eye. "I only want to help you."

"No— *No*—"

"Look at you," she whispered. "Look how you suffer."

"Please, don't come near me," he pleaded, hating the pathetic rasp of his voice. "Show me no mercy— Leave me here to die—"

"Abandoned," she said softly. "Neglected. Vilified—"

"*No*—"

"The injustice is too great."

She dropped to her knees before him, took his bloodied face in her hands, and he cried out, his head tipping back as a euphoric blitz filled his lungs, allowing him to breathe deeply for the first time. His chest heaving, his body trembled with abandon; the resulting ease was so extraordinary he struggled to remember why it was wrong. With excruciating tenderness she kissed his temples, then his forehead. Hot tears fell from his closed eyes, silent sobs wracking his body.

Always she healed him as she touched him, each graze of her fingers mending a bone, a laceration, erasing pain. He cried out every time, unimaginable feeling flooding his heart and mind, her very closeness sending him into a spiral of need so desperate he didn't recognize himself. He soon submitted entirely to her touch, leaning into her hands as she drew them slowly down his body. The sensations were so blissfully torturous that he wondered, for a delirious moment, whether he'd died.

"*Angel,*" he breathed. "My angel."

Carefully she prized from his body the remains of his tattered, bloodied clothing, discarding the lot before pressing a cool kiss upon his fevered chest. He jolted as if brought back to life, and when he looked at himself again he was shocked to discover that he was naked, entirely mended. His teeth had reassembled, his bone sat neatly in his arm. The pain had been lifted, but in its absence he was weak, filthy, and desperately parched.

She gathered his fragile body into her arms and gently laid his head against her chest, smoothing the hair away from his forehead even as he shook against her.

He swallowed over and over against the dryness in his throat, the feeling like coarse sand, and just when he thought he'd die of thirst, she touched her fingers to his neck. The small action seemed to slake his need at once, and he was marveling at this, at the extraordinary power she possessed, when she was suddenly wiping a clean, wet rag along his limbs, washing away the grime with almost impossible ease. From where she procured the water, he wasn't sure. He wanted to ask her, wanted to understand, but he was losing a battle with consciousness, his mind wishing to rest. Soon, he was entirely restored; his body gleaming in her reflected light, she the moon in his interminable gloom.

She stroked his hair, her fingers soft and cool against his heated scalp. "Tell me what happened," she said quietly. "Who did this to you?"

Cyrus struggled to keep his eyes open. "The devil," he said. "It's always the devil."

"Rest," she whispered, pressing a kiss to his forehead. "And leave the devil to me. I'll make sure he never hurts you again."

Cyrus exhaled with great feeling, the action dispelling the

tension he'd been holding for so long. It broke him to know that she understood the depth of his suffering, that she'd put an end to his pain.

No one had ever cared for him as she did.

Finally, his eyes closed. A feeling of calm overcame him, allowing him to rest as he never did in her absence. Here, he was safe. With her, he was safe.

When he opened his eyes again, they were lying in his bed.

She was naked in his arms, the silken crush of her lush curves a delicious relief against the hard planes of his body. She was smiling up at him, tracing the shape of his collarbone, and his heart ached at the sight of her. That she existed at all was a miracle; that she cared for him seemed impossible. What had he done to earn the love and affection of an angel?

When he expressed these feelings aloud she often laughed, accepting his adoration as a tender exaggeration; she had no idea how much he held back, how much more he wanted to say. He was in fact so in awe of her he could hardly breathe in her presence, and when she playfully nudged his chin upward with her nose, stretching to kiss the underside of his jaw, he thought his chest might cave in.

"You're awake," she said, drawing back to look at him.

"You're here," he breathed.

She laughed at that, then bit her lip, and her eyes were so joyous and beautiful the sight caused him physical pain. She noticed this change in him, and her happiness dimmed.

"What's wrong?" she asked.

"Nothing," he said, even as he felt the rise of something

fevered inside him, his heart threatening to beat through his chest. With great care he took her face in his hands and marveled at the feel of her, the glorious sight of her. He was enchanted by everything: not just her deep, limpid eyes, but the delicate arches of her brows, the fine shape of her nose, the soft pout of her lips. More extraordinary was that her beauty was but a vessel, physical majesty forged for a soul so tender it defied description.

"When you're here," he said, "nothing is wrong."

Her wry, responding smile said she didn't believe him, but she was merciful enough to spare him an interrogation. Slowly she turned her head, pressing a kiss to his palm, the pleasure of which he experienced with a sharp pang.

"Sad boy," she said softly. "What am I supposed to do with you?"

He stared at her mouth, the soft line of her jaw, the swell of her breasts against his chest. Her very proximity inspired in him a feeling of exhilaration so profound it left him dizzy. He dragged his eyes upward, meeting her gaze with a need that scared him. *"Anything."*

She almost laughed.

But Cyrus was shaken, watching her with a hunger he couldn't fathom into words. "You could probably kill me and I'd thank you for it."

She stiffened and drew back. "Don't say that," she said sharply. "That's not funny."

"I'm not joking."

"Cyrus—"

"I want it all, angel. Not just your joy but your sorrow. Not just your hope but your fear. I want your anger and disdain, your frustration and contempt—"

She made a breathless sound. "I would *never* treat you with contempt."

"I know," he said, sweeping his thumb along the crest of her cheek, his eyes following the gentle motion. He was hardly able to stay the tremor in his hands, or in his voice. "But I know, too, that you'll always do what is just. You'd never deliver me your scorn unless I deserved it, and should I be foolish enough to inspire your anger, I should also be honored to receive it."

She stilled, her lips parting in surprise.

She looked suddenly vulnerable as she shook her head, her eyes glistening with an evidence of feeling that seemed to gouge a hole in him.

"I love you," she whispered.

Always, this rendered him speechless.

Finally she smiled, small at first, then mischievous as she crawled on top of him and straddled his hips. He made a sound deep in his throat, his eyes closing as her weight settled against him; and then she slid her hands down his torso and he sucked in a breath, the collective pleasure so acute it rivaled agony.

She bent to kiss his brow, his closed eyes. She drew the tip of one finger down the sharp slope of his nose, and he opened his eyes in time to see that her cheeks were flushed. "So gorgeous," she said softly.

These words caused him nothing but anguish. He stared up at her, his mind detaching from reason as he drank in the sight of her naked body. He wanted to live here, with his face pressed against her, to breathe only in her atmosphere. He ran his unsteady hands up her back, terrified by the storm of emotion gathering inside him.

He felt *wild*.

She adjusted herself against him and he stiffened, gritting his teeth as he swore. She laughed, but he could feel her— could feel her own desire gathering between them. He was impossibly taut, afraid to move even an inch against her, and she gasped, suddenly, as he flipped her on her back, pinning her languid body beneath him. She was softness everywhere, silken skin catching his hard edges, and he shifted his weight, careful not to crush her. Her lips were still parted on a breath, her eyes darkening with hunger as she stared up at him. He felt the heat of her gaze along his body, then the sound she made when he touched her, stroking her sensitive skin with a featherlight caress. Her low moan set his blood ablaze.

He loved all of her: the shape of her lips, her hips, her slender hands and the freckle at the base of her throat. He'd kissed that freckle a thousand times, had spent countless hours learning her, loving her, discovering the desires of her body. It didn't matter how many nights he'd spent in her arms. Always, in her presence, he felt himself coming apart with a need that felt a great deal like madness.

He devoted himself now to kissing her neck, then lower, soothing the heavy curves of her, first with his hands, then his mouth. Her body trembled under his careful, focused attentions until she cried out, the sound of her unbound pleasure branding inside him, driving him to the edge of his self-control. He pressed his face to her neck, fighting for restraint as his heart beat violently against his ribs.

Even now he could feel her growing desperation, his own insatiable desire. He hardly knew himself like this, so intoxicated he thought he might die if he didn't taste her, everywhere.

"Cyrus," she gasped.

She reached between them, tried to close her hand around him, and he made a strangled sound, too overcome to care that his body was shaking.

"Please," she said breathlessly.

His heart was still beating at a dangerous pace, his own physical distress drowning out an ability to form coherent thought. Still, he forced himself to move slowly, drawing his hands down her legs with a quiet reverence, trailing kisses along her calves and ankles as he gently spread her open. He slipped his hands under her thighs, then hooked her knees over his shoulders.

The sight of her like this, vulnerable and trembling and ready for him—

Her eyes were radiant, her breasts lifting as she struggled for breath. She was so beautiful he could hardly bear to look at her.

"Cyrus—"

"Not yet," he said.

He lowered his head to the heat of her, and she nearly screamed, her hands grasping at the sheets as he tasted her, her soft cries rending the silence over and over. She'd chosen him—trusted him—to know her like this, to protect and pleasure her heart and body, and this astonishing reminder filled him with a blinding ecstasy. He loved watching her come apart, loved the way she gave herself over to him so completely. He loved that he could feel her spiraling, nearing release—

"I want you," she said, reaching for him. "Please—I want you now, I want to feel you—"

He retreated with torturous care, pressing a final kiss to her heated core as he shifted away, his hunger only intensifying as his eyes devoured the sensual lines of her supple body. He touched her where he'd tasted her, felt the evidence of her need and groaned, burying his face in her shoulder. She had so much power over him it was terrifying even to examine the way she owned his soul. When he finally managed to meet her gaze, his heart seemed to detonate in his chest—and her eyes, heavy with desire, shone briefly with amusement.

"Are you"—she bit her lip, fighting a smile—"Cyrus, are you trying not to look at me?"

His answer was breathless. "Yes."

"Why?" Her smile grew wider.

"You already know why."

She actually laughed this time, and he bent his head to her body and kissed her, everywhere, until her eyes were no longer entertained. Her breathing grew fast and shallow as her desperation peaked, and she reached for him where he needed her most, the feel of her hands offering a relief that only multiplied his anguish. Suddenly—urgently—she said his name, and he looked up, immobilized, caught in the crossfire of her attentions.

"Do you know what I love most about you?" she whispered. She was still touching him, and he was rocked by a fresh tremor of feeling.

"No," he rasped.

He could never quite believe this was happening. That she would look at him like this, want him like this. She was the rare combination of heart and beauty only ever encountered in dreams. And this—he blinked, then hesitated, confusion pulling at the edges of his mind—*this*—

Without warning his head clouded; his lungs contracted in his chest. He felt as if he was pitching forward, falling out of his body. He didn't understand—he couldn't sort through his thoughts—and what was he remembering? Gasping for breath now, remembering—

This was a dream.

Yes, a dream, but he knew that, didn't he? He knew he'd been dreaming, knew she was a figment of his imagination, a manipulation of his mind, a corruption installed in his head—

"No," he breathed. "*No*—"

He was going to be sick. His leg screamed with pain, his hand burned, his head pounded, he couldn't breathe, he couldn't breathe and he'd known—of course he'd known she wasn't real, he'd known she didn't actually love him, that she would never—*never*—

"Cyrus?"

"*NO*," he cried, jolting away from her. "No—*no*—"

"Cyrus—" She reached for him, alarmed, but he tore away, his limbs tangling in the bedclothes.

"Don't— Please—" He dropped his head in his hands. "Oh God—not again—I can't—I won't survive it—"

"What's happening?" she said, panicking. "What's wrong—?"

"No—no—NO," he shouted, falling off the bed. "This isn't real, this isn't real—wake up, you fucking idiot—wake up, *wake up, WAKE UP—*"

FIFTEEN

پانزده

"MILLIONS," HAZAN SAID AGAIN, HIMSELF thunder-struck.

Kamran processed this revelation as if from afar, both awed and horrified. His grandfather might not have been right about Alizeh—not precisely—but he'd not been alto-gether wrong, either.

Like a cold wind, he felt the rush of Zaal's voice, words from the man's final days coming to life inside his mind—

If you do not think there are others searching for her right now, you are not paying close enough attention. Pockets of unrest in the Jinn communities continue to disturb our empire. There are many among them deluded enough to think the resurrection of an old world is the only way to move forward.

Kamran swallowed.

All this time, he'd thought of her royal title as symbolic; he never thought she'd be truly recognized as a queen. But now—now that thousands of people had stormed the cas-tle to see her, and millions more might soon swear their allegiance to her—

He realized, with a shock, that he didn't know Alizeh at all. He'd fallen for a mirage of a girl. A version of her that had never truly existed.

Sarra was stunned into speechlessness, and Kamran felt much the same.

"How many millions?" Deen asked, blinking.

"I don't know," Hazan said quietly. "This is merely an estimate. There are very few empires that live in peace with my people. Many Jinn live and die undocumented, forced to live out their lives in prison camps. Others continue to live in hiding. We are a people with no nation, expelled from our own land, the earth under our feet stolen by Clay kings. For so long we've been waiting for the heir to our empire, the one who will protect and unify our people. I have no way of knowing for certain how many will come"—he shook his head—"but you may trust that those who can, will. By foot, by caravan, by ship or dragon. If they have to drag themselves, inch by inch across the earth to get to her, they will."

Sarra made a frantic sound, her skin now bloodless with fear. She was muttering half words and nonsense, something about how the city wasn't meant to hold so many people at once, that there weren't enough bathrooms, "and where will they *sleep*?"

Omid started crying.

"I didn't mean to hurt her," he choked out. "Honest, I never would've killed her— I was just— I was so hungry I couldn't think clear—"

Huda shifted her chair closer to the boy and pulled him against her, smoothing his hair and making shushing sounds as he wept. "It's all right, dear," she whispered. "She forgave you already, didn't she?"

"She showed me mercy, miss"—he lifted his head, eyes

bloodshot as he sniffled—"when I didn't deserve—"

"Pull yourself together," Deen hissed, looking distinctly uncomfortable. "You're embarrassing yourself."

"That's a bit harsh—"

Kamran watched this strange scene from a cold distance; he felt frozen in his seat, astonished by his own fear, his pulse racing as he was struck by another blow of memory.

His grandfather had tried to warn him.

If the girl were to claim her place as the queen of her people, it is possible, even with the brace of the Fire Accords, that an entire race would pledge their allegiance to her on the basis of an ancient loyalty alone . . . The Jinn of Ardunia would form an army; the remaining civilians would riot. An uprising would wreak havoc across the land. Peace and security would be demolished for months—years, even—in the pursuit of an impossible dream—

Hells, he'd been so naive.

When he first met Alizeh she'd been but a humble snoda, scrubbing floors in his aunt's grand house, taking beatings from a vile housekeeper. She'd been so vulnerable and small; Kamran had been unable to imagine her beyond the powerless servant girl she first appeared to be. He'd discovered, later—when she'd dispatched the assailants his own grandfather had sent to kill her—that she was perfectly able to defend herself. Still, she possessed no connections, no wealth, no obvious interest in recognition. She lived in the shadows.

That someone in her position had said no to his power, his wealth, his crown—that she'd *continued* to refuse him even after they'd made a clear physical connection, the embers of which still burned within him—

It had made no sense.

There exists no bridge between our lives, she'd said. *No path that connects our worlds.*

He'd been a fool.

In a matter of days she'd found a kingdom to crown her, the people to support her. Already her ascent had inspired the demise of his grandfather, had devastated his life. She'd strengthened as he'd been shattered, and now she would shake the foundations of his empire, too.

What would happen to his kingdom—to his armies—if the Ardunian Jinn swore their allegiance to a foreign sovereign?

He dragged a hand down his mouth. *They'd be torn apart.*

All this ran through his mind in moments, and he was returned to the present by the sound of a terrible whimper. Sarra had begun to pace.

"Heaven help us," she cried. "If they find out she's been injured—"

"Yes." Hazan had sobered a great deal. "This is grim, indeed."

"And you say you don't even know where she is? She's injured and gone? If she *dies*—"

"She won't die," Hazan said harshly.

"Cyrus sent her off on the back of a dragon," said Kamran. "The king is the only one who knows where she went, and as he is currently indisposed, we have no way of knowing what he did with her."

At that, Sarra regained a flicker of her edge, her anger. "So she did not fall off a cliff and *disappear*. My son sent the injured girl away."

Kamran narrowed his eyes at her tone. "Indeed."

"And yet you say you have no way of knowing what he did with her? Is your imagination truly so colorless?"

"I am not a mind reader, ma'am."

"And you," she said to Hazan. "What of you? Can you envisage no other explanation for his actions?"

Hazan stared at her with renewed concern. "You think he used dark magic on her? Or perhaps poisoned her?"

Sarra looked almost disappointed in Hazan then, shaking her head as she said, "Your every theory assumes as fact that he intends her harm. You've done a poor character study of my son."

"I disagree," Hazan replied, his concern displaced by anger. "King Cyrus has proven nothing but violent, aggressive, murderous, and manipulative. In a single night he slaughtered the king of Ardunia and an entire halo of Diviners, and this isn't even mentioning the destruction he left in his wake, having half destroyed one of the oldest palaces in history by allowing a dragon to—"

"Yes, all right," she said with a sigh. "I suppose you're not wrong to draw such conclusions. I confess, at first, I thought he meant to hurt the girl as well. But I no longer believe he'd cause her suffering. Not on purpose, anyway."

"What do you mean?" Kamran sharpened. "How can you be sure?"

Sarra opened her mouth to respond, then appeared to think better of it, saying only: "Have you never seen the way he looks at her?"

"No," he said, his mood darkening. "In fact I have not."

She offered a brittle smile. "Well. I suppose you'll see for yourself soon enough."

"What's that supposed to mean?"

Sarra looked at Kamran then as if he were not the impending heir to the largest empire on earth but an idiot child. "I'd bet my life," she said, turning her eyes to Hazan, "that he's entrusted one of his blasted dragons to help her. If the girl were badly injured, there's only one place he'd—"

"The Diviners," Hazan said. "Of course."

"Really?" Huda frowned. "You really think he was trying to help her?"

Omid rubbed at his tearstained cheeks. "I *was* wondering, miss, why he was hugging her so much. Seemed like an awful lot of hugging for people who don't like each other."

"He was hugging her?" Huda's eyes went wide.

"He was *holding* her," Deen corrected. "Probably to keep her from falling off the dragon. Though"—he hesitated—"I suppose if he did mean for her to die, he could've simply let her tumble into the ocean?"

Kamran felt himself growing angry, and he couldn't articulate why. He didn't realize that what he felt was a warped jealousy, his mind recoiling from the idea that *he'd* been the one to hurt her, that Cyrus might've been the one to save her. And it was with undiluted venom that he said, "If his intention was to help her, why send her off alone? Why not deliver her to the Diviners himself?"

Omid made a face. "And why did he ask her to marry him if all he wanted was to kill her?"

"Well, I don't know," said Huda, "but my parents have been married nearly thirty years and Mother is all the time going on about how much she'd like to kill Father, and in fact I worry, sometimes, that he doesn't seem to take her seriously—"

Kamran leaned forward, insisting: "It does not stand to reason. The king, too, was injured—had they gone to the Diviners, he might've received care for his own wounds. It makes more sense that he might've cursed her, binding her to the dragon before sending her off into the unknown, all so that we might never find her—"

"He's not allowed to set foot in the temple," said Sarra, her words dripping with condescension. "Cyrus is forbidden even from walking the grounds. Ever since he murdered my husband, the Diviners have refused him entrance."

Kamran stiffened.

It was the casual way she stated the horrifying fact that cast a brief pall over the room, and it was the reminder they all needed: the truth of who King Cyrus really was, how blackened was his soul. Kamran couldn't believe Alizeh would consider marrying such a criminal. If she was so desperate for a crown, why hadn't she appealed to him instead? He'd all but offered for her—and she'd chosen to align herself with this animal?

Even now, even with his head and heart muddled beyond reason, Kamran experienced a painful thrill at the thought of appealing to her, convincing her to join forces with *him*. In fact, the more he learned of her influence, the more he realized that an understanding between them would forestall his fears of upheaval in the Ardunian empire; if a Jinn queen and Clay king could join peacefully, perhaps the people, too, could live in harmony.

The idea took root inside him.

His interest in her would no longer be labeled impractical or emotional; marrying her would instead prove the perfect hedge against rebellion. He felt certain even his grandfather would've been convinced, for it wouldn't be a match born of base desire but a considered alliance made for the good of the people.

Something like relief began to expand in his chest.

Perhaps *this* was what the Diviners had meant for him to accomplish; perhaps proving his worth as king was bound up in the search for his queen. Perhaps the magic in his body had altered because he was not meant to be the sole ruler of Ardunia.

He felt a purifying clarity then, a feeling of ease cleansing weeks of tension. Kamran had been lost and confused, confounded by grief, by the machinations of Zahhak, the demands of the Diviners.

Now he understood.

His presence here, in this godforsaken empire, became suddenly tolerable. He would find a way to stay. He needed to speak with Alizeh at the first opportunity and make his intentions clear. After all, he'd never made her any formal offer. Surely such a proposal would appeal to her now; surely she would see the advantages of such a union—and would be sensible enough to leave this hellscape by his side, toward a future where they could both have exactly what they wanted.

"But—he's the king," said Huda, breaking the silence and his reverie. "The Diviners are obligated to serve the rightful sovereign." She looked around. "Aren't they?"

"They do as they please."

Kamran felt a chill pierce the room, his instincts awakening in a blaze of scorn for that voice. That *face*.

Softly, Omid screamed.

King Cyrus stood in front of the closed door, his wretched, haggard, and bloodied appearance doing nothing to diminish the blue blaze of his eyes. How he'd reanimated so quickly, Kamran couldn't imagine; though he supposed it had something to do with the devil. Black magic likely ran through the beast's veins. Perhaps he couldn't be killed so long as he was allied with Iblees. Perhaps that was the bargain he'd made.

"Whatever you're thinking," said Cyrus quietly, "you're wrong. Now leave my home before I rip you apart with my bare hands."

SIXTEEN

شانزده

"THAT'S NO WAY TO SPEAK to our guests," said his mother, her composure unraveling. Her eyes darted back and forth between him and the foul prince, and she moved briskly to the side of the room, just out of reach.

As if he would hurt her.

No matter her many steely performances, it had always been clear to Cyrus that his mother was afraid of him. Afraid of her own son. When this knowledge wasn't driving a stake through his heart, it made him want to put his head through a wall. He understood her reasons, of course, but understanding did little to diminish the pain. It was no easy feat for him to compartmentalize as he did, living every day with the knowledge that his mother wanted him dead.

"They've come for the wedding," she was saying. "You must invite them to stay at least through the Wintrose Festival."

"You celebrate Wintrose here, as well?" Deen perked up. "When I was a boy it was always my favorite time of the year."

"They will not be staying," Cyrus said thunderously. "There will be no festival—"

"When my parents were alive, we'd sleep outside in the rose drifts," Omid added dreamily. "The petals piled three feet high. Smelled like heaven."

"Oh, yes!" cried Huda. "My sisters and I would often travel to the rose fields in the third week of the festival—when the blooms are most fragrant—we'd pack a basket and steal away from Mother, and they'd actually be nice to me—"

"What is wrong with you people?" Cyrus said angrily. His chest was heaving. His hands were shaking. "Get. *Out.*"

"Forgive me," came a solemn voice. "But I will be leaving these premises under two conditions only: with my queen or with your head, and not a moment sooner."

This brazen pronouncement came from the young man adjacent to the prince, who'd risen to his feet only to pin Cyrus with a threatening glare. In response, the king narrowed his eyes.

This, of course, was Hazan. The one Alizeh had called her *friend.*

Cyrus spared a moment to look carefully at the unwelcome visitor, realizing now that this was a character more important than he once considered. The densely freckled face; the trio of crystal daggers slung from a belt at his waist. His posture, too, was of interest: he affected a casual stance, but Cyrus was not fooled. He was like a panther in wait; if provoked, the young man would certainly attempt to kill him.

"More to the point: how are you awake so soon?" Hazan pressed on. "You were practically dead when I delivered you inside, and that was just over an hour ago."

"And we were promised breakfast," added the child.

"Yes." Cyrus swallowed, hating the reminder that he'd

been carried inside by one of these imbeciles. "I heard I owe you my gratitude."

Hazan stared at him.

Cyrus stared back.

The Jinn crossed his arms. "Are you not going to thank me, then?"

"No."

Hazan did not laugh, though a shadow of a smile crossed his lips.

Softly, Cyrus said, "Now get out of my sight."

"Not without my queen."

"She is not beholden to you," Cyrus replied. "And you are not welcome here."

"You vile creature." The prince stood slowly from the table. "You would hold her here against her will?"

A flicker of amusement briefly animated Cyrus's eyes, and he turned, with pleasure, to face the idiot. "She is not here against her will. She has chosen to stay."

"That's a lie!" Kamran cried.

"Believe what you like," said Cyrus, his chest spasming suddenly as he spoke. He felt for the wall behind him and, finding purchase, leaned his back against its support. He was fighting to stay awake, hating the weakness in his limbs, the tortured emotion roiling in his gut. Like intermittent electrocutions, he was experiencing flashes of sensation from his nightmare: the sound of her crying out; the sight of her washing his body; the taste of her, *God*, the taste of her—

It was astonishing to him that he stood now on his own feet, alive and awake. He'd never before been able to stir himself from his nightmares; had he known such a thing was possible, he might've tried harder, sooner. That he'd awoken in his bed with a violent start—the sight of so many faces swarming around him like amorphous ghouls—was nothing short of a miracle.

It had been both touching and perplexing to see members of his staff gathered around him in concern, and though the king was mystified by their attentions, he'd thanked them for their care before swinging unsteadily upright. There was a brief outcry as they insisted he return to bed, but when he refused—falsely claiming his health was in perfect order—they took that as permission to pelt him with questions. They'd wanted to know what, precisely, had happened to him, what was going on, who the guests were, and—

"Was it really all for show, sire? Such a strange morning—"

"—tried to catch an arrow in your hand, sire? Might I be so bold as to ask why?"

"I once heard of a king who tried to catch a dagger between his teeth! He never said a word after that—"

"Shame you were injured, sire, terrible luck—"

"—my whole life, never dreamed I'd see Simorgh—"

"Heavens, their prince is frightful handsome, isn't he? It'll be work just to keep the maids from swooning at the sight of him—"

"Should we start preparing rooms, sire?"

"Cook will want to know—"

"What a spectacle it was! We're ever so grateful!"

"—be fighting each other for the chance to serve him, that's for certain!"

"Simorgh's children, too! I've still got gooseflesh, sire, look—"

"If I may—where has your bride gone, sire? She was out even earlier than the servants this morning—"

"Is it true they've come for peace talks? Do you imagine things will be different—"

"—then they just flew away! Five of them—in a shot of light!"

"Sire?"

"*Sire?*"

"Where are you going, sire?"

"Oh, sire, you really shouldn't—"

It had been an effort, politely evading their questions while synthesizing the pertinent revelations. How Kamran's unworthy team had managed to acquire, as transportation, the legendary Simorgh and her family was truly a wonder, but the knowledge was a gift, too, for it was comforting to know that only a literal miracle had allowed the Ardunians to breach their borders.

Cyrus had thanked his staff once more, promising answers before the end of the day. His injured hand and leg, he'd noticed, had been washed and bound; the cool salve under his bandages offering him considerable relief. He'd meant to tend to these wounds straightaway with magic, but when the butler informed him that his mother was breakfasting with the foreigners in the dining room, he knew his injuries would have to wait.

Now Cyrus felt himself sag a little more against the priceless wall paneling, its fabric woven with gold and lotus silk, a gift received nearly a hundred years ago from the Shon empire. He felt as if his brain was lurching in his skull, as if he were surviving a succession of small heart attacks.

"If you do not leave here of your own volition," he said with difficulty, "I will have you all forcibly removed. Should any of you refuse removal, you'll be thrown in the dungeons, to be executed shortly thereafter. You will, however, be allowed to choose your preferred method of execution—"

"Are you such a coward," interrupted the prince, "that you would leave my death to another? Are you so afraid to fight me yourself?"

Miss Huda gasped. Sarra's eyes widened.

Cyrus knew better. He knew better and still he rose to this weak bait, angrily shoving away from the wall as a burst of adrenaline blurred his better reasoning skills.

"No, you're right," said Cyrus, reaching for the scabbard still slung at his waist. "Best if I kill you now, isn't it? Best to do what I should've done the other night, and spare this world the heft of your useless, pathetic weight."

Another flare of remembered sound, of sensation—Alizeh laughing, smiling at him—and Cyrus flinched, looking up in time to see Kamran bolt out of his chair. Hazan threw out an arm to hold back the prince, catching him around the chest with painful force—but Kamran shook him off, breathing hard. He was staring furiously at Cyrus.

"What motivation do you claim for such blatant malice? You act as if we've ever been acquainted, as if you have any reason to harbor such hatred toward me, when it was *you* who murdered *my* grandfather—"

"*I have my reasons,*" Cyrus exploded.

Kamran tried again to lunge at him and, once more, Hazan grappled with the prince, wrenching him back. "*You have no reason,*" Kamran practically roared. "You're just a demented scion of the devil—"

"I don't need a reason to detest you," Cyrus said, making an effort to rein in his anger. "Nor do I need a reason to kill you, for it's provocation enough that you exist. Still, I need only to recall the events of this morning to fan the flames of my contempt—"

"You would deny me the right to revenge? After all that you've—"

"I speak of your actions toward Alizeh!" Cyrus cried. "I refer to your unmitigated arrogance! You expect to be king of the largest empire on earth, responsible for the countless needs and protections of innumerable citizens, and yet over and over you exercise that imperious, self-satisfied speck of a brain only in the service of yourself, putting the lives of your dependents—*innocents*—at risk, in order to slake the thirst of your revenge, meanwhile you needed only to ask if I would face you in a duel, for I would have readily accepted—"

"And who are *you*," Kamran thundered, "murderous, barbaric king that you are, to educate me on caring for the lives of innocents?"

Cyrus stilled, the familiar burn of fury scorching him from within. "King Zaal was no innocent."

Kamran began to speak before thinking better of it, his jaw visibly clenching as he sent a furtive glance at the former street child. Omid was sitting stock-still in his seat, his big eyes wide with manifest fear.

How many young orphans had the late king murdered in order to keep himself unnaturally alive? How many skulls had he shattered for the brain matter within? How many years had the man spent feeding the serpents at his shoulders in exchange for more time to rule upon this decaying earth? Killing Zaal had been the one task Cyrus had performed with pleasure.

"You admired your grandfather a great deal," he said finally, softly, "despite the horrors owned by his soul. If you would receive guidance from such a man, surely you might listen to a word of advice from me." Cyrus looked him in the eye. "Your thickheaded, self-righteous behavior has no place on the throne. If you do not learn to set yourself aside in the service of others, you will never deserve your crown."

Kamran recoiled at that, the anger in his eyes dissolving into something like alarm. He glanced at Hazan before saying urgently: "Why did you say that?"

Cyrus frowned. "I thought I made my reasons clear."

"Who told you to say that?" insisted the prince. "What do you know of my crown—"

"*Kamran.*" Hazan shook his head sharply.

The southern king looked between the two—from the prince's wild eyes to the unspoken warning in Hazan's—and did not understand. Kamran appeared deeply unsettled, genuine confusion unmasked in his expression when he finally turned to Cyrus and said:

"Why didn't you kill me? The night of the ball—you had every opportunity to be rid of me. Why leave yourself open to the consequences of your actions, to the retribution you must've known to anticipate?"

In response Cyrus only turned away.

At intervals, he continued to feel Alizeh flare to life behind his eyes; and the truthful answer to the prince's question was horribly enmeshed with this weakness. Worse, the prince's earlier accusations weren't unfounded: Cyrus had reason to dislike the prince, yes, but there was little logic to support his unchecked hatred of the Ardunian.

In fact, what intelligence he'd gathered of Kamran had been generally favorable; by all accounts he was a decent royal and a formidable soldier, and when Cyrus had first encountered the young man at the ball he'd felt no ill will toward him. It wasn't until he realized Kamran had won Alizeh's affections—that they'd known each other with some intimacy, that she'd cared for him enough to protect him—

Only then had he grown to hate the prince.

Somehow it didn't matter that Alizeh had been but a conjuring of his imagination. It didn't matter that they'd never known each other outside of the delusions of his mind. It didn't matter that she owed him nothing.

He'd *loved* her.

It was a hallucination, a fantasy. He knew that, and yet he could not reason with his emotions. Fiction or not, she'd embedded inside him, replaced the air in his lungs. That she'd proven to be real—more exquisite than he'd dreamed—and entirely ignorant of him, had been more than he could bear. To then discover that she'd given her heart to another—that he'd known her in ways Cyrus never would—had been nearly unsurvivable. And yet, it was the only reason he hadn't killed Kamran that night.

Because he suspected she cared for him.

In response to Cyrus's protracted silence, the prince made a sound of disbelief. "Do you know, I'm beginning to think you might be entirely unhinged," he said. "You should be locked in a tower, your eyes devoured by scarabs—"

Without fanfare Cyrus drew his sword, the slicing sound of steel halting the prince's speech as the room around them gasped; Deen released a faint, withering breath; and the southern king, who felt his heart was slowly atrophying inside his chest, couldn't bring himself to care about anything beyond this moment.

"Insult me again," he said, his voice dropping to a sinister whisper, "and I will not be merciful."

Kamran's eyes flashed with fury, and Cyrus almost respected him for standing his ground. The prince was reaching for his own weapon when Hazan shoved him, hard, against the wall.

"*Enough*," he shouted. "I've had enough of you two idiots!"

Then, turning, he focused his wrath on Cyrus:

"I don't understand why you dragged Alizeh here, nor do I understand your apparent need to marry her, but I do know that you went to great lengths to orchestrate this mess. The fact that you've allowed her a choice in the matter of wedlock tells me that you care, at the very least, whether she's forced to take her vows, so let me make something very clear, you blundering fool: if Alizeh finds out you've murdered her friends you may be certain she'll refuse to marry you."

Cyrus stilled, this obvious fact neutralizing his anger in an instant. He blinked, sheathed his sword and, his chest still heaving, reached once more for the wall behind him.

He was, regardless, in no condition to murder anyone.

And then he heard her again, her voice breathless with desire—

Do you know what I love most about you?

Cyrus felt his knees buckle before he caught himself. He couldn't remember if it had been this bad before; perhaps it was worse now that he actually knew her, that just last night she'd been in his bedchamber, that he'd glimpsed something like real affection in her eyes.

Perhaps this episode would finally drive him to madness.

"How easily managed you are," Kamran said acidly. "How desperate you must be."

Slowly, Cyrus lifted his head. "You have no idea."

This admission seemed to surprise the prince, whose glower slowly faded. "Why?"

"Why, what?"

"Why must you marry her?"

"An insightful question," Cyrus mused. "I hadn't realized you were capable of intelligent thought."

The glower returned. The prince opened his mouth, no doubt to make a scathing remark, when Cyrus's mother spoke instead.

"Shall I tell them?" she said to him, her smile saccharine. "Or would you like to explain it all yourself?"

Cyrus closed his eyes and scowled.

"He claims he's being forced to marry her," his mother announced, addressing the room. "He says that Iblees has demanded this of him."

He heard the boy gasp, then opened his eyes to see that the girl had covered her mouth with both hands while the apothecarist slid back in his seat in astonishment. Kamran's horror was so complete he looked positively ill, and the sight of this discomfort was so enjoyable Cyrus nearly missed the fury on Hazan's face.

"How can this be true?" Hazan demanded.

"Many terrible things are true."

"But why? Why would he want her to marry you—"

"So this is what you meant," the prince said slowly, the tension in his eyes cleared by understanding. "The night of the ball. I heard you tell her that Iblees wants her to rule. You said, 'A *Jinn queen* to rule the world. The perfect revenge.'"

"You didn't tell me this." Hazan turned to Kamran, alarmed. "Why would you not tell me this?"

"I forgot." Kamran shook his head, as if in a daze. "In all the chaos of that night— So much happened, I could hardly keep it all straight—"

"So she has to marry you?" The child now. "She has to marry you because the devil wants her to marry you? But why does she have to do what the devil wants? I don't understand."

"Me neither," said Huda and Deen at the same time.

"*She* doesn't have to do what the devil wants," Cyrus said irritably. "I do."

"Why?" said the boy.

"Because I owe the devil a debt."

"So you have, in fact, made a deal with the devil," Hazan said quietly, eyeing the king with renewed suspicion. "And this is what he wants in exchange?"

"In part."

"And what does he stand to gain from her rule? She would never act in his interests, or acquiesce to his demands."

Cyrus's expression darkened. "I don't know. Iblees, as you can imagine, has not confided in me the full extent of his hopes and dreams."

"Then she might be putting herself in danger," Hazan pointed out, "if she married you."

"And what incentive does she have to enter into such an arrangement," Huda added, "when the only person who stands to gain anything from this is *you*?"

"An excellent question," Deen said, nodding at her.

"Good God." Cyrus sighed angrily. He stared the lot of them in the eye. "Enough of this. Show of hands, who here wants me dead?"

"Is this some kind of joke to you—" Kamran began angrily, cutting himself off as the boy, the girl, and the older one began slowly raising their hands.

"You," Cyrus said, nodding at the prince, "need not cast your vote, given that you've already tried to kill me twice today." Then, to his mother, "And your feelings on the subject have never been subtle."

To her credit, Sarra looked appalled.

"But you," Cyrus said, turning to Hazan. "What reason did you have for helping me?"

"You mean why did I save your life?"

"You hardly saved my life," Cyrus snapped. "I would've sorted things out eventually."

Hazan's eyes were flinty. "You're deluded."

"And you haven't answered my question."

"Alizeh did not wish for you to die" was his cold response.

At the reminder of Alizeh's sacrifice for him, Cyrus experienced a painful cratering in his chest, and he grit his teeth against the feeling. "Excellent," he said to Hazan, the word hollow. "That is your only reason?"

"Yes."

"And you wouldn't mourn the loss of me were I to unceremoniously drop dead at your feet?"

Hazan sent him a scornful look. "Certainly not."

"Then you all have reason to rejoice." Cyrus took an unsteady breath before addressing the room. "Fear not a union between myself and your queen. The underlying reason she's deigned to consider my proposal is that, as incentive for accepting, I've offered her my kingdom."

"That is not news," Kamran said irritably. "By taking the throne, she would naturally have influence in the empire—"

"I mean to say," Cyrus bit out, "that I've offered her my kingdom *without* my involvement. She would be the sole ruler."

"*What?*" Sarra nearly screamed.

"What?" echoed the prince, who couldn't hide his shock.

"Oh my goodness," breathed Huda, blinking fast.

"But how?" asked the apothecarist. "You can't simply

recuse yourself. At best, you'd be cast out of society, stripped of your titles—at worst you could be tried for treason—"

"By the angels," Hazan said softly, shock and awe burning in his eyes. "You're willing to die for this."

"Once my debt to the devil has been fulfilled," Cyrus said flatly, "Alizeh would be free to kill me at her leisure. My empire would become hers, to rule over as she wishes."

"So this is why she wanted you to live," said the Jinn, subdued. "This is why she tried to save you."

"Cyrus," his mother gasped, looking at him with something like real feeling. "What are you thinking? You would simply hand over our empire to this girl? Have you well and truly lost your mind?"

"I still don't understand," said Hazan, his brows furrowing. "What would motivate you to act so recklessly—"

Cyrus turned away from this noise. He was most interested in the reaction of the prince, who regarded him now with steady silence.

"You cannot be trusted," Kamran said finally. "What's to stop you from reneging on such a deal as soon as your vows are spoken?"

"I offered to perform a blood oath."

Everyone, except the child, inhaled sharply.

"Cyrus!" his mother cried once more. "You cannot be serious!"

"That sounds disgusting," Omid muttered.

"It is," said Hazan, who looked troubled. "Blood oaths were outlawed in Ardunia centuries ago."

"Why?" asked the boy.

It was the prince who said, quietly, "It's a violent, dangerous magic."

"For as long as he remains in debt to her," Hazan explained, his eyes on Cyrus, "he will be physically bound to her. He'll have almost no free will. Blood oaths were responsible for long stretches of darkness throughout our history." He hesitated. "They're everlasting oaths. They cannot be broken."

"Are you really so desperate?" Kamran was studying Cyrus, too, though he appeared unbothered by the cruel limitations of the blood oath. "You would hand over your birthright for a single night as her husband?"

"No," said Cyrus. "Not a single night. She'd not be free to dispose of me until the devil releases me from my contract."

"This is outrageous," cried Hazan. "Kamran, you cannot consider it— It's nothing more than a scheme, and he'd doubtless force her to consummate the marriage—"

"I would *never*," Cyrus cut in viciously. "Think what you will of me in all other aspects, but even I am not so unworthy as that. She is entirely safe from me."

"You would put that in the oath?" Hazan was livid. "That you're not to lay a finger on her?"

Cyrus tamped down his anger. Condemned as he was, he knew it unreasonable to expect others to assume he possessed even a shred of decency, but the accusation still rankled. "Yes. I'll make it clear I won't touch her unless she wants me to."

Hazan looked disgusted. "As if such a scenario could ever exist."

"Miss," whispered the boy. "What does *consummate* mean?"

"Oh," said Huda, her color heightening. "You need not worry about that for now. I'll explain later."

"But—"

Meanwhile, Kamran was studying Cyrus, his eyes shrewd and calculating. "What bargain did you make with the devil?"

Cyrus only glared at him.

"He refuses to say," Sarra supplied. "I've asked him thousands of times, and he's never admitted the truth."

"I see." Kamran did not look away from the southern king. "And how long would it take for you to be released from your contract?"

"I can't be certain," Cyrus answered. "A matter of months, perhaps."

The prince took a deep breath, exhaling slowly as he processed this last statement. "Interesting."

"*No.*" Hazan was shaking his head. "Absolutely not. This is a dangerous, open-ended ploy—"

"I disagree," said the prince with immaculate calm. "In fact, I think it will do nicely for revenge." He met Cyrus's eyes. "You will die, she will inherit your empire, and then— I shall marry her."

Hazan shrank back, so severe was his astonishment.

The others, too, were making various sounds of bafflement, but Cyrus was somehow deaf to this, blind to all but the chaos flaring inside his body.

The statement had struck him like a whip.

Unmoored, it took every bit of Cyrus's self-possession to

keep from displaying his horror. He'd not considered such a manipulative tactic on the part of the prince, and he should have.

"It will require significant patience on my part," Kamran was saying, his eyes bright with triumph as he studied the king. "But then, I'm capable of extraordinary forbearance, especially for so great a reward."

A great reward, indeed.

What a master stroke it would be—what victory—for the Ardunian to inherit the Tulanian empire. The northern and southern kingdoms had fought many historic wars over access to resources—and in particular, the Mashti River. Cyrus knew how desperate Ardunia had been for a direct line to fresh water, and this would resolve the empire's greatest weakness in a single, peaceful move. No lives need be lost, no wars waged; Kamran would marry her and in the process marry the two nations, inheriting Tulan's every valuable natural resource, including the riches of their densely magical mountains.

It would make Ardunia, as an empire, nearly invincible.

His heart pounding madly in his chest, Cyrus couldn't believe he'd made such a misstep, and he couldn't see how to fix it. Even with this grand offer on the table, Alizeh hadn't committed to marrying him; if he were to retract his promise of Tulan, she'd surely refuse him.

It was a risk he couldn't take.

Horrible as it was to think of losing his empire, Cyrus had comforted himself with the knowledge that he'd be handing it over to one such as Alizeh; he felt certain that, in his

absence, she'd care for his people with unimpeachable compassion and justice. But to think that the Ardunian might
benefit—might absorb his land only to plunder it, to use
their precious resources in the pursuit of further expanding
their empire—

"What makes you so certain she'll marry you?"

Cyrus looked up sharply, shocked to discover that, of all
people, it was his mother who'd come to his defense.

"Why would the girl choose to share a crown, when she
could lead her own nation?" Sarra said, glaring at Kamran.
"What need does she have of you?"

Kamran narrowed his eyes, preparing to respond, but it
was Hazan who spoke, who appeared both distressed and
confused. He shook his head lightly. "Need would not motivate her," he said. "Duty might. For the sake of the prophecy,
for the good of the people— Yes, I believe she could be convinced that a union with the Ardunian empire—"

"What prophecy?" said Huda, looking around. "There's a
prophecy?"

"She *is* Ardunian, after all," added Deen. "Perhaps she'd
like to go home—"

"What prophecy?" Huda asked again.

Kamran was looking at Cyrus when he answered, darkly:
*"Melt the ice in salt, braid the thrones at sea. In this woven king-
dom, clay and fire shall be."*

Cyrus stiffened.

This was too much. He reached once more for the wall
behind him, his condition deteriorating by the second. Kamran had quoted the inscription from the Book of Arya, an

ancient tome known to hold the map to an extraordinary power. He'd been struggling for days to convince the book to reveal its secrets, all to no avail.

No one but Alizeh was even supposed to know of the book. Cyrus had only heard of its existence through Iblees; it was one of his tasks to discover the nature of Alizeh's purported magic, and he'd been commanded to steal the relic from her small room at Baz House.

"Where did you learn that?" Cyrus asked, struggling to suppress his panic.

Kamran only smiled. "She must already suspect her empire is to be woven with another—and we know it won't be yours," he said ruthlessly. "In fact, it's become clear to me now, more than ever, that she and I were fated to be together. It's been all but foretold."

"*Where did you learn that?*" Cyrus repeated, this time losing his self-possession. He felt he might choke on his own fury, so unraveled was his mind. That the devil had summoned him this morning to celebrate this loss, that it seemed obvious now it was all going to fall apart— He was too weak, too injured, too exhausted to endure it.

"It's from the Book of Arya," said Hazan, who was looking now at the king with some concern. "We found it among Alizeh's possessions."

"*Fucking hell,*" breathed Cyrus. He closed his eyes, his body sliding slowly down the wall. He finally sat, heavily, on the thick rug, and dragged his hands down his face. "You found the decoy."

"Decoy?" Kamran demanded. "What decoy?"

"What you discovered was an imitation of the real thing," said Cyrus, lifting his head. "It's physically identical—on the outside, at least—to the original."

"Where is the original?" Hazan asked urgently.

"I have it."

"*What?* Why? How—"

"No," said Cyrus vehemently, shaking his head. "I will bear no more of this. I began my morning by being shot nearly to death, so if you'll excuse me, I think I've earned a reprieve from the many delights of your company." He looked them over. Then, with a sigh: "If I can't kill you, and you're all refusing to leave—"

"We finally get breakfast?" Omid brightened.

"I'll have you all settled into rooms!" Sarra clapped her hands together. "Oh, we haven't had guests in ages! It'll be such a nice change." She was smiling with such warmth that, for a moment, Cyrus wondered whether his mother's enthusiasm was genuine. "You'll be quite comfortable, I'll see to it personally."

Omid opened his mouth again to speak, and Cyrus muttered an oath before saying, "Yes, for the love of God, we'll give you breakfast—" just as there was a sharp knock at the dining room door.

"Come in," Cyrus said angrily.

The butler, Nima, entered and hastily bowed. "Your Majesty," he said. "A trio of Diviners has arrived to see you."

Cyrus's head jerked upright, and at once, his adrenaline spiked. "What?"

"They've requested a meeting at once, sire."

Cyrus hauled himself up off the floor. He felt dazed; the Diviners had months ago refused to speak with him ever again. In fact, it had been so long since he'd communicated with one of his old teachers that his heart filled now with both joy and dread. The news must be dire indeed if they'd come to deliver it themselves.

Cyrus was paralyzed, struggling to process this, when he looked up to find Hazan standing at his side.

"If this is about my queen," said the Jinn, "I'm coming with you."

PART TWO

IN THE BEGINNING

در آغاز

THE SUMMER SUN HUNG LOW in a blue sky, heat so heavy it seemed to sink beneath flesh, cling to bone. A medley of buzzing sound filled the air, winged insects in frenzy. There was the smell of sod, the occasional flap of wings, and the rustle of fabric as Cyrus subtly shifted his weight in the tall grass. At least a dozen times he'd watched mosquitoes land on various aspects of his body, and at least a dozen times he'd struggled to remind himself not to kill the insects but to brush them away gently. This method was not foolproof.

Absently scratching at a bite on his arm, he peered up at the smudging sun before glancing again toward the horizon. He stood at the center of a meadow, acres of willowy grass interrupted only by a wild scatter of red poppies, their stems occasionally bending in the weak, welcome breeze. Cyrus leaned against the edge of a human-scale honeycomb; it was a massive wooden re-creation of the iconic hexagonal chambers, one of several seated on the sprawling back field of the Diviners' land. Cyrus didn't know when, exactly, the others were due to return, and his composure was unraveling. He drummed his fingers impatiently along his covered thigh, then tugged at the collar of his heavy black cloak.

"Too restless," came a deep, steady voice.

Cyrus stilled, then turned carefully to face his teacher.

The older man, Rostam, stood unflinching under the melting heat, his hood pulled back to reveal the shaved head, tanned skin, and unflappable calm of one who might be standing in the shade. Rostam did not sweat. He did not fidget.

Cyrus, meanwhile, didn't know how much more he could endure. The lesser, second son of Tulanian royalty had only recently acknowledged his fourteenth birthday, and he was neither fully at home in his body, nor was he yet in command of his mind. He'd not mastered the art of silent communication, either, and his voice, as a result, was one of the few that carried across the field.

"We've been waiting three hours," said Cyrus carefully, lest his tone register the statement as a complaint.

Rostam tilted his head. "Three hours," he echoed. "And all you've done is wait?"

Cyrus felt a prickle of unease.

"What have you been waiting for, little one?"

Even as he knew there must be more to the question— knew there was something he'd missed—Cyrus felt compelled to answer honestly. "I'm waiting for the others to arrive."

When this elicited no response from his teacher, he added: "They're due to return from the mountains with a fresh yield of crystals. We're meant to cleanse and sort the harvest before extracting the magic."

Rostam fixed the young prince with a piercing look, and Cyrus grew increasingly apprehensive. His teacher said again, even more softly: "What have you been waiting for?"

This time, Cyrus didn't answer right away.

He'd been at the temple long enough to know when he was being challenged, and though he withered under Rostam's unrelenting stare, he didn't push the overgrown locks out of his face, despite the sweat beading at his hairline; he didn't flinch, despite the buzzing creature that landed on his hand. He funneled all his energy into maintaining the pretense of calm when, more than anything, Cyrus wanted to unlatch his cloak and toss it to the ground. He wanted to run home and dive into the falls without pause, wanted to swim with his dragons until the moon rose high in the sky.

Cyrus wanted to fly tonight.

He wanted to fall asleep on Kaveh's back, wanted to open his eyes and be blinded by the stars. He wanted it to be tomorrow, when this hellish work was done and the crystals were ready for extraction, when he might try again to coax the magic free of its home and into his hands and— And then, he understood. Like a flickering bulb he brightened, then dimmed.

"I've been waiting," said Cyrus, "for this to be over."

A spark of approval animated Rostam's eyes. "And where have you waited, little one?"

Quietly, he said, "In the future."

"Three hours of your life, lost."

"Forgive me," said the young prince, lowering his head. "I've been consumed by thoughts of my own desires and comforts, when I came here today to be present for others."

There was a beat of silence before Rostam nudged the boy's chin upward, and Cyrus slowly met his teacher's gaze. "You do not require forgiveness. You require perspective."

Cyrus blinked at him, the question unspoken.

Rostam stepped back and opened his hands, turning his palms parallel to the ground. Slowly, he curled one of his hands closed, and a soft breeze drew toward them. Cyrus felt the breath of cool air curl around his neck, lift his limp hair, slide under his sunbaked cloak. The pleasure was so instant he went slack as Rostam lifted his other hand, turning his palm up to the sky where a cloud appeared overhead, suddenly casting them into shade.

The young prince enjoyed this respite for several seconds before Rostam said, gently, "You must not resist life when it becomes inconvenient to live. You cannot outrun fear. You should not ignore pain. You will not outlive death."

Cyrus felt a strange sense of foreboding. "What do you mean?"

"You spent three hours in a state of distress—focused solely on one emotion—hoping to discard those hours from your life as if your discomforts might expire with them. But life cannot be experienced one emotion at a time. It is a tapestry of sensation, a braided rope of feeling. We must allow for reflection even when we suffer. We must reach for compassion even when we triumph. If you spend your days waiting for your sorrows to end so that you might finally live"—he shook his head—"you will die an impatient man."

Cyrus only stared at him, his heart beating hard.

Rostam flicked his fingers and the breeze withdrew, the shade evaporated. Once more, Cyrus felt the sun bear down on him, the heat so oppressive he began to perspire at once.

Instead of fighting the feeling, he surrendered.

He closed his eyes and searched for the breeze. Beads of
sweat raced down his back and still he exhaled, releasing the
tension from his body. Finally he felt the gentle caress of a
current, the tall grass swaying against his legs; he listened
to the harsh *zizz* of a wasp hovering. The air was muggy, his
cloak suffocating, and he opened his hands to catch more
wind against his palms, heard the burble of a small spring in
the distance. There were birds, the gentle flutter of butterfly
wings.

By degrees, the world around him seemed to settle, its
thorns retracting, and though he was scorched and parched,
Cyrus finally felt present. When, after a time, he opened his
eyes, he discovered Rostam staring at him curiously, a skin
of water held in his outstretched hand. The prince accepted
this offering with deep gratitude before taking a long pull
from the vessel.

"You're not ready to endure the heat without water," said
his teacher. "But you exhibit great fortitude for one so young."

Cyrus caught his breath, ducking his head slightly as he
wiped his mouth. "Thank you, sir," he said. "I'm very grateful."

Rostam looked away as Cyrus took another drink, and
when he looked back, he said, "Do you know why we master
ourselves in order to master the magic?"

"Yes, sir." Cyrus handed back the empty waterskin and,
like an eager student, parroted the ancient Fesht line—

"Bel nekan nostad, nektoon bidad."

If it does not trust, it will not come.

"The magic will not release," the prince explained, "to

any person of unsound heart and mind. The Diviners act as intermediaries between the extraordinary realm and the ordinary, coaxing magic free from their crystals so that their power might exist safely in our world."

"What you've said is correct," said Rostam, whose countenance did not change. "But you've yet to answer my question. Once again: Why do we master ourselves before we can master the magic?"

Cyrus, who been certain he'd given a sufficient response, now faltered. "I don't— I'm not sure, sir."

"You've not yet seen how a man can be destroyed by weakness of the flesh," said Rostam, his timbre low and steady. "Desire, power, riches, immortality. You are still young and pure of heart—the world does not yet appear to you a misshapen place. But know this: magic has left in its wake a galaxy of dead stars. Even Diviners have not been immune to the allure of manifold power."

As if in response, there came a flurry of commotion in the distance, a storm of dragon feet hitting the ground with a series of small tremors. Cyrus was briefly distracted by the sight of two dozen dirt-streaked Diviners freshly returned from the mines. They dismounted the vivid beasts in perfect silence, the static of unrefined magic snapping all around them as they unloaded their wares. His heart soared at the sight. He wanted nothing more than to run to them.

Rostam settled his heavy hands on Cyrus's shoulders, startling the boy back to the present moment. His teacher's eyes were urgent, and when he spoke, the words thundered in the quiet between them.

"Master yourself so that you will never be mastered. Know yourself so that you might live with conviction. Live with conviction so that your steps never falter." He paused. "The mastery of self means never fearing the consequences of doing what is right."

Rostam released his shoulders, and Cyrus felt strange as he took a step back, as if the world around him had blurred. He blinked repeatedly, his heart pounding loudly in his chest as a faraway dragon gave a tired roar. It was a mercy that the prince was self-aware enough to understand even then— even as he failed to grasp the magnitude of what his teacher was saying—that he needed to pay attention.

"When you suffer," Rostam went on, "you can choose to endure, or you can choose to overcome." He gestured around them, to the vast expanse of the meadow. "Here, even in the midst of your discomfort, there existed elements of relief, if only you had bothered to search."

SEVENTEEN

هفده

AT FIRST, THERE WAS ONLY perfume.

The dizzying fragrance of intoxicating blooms had suffused the air and stormed her mind, and Alizeh, who was too disoriented even to know she was asleep, drew the decadent scent deep into her lungs. She licked her lips to taste this ambrosia upon her skin, as if it were an elixir for her drowsed spirit. Even in slumber her head was leaden, her thoughts clouded. She didn't know how long her eyes had been closed, nor could she bring herself to wonder about her whereabouts. Indeed Alizeh was conscious of precious little but the perfume that had roused her from her stupor; so much so that she'd forgotten even to be afraid.

It was in fact the first time in too long that she'd stirred, her fingers stretching, searching, as she was slowly returned to consciousness. She felt the give of a mattress as she shifted—and then she paused, for Alizeh had perceived the velvet of petals under her hands, and as she cautiously turned her head, her cheek pressed against more of the same.

Strange.

Everywhere, her body seemed to be touching flowers. Blooms skimmed the nape of her neck, adorned her breasts and torso and lower, all over. With a start, Alizeh became aware of her own nakedness, of the silky slide of petals along her skin, small drifts gathering in the dips and valleys of her body. Indeed her senses seemed to indicate that she was all but submerged in a bed of corollas, a possibility so absurd as to signify a fault of perception. Experimentally, she drew her hand down her body, and Alizeh was relieved to discover that she was not quite as exposed as she'd feared and yet still more vulnerable than she'd like: she wore a simple silk shift and nothing else, the gossamer material loose and billowy, enough that the petals had found a way to gather, like a second garment, against her skin.

It was disbelief that finally forced open her eyes.

A burn of tears followed this simple action, and as she blinked through the blur, a pink haze washed over her vision, each flutter of her eyes bringing into focus a sight so surreal she felt certain now that she must be dreaming.

She tilted her head back to take it all in, and gasped.

Alizeh was in a circular room of tremendous height, its aged, cream-colored walls almost obscured under cascades of thick, glorious pink roses. The distant ceiling, too, was hung with heavy adornment: more blossoms, more vines, more beauty. Ample blooms turned toward the iridescent light shot through a pair of ancient, stained glass windows; these oblong shafts of ethereal color highlighted, in particular, a curve of wall into which were built a series of floor-to-ceiling bookcases. The spare, battered shelves boasted but a few tattered volumes, and where once the sight of such a poorly stocked library might've inspired some melancholy, it was then only a source of delight, for the shelves were bursting with lush flowers so enchanting the sight of it all set Alizeh's heart aflutter.

She forced herself to sit up, her head swimming. All the while, loose petals had been raining down slowly, pirouetting as they fell, bringing with them that delicious fragrance. One landed gently on her nose, and she caught the satiny bit, absently rubbing it between her thumb and forefinger as she marveled at her surroundings.

Clouds of pink roses stretched across the floors and tumbled down a rough stone staircase, which descended toward an imposing, battered wooden door, which was, ostensibly, the exit. There were few other clues as to her location; the bed she occupied was the only freestanding article in the room. Old and nicked, its finish was faded in places, worn away in others—and its bedding was, as she'd suspected, covered entirely in rose petals. *She* was covered entirely in rose petals.

They were *everywhere*. Inescapable.

How long had she been lying here, receiving this gentle shower of beauty? It had to be magic—a tremendous enchantment—for there were no thorns present on the vines, and no decay among the fallen blooms. But then, what peculiar magic was this? What purpose did it serve? The bed covers, she noticed, were at least an inch thick with discarded flora; given the unhurried flurry from above, she suspected she'd been here, in this curious place, for at least a matter of days.

Strangest of all: Alizeh realized, with a shock, that she was not cold.

A feeling of frost had lived in her limbs so absolutely that she existed always in physical distress. She was always tense; often rigid. To a lesser degree this pain had persisted in her veins since birth; in childhood she'd struggled with the cold, but she'd not experienced the full agony until her parents had died, after which the ice had claimed her utterly. It had taken a long time to learn how to live around this constant suffering, and Alizeh had never dared to hope she might one day live without it. But now—now she felt at rest inside her body for the first time since her parents were alive. The dull, welcome warmth in her veins was one she never thought she'd feel again.

She struggled then to assemble her memories—to understand where she was and how she'd arrived here—but Alizeh's mind felt cobwebbed and dusty, her thoughts unsteady and slow to form. She pushed herself again for information, but her head, disordered as it was, instead dealt her a painful, unyielding blow of emotion. In quick succession she was delivered images of her mother in various states of heartache, the accompanying sounds and sensations so vivid she nearly doubled over in pain. Over and over the scenes changed, but the chords of agony only crescendoed:

Alizeh was six years old; she'd found her mother weeping on the kitchen floor, a letter clutched in her fist;

she was eight; awoken in the night by pounding at the front door, she'd tiptoed into the hall to find her mother sobbing in her father's arms;

she was eleven; her father's dead body had been discovered at the bottom of a well, and grief would not drain from their bodies no matter how much they cried;

she was twelve; everything was ablaze, her throat choked with smoke, her mother screaming, and she could smell it; she could still smell the charred flesh of her mother's body as the woman slowly burned alive in her arms—

Alizeh made a sound like she'd been struck, as if the wind had been knocked from her lungs. The pain was in fact so extraordinary it shocked her. Tears had fallen soundlessly down her cheeks, and she swiped them away with trembling fingers even as she struggled to draw breath. These unsolicited visits from grief were cruel, but somehow comforting, too, for Alizeh had no desire to forget. Indeed she often felt that her parents had vanished to all but her. True, she could no longer see them, yet she seemed to carry their bones on her back, their pain on her shoulders, their hopes in her heart.

Often, she still felt she could hear them whisper.

Even then she thought she heard her mother, the words like a caress against her cheek—

Do not fear, my dear, the fall

—just as the massive windows blew open. They groaned, then slammed against the pockmarked walls with violence, the blow cushioned only by the thick of flowers on either side. Another gust of wind blew the panels back on their hinges with an eerie whine, and instinct blazed bright within Alizeh, who pushed off the bed with an energy she did not own. She was shaking.

Flower petals whirled about her in a small shower as she steadied herself on the stone floor, then reached for a bedpost to better stabilize her body. Even in the midst of confusion she was not blind to the beauty of the moment, the ethereal drift of roses all around her, the gust of wind that had sent it all into a frenzy. She stood there, caught in this slow-settling whirlwind when her mind finally shook off the worst of its dust. Her heart now pounding in her chest, she was bombarded at once by clarity.

Hazan.

Her thoughts went first to him. She knew there was more to recall, more to unknot from her mind, but for now the image of Hazan would serve as her North Star. He'd come for her, she remembered that now. Which meant he must be here, somewhere, in Tulan— But then, where was *she?*

Was *she* still in Tulan?

She spun around, searching once more for any indication of her whereabouts. The windows were too high; even if she moved the bed she might not reach their ledge. She bit her lip, considering. If she were to climb the bookshelves she might be able to capture a discarded volume, the contents of which might provide some illumination. She squinted at what few spines were legible, but they appeared to be ancient tomes, written in a language she didn't recognize. Frowning, she studied her obvious escape routes once more: there was a door and a window.

But where would she go? How might she find Hazan? And there were others, weren't there? Her friends, yes— Where did they—

She touched a hand to her mouth.

She remembered, with a spike of fear, the anger in Kamran's eyes. She remembered the terror in Cyrus's, she remembered— Heavens, she remembered it all. The chaos. The horror.

The *pain.*

Kamran had shot her with an arrow meant for Cyrus. She'd felt it pierce through her back, felt the excruciating burn, the paralysis in her lower body, the drop to what had seemed a certain death.

Had she not died?

Of this final event she'd no strong recollection, nor could she recall what preceded it—but she was suddenly desperate for answers.

What had happened after she'd plummeted from the sky?

The sun, she noticed, appeared to have dipped into afternoon, but there was light yet in the heavens, enough for a half day's journey. She could open the door or scale the wall; either path could be terribly fraught, and she was still trying to decide between the two, when, suddenly, there came a delicate knock at the door.

Alizeh froze; her heart beat harder.

Very slowly, she turned to face the noise. Always she hoped for peace, but never did she fear battle. Even in this thin shift, she would fight if necessary.

Alizeh planted her bare feet firmly on the ground, then lifted her chin. When she spoke, her voice rang out soft and clear in the cavernous room.

"You may enter," she said.

EIGHTEEN

هجدہ

THERE WAS A GROAN OF wood and metal as the door was pushed open, and through the narrow gap appeared first a delicate hand, then a slippered foot, and, finally, a familiar face.

"Aliz— I mean, Your Majesty? Are you awake? They said you were, and oh, I dearly hope—"

"Miss Huda?" said Alizeh, startled. "Is that you?"

The young woman gave a strange, birdlike scream, slammed the door shut behind her, clapped both hands over her mouth, then ran up the stone stairs and all but tackled Alizeh in a series of exceptionally unladylike behaviors. Alizeh laughed at this, then stiffened as she was gathered up in a severe hug, for she was not wearing any underwear, and did not know how to extricate herself from the embrace without wounding the young woman's feelings.

Eventually, Miss Huda pulled back, her face bright with emotion.

"You're awake!" she said. "You have no idea how worried we've been! And you mustn't call me *Miss* anymore, just Huda will do, and anyway, we're friends now, aren't we?"

"Yes," Alizeh said softly. "Yes, of course we're friends."

Alizeh's mind was in turmoil. Her fears were so tangled and her confusion so great that she could hardly choose which question to ask first—and then she grew entirely distracted. There was something different about Huda, something vivid and fine, and Alizeh found herself staring at her friend, trying to understand this transformation before realizing the explanation was quite straightforward.

"Huda," she said on a breath, "you look absolutely *enchanting.*"

The young woman's color heightened as she pressed her hands nervously to her stomach. Huda was aglow, beaming as she stood there in a stunning velvet gown, the construction of which Alizeh couldn't help but admire. The dark blue fabric was of the highest caliber, its details exquisite, its stitches undetectable. The dress accentuated her lavish curves in so elegant a manner that Huda looked a great deal like royalty. It was precisely the sort of garment Alizeh might've designed for her, had she had the opportunity. Huda possessed far too statuesque a figure to be encumbered by the latest fashions, and now, released from the stays of the current styles, she was remade. Even her dark hair, too often pulled back in a severe knot, was newly arranged in a low, loose bun, artfully chosen tendrils framing the graceful planes of her face. Her eyes seemed bigger, her sun-kissed complexion more radiant. Everything about her ensemble allowed her best features to shine, but—

More than that, Huda seemed *happy.*

"Do you really think so?" she said, drawing a hand down her skirt. "Sarra says the dress suits me, though I'm not entirely— Goodness, look at me, my focus so easily diverted." She shook her head, then took Alizeh's hands. "It's just like you, isn't it, to emerge from a difficulty only to deliver me a kindness?" Huda beamed. "Much as I would love to discuss my wardrobe with you, dear, I must first tell you how very, very pleased I am to see you awake. I didn't believe it when they told me you were up, not at first, as we've been waiting weeks and weeks with no word and we've all been terribly distressed, and the Diviners haven't made it easy, you know, always warning us in their strange way that they can only keep the peace for so long before—"

"*Weeks?*" Alizeh blanched. "How many weeks? And what do you mean of the Diviners? And Sarra"—she frowned—"what do you know of Sarra?"

Huda paled. "Oh dear. I've really stepped in it, haven't I? *Please* don't tell me I'm the first one in to see you?"

Alizeh could hardly breathe around the mayhem in her chest. "Yes," she said. "You are."

"Oh dear," Huda whispered again.

"What's happening?" Alizeh said, backing away. "Where am I? Where is Hazan? Where is . . . everyone else?"

Huda went motionless, only her lips parting and closing as she prevaricated. She then clasped and unclasped her hands, looking around nervously, and jumped nearly a foot in the air when there was a sudden knock at the door. There was the whine of old wood, then—

"Miss? Can we come in, too? They said she's—"

"Not yet!" Huda spun around too fast, her voice too high. "I need another moment alone with her, but then, you know, after that, you might pop in to say hello—"

"But—miss—Deen and I would really—"

"Close the door, Omid!" she practically shrieked.

There was the sound of a long-suffering sigh, then another whine before the door slid heavily closed.

Huda looked at Alizeh, then, smiling horribly, said, "Perhaps you should sit down."

"I'd really rather not."

"Yes, well, perhaps I should sit down, then," she said, and sat heavily on the bed. Huda closed her eyes, drew a deep, bracing breath, and then coughed, her face souring as her eyes opened. "Good grief, how do you breathe in here? I can hardly think straight for all the perfume."

Of all the things Huda might've said, this observation came as an unwelcome surprise. "I think it's lovely," said Alizeh, her brows drawing together. "Don't you like the smell of roses?"

"A little, perhaps, is not so offensive to the senses," Huda rejoined, looking around the room with renewed revulsion. "But this, I fear, is egregious."

"I like it," said Alizeh, who was feeling oddly defensive. She shook her head. "Why are we arguing over the flowers?"

"I don't know, dear," she said, aggrieved. "I'm terribly nervous."

"And how do you imagine I must feel?"

"Better, I hope?" Huda raised her eyebrows. "Better than you did with the arrow in your back, anyway. I can't imagine that was very comfortable."

She laughed; Alizeh did not.

"Yes, well," Huda hurried on, "I don't know *all* the details, of course, as I am generally precluded from joining important meetings—and do you know"—she lifted her chin—"everyone is odiously self-important around here, as if I can't be trusted! As if I'd give away all the empire's secrets!"

Alizeh shot her a look.

Huda crossed her arms. "And so what if I do occasionally divulge my findings? A tiny secret shared among friends is not so awful, is it? Though perhaps if they shared more with me I might not be so inclined to snoop!"

"Have you been snooping?"

She dropped her arms. "Only a very little, entirely innocent bit!"

"Huda—"

"Perhaps later we can talk about all the discreet letters Prince Kamran has been writing"—she raised her eyebrows—"and all the mysterious trips King Cyrus has been taking—"

"You *have* been snooping." Alizeh's eyes widened.

Huda gave a brilliant smile. "I'm not entirely useless, am I? I don't care what Mother says about me. Anyway, to answer an important question: we are currently at the Diviners Quarters in Tulan. It turns out that the reason you were feeling so ill the morning of"—she made air quotes—"The Unpleasantness, was that you'd been poisoned by dark magic." She bit at her fingernail. "Which, you know, is why it's taken you so long to heal. Nearly four weeks you've been here at the temple—"

"*Four weeks?*" Alizeh cried. "I've been asleep for almost a month?"

"Oh, it's been torturous for all of us, let me assure you!

Certainly not more torturous than it was for you," she hastened to add. "I don't mean to imply that we suffered more than you did! I only mean to say that we did suffer, quite a bit, for even with the Diviners' intercession it wasn't a simple fix. No one was certain how long your healing might take, and it was the fact of not knowing that made it all the more brutal. They had to, erm"—she bit again at a cuticle—"*bleed the bad magic from your body*—"

Alizeh drew a sharp breath.

"Yes, disgusting! Grotesque, even! Though I don't know if they *actually* bled you, to be honest? But it sounds awful, just awful—and anyway the thing is, dear, no one can figure out why you'd have such a poison in your body to begin with, and, well"—she cringed—"naturally they've all been fighting over it."

"I see." Alizeh's heart was thudding painfully.

Huda sighed, released her tortured fingers from her teeth, and stared at Alizeh. "The boys have been awful. I quite hate them now. Not Deen and Omid, of course—but the others are always fighting and brooding and muttering and *ridiculous*. And to think, I nearly swooned the first time I saw Kamran!" She clasped her chest. "The way he'd parted the crowd the night of that horrific ball! I thought I'd die there in that fiery ring, and suddenly there he was—striding toward me like a hero, calling me a lady! Heaven help me, Alizeh, I thought I'd never seen anyone more magnificent in all my life." Huda dropped her hand, then made a disgusted face. "Can you believe, growing up in the royal city, I always dreamed of meeting him?"

Alizeh raised her eyebrows. She was still trying to digest the fact that she'd been half-dead for a month when she said, faintly, "Yes, I believe it's fairly common to be enamored of royalty."

Huda laughed. "It's generous of you to think of it that way. It makes my stomach turn to think back on the insipid dreams of my younger self, and yet—every time Mother was awful to me, or my sisters were cruel, or I discovered my pillows had been stuffed with rat entrails—"

"*Rat entrails?*"

"Yes, the rat entrails were particularly unimaginative," she said, pursing her lips. "Anyway, every time something terrible happened, I'd lock myself in my room and then lock myself in my closet and then lock myself in my head, where the stupidest of all my dreams lived, and I'd imagine that one day I'd meet the dashing prince and he'd be everything good and glorious and"—she hesitated, looking suddenly haunted—"well, I suppose I thought he'd be different. Kinder than everyone else." She was quiet a moment, fighting a flare of emotion before returning her gaze to Alizeh.

"Good thing that's sorted, isn't it?" she said with forced brightness. "Anyway, do you happen to have any recollection of being poisoned? It would solve a great deal of our problems, I think, if you could remember whether anyone had poisoned you."

Alizeh blinked steadily at the young woman, then sank down onto the bed beside her. She felt dazed; her mind was churning—*roiling.*

Had she been poisoned? She didn't know.

She couldn't remember.

Had she really been asleep for four weeks? What had happened to the world in her absence? What of her people, to whom she'd made promises?

Her heart was racing, her panic multiplying.

Unconsciously, Alizeh placed an arm around Huda's shoulder and squeezed, holding steady as the young miss yielded to this comfort. Alizeh listened as Huda sniffed sharply, retracting the feelings that had escaped her otherwise iron grip. The two of them were staring toward the window in silence when Alizeh said, softly, "If anyone puts rat entrails in your pillows again, I'll kill them."

Huda choked out a shocked, watery laugh.

Alizeh knew it hadn't been easy for Huda to be raised in high society as the unwanted daughter of a fallen woman; it hadn't helped that Huda's scandalous bloodline had informed the curves of her body, easily distinguishing her from her sisters. Huda's figure was voluptuous in a way that seemed to delight the worst vultures of a preying public, all while driving her stepmother to madness and cruelty. Alizeh had paid close enough attention to Huda to know that her loud, prickly facade sheltered a wealth of crushing pain—and a deep vein of untapped tenderness as well.

Why else would the girl have followed her all this way?

"I never thanked you for coming to save me," said Alizeh, whose own smile was faint. "Consider it a repayment for your kindness."

Huda laughed again, louder this time. She wiped her eyes

and said, "Goodness, I don't know why I've turned into a watering pot. I'm a bit overwhelmed, I suppose. It's been nearly a month of worry, then too much relief, and now this generous offer of murder—"

"What are friends for, if not to kill your enemies?"

Huda collapsed into a fit of giggles. "Oh, wouldn't it be lovely if we could choose our own sisters? I'd trade in all five of mine for just one of you."

Alizeh reared back. "You have *five* sisters?"

Huda nodded even as her shoulders shook, her laughter slowly abating. "I'm the baby, if you can believe it. Youngest children are supposed to be spoiled rotten, aren't they? But then Mother says I was born rotten and needed no spoiling to get there." Huda was still smiling as she spoke, but Alizeh stiffened.

She turned carefully to face her friend, for she was remembering an alarming conversation they'd once had—something Huda had said—

If Mother discovers I've hired you to make me a dress I'll be reduced to little more than a writhing, bloody sack on the street, for she will literally *tear all my limbs from my body.*

The nosta had glowed neither hot nor cold at this horrifying statement, leading Alizeh to believe that Huda had been uncertain whether her mother might deliver her such violence. Alizeh was beginning to worry that Huda's home life was a good deal worse than her sharp wit and untroubled air had led others to believe. She thought to test the nosta again now, to ask Huda a pointed question about her mother when she realized—in a blaze of fresh panic—that she wore nothing but a silk shift. All of Alizeh's things were gone: her cloak, her dress, her boots, her corset—

The nosta.

Had it fallen out of her clothes in this recent plummet to the death? Had the Diviners confiscated the magical object when tending to her wounds? How might she be sure? Perhaps she could find one of the priests and ask? Her mind was spinning now, her uncertainties escalating—

"Anyhow, dear, it really would be grand if you could try to remember. Do you even think it's possible someone poisoned you?"

Alizeh's head shot up at that. She could hardly think straight at the moment, much less remember anything useful. This conversation had dealt her so many emotional challenges she struggled even to flit from one thought to another, and yet—unfortunate as it was—a possible attempt on her life was the least shocking of Alizeh's concerns. She'd been nearly murdered enough times now that such an event was no longer cause for surprise, and, in fact, was becoming quite routine.

"Yes," she said, blinking. "Yes, I suppose it's entirely possible."

"In that case, I have to say—reluctant as I am to reward Kamran's terrible moods—that Cyrus *does* seem the likeliest suspect for such a crime, no matter how many dramatic displays"—Huda gestured dismissively to the room—"he's fashioned all around the city."

Very slowly, Alizeh electrified.

She felt the tremble of awareness in her fingers first, then in her chest and elsewhere, her body coming alive with a terrifying quaver of feeling. Her heart pounded dangerously as she looked around the room at the infinite blooms; the endless, devastating beauty. Her words were a breath when she said, "Cyrus did this?"

NINETEEN

نوزده

CYRUS SAT ATOP THE OLD, mossy roof of an outbuilding at the very edge of the Diviners Quarters, the damp of the sponge beneath him slowly seeping into his cloak. He pulled his knees up to his chest, stifling a shiver as the sun made a weak effort far above. Droves of clouds hovered before him, circling the grounds so completely that Cyrus could hardly see the temple below for all the white that obscured it—though this mattered little. He knew this property better than he knew his own home. He needed only to close his eyes to imagine the room she was in, to picture in detail its dimensions and contours. How many years had he all but lived here in his youth? How many times—*countless*—had he run freely into the arms of his teachers? Once, his life had been nothing but prayer and divination, quiet and contemplation.

Now—

Now he was but a tormented shade of his former self. His soul disfigured beyond recognition, his hands singed with dark.

He glanced at the newspaper in his hand, the headline screaming at him.

ALARM AROUND THE WORLD AS
JINN UPRISING IMMINENT

It was a copy of *The Daftar*, Ardunia's preeminent publication. Cyrus had been receiving copies of this, and other journals, for several months, for it was his custom to remain abreast of international news. He took a particular interest in the headlines from the north, for Ardunia had long been his greatest threat, but Cyrus himself had not been the focus of foreign interest since his first horrible month as king, a time in his life so dark it nearly eclipsed the era he was in now.

Nearly.

In four weeks, an estimated seventy thousand Jinn had gathered in Mesti, the royal city, and in the provinces just beyond. Every day this number grew. Despite his mother's well-warranted fears, the Jinn had arrived peacefully—for they'd arrived oblivious to their queen's injury. Cyrus had managed to conceal this fact through nothing short of a miracle, for the Diviners had consented to remain silent on the subject of Alizeh—only in the interest of protecting the greater peace. Even so, it was a risk, for the priests and priestesses were incapable of speaking falsehoods and would not lie if asked a direct question. In fact, the magic that bound Diviners to truth was of the same strain that enabled them to detect a falsehood. The latter was a talent that Cyrus, too, possessed to some degree, though his education in the priesthood was incomplete, and as a result his skills, too, were imperfect.

Still, he knew better than to try to deceive a Diviner.

They'd questioned him that terrible morning. Hazan on his heels, he'd met the trio of Diviners in a receiving room, the sight of their legendary, liquid-black cloaks sending twin pangs of dread and longing through him. In another life he would've been one of them, would've forsaken rank and prestige to occupy instead the liminal spaces of existence, where ego was eclipsed by the spheres of alchemy and prophecy. It was what he'd always wanted: to devote his life to the distillation of *being*.

He'd stared at them, at their hooded faces, their perfect stillness. They'd emanated a calm, tightly coiled energy, that steady pulse of magic beating within them like a second heart. Powerful and nameless, Diviners were an enigma to most; in fact, many found them terrifying. Yet Cyrus knew that those who were drawn to divination were often reserved and passionate, satisfied to spend their lives asking questions of the earth. Even so, it'd been so long since he'd stood in the presence of a Diviner that he'd been unnerved.

The southern king had greeted them as he once did— bowing his head as he pressed his hands to his chest—and though they'd returned the gesture, their disapproval was palpable.

He was not one of them.

Even then Cyrus had desired nothing more than to shave his head and shirk the world; he longed for their freedom. Longed for the hours he'd once spent in companionable quiet, for the backbreaking mornings excavating magic from the mountains, for the sun-soaked summer evenings cleansing and sorting the fresh crop of crystals.

Cyrus had learned years ago how to refine the precious material, how to gently conjure the magic free from the stone, whispering incantations under his breath when he was still too inexperienced to do so soundlessly. Thousands of times he'd injured himself in the process, nearly severing his right arm when he'd once summoned the power too quickly. Indeed, convincing magic to leave its crystal and enter the chaotic world was a great deal like taming a wild dragon. It was brutal and terrifying, and demanded not only immeasurable self-restraint, but tremendous heart—for the power was wise and would not release peacefully into the hands of any it deemed unworthy.

Bel nekan nostad, nektoon bidad.

Once released, magic proved a gentle presence. It had the energy of a cat in repose, weight like a lick of wind that curled around its keeper's neck, humming with pleasure.

Cyrus was the rare king on earth who knew this sensation.

Most royals had spent their lives as soldiers, or else engaged in merriment and frivolity; traditionally they received doses of magic from the Diviners as gifts, often in the form of comestibles, reinforced weaponry, or enchanted garments. Cyrus's years in the priesthood had earned him a rare authority and independence as a sovereign. He had access to great stores of magic while requiring no intercession from a Diviner; as a result there was no one to interrogate the ways in which he used his power. He was in fact so skilled at bonding with this precious matter that he lived much as the Diviners did: always ready to cast a spell.

And there remained bedrocks of magic yet untouched.

The most powerful crystals were so volatile they were nearly impossible to handle; the more potent the core, the more difficult the stone was to quarry. Some varieties were so temperamental they'd explode if so much as touched by the wrong person, causing an entire mine to collapse. Over the years, thousands had died in the effort to excavate these venerated strains from the earth—and Cyrus had long suspected that Alizeh's magic was of this untouchable stock. Even the greatest Diviners of Ardunia had been unable to access the crystals of the Arya mountains, and if the stories were true—if Alizeh were indeed able to unearth such power—she would be recognized by every holy order on earth as the greatest Diviner of their time. Her supremacy would be unmatched.

The world would bow to her.

Every day, this improbable theory grew stronger. Jinn everywhere had initiated a mass exodus. Those who could were fleeing their homes, traversing great distances to reach their queen. Already Cyrus had received thinly veiled warnings from neighboring allies and bald threats of attack from distant nations—simply for harboring her.

The existence of a Jinn queen was all but a promise of revolution.

Alizeh was a threat to the incumbent systems of oppression, to the cheap labor these empires received from those incarcerated, to the social order established on earth for a millennia. Few other kingdoms allowed their Jinn any measure of freedom; most were horribly persecuted, plainly hunted in the streets, subject to caste systems that denied them basic humanities, or else forced into prison camps where their powers were controlled by magicked shackles and systematic dehydration; thus, they were exploited for profit; there, they lived and died and bore their children. The empires of the world couldn't allow someone like Alizeh to rise. And though the southern king knew his truce with Ardunia to be little more than a sham, the rest of the world saw it as a political maneuver. Cyrus's pending marriage to an insurgent leader, coupled with his recent alliance with a force as mighty as Ardunia, had made him and his humble kingdom a target for malice.

He didn't know how long he might stave off an attack from an enraged empire, but the pact between Tulan and Ardunia had proven both a problem and a protection, for while this alliance had sent tremors of unease throughout the world, it was also the silent might of Ardunia's fabled army that currently kept Alizeh safe within Tulan.

It had become clearer to him, in these agonizing weeks, why her parents had kept her in hiding, and why the devil had been so adamant about this marriage. From birth, she had been marked. Without an ally, without an army, without an empire and resources and magic and *water*, Alizeh could not have withstood these external forces on her own. Great and necessary change had always been born in the blood of calamity.

Her life would be in danger for as long as she lived.

He'd been ruminating on this fact that wretched morning, imagining the real and figurative target on her back even as he'd stood before the Diviners, his body humming with apprehension.

Why is he here?

Cyrus had heard the voice in his head with a start, for it

was one he recognized. The priesthood demanded a dissolution of the material life and its mortal titles—over time, even given names were lost—but a man once known to him as Mozafer had stepped forward to speak.

"He insisted on coming," Cyrus explained. He'd glanced at Hazan, whose glower was almost violent. "He's concerned for his queen."

There's no time for this was the response.

At once, the receiving room disappeared; they were submerged in a smoky darkness where naught but four forms lit by an unseen light source. Hazan had not been allowed to join them.

Mozafer did not tarry.

The situation is grave, he'd said silently. *The girl will not heal.*

Cyrus, who'd expected terrible news, still sustained a savage pain at these words. "What do you mean?"

The priest drew forward, then held open his pale hand, upon which glittered a dusting of a blue shimmering powder.

Cyrus visibly stiffened.

Black magic was the only magic that left behind a residue. It was the cost of darkness, of selfishness: the toxic leavings were a by-product of the impure substance, and they filtered into the world as a faint poison. Every assault Cyrus had ever received from the devil had been delivered via this dark magic, but its leavings always evaporated; never before had they stained his clothes.

We found this lining the interior pocket of her cloak. Mozafer pulled back his hood a few inches, revealing shockingly white skin, to better study Cyrus's eyes. *It is a borrowed cloak.*

"It's mine," he'd confirmed, his heart racing now. "But I don't understand—there shouldn't have remained any trace—"

You have inflicted upon her a serious injury.

"I would sooner die than hurt her—"

It matters not whether you meant her harm. Mozafer pulled his hood back entirely now, baring his shaved head. His brown eyes were unflinching but not cruel. *The ice in her veins precludes her from absorbing such poison. While in others its effect is mild, in her it triggers an usual reaction. It appears her body would sooner destroy itself than metabolize a contaminated magic.*

Another blow of pain, straight through the chest. "What will happen to her?"

We don't know. We've never treated one such as her before.

"But will she live?" Cyrus asked desperately.

Mozafer hesitated. *Her body appears to have a natural healing mechanism, one that we feel will hasten her recovery. The exposure was minimal. She has a strong chance of rehabilitation. But it may take some time.*

"How much time?"

Mozafer shook his head. *Several weeks. Perhaps months.*

Cyrus had spiraled.

He'd lost his composure then as he hadn't since he was a boy. He'd doubled over, struggling to breathe, and made a sound of distress so severe that even the Diviners, who were not allowed to touch him, drew forward in sympathy.

There was so much to break him. His guilt, his shame, his

fear. That the evil in his life had bled through and harmed
her; that as a result he'd surely fail to fulfill his obligations to
the devil, that this failure would destroy everything. His life
was unraveling around him, the sinew of his body unbraid-
ing every day, leaving him threadbare, little more than bone.

"What will happen, Mozafer?" He'd fallen to his knees,
dropped his head into his hands. "What will happen when
I fail?"

We are not allowed to speak of it, came his gentle response.

"Will the Diviners continue to shun me?"

Yes.

"Will I ever be able to return to the temple?"

Not so long as you are tethered to him.

Cyrus lifted his head, fighting back tears. "And will you
not spare me a single word of guidance, when I am so desperate for your counsel?"

Mozafer kneeled before him, and Cyrus's heart constricted at the sight, at the warmth in the older man's eyes.
He said—

Sleep.

—before they vanished.

The smoke cleared. Cyrus had been returned to the
receiving room on his knees, the bright light of midday nearly
blinding him. He was at once pummeled by the intensity of
Hazan's angry protests, but he turned his gaze toward the
floor, ignoring the outburst as his mind reeled, as his heart
raced. He needed to pull himself together.

He needed to make plans.

He'd delivered himself without delay to his mother,

loudly informing her that his bride-to-be had requested a period of calm and reflection prior to the wedding—during which time she would be staying in the company of the Diviners and was not to be disturbed. This gossip, picked up at once by palace staff, quickly and efficiently disseminated throughout the land, reinforcing the mystery surrounding the arrival of the Jinn queen.

As for the pilgrims, they'd begun arriving that same day.

Slowly at first, then in droves, they asked for neither water nor shelter. They wanted nothing but space—and the Diviners had opened their vast grounds to them, where they'd gathered together in tightly arranged bouquets, the overflow spilling into the streets, the parks, the hills and mountains. They slept where they sat, no matter the weather.

In response to the many requests to see her, the Diviners had issued a single word, in an exceptionally rare statement:

Patience.

And so, the Jinn waited.

Cyrus studied them every day. He watched their numbers grow, watched them become restless and angry and ultimately subdued, only to repeat the cycle. In a short time they'd appointed a leader: a small, elderly woman who, after days of taking it upon herself to break up fights and settle arguments, became their intermediary. Her name was Dija, of Sorral.

Cyrus watched her now.

Her wizened face curtained by thinning sheets of milk-white hair, Dija stood on a high bough of a towering magnolia tree, her frame so slight she nearly blew away in the wind.

Her body feeble, her spirit ferocious, she'd grasped a nearby branch for support, and from her post, she conducted the chorus of voices. With her eyes shut, Dija placed her free hand atop her head as she cried out—

For the land that once was ours
For the millions who were slain
For the rivers red with blood
For the centuries of pain

Justice!
Justice!

For our parents in the ground
For the coffins that we built
For the tiny hands and quiet hearts
of the children who were killed

Justice!
Justice!

The mass followed her lead, hands placed atop their heads, eyes closed as they sang. Their voices had begun to haunt him throughout the day. Where once the heaving crush of the crowd had been a source of concern, now he felt nothing but astonishment. For her.

It was all for *her.*

And yet, she would not open her eyes.

In the general course of things, Cyrus was not one to steep

in his sorrows. But he'd been allowed to occupy this space at the edge of the Diviners' property precisely because his bouts of mawkish emotion were so pitiable. So long as his feet never touched the hallowed ground, he'd been granted permission to sit here and watch her from afar. During this time—precisely one hour—he brined in his own gloom.

It was a behavior so unlike him he'd come to resent it.

He shifted slightly then, lifting his head to look once more upon the masses, when a locust materialized as if from nowhere, a bright spark of green landing lightly on his hand. The insect settled its wings and stared up at him with its uncanny eyes.

Hello, friend, Cyrus said silently.

The locust jumped up in response, landing on his shoulder. They were fascinating creatures, known for listening deeply and saying little in response.

Have you seen her? Cyrus prompted.

The locust only adjusted its legs, twitched its head.

Will you check? Let me know if there's any change?

One more twitch of its head, and the locust took flight, disappearing into the clouds.

Cyrus watched him go, then tucked away the crumpled newspaper he still held in his hand. Every night for nearly four weeks he'd dreamed of Alizeh. Strong in body but fractured in spirit, Cyrus was so drunk on his dizzying, sensorial experiences of her that he could hardly see through the thick of his own mind to what was real. He'd gone against his own instincts and done as Mozafer had instructed, and he slept. It had been sound advice, for no magic could replace the curative properties of sleep, and Cyrus had felt the difference immediately: his body was steadier as a result. Still, the agony and the bliss of these strange nightmares had been a steep price to pay for a boost of physical endurance. He awoke every day aching and breathless, his body strained with need, his heart pounding so hard it scared him. Cyrus felt like an opium addict, desperate for these tastes of ecstasy even as he knew they were poison. He'd stopped fighting it. He willingly drowned in the feel of her, intoxicated by the taste of her. It was a torture he struggled to define. Every night he slept with his face pressed to her skin. Every night a new facet of his soul died for her.

He felt ill, all the time.

He was electric with impatience, with anxiety. Sometimes it felt as if he'd swallowed the sun, as if he was struggling to contain a fire that would kill him before it ever went out.

Finally, Cyrus stretched his neck, then shook his head.

"It's been days and days of this," he said. "I've grown tired of it. Surely *you've* grown tired of it."

There was silence at first; then, eventually, the slow crunch of vegetation under boot. It was several seconds before the young man finally showed himself, though Cyrus did not turn to face him. A gust of wind had pushed a bloat of clouds in his direction, and he gently pressed his fingers to the mass.

"You knew," said Hazan carefully.

"That you were following me?" Cyrus almost laughed. "Of course I knew."

"Then why not say something sooner?"

Cyrus did not answer right away. He was raking his fingers

through the vapor when he said, finally, "I suppose I was curious."

Hazan loomed over him a moment more, then settled himself atop the roof a small distance away, studying the southern king all the while.

"Curious about what?" he asked.

"You."

The young man bristled. "Why?"

Cyrus reached into his pocket, then uncurled his fist, within which sat the nosta the Diviners had found hidden on Alizeh's body. Weeks ago they'd delivered this magical object to Cyrus, and though the discovery had been a shock, it had also comforted him to know that so long as she'd possessed it, she might've known he was trustworthy.

He finally looked at Hazan. "She got this from you, didn't she?"

Hazan held very still, though panic flit in and out of his eyes. "Where did you get that?"

"I might ask you the same question," said Cyrus. "Considering this is *mine*."

TWENTY

پیسست

ALIZEH WAS STILL STUDYING THE surreal sight of the pink blooms all around her, astonishment driving the thunder of her heart.

"Cyrus did this," she said again, this time without inflection.

Just saying his name aloud left her with a strange, disembodied sensation. Alizeh felt suddenly desperate to see him, felt this need inside her like a physical ache.

Of course it was him.

How had she not realized right away?

"As I said, I find it egregious," Huda was saying. "He's acting like some wounded child—painting the city in flowers as if he's planning a funeral—"

"Where is he?"

"Who?" Huda startled. "Cyrus? Oh, I haven't the faintest. No one does, usually, and he certainly never tells *me* what he's up to. All I know is that he cannot be trusted."

"Why?" Alizeh asked, her eyes widening. "What has he done?"

"You mean aside from all his overt sins?" Huda laughed. "He hasn't murdered anyone yet, if that's what you're asking. But he's very, very secretive, and very irregular. Do you know, on several occasions I caught him speaking, with great feeling, to a *dragon*?"

Alizeh frowned. "That's not very irregular, is it? People talk to animals all the time."

"Yes, but who speaks to *dragons*?" she said, sounding exasperated. "Their ears alone are about a mile up their heads, which are about a mile from the ground. Imagine speaking to a dragon and thinking they could hear you! I'm certain you'd have to be deranged."

Alizeh's frown only deepened. "Surely you might choose some other reason to dislike him? This feels a bit unfair."

"Oh, I've *loads* of other reasons for thinking he's deranged, don't you worry." Huda waved a hand. "I needn't list them all."

At that, Alizeh felt as if something had flickered out inside her, taking her energy with it. "No," she said quietly. "You needn't list them all."

"Anyway, as I was saying, it likely *was* Cyrus who poisoned you, if you could only recall—"

"Huda," she said, staring into her hands, trying desperately to channel calm.

"Yes, dear?"

"I'd like to leave this room—to find Hazan—I'm feeling a bit faint, and I think fresh air would do me some good. Perhaps we might finish this conversation at a later time, preferably while I'm wearing undergarments."

Huda made another shrill, birdlike sound, then jumped from the bed as if she'd been branded. She spun around and said, "Yes! Of course, they *told* me to bring you a set of clothes— I'll be right back—"

"What? Who's *they?*"

Huda was halfway down the stairs when she called over her shoulder: "The Diviners, of course! They had to burn your other ones, you know"—she grabbed the door handle—"because of the contamination—though I wouldn't mourn the loss too much, as they were all covered in blood in any case—"

"Huda—wait—"

But Huda had already yanked open the door, called for Omid, exchanged a few hurried words with the boy, retrieved something out of sight, then slipped back inside the room, nudging the door closed with her hip. The heavy panel slammed shut behind Huda's back, and the young woman smiled up at Alizeh with great joy. In her arms she held a small, beautifully fashioned piece of luggage, the supple, powder-blue leather of the hard case fastened at intervals by brass hinges and clasps.

Stunned, Alizeh only stared at her.

"Can you not imagine my delight?" Huda said, ascending the steps in a flurry. "Now it's my turn to dress *you!*"

Alizeh felt the light fade from her eyes.

"Oh, don't look so horrified! Besides, if you don't trust my taste, you might trust Sarra's—she and I are a similar size, and she's been letting me borrow a great deal of her garments." Huda threw back her head and laughed. "I'm wearing the castoffs of a queen! If only Mother could see me now!"

"Your mother," Alizeh repeated softly, reminded that she'd overlooked an enormous detail. "Huda, if you've been here for almost four weeks, where does your mother think you are? Your family must be worried."

Huda's eyes went round. "Oh, no, it's quite incredible, really. Father is outrageously proud—he said he always knew the blood of an ambassador ran through my veins! And now Mother hasn't any choice but to sing my praises, for we're all practically famous—"

"Famous? What do you mean?"

"Yes, right, best to start at the beginning, isn't it?" Huda placed the suitcase on the floor. "Well, the news out of Ardunia is that the Diviners have stayed Zahhak's hand—"

"Who's Zahhak?"

"Ah." Huda's brows pinched together. "Can you remind me where you left off in all this? It's been a frantic few weeks, and I can't remember how much you don't know."

Alizeh stared blankly at the girl. "The last time I truly saw you, you were trying to beat Cyrus over the head with a candelabra."

Huda reddened at the mention of this, then laughed nervously, and before Alizeh could question her reaction, the young woman delivered her a mad rush of information. They passed a few minutes in this way, Alizeh prodding and Huda providing. Huda described all that occurred after Alizeh was whisked away from the ball on the back of a dragon, and how Zahhak—the oily defense minister of Ardunia—had tried to steal the throne out from underneath Prince Kamran, "who was basically locked in a tower by the Diviners—"

Alizeh gasped.

"—but then saved by Simorgh—"

Again, Alizeh gasped.

Too, Huda explained her coincidental presence during this difficult time at the palace—

"And then all of us, including me and Deen and Omid, flew to Tulan, even though Kamran did *not* want us to come with him, and he was adamant that he didn't care whether any of us died in the process, because he mostly just wanted to kill Cyrus—"

Except that he hadn't killed Cyrus, and instead the two young men had come to some impossible truce, which resulted in an open invitation for their group to remain at the palace. When Alizeh had asked to know the terms of this unlikely peace treaty, Huda's color deepened very suddenly, and she refused to say more except to explain that the prince, in an unexpected pivot, was being praised by the people of Ardunia as a compassionate peacekeeper, for it was now passing as common knowledge that he'd traveled all this way—against the interests of Zahhak—in the hopes of preventing war.

"And now," Huda said eagerly, "all of us are being credited for forging friendship between the two empires!"

"Heavens," Alizeh said softly.

"Incredible, isn't it?" Huda was nodding. "Our kingdoms have never coexisted so peacefully. It's been well over a decade since an Ardunian sovereign has even been invited to stay in Tulan. In fact," she added in an undertone, "I've learned from the servants—who are oddly tight-lipped when it comes to gossip about their king, by the way—that Cyrus has never hosted a single guest at the palace during his rule, which is quite unheard of, and makes our stay all the more exceptional as a result."

"And no one thinks it strange?" Alizeh asked. "That the Ardunian prince would choose to make nice with the person responsible for murdering the king of his empire?"

Huda considered this, tilting her head as she said, "Actually, now that I see how it's all developed, I think it would've been a great deal worse if Kamran had, in fact, killed Cyrus. Did you know that a mob tried to storm the palace before we left Ardunia?"

Alizeh shook her head, horrified.

"Well"—Huda nodded—"the people were so disgusted with Zaal after he was unmasked at the ball that they rioted for about a week. Even the royals were scrambling to distance themselves from the late king—some going so far as to praise Cyrus's actions, if you can believe it. A few even joined the fray to protest."

"What were they protesting? The possibility of war?"

Again, Huda nodded. "Most were refusing to die in the defense of a disgraced king; but they were also condemning Kamran by association, claiming they didn't want another corrupt sovereign who'd just as likely strike a deal with Iblees—"

"But that's terribly unfair—"

"Yes, terribly unfair, but the riots were quelled once word spread that the prince had already fled Ardunia—immediately after Zaal's death—to try to make amends with the southern empire. The general consensus is that he's wonderfully selfless to have spared his people unnecessary bloodshed, even while grieving his grandfather." She laughed, then shook her head. "Not at all the truth, of course, but my point is that if he *had* killed Cyrus, our empires would've certainly gone to war, and it would've been tragically unpopular. Kamran might've faced a veritable insurrection.

"Of course"—she leaned in—"we're the only ones who know the real reason it all worked out for him, and that's entirely thanks to you, isn't it?" She pulled back and smiled. "Cyrus really, *really* wanted to have us all executed, but Hazan pointed out that you'd be terribly cross with him if he murdered your friends, and he hasn't mentioned it since. And now here we are! Making peace! Best of all, Zahhak looks dumb and Kamran looks grand and—"

"And you and Omid and Deen have been celebrated," Alizeh finished for her, feeling dazed. It was a great deal to absorb.

"Yes!" cried Huda, who then quickly sobered. "Apart from being worried sick about you, of course, it's been the most exciting time of my life. I'm getting letters from fans! Can you imagine! People *love* me." She hesitated. "Well, it's mostly children. Some old men, too, I think, though it's sometimes hard to tell—"

"Huda?"

"Yes?"

"How does Hazan feel about all this?"

She stilled, her smile frozen. "I don't know."

"Surely you might venture a guess?"

Huda looked away then, biting the inside of her cheek before she said, "I think it might be best if you talked to Hazan about how Hazan feels." She looked back. "He doesn't share his feelings with me."

Alizeh softened. "Is he all right, at least?"

"I suppose so? He's been terribly grim. Not as bad as the others, but grim nonetheless."

"I see." Alizeh averted her eyes, taking a moment to study the shape of a particularly fine rose. She took a steadying breath before she said: "And Cyrus?"

"What about him?"

Alizeh struggled to meet Huda's eyes. Her interest in the southern king was almost impossible to hide, though she made an effort to appear indifferent. "What's he like?"

"*What's he like?*" Huda echoed, surprised. "You mean aside from being obviously cracked in the head?"

Alizeh suppressed a flinch. She couldn't explain why, but every insult Huda leveled against Cyrus seemed to prick her with its sting. And yet, she had no good reason to defend him.

"Well," Huda was saying. "I suppose you should know: he doesn't act at all like a king. He wears the same dreary clothes every day, no pomp whatsoever. He's *obscenely* quiet; he never sits down; I've never seen him eat; and he performs a shocking amount of magic. He's always disappearing, for example, or else appearing when you least expect him. I've seen more magic from him in this last month than I've seen in my whole life—and I'm inclined to agree with Kamran that he must get his power from the devil, for how else could he cast so many spells? And no one knows where he goes when he's all the time disappearing! Very suspicious." She lowered her voice. "Though I overheard Kamran in a rage

one day, telling Hazan how he'd witnessed Cyrus in some
ungodly state the night prior—something about him being
drenched in blood—"

Alizeh inhaled sharply.

"I know! Horrifying! Then again, when I saw Cyrus later
that day he appeared perfectly normal, so I fear Kamran
might've been exaggerating." Huda exhaled, deflating as suddenly as she animated. "Otherwise," she said, "he's boorish
and awful and wastes all his evil magic on stale displays of
imitation guilt. Heavens, if he feels so terrible about what's
happened to you, perhaps he never should've kidnapped you
to begin with!" she cried, angrily swiping petals off the bed.
"I swear, it's insupportable. He's enchanted every inch of the
city with the same pink roses, and he refuses to say a word
about it—he hasn't even accepted responsibility! The citizens, of course, think they're all elaborate displays for the
Wintrose Festival, but I know better. I caught him once, saw
him growing roses in his hands—"

"I see," said Alizeh with a quiet finality. She couldn't
bear to hear more about the flowers; her heart was already
too soft toward the notorious southern king. "I take it he's
treated you all poorly?"

Huda hesitated. "No," she said. "In fact, we've been well
cared for. Omid eats enough for ten of us, and Deen has been
delighting in the medicinal stores available in the castle.
Deen says that, in Ardunia, he's only allotted a very small
amount of magic from the crown for his business, but here,
they have access to a great deal. He asked the king one day if

he might try his hand at mixing potions, and Cyrus did not deny him access." She shrugged. "Anyway, Omid eats a lot, I spy a lot, Kamran skulks, Hazan broods, and Deen spends most of his days working with the palace alchemist. We all meet for meals, though mostly we don't see Cyrus at all. I suppose he has lots of secretive things to do, being king, et cetera."

Finally, Huda's small speech came to a close, and Alizeh turned to face her. A thousand more questions sat at the tip of her tongue, but she was prevented from asking, for Huda had pinned her with a curious look.

"Are you really going to marry him?" she asked.

Alizeh froze. She felt oddly breathless at the thought, and said softly, "I might."

Surprisingly, Huda did not condemn her for it. Instead, she canted her head and said, "I didn't understand at first, of course. Though I suppose now I can see the draw."

Alizeh's lips parted in astonishment. "You can?"

"Of course I can." Huda laughed, then frowned. "I might marry him, too, if it meant I got to kill him shortly thereafter and take his empire."

At once, Alizeh felt as if all the blood had rushed from her head. "How did you— How do you—"

"Oh, my dear, don't look so afraid! No one is upset with you! That is, Kamran was understandably distressed at first—but just until Cyrus told us about Iblees forcing him to marry you." She waved a hand. "Not to worry; he clarified the terms of your deal. He even told us he'd offered to make you a blood oath—which I think is a very good idea, by the way, no matter how brutal Hazan claims it to be." She raised an eyebrow. "I certainly wouldn't risk marrying such a man without a blood oath to secure my future."

Alizeh blinked, stunned. "So everyone knows? And no one objects to me marrying Cyrus?"

"Well." Huda bit her fingernail. "Perhaps you should speak with Hazan before you make your final decision. I fear he has a great deal to say to you on the subject."

Again, Alizeh blinked. "I see."

"Anyhow," Huda said cheerfully, and tapped the suitcase. "The gown I've chosen for you is *sublime*. Sarra showed me the trousseau she'd gathered in your honor, and together we went through the many articles she'd selected for your wardrobe. Most things have to be remade in your measurements, by the way—which I found shocking, considering how well that lavender dress fit you the night of the ball—but Sarra explained that Cyrus's gifts had been magicked to fit their wearer, while the garments she'd chosen were ordinary commissions—"

"Huda," Alizeh said, struggling to center herself, "I don't mean to offend, but I've grown weary under the weight of these many disclosures. I think I'd prefer to return to the palace and choose my own clothes. There are many important conversations ahead of me, and all I need for now is something decent and sensible—"

Huda scoffed. "As if you could wear something decent and sensible to face such a crowd! You're their queen, dear, and you have to look the part, especially as they've all been waiting so patiently—"

"*What?*"

Huda, who'd been unlatching the luggage, briefly froze. "Right," she said, wincing. "Did I forget to mention that part?"

TWENTY-ONE

یلست ویک

"THAT'S NOT POSSIBLE," SAID HAZAN, doing nothing now to conceal his apprehension. They were both staring at the nosta Cyrus held in his outstretched hand. "How could it belong to you? My mother left that to me in her will."

A flare of heat from the nosta confirmed these words—though Cyrus did not require the assistance, for he was fairly able to detect a lie. "Who was your mother?"

Hazan's jaw clenched. "I didn't come here to be interrogated."

"No," Cyrus said, and looked him over. "You came here to interrogate me."

"You can't be shocked to hear it," said Hazan, who was flushed with anger. "It's beyond evident that I don't trust you."

Cyrus almost smiled. "And you're hoping I'll put your fears to rest?"

"I want to know the terms of your deal with the devil."

"No."

"I want to know what you stand to gain from this arrangement—"

"No."

"—and I want to know whether she will be safe as your wife."

Cyrus stiffened at the words *your wife*. The sheer depth of feeling he experienced at the sound of the possessive *your* had briefly upended his mind. It was absurd, of course; for even if she consented to marry him, she would never truly be his. He knew that, and yet his heart would not slow its canter.

Slowly, he met Hazan's eyes.

"Always," he said. "She will always be safe with me."

The nosta flared red hot in his hand, and Hazan witnessed this color change with a mix of astonishment and alarm.

"My turn," said Cyrus, turning the small marble in his fingers. "Did you know that this is a royal heirloom? It's been passed down in my family for generations. That's why the Diviners returned it to me. My father thought we'd lost it ages ago."

Hazan's eyes hardened. "As I said, I received it from my mother."

"But you have some knowledge of its history."

To this, Hazan said nothing.

"You are no ordinary Jinn, are you?"

"What's that supposed to mean?"

"I mean it must be hard to lie, all the time, about who you really are."

Hazan was quiet for so long that silence gathered between them like smoke, choking. It was with unveiled anger that he finally said, "You know nothing about me."

The nosta flashed white, cold.

"Your mother was a courtier," said Cyrus, turning his eyes

to the clouds. "According to my sources, she spent a great deal of time in the Ardunian court and was a beloved attendant to the late queen. She did an admirable job concealing her identity as both a Jinn and a spy, and consequently received a number of precious gifts while in service. Some of which"— he tilted his head at Hazan—"had been stolen." He paused. "But who, pray tell, was your father?"

Hazan was fairly vibrating with rage. "I won't answer your questions," he said, "until you first answer mine."

"You're welcome to list them," said Cyrus.

"First of all, who the hell are you?"

"You might need to be more precise."

"You are yourself no ordinary man," Hazan said heatedly. "No ordinary king. I've been watching you closely these past weeks, and nothing about you makes sense—"

"Nothing?" He raised his eyebrows. "Really?"

"You never wear jewelry."

Cyrus glanced at Hazan when he said, "Is that a crime?"

"For a *king*? Are you mad?"

"I take it you have other complaints about how I dress."

"You never wear color. You often wear a hat. You possess only simple, plain clothes. No gold, no adornment, no crown in your hair. In fact, most days you walk with your head down—"

"This conversation bores me." Cyrus looked at his hands, then the tips of his boots, which had darkened with damp. "And I don't know what more you want from me. I've already given up my secrets."

"*Liar.*"

Cyrus lifted his head. "You would know what a liar looks like, wouldn't you?"

"I've lived at the palace in Ardunia my whole life—I've worked in service of the crown since I was a child—and you— You don't act like a king. You have no entourage, no valet, no menus prepared for your meals. You speak directly to your servants—"

"*Enough,*" Cyrus said curtly. "I don't know what you hope to accomplish with these accusations."

But Hazan had found his mark, and his eyes sharpened.

"Your people are loyal to you despite the brutal manner in which you took the throne. Your staff refuses to speak a bad word against you. You give your mother far too much control over your household, you pay your servants ten times the standard wage—"

"I said *enough*—"

"You love her, don't you?"

Cyrus was not quick enough to parry this and too stunned to sneer at the insinuation. Worse: he knew not how he appeared then, as if he'd been run through with a scimitar.

Hazan, to his credit, was dumbfounded. "It's true, then?" he breathed. "You really do love her?"

Cyrus said nothing. He didn't need to. The severity of his feeling for her could not be contained, and they both watched, in horror, as the nosta turned red in his hand. Cyrus closed his fist, but too late.

The silence between them grew thick and gnarled, but soon—somehow—lost its teeth. For the first time in weeks

Hazan seemed to relax, as if this wretched confession had somehow offered him comfort.

"Is it possible?" he said, his anger abating. "Can you love her when you don't even know her?" Hazan turned to face him, looked him directly in the eye. "*Do* you know her?"

Cyrus could endure no more of this. He hauled himself upright, eager to vanish—and as he stood he saw the sprawling grounds, the heaving mass of people, and then, through a part in the clouds, a rising swarm of locusts. It made for a dizzying horror show, like a surreal confetti spattered across the sky.

Cyrus drew a sharp breath.

"What is it?" asked Hazan. "What's happening?" He clambered to his feet, peering into the distance as the locusts slowly dispersed.

It had been a message, received.

"She's awake," Cyrus whispered.

TWENTY-TWO

بیست و دو

"I DIDN'T MEAN YOU HAD to *speak* with them," said Huda, who was chasing Alizeh down the hall with discernible anxiety. "I only meant that they'll *see* you as you leave the grounds, and I just thought you might like to look your best—"

"Nearly four weeks," Alizeh cried. "Almost a month they've been waiting for me, Huda, how could I possibly walk past them without a word? I *must* speak with them. Anything less would be cruel—"

"I—I, forgive me, but I don't know if this is such a good idea—" said Deen, who, along with Omid, was hastening to keep up. "I don't think Kamran would approve—"

Alizeh stopped, causing Huda to topple into her. She apologized before righting her friend, then turned to face the apothecarist.

"Why wouldn't Cyrus approve?" she asked.

Alizeh should've been embarrassed that she was so eager for any opportunity to discuss Cyrus; even then she couldn't understand her desire to hear someone say his name.

"I didn't"—Deen blinked. "Forgive me, did I say *Cyrus*? I meant to say Kamran."

"No, you're right," said Huda, even as she shot Alizeh a strange look. "You did say Kamran."

"Oh." Alizeh looked away, trying to hide her disappointment. She began walking again, the rustle of her skirts echoing in the stone hall. "I must've misheard you."

"We've sent word to him, by the way," said Deen, keeping up. "Last I heard he was preoccupied with some business, but he should be here shortly."

"Who? The king?"

"No, *Kamran*," said Huda, who sounded concerned. "Are you all right, dear?"

"Yes," said Alizeh, touching a hand to her throat. She was looking around blindly, searching for the exit. "Yes, I'm fine. How do we get out of here?"

"How can you move so quickly in that gown?" said Huda, gathering up her hem as she moved. "The train alone is four feet long!"

"Not that you don't look lovely," Deen added hastily. "Which you do. Quite lovely."

Alizeh glanced back at him, her anxiety briefly overpowered by gratitude. "Thank you," she said with feeling. "I've never worn a garment so exquisite in my life."

It was a masterpiece of pale pink silk, lace, and diamond-studded tulle. Every inch of the material was embellished with intricate gold patterns, fine stitches glimmering with yet more shining gems. The fabric of her bodice, with a high collar and long fitted sleeves, was a sheer illusion, artfully woven with shimmer and glittering rose-colored stones. Atop her head she wore a matching diaphanous veil, which had been weighed down by a gold circlet that glinted like a crown. She'd yet to glimpse her own reflection—there'd been no time—but all she had to do was look down at herself and her breath caught with wonder.

After all her years as a servant, Alizeh still struggled with splendor. She didn't believe a person was made better by wearing finery, but she could not deny the power of a garment. It was one of the things she'd loved most about being a seamstress: bolts of fabric could be fashioned into something like a weapon. An outfit might be used to build a person or break them down. Just then, this opulent gown had helped shift her mindset.

She rather *felt* like a queen.

"There's a door to a courtyard up ahead," Huda was saying, "and from there you can access one of the balconies—"

"This is a bad idea." The former street child was shaking his head, his long legs helping him keep pace easily. "I don't think you should do this. There's a million people out there, miss."

Huda rapped his arm and he flinched.

"I mean, Your Majesty."

"Huda assured me it was fewer than a hundred thousand," said Alizeh. "And you don't have to call me Your Majesty."

"I don't care how many people there are," Omid shot back angrily. "I don't want you to get hurt."

Alizeh stopped in place, she was so surprised.

Slowly she turned to face the boy, discovering genuine fear in his eyes. Laughing off his pain, she knew, would only wound him. She, too, had lost both her parents at a tender age; she knew how terror and loneliness propagated alongside grief like invasive weeds. There had never been another warm embrace. Never another loving hand to stroke her hair. Never a day she didn't struggle with the impermanence of joy. In a matter of months this poor boy had lost his parents, lived on the streets, saw his friends murdered for Zaal's profit, and then lost the Diviners.

He was afraid he'd lose her, too.

Alizeh watched Omid swallow back a knot of emotion before she drew forward, opening her arms to him. He towered over her by at least a foot, but she knew he was just a child—a child like so many others in need of comfort. At first he paled at her offer, but then, looking as if he might cry, he stepped into her embrace, turning a shade of red so bright it clashed with his ginger curls.

"I don't want to mess up your dress," he mumbled.

She only held him tighter.

"Don't you worry about me," she said finally, giving him a squeeze before holding him at arm's length. "I'll be all right."

He looked toward the floor, his face still blotchy with color. "I do worry, miss. I do worry. You already almost died. And I know what it's like in big crowds—me and the boys used to pull our best hauls at gigs like this. Thieves and rogues love to work a big crowd—"

"I hate to say it, but the child is right," said Deen. "You mustn't put yourself in danger. Besides, you've only just awoken—maybe you should take time to recuperate a bit more. I could brew you a medicinal tea to revive your spirits—"

"I appreciate your concern," said Alizeh, looking around at her friends. "Really, I do. But I must speak with my people, even if it endangers me to do so."

They only stared at her, their expressions registering varied levels of panic and resignation.

"There's something more you wish to tell me," Alizeh said, her brows pulling together. "What is it?"

"The whispers along the trade routes have been worrisome," said Deen quietly, though he wouldn't look at her now. "Many merchants of my acquaintance have written to me, asking about you, and the stories they've shared in return—" He shook his head. "Your Majesty, it is imperative that you know how many there are who wish you harm."

"It's true," Huda added, her eyes darting from her to Deen then back again. "Forgive me, dear, but a great deal has changed since you were injured. Even here in Tulan there are many against you. The sheer influx of migrants has been frightfully disruptive—it's angered the citizens, no matter how peaceful the crowds have been. They don't really . . . want you here."

"It's worse than that," said Omid angrily, retrieving a folded newspaper from inside his jacket, which he thrust toward Alizeh. "They want you to *die*."

"Omid!" Huda gasped, trying to snatch the paper out of his hand. "You shouldn't have brought that!"

His jaw set in a determined clench, Omid easily evaded this effort and handed the paper to Alizeh, which she carefully accepted. She knew from its dusty-green pages that she'd been handed a copy of *The Daftar*, Ardunia's most famous newspaper, though she didn't know how they'd procured a copy so far from home. She looked once more upon her friends' faces—worried, worried, and angry—before turning her eyes to the publication, shaking it open to read the headline.

ALARM AROUND THE WORLD AS JINN UPRISING IMMINENT
Tulan Under Fire, Prince Kamran Tries to Sow Peace, Threats of Violence Escalate

MESTI—In an unprecedented historical feat, tens of thousands of Jinn have swarmed the royal city of the southern kingdom, with the promise of more to come. These unwanted migrants, hailing from all over the world, are the first wave to descend upon Tulan, though they arrive with one purpose: to pledge their allegiance to the one they believe to be their queen. Jinn tradition has long hinted at the prediction of a savior, though many have cause to doubt the precipitous rise of a young woman who, according to numerous reports, has not yet claimed the mantle of leadership. Witnessed only briefly before a much smaller crowd, the alleged queen refused to offer any material information about her identity, evading direct questions and offering vague promises of explanation at a later date, which thus far have never materialized.

For nearly a month the reputed queen has been in hiding, reportedly citing a need for "calm and reflection" while her followers languish within Tulan's borders, and the empire's citizens live in turmoil. It is widely circulated as fact that the Tulanian king has chosen the mysterious young woman as his bride, an incendiary political decision that could throw Tulan into further chaos. It remains to be seen whether such a union will take place.

The Tulanian king, Cyrus, has refused to comment.

An uptick in criminal activity within Jinn communities has already been noted worldwide. This past week the empire of Zeldan struggled to quiet a series of riots at one of its largest camps, while two prison guards in Sheffat were reportedly murdered in an altercation with a prisoner. A Jinn uprising, according to Dr. Amira of Reinan, acclaimed professor of Jinn studies at Setar University, "could result in one of the bloodiest world wars in history."

Ardunia, sharing a border with Tulan, has seen the largest exodus of Jinn thus far, a cause for alarm in many communities throughout the empire. Gomol province, located in the north at the base of the Arya mountains, has been all but hollowed out, many homes and storefronts abandoned. Local shopkeepers have expressed fear for the future of their businesses, with bushels of fresh grain and produce going unsold.

Still, the popular vote remains with Prince Kamran, to whom many have expressed tremendous gratitude. A rare leader of a mixed kingdom, many Ardunians hope the prince will be able to sow peace beyond Tulan, helping to lead the world in a balanced approach to Jinn citizens everywhere. It is yet uncertain when he will return home for a long-awaited coronation;

though new information has led royals to speculate as to whether his delay is due to an altogether different interest. Some say the rumored Jinn queen is in fact the same young woman few were able to identify the evening of the royal ball—

Deen snatched the paper from her hands and Alizeh startled, looking up to find the apothecarist blinking nervously as he backed away.

"As a medical professional, Your Majesty, I cannot recommend reading the news—"

"*Deen*—"

"Give it back to her!" Omid cried, swiping at Deen to retrieve the newspaper. "She should know what they're saying—"

"Omid," said Huda patiently. "She doesn't need to know this much."

"She should know! You didn't even let her read the worst part—"

"All right," Alizeh said quietly. "That's enough."

Omid exhaled sharply, setting his jaw as he stared at the ground. His anger was a palpable thing, and it touched Alizeh to see him so concerned on her behalf.

Still, she needed to sit down.

Alizeh would be lying if she said she hadn't been affected by what she'd read. She was more than affected. She was disturbed and frightened and overwhelmed.

Certainly, she'd been naive.

She'd not anticipated such anger from the rest of the world; she'd never imagined the ways in which Cyrus and Kamran could be embroiled in her fate; and she'd been willfully blind to the far-reaching dangers of her role. Still, Alizeh was less offended by threats against her life than she was by the insinuation that she'd abandoned her people. Nearly a month they'd been waiting for her. Families. Children. The infirm and elderly. She had no idea what difficulties they'd endured.

She'd never meant to leave them for so long.

She closed her eyes on a sigh, then looked about herself in carefully contained agitation, feeling shaky and unsettled, but there was nowhere to rest. Like all else she'd seen of the temple, the stone hall they stood in was worn and weathered, but the pitted walls were broken up by a series of narrow windows that looked out onto an interior courtyard, where brilliant light and signs of life bloomed toward them.

Huda, who'd seemed to read Alizeh's mind, made as if to usher her toward that courtyard when Omid stepped swiftly between them, blocking the door.

"No," he said, his eyes bright with fury.

Huda placed her hands on her hips. "I know you're scared, Omid, but now you're being ridiculous—"

"I'm *not* being ridiculous," he countered. "If she goes out there, she's going to hear them, and then she'll never—"

"Hear them?" Alizeh said, peering through the window as if she might see sound. Only as she focused did she finally hear the soft hum of noise, a vibration of what might be a chorus of voices. "What are they saying?"

Deen shook his head at Huda. "I can't believe I'm repeating this, but, again, I agree with the child. It's dangerous for her to go out there, and we shouldn't encourage it—"

"It's not up to us!" Huda cried. "I don't agree with this, either, but neither do I think I have the right to force her—"

"So you're going to let her get killed?" Omid all but shouted.

"Omid—"

Deen shook his head again, this time more vigorously. "If Hazan finds out we've let her stand, unprotected, in front of a hundred thousand people, he'll murder us on principle—"

"It's fewer than a hundred thousand—"

"Please, I'm not as fragile as you seem to think," Alizeh objected. "I've always been able to protect myself—"

"No one thinks you're fragile, miss," said Omid, his voice grave. Heavens, she'd never seen him so serious. "Just because we want to protect you doesn't mean you're weak—it means you're important—"

Alizeh moved toward him and he fell silent at once, his words dying on an exhale. She took his hands as she met his fevered gaze.

The hall, too, went eerily quiet.

Omid had aged in her absence, she could see it in his face. She felt he was too old for a twelve-year-old, too tall, too punctured. Still, steady meals had filled out the hollows in body. His brown eyes were no longer overlarge and sunken; no longer skittish; no longer stricken with hunger. In fact he seemed broader, fuller, more concrete. It was terrifying to imagine that this vibrant young boy had once driven a crude dagger into his own throat—had once attempted to kill himself in the middle of a town square. Alizeh recalled this shocking fact with a painful spasm, her urgency fading as she heard the faint tremble of his breath, saw the tension straining his shoulders.

"You," she said softly, staring up at him, "will always be dear to me. For your kindness, for your loyalty—for your courage in the face of everyday cruelties. I wish you'd never suffered; I wish you a lifetime of ease. I wish for you to see your own strength—to see every difficult choice you made in order to forge your pain into an armor of resilience and compassion, when you could've used it instead to spiral into darkness. Should you ever want a place in my life, you will have it. But right now, in this moment, you must let me go. I will return to you, Omid. I swear it."

The boy looked at her for a long time, his eyes swimming with restrained feeling, then turned his gaze to the floor. "All right, miss," he whispered. "If you go, I'm going with you."

"No," she said, breaking away from him. "It's too dangerous—you said so yourself—"

"I'm coming, too," said Huda, squaring her shoulders.

"And I," said Deen, looking grim as he stepped forward.

"But"—Alizeh looked around at them—"you've just spent the last several minutes warning me away from the crowd—"

It was Huda who said, "Yet you are unafraid."

"Of course I am afraid!" Alizeh said, laughing even as her eyes teared. "But don't you see? If I let fear keep me from doing what is right, I will always be wrong."

"Spoken like a true queen," said Huda.

It was Deen who said, quietly, "Let us hope for the day when we might all remove our masks, and live in the light without fear."

Alizeh stiffened, turning to face him. Deen had recited aloud something she'd once said to him. She hardly knew what to say.

"Those words are emblazoned upon my cold, shriveled heart," he said, smiling faintly. "I'd quite like to live in a world where you are queen."

"Thank you," she said. "I'm so grateful for your friendship."

"And I, yours." His smile deepened. "I must say—I always suspected you were no ordinary snoda. But I never expected this."

"Ha!" said Huda. "Neither did I."

Omid shook his head, discreetly wiping his eyes. "Nah," he said, switching briefly to broken Ardanz. "You was always a queen to me, miss."

Alizeh looked at her friends, a tight joy unfurling inside her. She was reminded then of something her parents used to say to each other—when they dropped things; when they lost an argument; when they bumped into each other in the kitchen; when they made silly mistakes. They'd laugh, lock eyes—

"Shuk pazir ke manam, manam," said Alizeh.

Thank you for receiving me as I am.

Omid's eyes widened, then he laughed out loud. "I haven't

heard that since before my parents died."

"Ooh, I know this one!" said Huda. "Shuk nosti ke tanam, tanam."

Thank you for trusting me with who you are.

It was another well-loved call and response.

Alizeh studied her friends' faces a final time. Gently, she said, "I will go on alone. You will all stay here. And there will be no arguments."

She saw the flare of shock in their eyes, the fraction of a second before they could form fresh words of protest. It was her cue to leave—and she would've done—except that just then a dozen hooded men and women appeared suddenly and without a sound, as if conjured from smoke.

Diviners now stood sentinel at intervals all along the corridor, so motionless Alizeh wondered whether she'd imagined them.

More to the point, she was mesmerized.

It shouldn't have been a surprise to see Diviners in their own temple—certainly not when they'd cared for her with such dedication all these weeks—but Alizeh had never seen Diviners in the flesh, and she felt a strange thrill in their presence, a pull she couldn't name. Strangest of all: she couldn't see their eyes, and yet, somehow, she knew they were staring at her.

"Hello," she said quietly.

In response, the priests and priestesses pivoted toward her in unison, their black cloaks shimmering like molten steel. As one, they pressed their hands to their chests and bowed their heads.

Omid drew a sharp intake of breath.

Alizeh glanced at him, registering the alarm in his eyes before noting a similar agitation in Deen and Huda. She herself felt a prickle of anxiety, for this synchronized response from the Diviners was unfathomable to her.

Not knowing how else to acknowledge a greeting from such esteemed figures, Alizeh chose to mirror the motion, bowing her head as she pressed her hands to her chest. "Thank you," she said sincerely. "For everything."

This time, the Diviners only vanished.

There was a moment of unnerving silence in the aftermath, during which Alizeh struggled to straighten her thoughts. The Diviners had healed her and cared for her; she couldn't understand why they seemed unwilling to speak with her. Worse, she'd hoped to ask about her missing nosta, and now she wasn't sure she'd have the chance.

In the end, it was Omid who broke the tension.

"By the angels," he said quietly. "I didn't know you were a Diviner."

"Neither did I," said Deen, his voice breathless.

"Were you meant to keep it a secret?" asked Huda, who looked almost afraid of her now. "Were we not meant to know?"

Alizeh fell back a step, she was so astonished. "No—that is—you misunderstand. I'm not a Diviner," she said emphatically. "I've never even touched magic. They were only being polite—"

Omid was shaking his head. "When I lived with the

Diviners, miss, they didn't bow their heads at anyone except each other."

"That can't be true—"

"It is true," said Deen, watching her closely. "Diviners don't show that kind of deference to anyone outside the priesthood. They don't even bow their heads before the king."

TWENTY-THREE

بیست و سه

ALIZEH DIDN'T KNOW HOW TO process this latest revelation. Omid's limited experience with the Diviners of Ardunia surely didn't speak for all Diviners everywhere, but Deen's corroboration of the fact was giving her pause. Regardless, she wasn't sure it was the right time to argue the point. Her mind was already struggling to process the deluge of the day's declarations; it seemed impossible to add to this maelstrom the possibility that the Diviners might recognize someone like her as their peer— She, who'd never so much as touched magic—

Alizeh bit her lip, for that wasn't precisely true.

She'd never thought of her own peculiarities as *magical*, exactly, but she was forced to admit that the ice that ran through her veins was, irrefutably, a kind of magic. In fact, Alizeh had always been set apart from the other Jinn she'd known, for she'd been strange even among her own kind. It was only *her* blood that ran clear; only her body that healed itself; only she who could withstand the blaze of a fire. Her Book of Arya, too, was an enchanted object—one that came alive only in her hands.

Alizeh looked up at her friends; everyone was studying her warily.

This time, she really needed to sit down.

She moved unsteadily down the stone hall and pushed through the heavy wooden door of the courtyard, its entrance opening onto cracked travertine pavers. She heard the others following, their footsteps chasing hers, and as soon as she was outside she drew fresh air into her lungs, her legs nearly giving out as her body bore this latest shock.

The high walls of the courtyard, she noticed, were thick with flora, among them mature jasmine vines that released a honeyed fragrance carried by the breeze, and which brought her great comfort. At the center of the garden sat a large, circular reflecting pool, around which were arranged a series of crescent-shaped stone benches, fashioned in various phases of the moon.

Blindly, Alizeh sat down on one such bench. Huda sat down beside her. Deen and Omid took seats nearby.

She closed her eyes and took more deep breaths, and as the thunder of her heartbeat slowed, the muted chants of the masses grew louder. Outside in the courtyard the body of sound was more distinct; Alizeh listened closely as voices rose and faded like the swells of the ocean, the sorrow in their songs giving way to hope, reaching a crescendo so epic she could suddenly hear the words clearly.

We cried until our eyes went blind
We lost our voices, too
We slept each night inside our graves
always in hope of you

Alizeh stiffened, her nerves forgotten.

Justice!
Justice!

For the land that once was ours
For the millions that were slain
For the rivers red with blood
For the centuries of pain

Slowly, she got to her feet.

For our parents in the ground
For the coffins that we built
For the tiny hands and quiet hearts
of the children who were killed

Her chest heaved. She felt as if her parents had stood up inside her and screamed.

Justice!
Justice!

For our eyes as they went blind
For the voices we lost, too
For each night we slept inside our graves
always in hope of you

Our armor is our hope
Our weapon is the truth
We sleep each night inside our graves
We pledge our faith to you

Alizeh pressed a shaking hand to her mouth, fighting back tears. There was a roar of sound as the chant ended, jubilant shouts and cries. She wiped desperately at her eyes.

"I must go," she said, turning to face Omid. "Forgive me, but I must go to them now—"

"Wait—miss—"

"But—"

"What will you say—?"

Alizeh picked up her skirts and ran through the courtyard, which wrapped partly around the side of the central building. She searched for the balcony, encountering it so suddenly she gasped just as someone screamed, drawing back a step as the sheer size of the crowd overwhelmed her. Alizeh had never seen so many people in one place in all her life, and the idea that they'd come for her—that they were all there to see her—

It filled her with feeling so severe she could hardly breathe.

Jinn of every race and age and station— Scores of men and women with children in arm or else on their backs; young ones napping in the grass; crowds of youth tightly gathered in shock, the elderly struggling to their feet to get a better look.

The mass seemed to stretch on endlessly.

There were more sharp screams, fingers pointing in her

direction, but it was a moment before the crowd truly saw her, before their cries quieted to a silence so complete it was frightening. They turned to her as one, the breathless focus aimed in her direction driving home, for the first time, the magnitude of her responsibility. Alizeh had never seen Jinn gathered like this, never known with certainty whether anyone would even accept her as a leader.

She took a steadying breath, trying to find her voice, and as she drew closer to the balustrade, the silence broke. People began shouting—

"My queen!"

"Is it really her?"

"Your Majesty!"

"She's here!"

Only then, as she parted her lips to speak, did she realize the enormity of her error.

She was not yet a crowned queen.

She had no throne, no kingdom, no authority, no real magic. Even her clothes were borrowed. The last time she'd stood before her people she'd had good reason to delay answering their questions. But now—

"When will you take the throne, Your Majesty?"

"Will you marry King Cyrus?"

"Will we go to war?"

"We *will* go to war!"

Another roar from the people, their fists rising in the air.

Her heart pounding madly in her chest, Alizeh's mind was a swarm of tangled thought. She wanted to answer them, wanted to—

She saw the dagger before she fully understood what it was, the gleam of silver in the distance appearing like a glimmering bird before it focused into a blade, aimed directly at her throat.

Alizeh froze.

Perhaps if her head hadn't been so splintered—if her heart hadn't been afflicted with myriad pains—if she hadn't been so recently astonished by her own shortcomings as a leader—

Perhaps if she'd been in better possession of herself, she might've gathered her wits about her, harnessed her supernatural strengths, and simply moved out of the way. Instead, she fell back on old instincts, doing what came naturally to her when attacked:

She fought back.

Alizeh threw out her arm with unthinkable speed, adrenaline heightening her focus as she watched the dagger, as if in slow motion, spin with exceptional aim toward her throat. She caught the weapon at an unnatural angle, the hilt hitting her palm with a hard *thwack*, so forceful the impact she was swung off her axis before being slammed cruelly against the wall. The breath knocked from her lungs, she made a soft sound of pain as she heard the crowd scream, their frenzied voices clamoring. They were already turning on each other, searching for the perpetrator, and even in the midst of her own trials Alizeh knew she needed to calm them— knew that if she did not, violence might soon erupt—but she couldn't seem to pry herself from the wall. She knew without a doubt that the weapon had been enchanted, for the dagger continued to shudder in her hand, its unnatural power more than matching her own. Even as she fought it, the shaft twisted her fist inch by inch, the blade soon pointing again at her throat.

Alizeh closed her eyes, called upon her strength, and with a violent cry managed to shift away from the wall, using gathered momentum to pivot—and bury the blade in the stone behind her. It lodged, to her great relief, with a terrible sound.

Alizeh staggered back around, facing the crowd in a daze, her tired arms trembling, her heart racing. She couldn't seem to focus her eyes as she listened to their raucous cries; she was busy trying to catch her breath when— There, *again*—

Like déjà vu, another gleam of silver.

She blinked, certain she must be imagining it, and the moment she took to steady her mind cost her the only opportunity she might've had to react. She heard a bloodcurdling scream as she registered, too late, a need to fall back.

Suddenly, she was knocked to the ground.

Alizeh hit the stone floor with a muted cry, the weight of another body landing heavily against her. She heard the uproar of the masses, the chaos exploding. She tried to get up and was immediately pushed down again, though out of the corner of her eye she glimpsed the profile of Hazan's familiar, freckled face, and then, just above her head, buried in the wall behind her: two daggers. The second one had missed her by inches.

"Hazan?" she gasped.

In response he rendered them both invisible, hauled her up into his arms, and moved her with lightning speed back into the walled courtyard, where he set her down at once.

Even then he was careful not to disturb her dress as he steadied her, though her veil and its accompanying crown were
falling off her head, and she caught them both before they
hit the ground.

"Hazan—"

"Forgive me, Your Majesty." He cut her off, his fists
clenching as he avoided her eyes. "I'm too angry right now to
speak to you in the manner you deserve."

Alizeh felt a wash of mortification. She never thought
Hazan could be so cross with her.

"*You idiots!*" he bellowed without warning, spinning away
from her. "I can't believe you let her go out there!"

Alizeh turned to see her trio of friends rush into view.

"She insisted!" said Deen, striding forward. "We couldn't
physically stop her—"

"I tried to tell her!" Omid yelled, his face mottled with
color. "I tried to go *with* her! I told her it was a bad idea— I even
wanted her to read the paper—but no one listens to me—"

"Are you all right, dear?" Huda hurried toward her and
grabbed her arm, guiding her to a bench. Then, to Hazan, "Is
there any chance we can see the weapons?" And, "Omid, can
you ask the Diviners for a glass of sugar water?"

Hazan glanced at Huda, then left to retrieve the blades;
and though Omid clenched his jaw in response, he nodded
before walking away.

Alizeh watched them branch off as the cold of the bench
seeped through her clothes. She was suddenly freezing
again, and she didn't understand the shift. She was fatigued
from a depletion of adrenaline, her back aching where she'd

slammed against the wall. Her right arm was so tired she could hardly lift it to adjust her veil, which was still slipping off her head. She didn't even realize she was shaking until she saw her hands tremble; she would have to sit a moment with the fact that someone had tried to kill her. Twice.

Heavens. For as long as she could remember, someone had been trying to kill her. She was, quite frankly, tired of it.

Hazan returned a moment later, holding up the murderous daggers for all to see. They were identical, though they looked simple enough: steel blades, gold shafts.

"They're an enchanted pair," he said. "They've been vibrating since the moment I yanked them out of the wall."

"Vibrating?" Huda asked.

"Trying to finish the job." He kept a tight grip on the hilts even as he strode to the door. "I need to hand these off to the Diviners immediately."

Trying to finish the job, Alizeh repeated softly, almost to herself. She flinched when the door slammed shut behind him, and looked up to find that Deen was watching her closely.

"I think you need something stronger than sugar water," he said. "I'll go fix you a strong tea, miss. I mean, Your Majesty—"

"Please, call me Alizeh," she said, tensing to keep her teeth from rattling. "And tea sounds wonderful. Thank you."

Then, with another nod, Deen was gone, too.

Huda sat beside her, took her hand, and squeezed it. "How are you feeling?"

"Foolish." Alizeh suppressed a sigh as she removed her

circlet, then her veil, setting them both on the bench beside her. She dropped her head in her unsteady hands. "Hazan is mad at me. Hazan is never mad at me."

"He was scared. Imagine, he'd gotten word that you were finally awake, rushed over here to see you—only to find that someone was trying to kill you. You nearly died, dear. *Again.*" Huda clucked her tongue. "His poor nerves. *Your* poor nerves."

Alizeh looked up. "It was all for nothing," she said. "I didn't even say anything. I had nothing to say."

"I wouldn't say it was entirely fruitless," Huda countered gently. "At least they saw you make the effort. Certainly no one can blame you for what happened—they'll understand if you're not rushing to stand before a crowd again." She tilted her head. "Perhaps going forward we can communicate any messages via Dija."

"Who's Dija?"

"She's sort of a leader of the masses. She and a few others help keep the crowd in order. Cyrus has spoken with her several times, as far as I'm aware."

At the sound of his name, Alizeh averted her eyes. "I've made a decision, Huda. I know it might not be a popular decision, but—"

The door whined opened then, and Huda, who'd opened her mouth to speak, suddenly shot upright.

Hazan had returned.

"Yes, I'll, um, speaking of Dija, I'll just pop down to see her, shall I? Best to get a feel for what's happening outside."

"You're going into the crowd?" Alizeh said, alarmed. "But—isn't it dangerous?"

"Oh, not for me! No one cares who I am!" she said, and rushed off.

The door slammed shut for the fourth time, and once again, Alizeh flinched. She and Hazan were alone.

He stood just off to the side, one hand pushed through his hair as he stared blankly at the wall. The sounds of the crowd still carried in the distance.

"Hazan," she said softly.

"Yes, Your Majesty."

"Do you think you'll be mad at me for a very long time?"

She heard him sigh.

"I'm not mad at you," he said, his voice hard. "I'm mad that someone tried to kill you. I simply don't understand why you'd put yourself in so dangerous a position—"

"Please," she said desperately. "Please understand, I had to speak with them. Not only because it was my duty to try, but because I needed to learn that I never, *ever*, want to be in that position again."

Hazan turned to face her. "What do you mean?"

"The next time I stand before my people," she said, "it will be with a crown and a plan. I can have nothing to say to them until I secure both. I need to find my magic, Hazan— I need to go to Arya at once—"

"We'll go," he said, moving briskly toward her. "We'll return to Ardunia tomorrow, if you like. Say the word and we'll go."

"I wish it were that easy," she said, attempting a smile. "It's going to be a long, difficult journey—"

"Not if we travel by dragon."

"—and I need to get my book back from Cyrus. He's refused to give it to me."

Hazan shook his head. "I'll kill him."

Alizeh laughed, her heart warming with affection. "You can't kill him. I need him."

Hazan stood before her, tall and looming. "All due respect, Your Majesty, you don't need him. You have me."

She looked up into his eyes and smiled. "If only you had an empire."

Hazan sighed heavily, then turned away. "If only."

She reached for his hand, meaning to clasp it in friendship, and he recoiled. She realized then that he'd recoiled before when she'd touched him, and withdrew her hands immediately.

"Forgive me," she said, embarrassed. "I didn't mean to make you uncomfortable."

"I'm not uncomfortable," he said, though his voice was rough. "It's only that I'm not used to being touched."

She looked up, but he would not meet her eyes.

"Hazan," she said softly. "Will you look at me?"

She watched him swallow, watched him hesitate before dropping slowly to one knee before her. He lifted his head and their eyes locked. He seemed to drink in the sight of her, fear and affection at war in his gaze.

"Hazan," she said again. "I'm worried you're not sleeping well."

This disarmed him so completely he almost laughed, the intensity in his eyes melting into something gentler. His chest caved as he exhaled, and he lowered his head once more. "I will try to do better, Your Majesty."

"Thank you," she said softly. "For saving my life."

"You need not thank me," he said, "for the actions I perform in my own self-interest."

She laughed, and they shared an easy, fleeting moment of silence.

"I feel you should know," she said, her voice quieting to a whisper. "That I've made my decision."

He looked up sharply.

"I'm going to say yes. To his proposal." Alizeh clasped her hands in her lap. "I'm going to marry Cyrus."

Hazan seemed to stop breathing.

"I know you were against the idea—and I know he's not trustworthy—but I hope you can understand why, especially after today—"

The door slammed open without warning, and they both spun toward the sound. Alizeh fought back a gasp.

Kamran had arrived.

TWENTY-FOUR

بیست و چهار

ALIZEH WENT RIGID, SURPRISED BY the intensity of her reaction to him. Kamran was as handsome as ever, the vein of gold branching up his face giving him a magical, mysterious air. He'd always been striking, but her memories had done him an injustice. His bearing impressive, his eyes gleaming— Kamran radiated the kind of glory that could only be born from a lifetime of power and privilege. The young man who stood before her now was truly a wonder to look upon, and yet, the idea of speaking with him filled her with dread. The last time she'd seen the prince he'd been enraged and unreasonable. He'd refused to listen to her, refused to be rational, and then he'd shot her with an arrow, nearly killing her in the process.

Kamran kept his eyes on Alizeh as he moved slowly forward, as if afraid to spook her. Still, there was something gentler in his countenance today, the fire in his eyes dampened, and she felt herself unclench as he approached, even as she remained wary.

"Forgive me," he said, glancing between her and Hazan. "I hardly know what to say. I heard the good news, then the bad. I'm so relieved to see that you're unharmed."

"Yes," she said, feeling oddly wooden. "I was lucky a friend arrived in time to spare me a much darker fate." She softened, smiling at Hazan with real warmth. "I owe him my life, over and over."

Hazan only bowed his head.

"Indeed." Kamran nodded, glancing at his old minister before refocusing on her. "How—how are you?"

An array of answers flowered in her mind, but Alizeh only appraised him before saying, politely: "I'm fine, thank you. How are you?"

"I'm— Yes. Fine." Kamran hesitated, then laughed with a charming self-consciousness. "Heavens, this is awful, isn't it?"

"Yes," she said, and sighed.

Kamran shook his head, lost his smile. "Will you ever be able to forgive me?"

She looked up at him, surprised. "I've already forgiven you."

"You have?" His brows lifted. "Yet you don't seem at all pleased to see me."

Alizeh looked away. She knew his actions that awful morning had been unintentional—knew he hadn't meant her any harm—but Kamran's conduct had been indicative of a man unable to think beyond his own desires. She'd tried to reason with him, had begged him to imagine the situation more complexly, to see how killing Cyrus would have far-reaching consequences—and he'd shaken her off without care or consideration.

This had bothered her almost more than the injury itself.

She'd lately been trying to understand her burgeoning hesitations toward Kamran, and the more she interrogated her feelings, the more she'd begun to wonder whether it was, in the end, less that he'd wounded her vanity and more that he hadn't respected her mind. Certainly she didn't expect him to exchange his every thought and opinion for hers— but her fears and concerns should've *mattered* to him. They should've mattered at least enough to give him pause. To warrant a discussion.

It bothered her that they hadn't.

"I'm not displeased to see you," she said, and meant it. "In fact, I'm truly happy to see that you're well. I know how much you've suffered these last several weeks, and I can imagine it hasn't been easy for you." She hesitated. "It's only that . . . I suspect our book has closed, Kamran."

He seemed stunned by this response, his chest lifting slightly as he breathed. "I see," he said.

Alizeh looked into her lap, then glanced at Hazan, whose expression was inscrutable. She realized then that she had no desire to continue this conversation, for not only was it intolerably awkward, but there were a thousand things she'd yet to accomplish.

She stood up at once.

Kamran leaped forward to help her, taking her hand as she tried not to trip on her train. Alizeh steadied herself with his assistance, then stared at their clasped hands in a dizzying moment of disconnection. She wasn't repulsed by Kamran, not even a little—in fact, he radiated warmth and strength, and smelled of something rich and honeyed that beckoned her. It was only that it seemed strange to her that she'd once kissed him—had once nearly swooned in his arms. The memory of that moment seemed to belong to a different girl, a different life.

Was it possible she'd been but a servant then? And a queen now?

She drew back her hand, shaking out her skirts before collecting her crown and veil. "Hazan, how might I return to the palace?"

He stepped forward at once. "I'll call for the carriage, Your Majesty. It shouldn't be but a moment." He moved briskly toward the door, but then, glancing at Kamran, he paused. "Unless you'd wish to accompany me?"

"Yes," she said, brightening. "I'd like that."

"Please, Alizeh," Kamran said quickly, drawing forward. "Might I have a moment alone with you?"

Alizeh hesitated. She was just opening her mouth to speak when Huda's head poked through the open doorway.

"Oh! Are we allowed to come back in—" Her words died when she spotted Kamran, her smile turning brittle. "Ah. I see the prince has arrived."

Kamran stiffened at the sound of her voice, his mood darkening as if he'd been doused with cold water. He turned to her slowly, his eyes flaring with hostility. Alizeh marveled at this brief, heated exchange, wondering what, precisely, had happened between them in her absence.

Huda had failed to be specific.

"The prince is here?" Omid's voice preceded his body as he reentered the courtyard, his eyes gleaming when he spotted Kamran. "Sire! You're back! Did you have any trouble with the—"

"What have I said to you," Kamran said sharply, "about closing your mouth?"

"Right," the boy said quickly, his ears turning red. Then, "Oh, and sorry about the water, miss," he said to Alizeh. "Miss Huda told me not to interrupt your conversation with Hazan, so I didn't bring it, but if you'd like—"

"Not necessary," said Deen, entering the courtyard with a flourish. He was holding a metal flask, which he eagerly pressed into Alizeh's hands. "This will do the trick nicely."

"Thank you," she said, unscrewing the cap. Delicately, she sniffed the contents, then fought back a wince. "You said this was *tea*?"

"In a manner of speaking." Deen grinned triumphantly, and Alizeh realized that in the brief time she'd known him, she'd never seen Deen smile so much. "It's a warm brew of lotus root, crushed sapphire, river water, a bit of saffron, and just a *touch* of frost."

"Frost?" She stared at the flask. "Do you mean ice?"

"A specific strain of magic," he said, shaking his head. "I'll spare you the tedious details, but I've been working with the palace alchemist on a number of new elixirs. I must say, I've never studied under such a talent before and the experience has been *enlightening*. I'm hoping to publish my findings when we return home."

"How wonderful," she said, breaking into a smile. "I'm so happy for you."

"Go on, then, take a drink"—he beamed—"I usually recommend it as a sleeping draught, but I think it'll settle your nerves nicely. The effects are fairly immediate."

"Oh," she said, clasping the bottle to her chest. "Would it be all right if I saved it, then? I'm eager to return to the palace, and need to have my wits about me—but a sleeping draught might be lovely for later."

He bowed his head slightly. "As you wish. Just be sure to tell me how you like it in the morning."

"Yes, of course, I—" She startled, then, at the press of a hand against her waist. She turned. It was Kamran.

"Would you allow me to accompany you back to the palace?" he said, looking at her with an intense focus. His eyes—one gold, one brown—were a disorienting kind of beauty. "We could share a carriage."

Alizeh hesitated.

She didn't want to be locked into another uncomfortable conversation, but she did want to tell him about her decision to marry, and, given his general feelings about Cyrus, she didn't know how he'd receive the news. Ultimately, Kamran's opinion on the matter would not move her, but Alizeh was not cold to the fact that Cyrus had murdered his grandfather. She felt she should be the one to deliver him the news; she felt she owed him this much. All this she considered in a matter of seconds, and was preparing to answer when Huda made a choking sound, something like a terrible laugh.

Kamran turned to face her, scathing as he said, "Was my question funny to you?"

She shook her head in an exaggerated motion, eyes widening in fake innocence. "Not at all, Your Highness. Nothing about you is funny. You're a very serious prince. Everything you say is of the utmost seriousness."

"That's interesting." A muscle jumped in his jaw. "I didn't realize you even knew what the word *serious* meant."

She gasped, then fell dramatically against the wall. "Oh, your words have wounded me! I'm bleeding!"

In a shockingly unrefined action, Kamran rolled his eyes, turning away from her as he muttered, "You're insufferable."

She drew away from the wall, then crossed her arms. "*You're* insufferable."

"Miss, you really shouldn't talk to him like that," Omid whispered, tugging at her arm. "He's going to be king of the largest empire on earth—"

"Yes," she said, sounding bored. "I think we've all been reminded of that fact a million times."

Kamran spun around angrily. "What is that supposed to mean?"

"What's that? I can't hear you," she said, and cupped a hand to her ear. "Maybe if you got off your high horse I might be able to—"

He strode in Huda's direction with lightning speed, looking as if he might tie her to a tree and leave her there. "You brazen, unmanageable *delinquent*—"

"*Delinquent?*" she cried. She quickly backed away from him, her face bright with color. "What crimes have I committed? None! You, on the other hand, nearly killed the prophesied Jinn queen of the entire world and then expect her to go on a carriage ride with you—"

He stopped in place. "*I apologized!*"

"My condolences!" she shot back. "That must've been hard for you!"

"Heavens," said Alizeh, who could no longer contain her laughter. "When did this tender relationship begin?"

Everyone, altogether, turned to look at her.

The spell broke. In fact, Kamran appeared startled by the sound of her voice, shaking himself free of the moment before putting the length of the entire courtyard between himself and Huda who, for her part, was staring at the door, looking almost embarrassed.

"It's been this way since before we left Ardunia," Hazan offered, his eyes glinting with humor. "Though in the last few weeks it's grown a great deal worse."

Huda opened her mouth to protest and Kamran shot her a withering look. She glared back.

"Yes, all right," Alizeh said to Kamran, still smiling. "Let's ride back together. Perhaps you can tell me more about all that's happened in my absence."

TWENTY-FIVE

بیست و پنج

ALIZEH NUDGED THE CARRIAGE CURTAINS open an inch, hoping to glimpse the scenes out the window. She'd been assured it wasn't a long drive back to the palace, and she'd missed so much in the last month that she was desperate to drink in the sights before they lost the sun. The day was steadily dipping into night, a hazy bloom of color casting the royal city in a surreal light, while a soft, brief rain had given it a liquid glow. Huda, she soon discovered, had not exaggerated.

Everything was covered in roses.

They'd grown nearly everywhere, pink blooms on roofs and doorways gleaming gold in the evening light; massive, blossoming vines reached up the sides of buildings, snaked along sidewalks, circled lampposts and trash bins, beautifying everything.

The more she saw, the more her heart hurt.

Cyrus had left a mark everywhere. Remnants of him lived in eternal bloom in the outside world and inside her veins. At the thought of him she experienced a relentless ache she didn't understand, and it scared her.

There was a shout, then the sound of muted laughter, and Alizeh peered once more out the window. The streets were so thick with petals that children had stopped to jump in the drifts, tossing handfuls into the air while their parents apologized to those trying to shove past. Traffic was thick and slow, and Alizeh, whose life had been so recently ripped apart, marveled that the world could spin on as usual. There was something comforting in the sounds of hurried pedestrians; the whinny of horses; the angry shouts of carriage drivers blaming each other for the jam. She bumped along, watching, with a twinge in her heart, as groups of young people laughed with abandon. Men pulled their hats lower, frowning at the sky; children giggled and giggled, then screamed; shopkeepers locked their doors, squinted at the street, and set off for home.

Despite recent horrors, Alizeh smiled.

She was feeling hopeful. Finally, after so long, she had a firm plan. Her smile dimmed, however, at the prospect of speaking with Cyrus.

Her complicated feelings for him felt like a horrible failure of her good sense. All she had to do was *imagine* him touching her to stir up a tempest in her heart. When she recalled the sight of him—his powerful, gleaming body, the ferocious need in his eyes—not only did she struggle for breath, but she was possessed by a mortifying impulse to make an indelicate sound, and had to bite her lip to keep the tortured whimper trapped in her throat. It ached beyond reason to remember the pull between their bodies, the fever of him so close; his desperate confession and the resulting devastation. She had no idea what would happen when she saw him. He'd once told her that if she married him in name only, she'd make him the most wretched man alive. If that was true, then she was about to destroy him.

She breathed, trying to keep her exhale steady.

As the sky slowly darkened, fireflies lit the world, dotting everything like glittering jewels. The sight had been particularly astonishing as they'd left the temple, where tens of thousands of the glowing insects had winked throughout the crowd like a map of the stars.

"It's so beautiful here," she whispered, forcing herself to draw away from the window. She pulled the curtain closed, deciding to break the silence herself. "It even smells lovely."

Kamran only stared at her from where he sat, on the opposite bench inside the carriage. She'd felt his eyes on her these last many minutes, the energy between them strange and fraught; despite his insistence that they have a moment alone together, he'd said nothing at all. Even then, as she studied him, he did not speak; it was as if he hadn't even heard her. Still, he made no effort to hide his overt interest. He also seemed unaware that he was tapping his gloves against his thigh, and the buzz of tension in his body put her on alert.

It had been a small production delivering her into the simple, unmarked coach, but the conveyance was meant to be reinforced with layers of defensive magic, including an enchantment that repelled glances from passersby. Both Kamran and Hazan had assured her they'd been traveling back and forth this way for weeks, with palace guards in plain clothes riding alongside at all times. But perhaps the situation was more precarious than she realized.

"What is it?" she said, sitting back in her seat. "Is something wrong?"

"Yes," he said quickly, then hesitated. "I mean, no—nothing is wrong. I don't know why I said that."

She stared at him a beat. "Are you all right?"

"Forgive me," he said, and sighed. He finally set down the gloves and stared blankly at a curtained window. "I've never done this before, and I'm afraid I'm going to botch it."

"Botch what?"

He took a shallow breath and said, "I want to marry you."

The words came out in a nervous rush that was so unlike the assured, polished prince she'd known that Alizeh's astonishment was doubled. In fact she was so stunned that she said nothing at all for several long, excruciating seconds before she realized she should absolutely say something, and quickly.

"Are you"—she blinked—"are you joking?"

He recoiled. "Absolutely not."

"Forgive me," she said. "I'm just— I'm afraid I don't understand."

He parted his lips to speak, then frowned. "Can you really not understand?" he said. "I wish to marry you. I want to marry you."

"But—why?"

He froze, his frown deepening. He turned this frown upon the curtained window again as he said, quietly, "I didn't think I'd need to provide a reason, if I'm being honest."

She touched a hand to her throat, feeling slightly ill. She could hear a peddler hawking his wares on the street. "Can you try to think of a reason?"

"You're— Well, you're everything I've ever looked for in

a queen," he said, relaxing a little as the words came to him. "You're beautiful and intelligent and poised and elegant—"

"Do you love me?"

He lifted his head, then faltered as he said, "I— I admire you deeply—and I'm certain that, in time, we would come to love each other. The truth is, I've thought of you almost constantly since we first met. I've never felt for anyone what I've felt for you, and I'd be honored to spend my life by your side." He paused, his gaze briefly dropping to her lips. "We've already proven we're well-suited in many ways. I believe it would be an excellent match."

"I see," she said, the chill in her bones overwhelmed by the tide of heat moving through her body. "Thank you."

He hesitated. "Thank you?"

"For the explanation," she said, distracted. "It helps."

"Ah." There was another taut silence before he said, "Might you have an answer for me?"

She clasped and unclasped her hands, a feeling of misplaced guilt twisting her heart. "Yes, I'm—"

The carriage jolted.

"Yes?"

"—deeply, *deeply* flattered," she said, holding on to the seat to steady herself. "But no, I— That is, I think—"

"*Hells,*" he said quietly. "You're refusing me."

She lifted her head at the hurt in his voice. "It's not you, Kamran. Truly, it isn't. Honored as I am by your offer, I cannot be your wife. I must put my people first. I have a responsibility—a role I must fulfill—"

"You would be much more than a prize to me," he said,

leaning forward to take her hands. "You would rule by my side. You could care for your people with the might of Ardunia behind you—"

"But I don't wish to share a crown. I want my own kingdom," she said, hating the words she knew she would deliver next. She steeled herself, then took a sharp breath. "I've decided to marry Cyrus."

He astonished her by saying, with an air of confusion, "Yes, I imagined you would. I meant I'd like to marry you after that."

She withdrew her hands from his grasp, sitting back with a shock. "*After* that?"

"Yes. After you kill him."

"After . . . I kill him," she repeated, the words little more than a whisper. She stared blindly at the carriage floor, the glimmer of her long skirts winking in the dim light. "Of course. You know about his offer."

"It's a good offer," he said. "You should take it."

She lifted her head so fast she nearly sprained her neck. "You think I should marry Cyrus?"

"Absolutely you should." Gone was the uncertainty in Kamran's eyes, replaced by a hawklike gleam. "Make him perform a blood oath, become queen, take his kingdom, kill him when it's done, and reign supreme."

She stared at him in astonishment. "You say it like it would be easy for me to be so ruthless."

"You have a difficult climb ahead of you," he said with some nonchalance, his composure returning as his mind shifted into politics. "I'm afraid you must learn to be ruthless.

Tulan is one of the richest empires in the world; any sovereign on earth would've died for such an opportunity. You'd be mad not to take it."

Alizeh tilted her head at him, fascinated despite herself. She'd never interacted with this methodical, intellectual side of Kamran, and she realized only then that he might be an excellent resource, for she knew little about geopolitics. She might learn a great deal from him.

"Why would I be mad not to take it?" she asked.

He ticked the answers off on his fingers. "Volcanic soil; fresh water; great stores of magic. There are so many microclimates here that the kingdom is practically self-sustained. They grow nearly all that they require; Tulan imports next to nothing and has little debt. Smaller military, yes, but robust and well-trained. Historically it was a land constantly under siege, ruthlessly invaded and plundered by external forces, but the Nara line—Cyrus's family line—was the first to fight back and win. They've staved off every foreign invasion in nearly a hundred years, giving them the stability they needed to flourish, build advanced weaponry, and develop modern magical defense systems.

"There's very little unemployment; the people have high literacy rates; and there's advanced medical care accessible across the nation. As a whole, the empire is an extraordinary asset not only for its rich land and abundant resources, but because it comes with educated, happy, and productive citizens. There's a reason Ardunia has tried to claim it for so long. If Cyrus is offering it, you should take it." He shook his head sharply. "Without a doubt."

Alizeh's lips parted, surprise rendering her virtually speechless. "This is it, isn't it?" She blinked at him. "This is the reason for the truce. The reason you and Cyrus made peace."

He shifted in his seat, briefly uncomfortable. "Yes."

"You don't want *me*," she said, a faint smile touching her lips. "You want Tulan."

"I want both."

Now she laughed. "I appreciate your honesty—really, I do—but you've just outlined all the reasons Tulan makes for a remarkable nation. What could possibly motivate me to share these riches with you when I might have them all for myself?"

"In this woven kingdom, clay and fire shall be."

Alizeh lost her smile. She looked at him then with a pinch in her chest, her body stiff with alarm. "You've seen my book," she whispered.

"I found it in your carpetbag," he said, "which you'd left behind in Ardunia."

"Yes. I'd left it at Huda's house."

Kamran reached into his pocket and procured her handkerchief, which she accepted from his outstretched hand.

"Thank you," she said, her heart pounding. She rubbed her thumb over the embroidered firefly, remembering her mother, her father, her fate. "I never thought I'd see this again."

They came to a sudden and nauseating halt, the stop so sudden they flew into each other's arms. Kamran caught her before their heads collided, holding her closer than they'd been in what seemed like a very long time. She felt the heat of his hands through her sheer bodice, the brawn of him through his clothes. He was strong and safe and assured, and for a moment she remembered exactly why she'd once kissed him.

"*Marry me*," he whispered ardently. "Marry me after we've buried him, and we might bring together two of the greatest empires on earth. Together we would be an indomitable force. We can work together to change the fate of Jinn all over the world."

She swallowed, overwhelmed by the feel of him. It was too much for her mind to sort. "Kamran— I don't—"

The carriage door was yanked open with a flourish, a palace footman standing before them with a bright smile and an eager welcome. At once Alizeh pulled free of Kamran's embrace, but not before she saw a familiar copper head in the distance, briefly there—then gone.

TWENTY-SIX

بیست و شش

CYRUS HAD MADE A TERRIBLE mistake.

He stood stock-still in the middle of his private sitting room, his head bowed as if struck down by his own stupidity. He heard a faint ringing in his ears, his body tensing as it absorbed shockwaves of pain. He'd materialized in this room on instinct, for this was where he often retreated when he needed to escape the performance of his life—but he felt blind just then to its details. Where once the warmth of the space would calm him, now he couldn't focus on the tangible objects within reach. He was too aware of his clothes, heavy against his body; the collar of his sweater, choking him; the resistance of his bones, straining against skin; the weight of his feet, concrete in boots. His hard teeth, his grainy tongue, the heft of his hair on his head. His heart pounded so hard he wanted to reach inside his chest and rip it out. It was tempting indeed, he thought, to use magic to spare his mind of such moments.

He shouldn't have gone.

He'd known better than to try to see her, but in the end he was a disappointment even to himself, only capable of so much self-restraint. Nearly a month he'd been kept from even seeing her face while she suffered, forced to remain at the farthest edge of the Diviners' property while the others came and went at their leisure. It'd been hard enough to endure this separation when he knew she was safe and healing—but when he'd heard of the attempt on her life he'd nearly lost his head. All he could do was wait—wait for a signal that she was all right, wait for word that she was leaving the temple, wait at the door for her to arrive—

It was annihilating, the power she held over him.

He finally exhaled, his body shaking slightly. She'd been here once, had broken his door, shattered his things. All this had since been mended, but the echoes of that evening persisted. He blinked as he looked around the room, its details beginning to come into focus. The towering bookcases; the velvet couches; the prodigious fireplace. His desk was a disorganized mess of unbound manuscripts, uncapped wells of ink, and unsorted crystals, the chaos of which only heightened his anxiety. When he wasn't being tortured by Iblees he often buried himself in work as a means to occupy his mind. Tulan was a small enough empire that he need not rule by committee, but he met weekly with the heads of his noble houses and took his responsibility to the people—from the soldiers to the farmers—very seriously. At the moment, they were all voicing the same concerns about the steadily growing masses, the increase in external threats.

The matter of his impending marriage.

Cyrus sat down blindly on the nearest sofa, disturbing a sheaf of papers as he sank into the cushions. There was a small, cut crystal bowl of apricots on the low table before him, which he focused his eyes upon now. He'd picked these apricots just this morning; there was a lone tree along the overgrown path that led to the Diviners Quarters; it had been growing there since he was a child, and he'd been pocketing its fruit for as long as he could remember, for it never stopped blooming.

He reached for one of the apricots now, closing its soft, small shape into his hand as his thoughts raged. His mind kept returning to Alizeh and Kamran, to images of their embrace in the back of the carriage. The way she'd looked at him; the way he'd held her. Cyrus relinquished the apricot, which rolled to the floor, then dropped his head in his hands, his chest caving as he exhaled.

They'd reconciled, then.

Doubtless the Ardunian had told her everything, had talked it all through. Any minute now Alizeh would be along to bring Cyrus the good news that she'd be accepting his offer of marriage. She'd likely spare him the rest—too merciful to announce that she'd be marrying him while being quietly betrothed to another, the two of them conspiring to kill him and combine their empires.

Cyrus knew he was unworthy of her—knew he had no right to hope for more than the terms he'd offered—and yet he could not calm the commotion in his chest, his heart thudding so hard he almost didn't hear the gentle knock at his door.

He turned toward the sound like a stone unearthed. He stood slowly, as if soaked in water, and moved through room after room in a stupor, reaching the main door without remembering how.

He stood before the closed panel, his hand on the handle.

He recoiled slightly when the knock came again.

"Cyrus?" she said softly. "Are you there?"

The sound of her voice nearly unhinged him.

For weeks he'd lived in dreams of her; he'd memorized her laughter, held her naked in his arms, had known her gasps and cries of pleasure. She'd healed him and loved him. Touched him. Tasted him.

Fuck. This was going to kill him.

He took a shaky breath and pulled open the door.

TWENTY-SEVEN

بيست و هفت

ALIZEH LOST HER STRENGTH AT the sight of his face.

His golden skin and startling blue eyes, the sheen of his coppery hair, his luminous features juxtaposing harshly against his black attire. She'd forgotten how tall he was, how arresting. She couldn't remember if she'd ever stared at him straight on like this, free to map the cut of his cheekbones, the sharp lines of his jaw. He looked better rested than she remembered; more radiant as a result.

Heavens, he was breathtaking.

She watched him take in her elaborate gown, lingering almost imperceptibly along the details of the sheer bodice, its artfully placed beading and appliqués. She'd left the crown and veil behind, and her hair, in its simple updo, had begun to come undone; he focused on one of these loose tendrils, his face gilded by the warm glow of nearby lamplight. His lips were soft, and they parted when he swallowed, the movement drawing her eyes to the column of his throat.

"Hello," she said softly.

In response he only exhaled, turning his eyes to the doorjamb. She waited a moment for him to speak, and when he said nothing, she was surprised. She realized with creeping, prickling mortification that she'd expected Cyrus to convey great emotion at the sight of her. She'd expected him to ask after her health, to express pleasure at her recovery, to show concern about the recent attempt on her life. Instead, he radiated a tension that seemed to indicate only a growing impatience, which left her stunned. After his devastating confessions, his proprietary actions toward her; after he'd saved her life and all but painted the city with flowers in her honor—

"Was there something you needed?" he said quietly. "It's rather late."

"I— Forgive me," she said. "I didn't mean to disturb you."

He glanced at something out of sight, then returned his eyes to the doorjamb. "I take it you've just arrived," he said. "Whatever you require may be procured. You need only ask; the servants know to attend to you without limitations. If you're in need of a lady's maid—"

"No," she said, unnerved. "No, it's not that—"

"Very well. Please let me know if I can be of service." He withdrew with a respectful nod, and Alizeh, her mind finally catching up to her body, threw out her hand to keep the door open.

"Cyrus," she said, alarmed. "Will you not look at me?"

He froze briefly before meeting her eyes, and when he did it was with a politeness so detached it astonished her. "Yes?" he said. "Was there something else?"

She heard the scurry of passing snodas, and drew closer to the door. "May I come inside? And speak with you privately?"

Fear awoke in his gaze, so fleeting it was gone before she was convinced it had even existed. She searched for it again in his expression, but he only looked at her steadily, his composure cool as he said, "Of course."

He stepped aside to let her pass.

Alizeh had once been worried about the impropriety of visiting Cyrus in his bedchamber, but now that she knew she would marry him, the potential gossip no longer bothered her. Glancing once more at a passing snoda, she crossed the threshold into his room. As soon as she heard the door snick shut behind her, her heart took flight.

She hadn't been alone with him since that night. The night everything and nothing had happened between them.

Cyrus moved with ease, striding away from the door into the decadent antechamber. There was lush seating gathered around a pair of low tables, and Cyrus stood behind a chair while gesturing deferentially to another. He was waiting for her to take a seat before he sat down, and the attentive action was so unlike an imperious king it shocked her. Just earlier, Kamran had boarded the coach before she did, and Alizeh had thought nothing of it; expected nothing more. Always Cyrus was confusing her, and she was made so anxious by this simple gesture that she shook her head at him, too nervous to comply.

"You'd rather stand?" He seemed surprised. "I take it this will be brief, then."

"I— Yes—" Her heart would not slow its pounding. She felt feverish in his presence, and it was destroying her capacity for calm. "Yes, I've come to tell you— That is, I just wanted you to know that I've decided to accept your proposal," she said finally. "Of marriage."

He looked at her, his eyes placid. "Excellent."

"Is it?" she said, attempting a smile. She clasped her hands against her waist, not knowing where to look. "I thought you'd be more pleased to hear it."

"I don't mean to offend," he said, lowering his head. "It's only that I find it hard to celebrate the orders of the devil."

Alizeh nearly winced; she felt so stupid. Of course he wouldn't rejoice at the news; it was a terrible bargain for him, one that ended, theoretically, with his murder. She supposed she'd only hoped to see more of a reaction from him in general, for he'd been so passionate the last time they'd spoken, except—heavens, that felt unfair, too, for he owed her nothing of his emotions. She'd made it clear she wanted him only for his empire, and expecting him to fall apart at her feet was nothing short of sadistic.

Angels above, she was disappointed in herself.

"Forgive me," she said, her eyes catching on the soft glow of a sconce. "That was a foolish thing to say."

"There's nothing to forgive," he said quietly. "Thank you for informing me of your decision."

Alizeh nodded, even as she felt a disturbing desire to scream. She didn't understand this coldness between them, for it had never been this way, not even when she'd hated him. She averted her eyes, knowing she should leave even when some part of her longed to stay. "I'll bid you good night, then," she said quietly, and headed for the door.

"When?"

She turned, stunned, for the single word was charged with more feeling than any she'd received from him tonight.

"I beg your pardon?" she said.

"When," he said, "will you be ready to take your vows?"

Alizeh blanched. She'd never thought of it that way: that she would *vow* to marry this man. That she'd promise aloud to honor and love and care for him for the rest of her life. To all the world thereafter he'd be known as her husband.

She, his wife.

The idea should've been offensive to her—but she was drawn, inexorably, to the idea of being with him. He, who was unproven and untrustworthy. He, whose life was braided with the devil's. She'd never thought of herself as someone with such poor instincts, but she could imagine no other explanation for the ineffable pull she felt in his presence, the soul-deep reach. It was dangerous, how her heart beat at the sight of him. She knew she shouldn't allow herself to feel such things when their marriage was destined to end in murder. And yet. When had she ever been so heavy with want?

"As soon as possible," she whispered.

"Tomorrow?"

"Yes— *No*," she corrected, trying to center herself. "The servants will need at least a couple of days to prepare, I think."

He studied her with something that approached bewilderment. "Prepare for what? We need only a pair of witnesses and a Diviner to bind us."

She hesitated. "Certainly some arrangements will need to be made. I realize it might be difficult to wed publicly—as I can't imagine how we might secure such an event—but if at all possible, I wish for my people to bear witness. And maybe we could have a small cake? I think Omid would like that. And the staff, too, surely they'd enjoy—"

"No."

She stared at him in surprise. "No? You don't want cake?"

"No," he said angrily. "I don't want cake."

"Very well," she said, lowering her eyes. "I, myself, have never had cake. I don't know whether it's any good, but as it's traditional in Clay weddings, I assumed—"

"You've never had cake?" he said, sounding suddenly bleak.

"My parents didn't know how to cook or bake," she said quietly. "And later, of course"—she looked away—"such luxuries were not within my reach." She took a bracing breath, forcing herself to brighten as she met his eyes again. "Anyway, perhaps instead you might consent to wear something other than this black uniform—"

"No."

"Cyrus—"

"*No.*"

"I don't understand," she said. "This was your idea—you wanted to get married—"

"Are you trying to punish me?" he said, his voice rising in anguish. "Do you really think me capable of pretending our wedding day is the happiest day of my life?"

She tried to maintain her composure then, steeling herself as she said, "Would you instead disgrace me in front of the world, making it seem as if marrying me is a chore? Will you spend our wedding day in a foul mood and funereal clothes? Would you have your household believe you detest me by denying them so much as a bite of something sweet in my honor?"

She saw the fight leave his body then, heard his unsteady exhale.

"Fine," he said, the word so soft it was hardly a whisper. "Do what you will."

"Thank you."

Again, he exhaled, this time turning away from her as he dragged his hands down his face. His self-control seemed to be crumbling, for he was almost visibly shaking now; but with each passing second Alizeh, too, felt herself grow weaker before him. There was an unmistakable heat between them, an electric pull she lacked the strength to resist. She didn't even realize she'd drawn closer to him until he suddenly backed away, his eyes devouring her as she approached, darkening with a need so palpable she felt as if he'd stripped her bare.

Finally, she saw a shade of truth in his gaze, and she could hardly breathe in the face of it.

"Cyrus—"

"*No,*" he said sharply. "Don't."

She stopped in place, just inches separating them now. "Don't what?"

"Alizeh," he said. His chest was heaving, his body rigid with tension. "Be merciful."

These words lit a dangerous fire within her.

She told herself to withdraw, but just then she couldn't seem to move. She was in his orbit now, so close she could see the sharp wisps of his copper lashes, her head humid with sense memory. She wanted to touch him, to know the heat of his skin. She knew what his body was like under those clothes, how much power and passion he kept tightly leashed inside him. It was a revelation she'd been slow to unravel about Cyrus: that he possessed such careful control, such extraordinary discipline over his own body. Cyrus's desire for her had been as scorching as a summer heat; she'd felt desperate under the weight of it, yet he'd not lifted a finger to her body. He'd never kissed her, never simply claimed what he wanted. Not the way Kamran once had.

This was a fascinating discovery indeed—for royals, so saturated in overindulgence, seldom knew *how* to deny themselves. Having worked in a number of prominent houses, Alizeh knew firsthand that the rich and titled were gluttons of the worst variety. Upon first engaging with Cyrus she'd been so distracted by his perceived monstrousness that she'd failed to notice the inconsistencies in his royal character. His modest presence was perplexing enough: his plain clothes, his conspicuous lack of jewels or adornment—even the common way he'd tended to his own dragon. More interesting was that he had no attendants, no entourage trailing him, no snodas supplicating at his heels. But perhaps most unaccountable was that the servants did not quaver around him; they didn't fall to their knees in his presence.

She marveled at these realizations now, and very carefully, she stepped back, putting at least two feet between them.

This distance seemed to accomplish nothing.

A dam had broken, and there was no repairing it. Gone was his cool exterior, his eyes bright now with the fire of pain and hunger. The longer she looked at him the more unsteady she felt, and soon the fever between them reached a dangerous pitch, her own torment growing so acute she felt desperate to sit down. She wanted relief she didn't understand, wanted something from him she couldn't name. Her every feeling was so heightened she worried she might cry out if he so much as walked toward her.

"Cyrus—"

"We should perform the blood oath tonight," he said, turning his body away.

"What?" She blinked; her head was swimming.

"If we're to be married so soon, we should not delay." His voice was rough, and he paused to clear it. "I'd prefer to have a couple of days to recover before the ceremony."

This shocking statement produced precisely the cooling effect Alizeh required. It was an ice bath of reality, one she'd nearly overlooked.

Blood oaths were morally reprehensible, and yet she could not see a way around such a provision in this circumstance. It was the only way to be certain Cyrus would uphold his end of the bargain.

"I've never seen it done before," she said, sobered. "I've only heard stories. Will it be very bad for you?"

He kept his eyes on the ground when he said, softly, "It is my understanding that, in the beginning, there will be a great deal of pain."

"Will it get better?"

"It depends."

"On what?"

He shook his head, still avoiding her eyes. "These details are of little importance. If it's amenable to you, I'd like to perform the oath tonight."

She tried to adjust to the idea. "We'll need a Diviner, won't we? Is it too late?"

Again, he shook his head. "I can do it myself."

Another shocking revelation. Blood oaths required an enchantment so advanced Alizeh had never heard of one being performed by anyone outside the priesthood. "Really?"

"Yes."

She was quiet a long moment before she said, "Cyrus, will you never tell me the truth?"

He startled, lifting his head to reveal an unguarded fear. "The truth about what?"

"About who you really are. There's so much you're not telling me—so much that doesn't make sense. Every time I speak with you I'm left with more questions."

"Do you think I've been lying to you?"

"Yes," she said, and paused. "Except that I have the strangest feeling you might be lying about how horrible you are."

Cyrus almost smiled, though the action was weighed down by an unspoken grief. "Give me twenty minutes," he said. "I need to prepare some things."

"Are you going to ignore what I just said?"

He strode to the front door, which he opened in a fluid motion, shifting aside so she might exit.

She stared at him. "You want me to leave?"

There was a weakness in his eyes when he said, "No."

"Cyrus—"

"We'll need at least three witnesses," he said, lowering his head. "Though I'm sure you'll have no trouble convincing your friends to watch me suffer."

Alizeh frowned, then moved to the door in a daze, her skirts whispering along the floor. She came to a halt in front of him, their bodies only a hand apart—and she studied his chest, then his throat, his jaw, the curve of his lips. Her voice was a little breathless when she said, "You can't just ignore the things I say and hope they go away."

"I'll meet you in the library downstairs," he said.

It was unconscious, what she did next; she didn't mean to touch him, not exactly. In fact, she couldn't even remember lifting her hand to his body. She only remembered the softness of his sweater, the heat and hardness of his torso beneath—and then *relief*, intoxicating relief when he finally touched her, when he dragged his hands down her body with a tortured sound, his palms branding her through the thin tissue of her dress before he gripped her hips, hard, and she bit back a cry, startling as the door slammed shut only to discover, with a shock, that she was pressed against it, held in place by the hot length of him, his chest heaving so hard it seemed to mirror the chaos inside hers. He looked wild and barely leashed, as if the effort to keep himself still was actively killing him.

"You don't know what you're doing," he said, his voice so rough it was unrecognizable. "You don't know what I want from you, angel. You can't even imagine."

"What do you mean?" She stared up at him, her heart hammering in her chest. "What is it you want?"

His eyes seemed to glaze over at that, the blue of his irises blown out by black, and he dipped his head, nearly touching her lips as he exhaled, his body shaking. *"Everything,"* he whispered, releasing her suddenly, backing away as if she'd run him through with a blade. "I want *everything.*"

Alizeh felt liquefied. For all the frost in her veins, she'd never known this kind of fever, never felt such desperation. And he'd never even kissed her.

She made a breathless, anguished sound.

"I'll see you downstairs," he said, staring at the floor. "Twenty minutes."

This time, she fled without a word.

TWENTY-EIGHT

بیست و هشت

"SO?" HUDA WAS WAITING FOR her at the bottom of the staircase. "How'd it go?"

Alizeh kept walking, her eyes averted even as Huda chased after her. She felt shaken. Unwell. She wasn't quite ready to speak, and she didn't know what to do with her heart, which was battering her ribs so hard she thought they might bruise.

"Fine," she said. "It went fine."

"*Fine?* What do you— Heavens, look at your face," Huda gasped. She stopped Alizeh in place, holding her at arm's length for an inspection. "What did he do to you?"

"What?" Alizeh, who felt unreasonably vexed by this question, looked into Huda's steady brown eyes. "What do you mean?"

"Did he try to hurt you?" Again, she gasped. "Was he horrible? Oh, I knew you shouldn't have gone in there alone—I tried to tell you—"

"No, he didn't try to *hurt* me," she said, delivering the words with more heat than she intended, and regretting it the moment she saw the astonishment on Huda's face.

"Forgive me," she said. "I didn't mean to direct that anger at you. It's been a difficult day."

Huda softened at once, her eyes heavy with sympathy. "Of course, dear. I understand."

Alizeh had never been in such a bad mood.

She drew away from Huda, wrapping her arms around herself. She felt frustrated and confused; she wanted the world around her to make sense, and it didn't. Cyrus was supposed to be evil. She wanted him to act evil. He wasn't supposed to be kind and deferential and considerate. He was the character she was meant to kill without a crisis of conscience. She wasn't supposed to lose her head. She wasn't supposed to feel like *this*, like there was an open wound inside her, like she wanted to sit down and cry.

The feeling came dangerously close to grief.

She moved blindly down the hall, not knowing where she was headed. She didn't want him to die. She didn't want to perform a blood oath. She didn't want to kill him. *The library*. Where was the library? Was it necessary for her to kill him? *Yes*, she considered, for if she didn't kill him, she'd be married to a man bonded with Iblees, which meant she could never fully trust him; he might one day hurt her if only to please the devil—Cyrus himself had not denied such a possibility. Then again— Kamran had offered to marry her, hadn't he? That was an interesting alternative, but then she'd have to be married, forever, to Kamran—which, while not so terrible a prospect, did make her feel a bit claustrophobic. Yet, if she married Kamran, perhaps Cyrus might not die. Except *no*, that wasn't right, because the devil would kill him anyway, wouldn't he? And would Kamran still want to marry her without the jewel of Tulan in her possession?

She made a pitiful sound.

Where on earth was the library? She'd only seen it once,

in passing, on her first day at the palace. She supposed she could ask a servant, but she didn't want to draw attention to their evening plans. If only she could remember—

"Did you set a date, then?"

"A date?" Alizeh echoed, distracted. Huda was keeping up with her, the look of concern in her eyes growing only stronger.

"For the wedding." Huda frowned. "Are you sure you're all right?"

"Oh," said Alizeh, blinking. "Yes, of course. Huda, do you know where the library is?"

"The library?" she repeated. "Head straight down the hall and make two rights, then a left, but wait—" She tugged gently at Alizeh's arm, drawing her back. "What did he say? When will you marry?"

"In two days."

"*Two days?*" Huda nearly cried. "Isn't that terribly soon?"

Alizeh tensed. There were servants everywhere, by all appearances attending to their various tasks. When she'd worked as a snoda, it'd always been astonishing to Alizeh what people would say in her presence. They simply didn't think of her as a person. They paid her as much attention as they did the wallpaper—and yet she was always, always listening.

"Gather the others," she said quietly, "and meet me in the library as soon as possible. I have a great deal to tell you."

Huda smiled brilliantly. "Excellent! Shall I ring for tea? Should I wake Omid? He went to bed, but I—"

"No," said Alizeh quickly. "It's better that he's asleep, I

think. And no tea. No servants at all. It won't be that kind of an evening."

"Whyever not?" Huda's smile dimmed. "Are we not gathering to gossip?"

"No," said Alizeh, squeezing the young woman's arm. "Not exactly."

"Your Majesty," came a familiar, agitated voice, and Alizeh spun around to see Hazan all but running toward her. He reached her in moments, taking a beat to study the sight of her before he said, "Are you all right?"

"Why wouldn't I be?" she said, surprised by his concern. "Has something else happened?"

"I was informed that you went up to his quarters alone—I didn't realize you'd be in a closed room when you spoke with him— I swear, if he laid a finger on you—"

Alizeh's bad mood returned. "Why is everyone so concerned he's going to hurt me? Prior to your arrival, I spent a great deal of time alone with Cyrus, and I never came to harm."

"Respectfully, Your Majesty," Hazan said with forced calm, "when we found you, you were unconscious, your throat had been cut, you'd suffered a head wound, and you were covered in blood."

"Must we speak like this in front of the servants?" she said desperately.

He lowered his voice. "The Diviners said they found half-healed dragon bites along your leg and torso—"

"And then you woke up," Huda added in a dramatic whisper, "only to be shot in the back and tossed off a cliff."

"That was Kamran's doing!"

"What was my doing?"

Alizeh looked up to find Kamran approaching their group. He smiled at her with genuine pleasure, then caught sight of Huda and scowled.

"What are you doing here?" he said, turning his eyes to Hazan. "You were supposed to meet me in the parlor. Why are you all standing in the hall having a heated discussion?"

"How interesting that you should ask," Huda said sweetly. "Alizeh was just reminiscing about the time you nearly killed her."

Kamran's expression only darkened. "I doubt that."

"Indeed I was not," Alizeh said, frowning at Huda. "Please don't fight tonight. There's too much ahead of us."

"Ahead of us?" Hazan looked suddenly alert. "Did something happen?"

"Yes, I—"

Kamran came to stand beside her, briefly touching her lower back in a move that felt almost possessive. She looked up at him, surprised. It was not that she felt uncomfortable, exactly; she cared for Kamran, and felt quite safe with him. It was more that she wanted to be clear that she did not, at this time, consider him anything more than a friend. She thought to say something, but couldn't decide whether she'd be overreacting to so small a gesture, and resolved to ignore it. Her mind was full enough as it was.

"Hazan," she said, trying again. "Could you lead us to the library? I'll explain everything when we have some privacy—"

Just then she heard a scream; she turned toward the sound to find that a snoda had gone rigid at the sight of her, and when Alizeh looked upon the girl, she made a choking sound and collapsed in the middle of the hall. Alizeh panicked, remembering then that a handful of Jinn servants worked in the palace, and moved as if to go to her, but Hazan tugged her back.

"You can't," he said.

"Why not? She could've hurt herself—"

"We haven't caught the assassin yet—I won't take any risks with your life—"

"She's a *servant*—"

"It's a convenient uniform," he said, shooting her a knowing look.

"But— Hazan, we can't simply leave her there—"

A cluster of snodas rushed into the hall at the commotion, two more of whom spotted Alizeh and promptly screamed. One of them clapped a hand over her mouth, fighting back a sob, while the other struggled to speak, then fainted.

The remaining servants, who were ostensibly not Jinn, stood and stared at Alizeh in open-mouthed astonishment, their appraisals all the more unnerving for the fact that she couldn't see their eyes.

Hazan shook his head. "I'm taking you away from here. You can't wander these halls alone anymore." Glancing at Huda and Kamran, he said, "You two, meet us in the library." Then, "And try not to kill each other before you get there."

"But, Hazan—wait—someone has to help the snodas—"

"I'll do it," came a familiar, saccharine voice. Alizeh

turned, unnerved, to see Sarra striding toward their group at a leisurely pace.

Sarra shook her head, her eyes fixed on Alizeh as she said, "What a strange and fascinating surprise you've turned out to be. Lately everywhere I turn there seems to be some drama, and you, my dear, at the center of it."

Alizeh said nothing to this, only watched Sarra warily as the woman sashayed past them toward the fallen snodas, snapping her fingers for someone to fetch "that Ardunian apothecarist." Alizeh still had no idea what to make of the woman, and she was afraid anything she said would be heavily scrutinized, for they were in the presence of at least twenty servants at the moment, a dozen of whom had filed into the hall in the last seconds alone. The longer they stood here, the more of a spectacle they were becoming. Whispers were gathering around them like a storm.

"Let's go," Hazan said, placing a hand on her shoulder.

"Yes," Alizeh said, distracted. "Yes, we should go. We're going to be late."

"*Late?*" Kamran and Huda turned toward her at the same time.

Beside her, Hazan stiffened. "Late for what, Your Majesty?"

TWENTY-NINE

يستونه

WHEN THEY PUSHED OPEN THE heavy door to the library, Alizeh knew at once that he was inside. She could feel him somehow, as if she were magnetized to his presence. She moved with confidence through the unfamiliar space, its cavernous dimensions lit by warm pools of light.

"This way," she whispered.

"Are you sure?" Huda whispered back. "Good grief, this room feels haunted at night."

"Maybe that's because you're here," Kamran said in an undertone.

Huda gasped. "Maybe *you*—"

"Enough," Hazan said sharply. "Keep your stupidity to yourselves this evening or I'll have you both thrown in the dungeons."

"You have no authority to do such a thing," Huda protested.

"You think Cyrus would deny me such a request?"

Huda looked affronted; Alizeh couldn't help but smile.

In the end, the four of them had headed to the library together, for when Alizeh had explained, vaguely, that Cyrus was waiting for her, Hazan had been inexplicably angry; Kamran had expressly refused to leave her side; and Huda had said, "Should I bring my throwing stars?"

The imposing, soaring shelves towered over them as they went, the smell of old books and aged leather filling her nose. It was a well-loved room, clearly a place meant for more than display, dotted throughout with worn chairs and rugs. As she pushed on, Alizeh discovered the heart of it: at the end was a discrete space anchored by a mammoth, unlit fireplace, around which were a collection of plush sofas and low tables lit by golden light from nearby lamps. The back wall, however, was a masterwork of glass: massive windows and doors looked out upon a heath crowned by a brilliant moon, the glow of which cast an ethereal spotlight upon a single figure.

Leaning against the mantel, was Cyrus.

Like a lit matchstick, his bright hair shone against the dark of his clothes; he radiated power and elegance even in repose, his gaze almost languid as he watched them enter. He looked at Alizeh first, but he stared longest at Kamran, the two men sharing a look that came very close to hatred, even as they exchanged silent nods of acknowledgment.

Alizeh had to force herself to stand back, to give Cyrus a wide berth. It was better for her when there was distance between them, when her mind could think beyond the space he took up inside her. Even now she fought for self-possession. Heat had gathered low inside her cold body as it never had in her life, a frantic need building within her, quickening across her skin. She struggled not to stare at his mouth, which drew her eyes over and over; struggled to shove aside the memory of his words, still unprocessed.

Everything, he'd said.

I want everything.

She startled, suddenly, at the feel of a hand at her back, and looked up to find Kamran standing beside her once more. Twice now this had happened, which registered in her clouded mind as worrisome, for he seemed to think she welcomed these proprietary touches, despite the fact that there was no understanding between them. She'd need to take him aside soon and make it clear that she'd yet to make a decision about his offer. In fact, she didn't think she'd be able to give it more thought until she'd first dealt with the pressing issues before her.

"You're late," Cyrus said without preamble, drawing away from the fireplace as he did. He approached them as an apparition might, his movements slow and liquid. His eyes, she thought, were almost angry—except she blinked, and he appeared unflappably calm.

"Your Majesty," said Hazan, turning to her. "Perhaps now you can tell us why we're gathered here."

Cyrus came to a halt. "You haven't told them?"

"I didn't want us to be overheard by the servants," Alizeh explained, looking around at the others. She took a breath. "Very well, then. I've brought you here because we've decided to perform the blood oath tonight."

Huda stifled a small scream.

"You son of a bitch," Hazan said, stalking toward Cyrus as if he might kill him. "*How dare you*—she's only just awoken—she's hardly had a chance to recover, to spend time in her own head—"

"Hazan, please, it was my choice—I agreed—"

"She won't be affected by the oath," Cyrus said, his voice clipped. "I'm the one who will bear the burden of pain."

Hazan stopped. "Have you ever witnessed, firsthand, the consequences of a blood oath?" He gestured to the room. "Or have you only read about it in your precious books?"

Cyrus stared stonily at Hazan. "I've read about it widely. I've heard personal accounts from the Diviners— I'm perfectly capable—"

"I've seen it with my own eyes!" Hazan exploded. "You think this is a simple matter? You will be giving up a piece of your soul, of your free will—"

"*I am well aware*—"

Hazan turned once more to Alizeh, beseeching her. "Your Majesty, you must understand—the cost of such a magic is too great. Once this is done, you will all but own a piece of him. You'll carry him with you as deadweight; he'll be physically incapable of being apart from you—"

"And she'll have to kill him to put an end to it." This, from Kamran, who'd drawn somehow closer to her. "I don't see that as a bad thing, Hazan."

"What do you mean," Alizeh said, her thoughts racing madly, "that he'll be physically incapable of being apart from me? I knew there was a tether, but I didn't realize it manifested in such a literal way."

"Yes, Your Majesty," said Hazan, who seemed relieved by her shock. "It's a merciless bond, used throughout history only by the most desperate creatures, with grim results for both parties involved—"

"He exaggerates," Cyrus interjected. "In the beginning, yes, it will be difficult, which is why I've asked to do this as soon as possible—"

"*Always!*" Hazan cried. "It's *always* difficult! It's worst in the beginning, yes—at first, the pain of separation will be unendurable—and perhaps, in a matter of days, you'll be able to stand a dozen feet apart from her without wanting to drive a dagger through your skull. In months, if you're lucky, you might endure the distance of a wheat field—but you will *never* be able to part from her for long. Until your debt is paid you will never again have independence. It is the very nature of a blood oath to keep a debtor chained to their creditor, and I am appalled that you'd commit to such magic without knowing the facts."

"I know the facts," Cyrus said darkly. "I simply have no choice. My debt to her is my death. When it is done, I will be, too."

"Cyrus," she whispered. "Are you certain—"

"It's the only way," said Kamran. "We can't trust him without the oath. You cannot marry him without the guarantee—"

"Then perhaps she shouldn't marry him at all!" Hazan said furiously. He fought for composure, then turned to Alizeh as he said, "Is it truly so imperative that you wed him, Your Majesty? Can you not accept Kamran, instead, when he's already offered for you—"

"How did you know that?" Alizeh glanced at Cyrus, whose body was rigid even as he stared silently at the floor. "I haven't— I didn't tell anyone—"

"Oh, my dear, we've known of his intentions for some time," said Huda, putting an arm around her shoulder. "The prince has only been talking about it for weeks."

Alizeh looked at Kamran, at the steady look in his eyes, and her mind went blank. "Forgive me," she said to him. "But I—I haven't made a decision with regard to—that is, I only know that if I don't marry Cyrus, the devil will kill him anyway." Her heart wrenched in her chest, her voice dropping to a whisper. "He is doomed to die one way or another."

"Precisely," said Kamran, unmoved. He turned to the others. "If he is to die regardless, why shouldn't she walk away with a prize? I've already advised her to take the offer—"

"You *advised* her?" Cyrus said darkly, his eyes flashing with unchecked hatred. "You mean you advised her to marry me?" It was the first time Cyrus had addressed Kamran, his voice so heavy with loathing it radiated tension throughout the room.

"Yes," said Kamran, whose own eyes were mocking. "I encouraged her not to lose an opportunity to reap the reward of killing you."

"At least I have something to offer her. Meanwhile you dare to promise her a kingdom you've yet to inherit. Empty promises from an ousted prince who might never be king."

Kamran stiffened.

Cyrus studied him, his voice soft and lethal when he said, "Did you think I wouldn't find out what really happened when you left Ardunia? I don't care what the papers say about your popularity among the masses. Your Diviners don't think you worthy of the throne."

"What?" Alizeh said. "Is that true?"

Kamran stepped forward, looking murderous. "I didn't realize we were sharing secrets," he said to Cyrus. "Perhaps you'd like to explain to everyone why I once found you collapsed on the grounds in the dead of night, every inch of you so covered in blood you could hardly open your eyes?"

Cyrus tensed, and Alizeh inhaled sharply.

"How many other enemies do you have?" Kamran was saying. "How many other revolting vices? Do you spend your nights gambling? In the arms of prostitutes? You're so depraved you have no protection from the violence of thugs even as *king*—"

"*That's enough*," said Alizeh, experiencing a rare flash of anger. She, who knew exactly why such a thing had happened to Cyrus, could listen to no more of this slander. "You cast aspersions upon his character without possession of the facts—"

"His character?" Kamran was stunned. "What character? The man murdered his own father for a crown! He murdered my grandfather. Murdered our Diviners! I have reason to suspect he's been sending spies into Ardunia for months— has he mentioned that? Has he offered any explanations for launching covert missions into our empire? For breaking the Nix accords by drawing magical boundaries between our lands? His every action is a manipulation! His every word is chosen in the pursuit of his own self-interest. Heaven knows what else he's done in the course of his dissipated life!"

Alizeh absorbed these horrible facts, hating that she could

not deny them, that Cyrus refused to speak of his father, to explain his actions. She hadn't known about the spies, and when she glanced at Cyrus for a reaction to this fresh accusation, she found him staring impassively at the wall. He made no move to refute the charge, and yet these assertions felt at odds with all that she'd learned of him; he did not, in fact, strike her as the kind of person who acted only in his own self-interest. The tense moment inspired a memory as evidence; when she'd first arrived in Tulan, she'd pressed Cyrus for information about his deal with the devil and he'd said—

I must live long enough to accomplish something crucial. Beyond that, my beating heart is of no consequence. You have no idea what's at stake. My life is the least of it.

The nosta had confirmed this as truth.

Alizeh couldn't decide whether she was stupid or perceptive for thinking there had to be more to Cyrus, more to his actions. She'd discovered him to be too intelligent, too reasonable. He was reserved and thoughtful, and had betrayed a great deal about himself in the small, human moments they'd shared. Someone in possession of such careful self-control, she reasoned, would never lose his head long enough to commit thoughtless violence. Indeed it now seemed bizarre to her that he'd entered into a deal with the devil, for Cyrus appeared to have no material desires, no interest in the profits of the world—and worse, he seemed to receive nothing but torment from Iblees. Where were the rewards of his bargain? It drove her crazy that she couldn't understand.

"Nevertheless," she said finally. "His torture was inflicted by the devil—I know this because I saw it happen myself—"

"We need not discuss this," said Cyrus, flashing her an inscrutable look. "The opinion of a worthless royal means nothing to me."

"You would truly defend him?" Kamran said, ignoring this as he turned to her. "It's a great credit to your compassion that you would pity someone as corrupted as he, but I would implore you not to spare another thought for his foul soul. I don't care if Iblees roasts him over a spit every night. *He* put himself in this situation—he capitulated to the devil, he sold himself to darkness." Kamran gestured widely. "These are the consequences. He will lose Tulan, which we should be happy to claim upon his death. I refuse to be sorry for capitalizing upon another man's stupidity."

"Well," said Cyrus, taking a sharp breath. "As much as I enjoy listening to your plans to feast upon my corpse, I've grown tired of this conversation."

Alizeh was shaking her head. "Cyrus, please— I don't share his sentiments—"

"And I don't care to discuss it," he said quietly, turning away. "It's getting late, and I'd rather return to the task at hand."

"Yes," she said, hesitating. "Of course—"

"Your Majesty," said Hazan. "Must this gruesome deed be done tonight, of all nights, when you've only just returned to us? Could we not take more time to consider the other options available?"

Alizeh sighed heavily, closing her eyes a moment before

turning to her friend. "What options, Hazan? What other options do I have? Already I've been missing for a month. Already there's been an attempt on my life. Today we have seventy thousand Jinn gathered, but soon that number will double, and double again. What then?" She shook her head. "Am I to remain silent forever? Am I to haunt the halls of this palace, letting my people languish without leadership, without answers—without hope? What of the external pressures facing Tulan? What of the needs of Ardunia? We cannot remain here, in this in-between place forever. Clearly Kamran needs to return home to address the turbulence he left behind; Huda and Deen have families waiting for them—"

"Oh, please don't rush things on our account," Huda piped in. "I've absolutely no desire to see my family, and Deen is rather going through something, actually, and though he's been vague about the details, he doesn't seem in any hurry to—"

"Yes, thank you, Huda," Hazan said quietly.

Again, Alizeh sighed. "It kills me that I'm not yet ready to lead. That I have nothing to say, that I can offer only empty promises. I need a crown, Hazan, and I need it now. Cyrus and I have discussed it, and we will marry in two days' time."

"*Two days?*" Hazan paled, his eyes wide with shock. Even Kamran turned sharply to look at her.

"Yes," she said steadily. "Two days. I want to return to Ardunia immediately after the wedding."

"What?" said Cyrus, straightening. "You didn't mention—"

"That means he'll have to come with us," said Huda. "Right? If the blood oath makes it so he's unable to be parted from her, he'll be forced to come back to Ardunia with us, won't he?"

"Yes," Kamran said darkly.

"Your Majesty," said Hazan, who was not yet convinced. "We can embark on a quest to the Arya mountains straightaway—you need not marry first. We can leave for Ardunia tomorrow—"

"No," she said. "I must secure my crown before departing Tulan. I need to know who I am and where my home will be. I cannot leave my people without a show of faith; I need them to trust that I'll return—that I'll not abandon them. *This* is the way."

Hazan stood before her, astonishment rendering him absolutely still, and Alizeh knew she'd won the fight when he responded only with an unsteady breath. Blindly Hazan retreated, sinking into the nearest chair.

"I understand," he whispered. "I hate it, but I understand."

"Excellent," Cyrus said, the word charged with heat. "Are we finally done? Or are there more debates to be had? Please let me know now, so I might schedule time to lose the rest of my mind."

"No," said Alizeh gently. "We're done."

He looked at her then, finally looked at her for more than a fraction of a second, and she was surprised to find in his gaze something that looked a great deal like fear. Her heart broke at the sight, and she moved instinctively toward him when he suddenly pivoted, then walked away. She watched in silent confusion as Cyrus went to the door along the back wall, pushing it open to let in the night air.

Alizeh stiffened, then shivered.

"What are you doing?" asked Hazan, who'd risen to his feet. "Will you not be performing the ceremony here?"

"No," Cyrus said, his voice low and dark. "I don't want any blood near my books."

And he stepped outside.

THIRTY

سی

CYRUS STRODE INTO THE ENDLESS dark, fireflies hung in the air like ornaments all around him. Firm grass crunched under his boots, the skies heavy with the sound of crickets and the hush of distant waterfalls. He couldn't name this storm inside his chest; there were no words to describe the tumult of feeling he struggled then to tame. He only knew that he felt feral and scorched and terrified, and every minute demanded more of a withering self-possession he fought desperately to maintain.

He hated these people. Hated that he had to show restraint before them, hated that he couldn't simply kill the odious prince, whose every breath was an effrontery. Even then, even as he followed an old path to an old cottage to lay the foundation of his own pitiful end, he wanted to turn around and slit the idiot's throat.

More than that, he wanted to fall to his knees.

This tremble inside him, this madness in his heart—it was all for her. *All for her.* He could hardly look at Alizeh without losing his mind; nearly four weeks he'd seen her only in his dreams, and he'd all but forgotten how finely wrought she was in real life, how delicate her features, how soft the curves of her cheeks. He came to life when she smiled, drew breath when her eyes brightened, died when she left a room.

She'd smelled like roses.

His roses.

And she would marry him, would become his wife in front of the world, and he would never have her. Never touch her. He would watch in silence as another man put his hands on her, the two of them counting the days until they could kill him.

He exhaled, shakily, the crisp air biting his skin.

It caused him physical pain to remember how little it had taken to unravel his restraint. She'd all but pressed a hand to his torso and, like a man unmoored, he'd wanted to rip her dress down the middle, sink to his knees and taste her. He wanted to feel her legs tremble around him, wanted to hear her cry out, wanted to watch her come apart—wanted things that would likely terrify her even to imagine.

A gust of wind pushed against his body, and he glanced up at the stars, his body still so dense with heat he could hardly feel the chill. Cyrus was out of his head, and she— She was a vision crafted by a generous maker. She was everything sweet, her every instinct to be kind. Even her anger was exquisite. Knowing he was to die by her hand made the reality almost bearable.

He heard hurried footfalls as someone approached him, the movements heavy enough to indicate a certain height and mass. Cyrus turned slightly to see that Hazan had come up on his left.

"How much longer will this take?" said the Jinn impatiently. "I was unaware we'd be required to tramp through a field in the freezing cold, otherwise I would've brought a coat."

"I was unaware you were so easily fatigued," said Cyrus. "I admit I'm disappointed. I thought you were more resilient than that."

"Alizeh," he said angrily, "is nearly blue with frost. Her gown is made of tissue. She is frozen enough in the general course of things without this added—"

Cyrus stopped, then turned to look at her. In his haste to exit the abhorrent conversation he'd been thoughtless; Alizeh was visibly struggling, her arms tight across her chest, fighting over and over an impulse to tremble as she moved. Kamran, he noticed, was hovering nearby looking chagrined, leaving Cyrus to wonder whether his offers of aid had been rejected.

This mattered little.

He went to her in a few strides, removed his coat without a word, and laid it gently over her shoulders. All this he did so quickly she looked up at him just as he turned to walk away, and she caught his arm before he could go. He felt the press of her hand through his sleeve like a branding iron, his heart picking up as he halted, then watched as she gestured to Huda and Kamran to go on ahead. Only when they were alone did she release him, and he felt almost as if he'd been tricked.

"Cyrus," she said.

He was afraid to look at her face. He would not look into her eyes. "Yes?" he said to the dark.

"Thank you," she said softly. "Your coat is so warm I fear I could fall asleep inside it."

He swallowed, hating the way this gratified him. "You're welcome."

"Can I ask you a question?"

"No."

She laughed, and he wanted to dissolve.

"Here is my question," she said. "If you cannot bear to be near me now, how will you survive what's yet to come?"

Now he did look at her, his breath catching as he stared into her eyes, soft and gleaming in the reflected moonlight. He seemed to sink into the grass as he gazed at her, the world blurring beyond the space she occupied. There was something so gentle about her presence, something that reminded him of magic: all curves, no edges. He wanted to press his face against her neck, wanted to breathe in the fragrance of her skin, the perfume of the flowers he'd grown himself. He wanted to make her laugh. He wanted to hold her hand. He wanted to bring her tea and walk with her through the seasons. He wanted to watch her conquer the earth. He wanted to glide his hand down her naked back, wanted to taste the salt of her, wanted to bite her bottom lip and lose himself inside her.

God, the things he wanted.

The longer he looked at her, the worse he felt, and the more unsteady she appeared. Her breaths had grown shallow, her eyes deeper; darker.

"Cyrus," she whispered.

He shook his head, inhaling sharply as he finally tore himself away. "I won't survive it," he said. "It's your job to make sure I don't."

THIRTY-ONE

سی ویک

IT WASN'T LONG AFTER HE left her that a neat cottage came into view. Nestled between two towering trees in a private corner of the palace grounds, the stone edifice was all but buried under overgrown moonflower vines, whose circular white blooms released a soft, sweet smell that beckoned as they approached. Warm light shone in the warped windows, a curl of smoke escaping from the chimney stack. It appeared Cyrus had prepared for their arrival.

The five of them had fallen into a tense silence these past few minutes. Even Huda, who'd returned to Alizeh's side, was exercising a rare discretion by not demanding to know the details of her conversation with Cyrus. Instead, the young woman sent her sly, questioning looks that Alizeh acknowledged only once, with a wary smile. There was so much to say, and nothing to discuss.

What Alizeh was feeling for Cyrus had begun to frighten her, and she needed to accept that her affection for him was both dangerous and pointless. She was making a choice, with every step she took this very moment, to perform an irreversible oath that would change both their lives forever; they'd be bound to a morbid ending that could never be undone. What was the point of continuing on in this vein, torturing herself for glimpses into his heart, for pieces of him he'd never be free to give? In order to trust him she'd need answers he could never provide—for the devil had forbade him from speaking the truth.

It didn't matter that she wanted to trust him anyway.

It didn't matter that he'd given her the coat off his back, that she was warmed even then by the heat of him, her head dizzy with the lingering scent of his skin. It didn't matter that she watched him now with a longing that was as painful to her as it was confusing.

Alizeh had made a decision, and she would not diverge from the path before her. She'd been born to lead her people to freedom, to protect them from the cruelty of a world that sought to misunderstand and destroy them. Nothing else could matter. She had to accept as fact that sometimes revolution demanded darkness in exchange for light.

Here, tonight, was proof.

Cyrus came to a stop in front of the cottage door, reaching for the handle when he suddenly hesitated, then turned back to look upon their small party. "Have any of you experienced magic before?"

"*Magic?*" said Huda drily. "You mean like that nasty trick you pulled that made me lose my voice?"

"Or when you left the prince paralyzed," Hazan added, "and half-dead in his own home?"

"Bastard," Kamran muttered.

"I'm referring to organic magic," Cyrus said impassively. "Have you ever felt it in its pure, unprocessed form?"

"No," said Alizeh, who felt a prickle of unease. "Why?"

He shook his head, turning back to the cottage. "It can

be a little unsettling if you're not expecting it. Do not be alarmed."

He turned the handle, pushed open the door, and a wash of warm, marbled light spilled out into the darkness, casting them all in a delicate glow. Cyrus stood aside to let Alizeh pass before him, and as she stepped across the threshold her breath caught with wonder.

They'd entered a room with soaring ceilings supported by heavy wooden beams, the scent of earth and perfume filling her nose. Nature had pushed inside, climbing vines sprawling from cracks in stone corners and creeping toward the floor, which was covered by a massive, richly colored rug that was threadbare in places, singed in others. A roaring fire blazed in a hearth so large she might stand in it, and Alizeh startled at a sudden *pop* of a log, darting aside in time to keep her skirts from catching a stray ember. The air was thick as she moved deeper into the space, as if she were wading through thinned water. It wasn't unpleasant, only disorienting, and once she'd fought back a shiver of unease, she relaxed into the sensation. Curious, she pressed a finger to the air and felt a thrill of resistance, so soft it recalled the plump cheeks of small children. Alizeh looked around in a daze, possessed by a peculiar feeling that if she let herself fall, she might float.

The walls were lined with mismatched cabinets and wooden shelves heavy with dusty books; tapered candles; an assortment of earthenware; and dozens of sealed jars in various sizes, whose bright and unfamiliar contents brought to mind the storeroom of an apothecary.

Hazan pulled down one such jar from the shelf, turning

it over in his hands as he said, quietly, "I haven't seen silver ash in years." He looked up at Cyrus. "What is this place? Is it all yours?"

Cyrus only averted his eyes and said, "I'll be ready in a minute."

He allowed them to explore the cottage without further comment, though Alizeh watched him carefully. His eyes were unreadable as he crossed the room to a closed cabinet, pressed his hand against the wood, and stepped back as a series of locks audibly unlatched. The door swung open with a whine, and he quickly withdrew something from its interior, pocketed the item, and closed the compartment. He pressed his hand once more over the wood, resealing the door.

Alizeh watched in awe as he did this, for she realized then, as she turned her eyes again to the room, that she continued to underestimate him. She thought she'd already given Cyrus more credit than he'd rightfully earned, but she saw now that she hadn't even grasped the full depth of his person. Indeed the more she learned about Cyrus the less she understood him; he was like a destination in the distance that grew farther away as she approached.

Certainly no ordinary person knew magic like this.

"*Wow*," whispered Huda, who stood before a massive worktable that spanned the length of the room. Upon its weathered counter were sundry tools and objects, among them a cracked mortar and pestle, a stack of moth-eaten books, a sheaf of crumbling papers, and desiccated wells of ink. Alizeh drew closer to the table and blew away a layer of dust from a rack of glass vials, the glittering, jewel-toned liquids sloshing eagerly inside their containers.

"*Ha*," said Kamran, who'd plucked a book of nursery rhymes from a shelf. He turned the aged, leather volume over in his hands with a reluctant smile. "My father used to read me these stories."

"Really?" Huda went to him as he opened it, standing on tiptoe to peer over his shoulder. "But Kamran, these pictures are terrifying."

"That's why he liked them," he said, laughing as he turned a page.

Huda glimpsed the next image and gasped, drawing away from him as she crossed her arms. "I would never read such horrifying books to my children."

Kamran snapped the book shut with a scowl, turning to face her. "Are you criticizing my dead father?"

"I suppose I am."

"And am I to tolerate your impertinence, as if I have any interest in how you might raise your hypothetical children— the acquisition of which, I should note, would first require you to convince a man to part with his mind long enough to spend his days in your infuriating company—"

"Infuriating? You think *I'm* infuriating? Meanwhile you've never so much as unplugged your aristocratic ears long enough to hear the opinions of others, much less the odious sound of your own voice—"

"Would you two please shut up," said Hazan lazily, plucking another jar off the shelf. He smoothed out the peeling label, squinting at the writing. "This is hardly the time or the place."

Huda and Kamran shared a dark look before stalking off in opposite directions, the tension between them so fascinating, Alizeh was briefly distracted from the weight in her chest.

She was experiencing a rising apprehension as the minutes ticked on, knowing she should ask about the task ahead of them even as she preferred to wander this mysterious space. Cyrus might not choose to admit it, but it was clear enough to her that all these magical implements and ingredients had once belonged to him—still belonged to him, in fact—even as it was evident that the cottage had been abandoned. Something had kept him from coming back.

More mysteries.

Still, it was a rare opportunity to peer inside a magical keep such as this, for she didn't know whether she'd have such an opportunity again. There was so much here in this one room she'd need weeks to go through it all, and everything she looked upon inspired so many questions she hardly knew where to start.

Most astonishing, of course, were the crystals.

They were everywhere—sorted by size and color and formation—some heaped in cracked bowls like so much rock candy, others displayed under bell jars with care. One prodigious cluster of blue crystal sat directly on the floor, so vast were its dimensions, and Alizeh moved toward the specimen, reaching out gingerly to trace its edges.

"It's empty," said a voice just behind her.

Alizeh turned with a start to discover Cyrus reaching past her; he snapped off a brittle piece of rock, which he held up to the light. "These are very old."

"What do you mean it's *empty?*"

"Its magic has already been extracted. This is but a husk now." He offered her the hollow bit of crystal, and as she took it from him, her fingers grazed his, this brief contact sending a thrill through her body. She thought she imagined the quiet breath he took then, the way he closed his fist and pocketed his hands.

"Good God, how on earth did you source so much powdered heart?" said Hazan suddenly, turning to search the room for Cyrus. He was holding a glass jar full of something that looked like scarlet sand. "This is illegal in Ardunia."

Cyrus only stared at him in response, then flicked his wrist as if shooing a fly, and the contents of the room disappeared. The fire in the hearth still blazing, they now stood in an empty cottage, not a stick of furniture in sight. Everything— all the magical impedimenta—was gone.

Hazan gaped at his now-empty hands.

Cyrus approached the center of the room with an eerie calm. "If you're ready," he said with a nod to Alizeh, "I'd like to begin."

Alizeh felt at once a shock of nerves, dropping the small piece of crystal in her haste to steady herself, the dull plink echoing in the newly deserted space. She bent to retrieve it, realizing as she did that it was the only item in the room that hadn't disappeared. Alizeh looked up into Cyrus's heated eyes and knew, without knowing why, that he'd allowed her to keep it.

"Very well," she said softly, discreetly tucking the bit of

crystal into her boot before she straightened. "What do I need to do?"

"Nothing," said Hazan, who was striding toward Cyrus. "Not yet. This first part will only affect the debtor."

Cyrus looked at him. "Have you come to chaperone?"

"Joke if you like," said Hazan gravely, "but I'll be here to make sure you don't die in the process."

"*Die?*" said Alizeh sharply. "Has that happened before?"

"Yes," they both said at the same time.

"But—"

"There's nothing for you to do if it comes to that," Cyrus was saying. "Once the oath is spoken aloud, the magic cannot be stopped."

"If your skin comes detached from your body, perhaps not, but you won't speak until later. Should there be any early sign of danger, I'll intercede." Hazan hesitated. "You're certain you'll be able to manage the enchantment even as it tortures you? Traditionally, this sort of thing is conducted by a Diviner, as most people wouldn't be able to endure the pain long enough to complete the oath—"

Cyrus looked irritated. "I'll be fine."

"Wait," said Alizeh, trying to hold on to calm. "I just— Cyrus, is it common for people in Tulan to be so magical?"

He hesitated before saying, "No. Not exactly."

"Then is it safe, what you're about to do? If there are so many risks involved, should we not wait, perhaps, for a Diviner? Someone professionally trained?"

He turned his eyes to the floor. "I am professionally trained."

"But you are not a Diviner—"

"No," he said, lifting his head. "I am not."

"Then—"

"He trained at the temple for almost seventeen years," Hazan offered before glancing at Cyrus, who stiffened. "He was enrolled at the temple by age three, and took preliminary vows to join the priesthood when he turned eighteen. He's as close to a Diviner as a person can be."

Alizeh experienced a sharp pain in her sternum, so shocked she could hardly find the words. "What?"

"A Diviner?" said Kamran, stunned. "*Him?*"

"Rather a fall from grace, I think," muttered Huda.

"You wanted to become a Diviner?" Alizeh shook her head. She felt inexplicably heartsick. "Heavens. Your mother once told me you'd been studying magic since you were child. I can't believe I didn't understand then what she meant."

Cyrus returned his gaze to the ground. He sounded angry when he said, "I don't care to discuss it."

"Surely we *must* discuss it," Huda insisted. "What a fascinating revelation. Oh, how I wish I had a cup of tea—"

"I don't understand your reticence to speak of it," said Hazan. "You guard this truth as if it's a secret, when in fact it's widely held information. Just earlier I asked your mother whether she knew why you never wore a crown, and she told me right then that you'd refused adornment since the day you decided to take your vows. It took little prompting to come by the rest of the details. Hell, I was offered firsthand accounts from your otherwise tight-lipped staff—some of whom have worked in the palace since you were a boy.

They heard us discussing your past and offered to tell me the story of your old nursemaid, how you once bounced off the roof—"

"*That's enough.*"

"He bounced off the roof?" said Huda, delighted. "Who told you this? Was it the housekeeper?"

"No," said Hazan, "though I did ask, then, if any of them knew why he wore black all the time, and the housekeeper said he'd once told her that he was in mourning."

"What?" Alizeh looked at Cyrus. "In mourning for what?"

"*Good God.*" Cyrus pushed both hands through his hair.

"Hold a moment—this makes no sense," said Kamran. "You were heir to the throne. How could your parents allow you to pursue a path to priesthood? No respectable kingdom would allow their firstborn to relinquish a duty to the empire—"

"Oh, also"—Huda lifted a finger—"and forgive me for being so blunt about it—but if you didn't want to be king, why did you kill your father? You might've let him keep his crown if you weren't keen to follow in his footsteps."

"He's not the firstborn, actually," supplied Hazan. "He's the spare. It turns out he has an older brother—though, interestingly, it was the one subject everyone refused to discuss—"

"I said, *enough.*" Cyrus was furious now. "This is why I don't speak of it. This is why I detest talking to people. This is why I never host guests at the palace. I have no interest in explaining my life or my choices to anyone. I will not be interrogated," he cried. "And I will not answer your questions.

Leave me the hell alone."

Everyone fell suddenly, deathly silent.

Cyrus's anger was as palpable as the weight of magic in the air, and Alizeh was distraught as she looked at him. It changed nothing to know these things, and yet, somehow, it changed everything. She longed to know what'd happened— what had shifted in his life to bring him to this moment?

How had he gone from the Diviners to the devil?

Cyrus was fighting to regain his composure. "I'm sick of talking. I'm tired of delaying. I want this wretched night to end. *Now.*"

Hazan, who appeared uncharacteristically chastened, said quietly, "Let us carry on, then."

But Alizeh could not be calm. How was she meant to live like this, always at the edge of a precipice? She needed more information, needed to understand—yet Cyrus would not reveal his secrets, and she certainly couldn't force him to speak. She only felt, with greater conviction every minute, a burning suspicion that he was not as villainous as he wanted the world to think he was, and this was enough to drive her mad.

"Cyrus," she said desperately, "I'm so sorry."

He looked at her, then looked away, his voice rough as he said, "Why are you sorry?"

"I don't know." For some unfathomable reason, she felt close to tears. "I just know that I am."

He lifted his head, meeting her eyes for a moment with unguarded anguish, and she glimpsed inside him then what she'd seen once before: a staggering, breathtaking grief.

A moment of truth, there—then gone.

Alizeh's heart broke when he looked away from her, and she watched, spellbound, as he tugged up his shirtsleeves to reveal powerful forearms, his golden skin dusted with fine, copper hair. He closed his eyes and held out his hands, palms up, and soon there came a spine-chilling sound, like a skitter of insects, as a skin of darkness formed slowly along the ceiling.

"Wait—what are you doing?" Kamran asked, alarmed.

Cyrus threw up his arm and, in a move that seemed to require sheer physical strength, he dragged the heaving black shadow down the wall. The strain of this exertion was evident in the lines of his face, the veins in his neck. He pulled at this skin until it finally fell into place beneath their feet, and when it did, Alizeh felt the world tilt.

Then she heard Cyrus scream.

THIRTY-TWO

سی و دو

AT FIRST, ALIZEH THOUGHT SHE'D gone blind.

Darkness had consumed her eyes, her mouth, filled her nose and throat and seared her lungs. She was drowning, she couldn't breathe, she could hardly find the strength to make a sound beyond a whimper. She tried to tell herself it was a trick, that her fear of the dark lived only in her mind, but there was no reasoning with the illogical, and Alizeh was soon convinced she would die here, compressed by the weight of the universe just as her ancestors once were, left to wilt and wither without light, without warmth—

She drew a desperate, gasping breath as the dark suddenly drew back and the room returned, the fire crackling in the hearth. Alizeh was doubled over, one hand pressed to her chest as she tried to calm the clamor of her heart, when she heard Huda say, in a horrified whisper—

"Is this black magic?"

Very slowly, Alizeh looked up.

Cyrus hung in the air unclothed, naked save a shroud that coiled around his body like a ribbon, so dark it appeared almost to sever him in pieces, choking his throat, his arms, part of his torso, and his hips—the magic sparing him a modicum of privacy.

Alizeh fell back, aghast.

"No," said Hazan, his voice grave. "It's not black magic. It's simply barbaric."

It frightened her to see him so defenseless, yet even in this nightmarish scene Cyrus looked otherworldly. His powerful, muscular body was bathed in firelight, the golden glow of his skin a shocking contrast to the spiral of gloom that restrained him. She felt almost as if she shouldn't look at Cyrus, exposed as he was, though neither could she look away; he was breathtaking even in agony, his broad chest straining against his binds as he suffered.

And it was clear that he suffered.

Pain was printed upon his face, though he bore it well, his eyes squeezed shut as he grit his teeth against assaults from an unseen force. Occasionally he gasped, making short, choked sounds of anguish, and just then he went so rigid with torment it killed her even to bear witness.

"Hazan," Alizeh said desperately. "What's happening?"

Hazan looked weary.

He glanced at her before returning his eyes to Cyrus, resignation in his voice when he said, "I suppose you must first understand that only a truly desperate person can perform a blood oath, for the chains that bind a debtor can only be woven from the darkness within them. The more desperate the debtor, the darker the coil." He exhaled, heavily. "Your Majesty, you must prepare yourself. This will be brutal for him when it's over. If he survives the first night, each day will get easier. If he does not—"

Cyrus cried out, his head jerking back violently.

Alizeh gasped, clapping a hand over her mouth as she saw

the tide of color rushing to the surface of his skin. Cyrus's body was soon glistening with blood, the sheen of scarlet thickening as it knit together, weaving what looked almost like a gruesome garment around his naked figure. He made another choked, guttural sound as blood dripped steadily from where he hung, a slick pool forming on the floorboards beneath his feet. Soon, he was draped in a liquid cloak of his own blood, and then, without warning, the cloak dropped to the ground.

Alizeh stared in mute terror at the article, which had hardened into something real and substantial. Cyrus was still suspended in the air, the black ribbon still bound around his body; and though the strain of anguish was gone from his face, he was ashen and trembling, limp from exertion.

"Your Majesty," said Hazan quietly.

She turned to him, not wanting to hear what he said next, for she already suspected what she was meant to do. "No," she breathed.

Hazan nodded to the ground. "When you put on this cloak, you will absorb his blood into your body. This piece of him will belong to you until his debt is repaid."

Alizeh stared at the grotesque garment, bile rising in her throat. The cloak had solidified into something that looked almost like leather, the gleam of it turning her stomach. "Must I wear it now?"

"No," said Hazan. "Not yet." He looked up then, his voice imbued with a surprising compassion when he said, "Cyrus, are you able to speak?"

Cyrus did not open his eyes, though he made an effort to swallow, then nodded his head. Alizeh looked from Hazan

to Cyrus, her heart hammering in her chest. The realities of
this disturbing night were becoming too monstrous, and she
was suddenly stricken with fear.

When Cyrus finally spoke, his voice was ravaged.

Freely I bind my body,
these chains of my own design.
I offer my blood as bond,
until I repay this debt of mine.

"Now," said Hazan softly, "he will speak aloud his promises."
Cyrus looked nearly wrecked, his chest straining as he
struggled to draw breath. "I offer you my kingdom," he said,
the rasp of his voice unrecognizable, "in exchange for your
hand in marriage. And I vow never to touch you unless you
should desire that I do. Once I'm discharged of my debt to
the devil, I offer you my life. You are free to kill me then at
your discretion, for I will die willingly at your hand."

Hazan exhaled shakily beside her, looking uncharacteristically distressed. Out of the corner of her eye, Alizeh
glimpsed Kamran and Huda, too, who'd been so silent she'd
nearly forgotten they were still in the room. Everyone looked
rattled and grim, though none were as disturbed as she. Once
more, Cyrus spoke:

Should you choose to accept my oath,
my blood is yours to claim.
Wear my pledge upon your back,
then speak aloud my name.

Alizeh was breathing hard now, her eyes wild as she turned to Hazan, who offered her a nod of confirmation. With trembling hands, she reached for the cloak, which was warm and slippery under her hands. A powerful wave of revulsion nearly unbalanced her then, and she worried she might actually be sick.

"Your Majesty," said Hazan. "Are you all right?"

She shook her head, staring at the cloth of blood she held. "Hazan, this is— That is, I realize I made the decision to do this against your better judgment, but this is so much darker than I thought it would be—so much worse—"

"I did try to warn you," he said, his eyes heavy.

"I know—I know you did—"

"You can still walk away. You've not yet accepted his oath. He will still suffer for a time, but not to the same degree." He looked away. "But it's cruel to leave him in agony like this. Even someone like him. Whatever you choose, you must make your decision now."

There was no decision to make.

Alizeh could not walk away; she'd already made her choice. She'd already promised herself she'd stay the course, that she'd do what was best for her people—what was necessary to secure their future, their safety. She'd already argued this decision to its end, and she knew what she needed to do.

She simply wished she didn't have to.

Shaking, she shook out the cloak, then whipped the heaving mass of it around her shoulders, where it settled and clung like a second skin, molding to the shape of her back. Her heart was frenzied now, beating so hard it was making her dizzy. She drew a deep, steadying breath, then turned her eyes to the man she would soon marry.

"*Cyrus,*" she whispered.

He gasped, his body seizing as some new pain assailed him, and then, with a suddenness that shocked her frozen limbs—the cloak melted into her body, flooding her veins with a rush of blood so potent she recoiled with fright.

The feeling soon settled into something altogether pleasurable, leaving her light-headed and steaming, unsteady on her feet. It was with a delicious relief that Alizeh felt as if she'd been set on fire. Her cheeks were hot, her head drowsed and heavy. It was surprisingly intimate, the feel of his blood in her veins, the fever of him now living inside her. She wondered whether this warmth would linger always, for the change within her had occurred with astonishing speed. It was as if something had been hooked inside her soul, tethering her to a heart whose beat she could almost feel. She knew without lifting her head exactly where Cyrus hung in the air above her. She knew that, no matter where he went, she could walk a path to him blindly.

"Your Majesty?" said Hazan, watching her closely. "Are you—"

There was a violent sound, like a gust of wind, and without warning Cyrus was released from his bonds, his limp body hitting the bloodied floor so hard the horrible *crack* echoed all around them. Like a desperate moth, his black shroud fluttered as it fell with him, cloaking his naked figure.

Alizeh drew a sharp breath.

She imagined she could feel the pulse of him inside her, the heat of his blood pumping in her veins. She moved toward him with rising fear, not knowing who she'd discover when he opened his eyes.

Hazan, Huda, and Kamran closed ranks steadily behind her, the four of them cautiously approaching his fallen body.

Only his face and part of one shoulder were visible, the rest of him still veiled in black. Cyrus stirred, the metallic locks of his hair glinting in the firelight, his face drawn and pale. He made a low, anguished sound, the pain of which seemed to reverberate in her bones.

"Why does it not help him that I am near?" she said, turning to Hazan. "I thought he would only suffer in my absence."

"The bond is too fresh." Hazan shook his head. "I'm afraid you can only quiet his pain at the moment. He will endure this agony regardless; it's only a matter of how much."

Alizeh absorbed this information with an ache, then dropped to her knees beside him, sinking into a shallow pool of his blood. She clasped her hands to keep from stroking his hair, smoothing his furrowed brow.

"Cyrus," she whispered.

He fought to open his eyes then, and when he did, her heart wrenched in her chest. His eyes were bloodshot and red-rimmed, his pupils blown out, dilated to a disturbing degree. He still appeared to be suffering despite her proximity, his body rigid with strain.

"Does it hurt terribly even though I am here?" she asked him, searching his face.

He merely blinked at her, the action slow and tired, before

his eyes closed once more.

"Cyrus?" She was panicking now. "Cyrus, can you speak?"

"It's best if you don't force him," said Hazan quietly. "For him, the hell of this night has only just begun."

THIRTY-THREE

سی و سه

CYRUS AWOKE WITH A START.

His principal thought was for the emptiness of his mind, for it was the first time in months he'd not risen from a nightmare. This fact alone was strange enough to occupy his fears for days, but then, as he felt the shape of things around him, he perceived that he was lying in an unfamiliar bed, in an unfamiliar space. The room was large and dark, its details vague in the rheumy glow of an unborn sun, dawn pushing against the horizon. This burgeoning light pitched through a pair of windows whose curtains had not been closed, a detail that struck him as strange even as pain throbbed steadily throughout his body. His head was heavy, so disjointed he felt almost drugged, and as he blinked slowly against a rising tide of dread, he realized he had no idea where he was. His cheek was pressed against a strange pillow, his body tucked between the sheets of a bed he did not recognize.

Images of the evening came back to him slowly and with a blaze of feeling, and as he recalled these recent delights of his life he became slowly aware of the fact that, under these linens, he was half-wrapped in his own shroud—beneath which he was entirely naked.

This filled him with no small amount of horror.

Someone had delivered him to this place as if he were a

newborn babe, swaddled in a skin of darkness. What had happened to him? He was not supposed to have been so immobilized; he should've had strength enough in the end to have returned to his rooms. He'd planned for it. Even now he felt the thrum of latent magic inside him, stores of which lived in his veins almost constantly.

He'd had a plan.

He'd meant to cast himself back to the privacy of his quarters, where he'd intended to suffer the torment of this first night in the company of his own unraveling mind. When preparing for Alizeh's arrival—long before he knew who she was—he'd asked his mother to choose a room for this bride of the devil as far away from him as possible. It had seemed a wise enough choice at the time, but just yesterday it struck him as a terrible mistake. The impressive size of the palace made it so that their rooms were dangerously far apart, and Cyrus had worried that, in the aftermath of the blood oath, he'd have to endure a torturous degree of separation from Alizeh—for there was no magicking away the pain of such a vow. He'd expected to pass these hellish hours wide awake and retching into a basin. Never did he think he'd fall asleep. Neither did he think the agony would be so manageable. He hurt, yes—everywhere—but it was not so intolerable that he was unable to function.

He wanted to celebrate this fact, except that he was ill at ease in this foreign space. He felt certain he was in the castle, for there were aspects of the room that seemed familiar to him, but he needed to know where, precisely, he was—and whether he was alone.

He had a strange feeling he was not.

With great effort he levered himself upright, shifting onto his elbows to look around. The sheets fell to his waist, exposing his upper body to the cool air, a welcome balm for his overheated skin. Half the room was cast in deep shadow, the rest touched with just enough light that he could make out general impressions of furniture. All the suites in the palace were well-appointed, but this one appeared, by all accounts, nonspecific. There were no personal effects to be seen, no discarded items on the bedside table, no shoes, no glasses of water or articles of clothing lying around.

No one, it seemed, lived here.

With a dawning relief, Cyrus realized he'd been delivered to one of the many guest quarters in the palace. Presumably they'd not wanted to invite the curiosity of a snoda, for a servant would've had to unlock his bedroom door. He nearly smiled at this discovery as he stretched his neck, closing his eyes as he drew a deep, cleansing breath.

Finally, he might simply exhale.

Horrified as he was to have been carried to this strange room like a child, he was cheered beyond measure to find that the resulting discomfort was reasonable. Hazan's protests had been so theatrical that Cyrus had almost believed the pressures of the oath would kill him. Yet he'd awoken just now much like an ordinary person from an ordinary sleep—somehow arising without unspeakable pain.

This was reason for gratitude.

Slowly, he untangled his legs from the terrible shroud, then stood with great care, grasping the bed post as he straightened. His body was still trembling slightly, and it was a moment before he blinked away a sudden head rush, but he soon felt at least well enough to put weight on his legs. Even in private he felt uncomfortable being so exposed in a strange space, and he reached for the cashmere throw draped at the foot of the bed, wrapping the soft length of it around his hips before taking an exploratory step forward.

His first thought was to magic himself back to his own room, but he was struck by an alarming thought: that his earlier theory might've been wrong, that perhaps he'd been brought to this guest suite as a mercy, not a convenience. He wasn't certain where he was positioned just then in the palace, but there was a chance his pain was only tolerable because of his proximity to Alizeh's rooms; if so, he didn't wish to upset this balance.

He thought instead to search the space a bit more, hoping to find a pile of his discarded clothes, or at least a dressing gown. He'd made it to the hall when something snapped inside him, the lash so electric it spasmed violently in his chest. He gasped, biting back a cry as the pain blinded him, radiating in his eyes, his tongue, his spine. He staggered forward, catching himself too late against an opposite wall as the whip of what felt like lightning cracked once more inside him, this time so severe he made an anguished sound as he fell to his knees.

He was gasping for air, his body shaking so violently he could hardly gather the strength to return to bed; the pain was strange and breathtaking, a torture unique from the other experiences he'd known, for once started, it did not cease, not even for a second. Over and over he was struck by the explosive force of an unseen strap, as if someone were attempting to leash his soul, to drag him back to his possessor.

Cyrus realized he must be locked in the wrong place—too far from the safety of where he'd started. He managed, in his agony, to heave himself a few inches closer to the bed before he was clipped by a gut-wrenching shot that caused him to cry out desperately. He collapsed, catching himself on his hands and knees, panting and nearly blind.

He had a sudden vision of his nightmares: the dark bands of smoke around his body, the fall from a great height, the endless torture, crawling in the dark like an animal in search of escape. At least in these terrors there was the promise of relief, the vision of an angel that arrived, always—

Out of the corner of his eye he glimpsed movement, straining to lift his head only to witness the first burn of dawn, golden rays of light lifting against the windows, glazing the room in an ethereal glow. He knew he'd gone mad when he saw her then, when she moved toward him in a vision of radiance, just as she always did in his dreams.

It had finally happened.

He'd finally lost his fucking mind.

"Cyrus," she whispered, drawing closer. "Where are you?"

Disbelief paralyzed him utterly. His mind was ravaged by the impossibility of this vision, the disorienting déjà vu.

Cyrus. Where are you?

The words she spoke, the way she moved, the blaze of

light. Was he, in fact, dreaming? From his vantage point on the floor he noticed then, for the first time, a side table upon which sat a potted orchid, a bowl, and a gold-rimmed dish— within which sat a heap of blood-stained towels.

Had she washed the blood from his body?

Were he capable of movement, he might've inspected himself—might've drawn a hand down his limbs to confirm the theory. Instead he grit his teeth so as not to scream as pain continued to thrash him. His instincts insisted something was amiss, even as the violence of his torture abated at her approach. This was literal delusion, he knew it was— knew it *had* to be, even as he felt very much awake, his heart beating in his chest with concrete force. She spotted him on the ground and moved toward him like an angel, the silhouette of her graceful body backlit by the rise of a brilliant sun.

This was impossible.

"No—*no*—"

"Cyrus," she said again, crouching now to look him in the eye, worry creasing her brow. "I only want to help you."

I only want to help you.

He heard her voice as if from a great distance, her words echoing in his head over and over, raising a clamor within him that made his head feel as if it might explode.

"No—no—NO," he shouted, falling back, scrambling out of reach.

More of the same words she'd spoken in his dreams— except he'd never had a nightmare like this one; always they were in the same location, always beginning in precisely the same way. It was perhaps the slight inconsistencies that unbalanced him now, for he'd been confident he was awake before she'd entered the room—but now he couldn't be certain. He felt frantic, for he knew not whether this was some new game the devil was trying to play.

"This isn't real," he said desperately. "This isn't real—"

She drew close and touched him—a single stroke of her hand along his arm—and the feel of her bare skin against his tortured body was so exquisite he fought back a groan, his chest heaving as he ached.

"Please," he said, begging himself now. "Please wake up—"

"Look how you suffer," she said, her voice heavy with grief. She shook her head. "I didn't realize it would be this awful."

Look how you suffer.

Look how you suffer.

She dropped to her knees before him, took his face in her hands, and he cried out as he caught fire. Always she healed him when she touched him, but this time the press of her skin felt so real it was terrifying, his heart battering his ribs as her delicate fingers spread along the lines of his jaw, her thumb grazing the slope of his cheek. He made a tortured sound deep in his throat, his eyes closing as relief flooded his veins. He felt as if he might die from this simple pleasure, which awakened within him a bliss that drowned out any last vestiges of pain.

He wanted to live here. Dig his grave and die here.

"*Angel,*" he breathed. "My angel."

"Come with me," she said softly, withdrawing only to take him by the hand. This small gesture frightened him, for it was unbanked in his memory. Never in his dreams had she done something so ordinary as hold his hand, and the press of her small, soft fingers was so gentle—so intimate—he was almost convinced she was truly here.

With excruciating tenderness she helped him rise to his feet, letting go of his hand only to catch the loosened wrap around his waist, tucking its ends neatly so as not to expose him. He felt as if he was apart from his own body, half-alive, reduced to nothing but heat and sensation. He watched, transfixed, as she tended to him with a benevolence he did not deserve, and then he went with her blindly, their hands clasped once again, as she guided him back to the bed. It occurred to him then, with a vague panic, that he'd follow her off a cliff if she were the one to lead him there.

She helped settle him back onto the mattress, searing him where she touched him, then tucked him in, pulling the sheets up to his waist. It was by far the strangest dream he'd ever had, a path with her he'd never before traveled.

He was afraid she was going to leave, but then she sat, lightly, at the edge of the bed, and looked at him with an easy smile. He felt like he was falling backward inside his own body as he stared up at her, gazing into her eyes with the freedom of a man happily detached from his mind. He was surprised to feel the slight tremble of her fingers when she pushed a lock of hair out of his eyes, for she'd never been nervous with him.

"What is it?" he said.

She only shook her head and said, softly, "You're so beautiful."

These words detonated inside him, the resulting pang so severe he flinched.

"What's wrong?" she said, brightening with alarm. "Are you hurting again?"

"No," he said. "Yes. I don't know."

She studied him a moment more, deliberating as she searched his face. "I've been sitting just there," she said, nodding to a chair in a corner, its heavy shadows lifting as a starburst of color shattered across the room. "I must've fallen asleep earlier, but I promise I'm not going anywhere. Okay?"

"Okay," he said.

"You need to rest."

He swallowed, still staring at her. He wondered if she had any idea what he'd do for her, the worlds he'd destroy for her. "Okay."

"Good," she said, almost smiling as she drew her hand over his brow, stealing his breath in the process. "If you need anything at all, I'll be right over there."

She stood up to leave and he panicked.

"No," he said quickly. "Please stay."

"I am staying," she said, fully smiling now. She pointed to the chair. "I'll be right there—"

"No," he said, shaking his head. "I want you next to me."

She froze, her smile slipping as she frowned—as if she were unearthing a memory.

Carefully, she sat beside him.

"Cyrus," she said, drawing the back of her hand down his cheek, this contact calming him at once. "Do you think you're dreaming?"

He felt out of his mind. "I don't know."

"Sleepy boy," she said. "This is not a dream. I'm really here. And I promise I'm not going anywhere."

Cyrus sat with this, trying to absorb her words, but he was unconvinced—for a person in a dream always thought they were real. Besides, he felt intoxicated by her closeness, and by some heaviness he could not explain. She was still touching him, though only slightly, her hand having retreated from his face to rest against his chest, under which his heart beat at a dangerous pace. Every shaking breath he took lifted his upper body, pressing her fingers against him anew, provoking in him a pleasure so acute it seemed to be burning him alive.

God, he wanted her.

He noticed then that she wore a soft dressing gown cinched over what appeared to be a nightdress, her hair pinned partly away from her face. Loose, silky curls grazed his skin as she leaned close to him, and he wanted to pull her on top of him, wanted to feel more of her, everywhere. If this was not a dream, and she'd really been here all night beside him, how had she changed out of her opulent gown?

He gasped when she withdrew her hand, catching her fingers without thinking, then closed his eyes as he pressed them to his lips, kissing them, softly.

She made a sound and he opened his eyes to find her staring at him, looking faint and unsteady.

"What's wrong?" he whispered.

"Nothing," she said quickly, then hesitated. "Everything."

With some difficulty he pushed up on his elbows, then pulled himself into a seated position. His head was swimming, a dull pain branching through his body, but he needed to look at her properly. He took her face in his hands and she gasped, her body trembling even as she leaned into him, her eyes closing on a breathless sound.

"Tell me what's wrong," he said. "Tell me what you need."

"I n-need you to know," she said, her voice catching, "that this is not a dream."

His pulse was racing.

He felt frozen by fear and indecision, his head disordered by figments of memory and sensation. He didn't know what was real anymore. Her skin was so soft under his hands, so soft it amazed him. He'd touched her like this a thousand times but those memories paled in comparison to this, to *this*— Had it ever felt like this, the sensation of her so bright it burned him? He held her face and marveled at her, at the elegant lines, the lush curves of her lips. He leaned in, grazing her cheek with his nose and when she gasped he watched her throat move, watched her hands shake as she reached for him, her small fingers pressing against his ribs, then slowly drawing up his back. He was drugged by this tender touch, by this searing heat that soothed him, each caress lulling him toward something that felt like home.

He was safe here. With her.

He blinked slowly, the dense weight of exhaustion returning to his body, pushing him down. His head fell heavily against his pillow. He wanted to sleep, but he was afraid to close his eyes, and he hadn't realized he'd said as much out loud until she said, softly—

"Why are you afraid?"

He shook his head, his eyes closing against his will. "Because," he said, and sighed. "You're never here when I wake up."

He felt the whisper of her breath against his forehead, then the press of her lips, so gentle against his skin, and he felt certain now, unequivocally, that he was dreaming.

"I'll be here," she said. "I'm not going anywhere." Then, softer, her lips grazing the curve of his ear: "You can't lie to me forever, Cyrus. I'm going to find out the truth about you, and when I do, I promise you this: I'll ruin him. I'll make the devil regret the day he was born."

Don't miss these stunning novels from the *New York Times* bestselling author of the **SHATTER ME** series.

"The very best books move you to reconsider the world around you, and this is one of those."

—Nicola Yoon, #1 *New York Times* bestselling author

HARPER

An Imprint of HarperCollinsPublishers

epicreads.com

An epic, romantic fantasy series inspired by Persian mythology from #1 international bestselling author

TAHEREH MAFI

"Prepare to be destroyed."

—Stephanie Garber, #1 *New York Times* bestselling author of the Caraval series

HARPER

An Imprint of HarperCollinsPublishers

epicreads.com